STRANGE | HORROR...

Pulling myself together, I turned the *Torn-ga* over. Sticking out under his left shoulder-blade was a harpoon-head. I set my foot on the body and drew the lance out at his back, and turned to examine more fully the body of my grim foe.

He was perhaps an inch over five feet in height, and was covered with short, fine seal-hair of a grayish-brown colour. The eyes were enormous, with no eyelashes, very like a seal's, the hips tremendously developed, and the legs disproportionately long; the instep was very broad and flat, and both the toes and the fingers very long, webbed, and ending in thick nails like claws.

The face was hideous; it had a wide receding jaw, with very prominent eyebrows overhanging the huge eyes, a low forehead, and small furry ears. I noticed, too, the teeth were sharp, the dog-teeth much developed, and the front-teeth of the lower jaw noticeably longer than the others. He had died with his lips drawn back in a savage snarl...

—from "Spirit Island" by Henry Toke Munn

STRANGE ISLAND STORIES

EDITED BY
JONATHAN E. LEWIS

STARK
HOUSE

Stark House Press • Eureka California

STRANGE ISLAND STORIES

Published by Stark House Press
1315 H Street
Eureka, CA 95501, USA
griffinskye3@sbcglobal.net
www.starkhousepress.com

ISBN-13: 978-1-944520-43-4

Book design by Mark Shepard, shepgraphics.com
Cover illustration and design by JT Lindroos: jtlindroos.carbonmade.com
Proofreading by Bill Kelly

First Stark House Press Edition: March 2018

Table of Contents

INTRODUCTION

Islands are everywhere, but we often don't stop to think of them as being particularly unique places. After all, they aren't uncommon. Islands can be entire countries such as Great Britain, Iceland, and Japan. They can also be isolated tropical paradises or small rocky lands under gray skies in the middle of cold, northern European waters. The booming cosmopolitan metropolises of Manhattan and Montreal are both located on islands. There's also the now uninhabited Alcatraz Island in San Francisco Bay, home of the eponymous infamous prison that has provided a great setting for numerous crime films. The list goes on.

But there are other islands that solely exist in literature and genre fiction. These are strange and mysterious places, small bits of land surrounded by water on all sides, where the rules that govern human conduct and nature itself are often bent, if not broken entirely. Think about it. Islands are, in many ways, the perfect settings for authors looking to craft stories that explore themes such as human isolation, lost civilizations, strange and unusual animal life, the power of nature, the cruelty of man to his fellow man, and human nature itself. What better setting than a small isolated piece of land in which to place characters and let them have a go at each other? Indeed, the more uncanny the island setting, the stranger the animal or plant life, the better atmospheric backdrop for a strange tale to unfold.

In his introduction to the Oxford World's Classics edition of **The Island of Dr. Moreau** (Oxford University Press, 2017), Darryl Jones contends that H. G. Wells's novel about a mad scientist conducting bizarre experiments on a remote South Pacific island "very self-consciously partakes in another important literary subgenre. It is an island novel." He goes on to define the form of the island novel. "Traditionally," Jones writes, "this form uses its remote, isolated, exotic locations as vehicles for the examination of human society, or even of human nature itself." Among the works cited by Jones as being important representatives of the island literary subgenre are Daniel Defoe's **Robinson Crusoe** (1719) and William Goldings's **Lord of the Flies** (1954), both of which would be of considerable interest to readers of this anthology.

If there exists a specific island literary subgenre, then it follows that there exists the possibility of different types of narratives within the subgenre. One such form is that of the strange island short story. This is the subject and theme of this anthology. The strange island short story form, like the island novel, utilizes island locations to examine human society and human nature. But it pushes far beyond that and takes the reader on a journey into the weird, the bizarre, the scary, and the unsettling. It allows authors to create alternative worlds, places where cannibalism, lycanthropy, and voodoo exist. Places where islands can literally come alive. On islands, women, rather than men, can be the dominant sex. Islands can also defy the normal rules of geography and topography. Limits are only constrained by the human imagination.

Some of the works herein are what might be called straightforward horror fiction, designed to be enthralling tales that provide busy people with some escapism from their humdrum lives. Others are largely metaphorical and examine such themes as the division between past and present, differing gender roles, and the division between the city and the country. I have assembled a diverse array of short stories, most written by British or American authors in the late nineteenth- or early twentieth-century and all of which are set, in whole or in substantial part, on islands. Sometimes the strangeness lies in the realistic portrayal of a human horror, such as that of leprosy in Jack London's "Good-by, Jack." Most often, however, the stories are works that push far past the boundaries of realism and take the reader on a fantastic journey into strange and unsettling realms.

Although some of the authors whose stories are included here are well-known literary figures, others are better known as authors of pulp or "lowbrow" fiction. Readers will have an opportunity to decide for themselves whether there is any real distinction between the stories when it comes to their literary merit, or whether some of the best works are those that simply offer up a good scare. The reader will find each story preceded by a short introduction in which I provide biographical information about each author and some historical and literary context that will help the reader better appreciate the themes found in the work. Some may find it useful to read these introductions both before, and then again after, reading each story.

In terms of structure, I have chosen to divide **Strange Island Stories** into four distinct sections. The first, "Ghosts and Shape Shifters," includes classic ghost stories, tales of lycanthropy and werewolves, and supernatural tales set on islands. These short stories are proto-horror or horror stories par excellence and should highly appeal to fans of horror fiction. This section includes my personal favorite in the anthology, Algernon Blackwood's "The Camp of the Dog," a story that utilizes a northern European island setting to great effect. Connoisseurs of contemporary Scandinavian crime fiction in particular might find much to appreciate in Blackwood's darkly atmospheric tale.

The second section, "Bizarre Creatures and Fantastic Realms," includes short stories in which bizarre animal and plant life play an important role.

Devotees of cryptozoology may find much to appreciate in these works of weird fiction. Among the authors whose works are included herein are Arthur Conan Doyle (best known as the creator of the fictional sleuth Sherlock Holmes) and Robert Louis Stevenson, the author of **Treasure Island** (1882), as well as H. P. Lovecraft, whose vast output is now appreciated by horror fans and literary critics alike.

The third section, "Human Horrors," as its title indicates, includes works that are not necessarily "weird," but are nonetheless horrific and deeply strange. Readers might find these stories, all of which evoke a sense of foreboding dread, to be deeply chilling. Among the stories included in this section is George G. Toudouze's lighthouse story, "Three Skeleton Key," a story that was adapted several times into a chillingly effective radio show.

The fourth, and final, section of **Strange Island Stories** includes an original work of short fiction I have written entitled "An Adriatic Awakening." An homage to the authors whose stories appear in this volume, "An Adriatic Awakening" takes place on several islands, notably Manhattan, Long Island, and two islands off the coast of Croatia, one of which is purely fictional but which I hope will linger in the reader's subconscious for a time after reading. In writing this tale of psychological dread, I realized how many of the "rules of the game" for writing strange island stories were very much set in stone by the writers whose fictional works are included in this anthology. Islands, in those short stories as well as in mine, are both real places and metaphors for territories untouched by human civilization and by the unwritten laws and rules that guide human behavior.

At the very end of the anthology, readers will find a "Notes for Further Reading" in which I include a list of other stories and novels, as well as some films, that might be of interest. I am sure that scholars of pulp fiction know of many other island stories that are themselves enthralling and worth a look. Space considerations, however, always necessitate that some stories are included in an anthology while others are left out. That doesn't mean that there aren't other strange island stories out there, some all but forgotten, that aren't waiting for rediscovery. Similarly, there are adventure stories and crime stories set on islands that are definitely worth reading, but are beyond the scope of this particular anthology.

As you read these stories, it is worth keeping in mind that the vast majority of them were written at a time of heightened advances in both the natural sciences and the social sciences. This was the era of Darwinian evolution, when biology and botany were fields that grew in stature and importance. Similarly, it was in the late-nineteenth century when the social sciences, designed to both explain and to understand human behavior, became specialized fields of academic study. Anthropology and psychology, for instance, became distinct fields. Many of the stories in this anthology should be understood as reflecting the era in which they were written, when explorers and scientists were notable public figures in their own right.

Completing **Strange Island Stories** was a multiyear project that involved a significant amount of reading on my part. I had to first discover the stories I wanted to include in this anthology and to introduce to a new generation of readers. I know how thrilled my mother would be that I finished this second book for Stark House Press. My father Steve Lewis, who runs the Mystery*File blog, helped me with the scanning of the stories included in this anthology and making sure that I had properly edited copies of these works. Greg Shepard at Stark House, who also published my previous anthology **Ancient Egyptian Supernatural Tales** (2016) was excited by this project idea from the get go. I especially want to thank him for allowing me to include an original short story. Taking Stephen Cooper's short story writing class at UCLA Extension provided me with the writing skills needed to complete an original fictional work. His seminar definitely helped me in more ways than one. Stefan Dziemianowicz was kind enough to provide me with some useful information about David Eynon, whose "The Sixth Gargoyle" is reprinted in this anthology. Mike Ashley, who was instrumental in helping me with my previous anthology, was likewise supportive of this current project and provided me with a copy of James Francis Dwyer's "The Isle of Doom." Similarly, my fellow horror fans, many of whom I have met through social media, have made the rather solitary nature of editing and writing easier. It's a lot easier to spend time inside working on a laptop when it's bright and sunny outside when you know that there are so many passionate horror fans out there who are interested in your project.

So let us now cast off into uncharted waters and sail away to islands of the imagination. Places of rapturous wonder and enchantment where dark forces lurk in wait for those readers intrepid enough to set foot on some very strange islands. Who knows what we may find there.

Jonathan E. Lewis
Los Angeles 2017

GHOSTS AND SHAPE SHIFTERS

Introduction to Monos and Daimonos

The British author Edward Bulwer-Lytton (1803-1873) not only wrote bestselling novels, but also plays, poems, and short stories. Today, he may be best remembered for coining the aphorism "the pen is mightier than the sword" and for the famous (or infamous) seven words with which he opened his novel, *Paul Clifford* (1830): "It was a dark and stormy night." The very same year that *Paul Clifford* was first published, Bulwer-Lytton, under the byline "Edward Bulwer" published an exquisitely bizarre short story in the May issue of *New Monthly Magazine*. Entitled "Monos and Daimonos," the story is about solitude and the demonic.

At once a ghost story and a phantasmagoric sojourn into one man's ceaseless quest to be alone, this tale may be economic in length, but is nevertheless rich in thematic elements, one such being man's complex relationship with Nature. In "Monos and Daimonos," Bulwer utilizes a remote island setting to vividly contrast harried urban life with the supposed bliss of being alone, apart from the needs and whims of one's fellow man. Indeed, the story is prescient for its insight into human psychology.

With a shipwreck acting as the transformative event that forces the narrator-protagonist onto a remote, supposedly deserted island, "Monos and Daimonos" explores both the dark side of human nature and the impact that extended solitude can have on a man's psyche. No wonder then that Edgar Allan Poe, an admirer of Bulwer-Lytton's work, paid homage to this proto-weird tale in "Silence: A Fable" (1838). Reading "Monos and Daimonos," you may find yourself asking what in this story is truly "real" and what is merely an extended allegory about the man's capacity for evil in a primitive state of nature.

MONOS AND DAIMONOS
Edward Bulwer

I am English by birth, but my early years were passed in a foreign and more northern land. I had neither brothers nor sisters; my mother died when I was in the cradle; and I found my sole companion, tutor, and playmate in my father. He was a younger brother of a noble and ancient house: what induced him to forsake his country and his friends, to abjure all society, and to live on a rock, is a story in itself, which has nothing to do with mine.

As the Lord liveth, I believe the tale that I shall tell you will have sufficient claim on your attention, without calling in the history of another to preface its most exquisite details, or to give interest to its most amusing events. I said my father lived on a rock—the whole country round seemed nothing but rock!—wastes, bleak, blank, dreary; trees stunted, herbage blighted; caverns, through which some black and wild stream (that never knew star or sunlight, but through rare and hideous chasms of the huge stones above it) went dashing and howling on its blessed course; vast cliffs, covered with eternal snows, where the birds of prey lived, and sent, in screams and discordance, a grateful and meet music to the heavens, which seemed too cold and barren to wear even clouds upon their wan, grey, comfortless expanse: these made the characters of that country where the spring of my life sickened itself away. The climate which, in the milder parts of —— relieves the nine months of winter with three months of an abrupt and autumn-less summer, never seemed to vary in the gentle and sweet region in which my home was placed. Perhaps, for a brief interval, the snow in the valleys melted, and the streams swelled, and a blue, ghastly, unnatural kind of vegetation, seemed, here and there, to mix with the rude lichen, or scatter a grim smile over minute particles of the universal rock; but to these witnesses of the changing season were the summers of my boyhood confined. My father was addicted to the sciences—the physical sciences—and possessed but a moderate share of learning in any thing else; he taught me all he knew; and the rest of my education, Nature, in a savage and stern guise, instilled in my heart by silent but deep lessons. She taught my feet to bound, and my arm to smite; she breathed life into my passions, and shed darkness over my temper; she taught me to cling to her, even in her most rugged and unalluring form, and to shrink from all else—from the companionship of man, and the soft smiles of woman, and the shrill voice of childhood; and the ties, and hopes, and socialities, and objects of human existence, as from a torture and a curse. Even in that sullen rock, and beneath that ungenial sky, I had luxuries unknown to the palled tastes of cities, or to those who woo delight in an air of odours and in a land of roses! What were those luxuries? They had a myriad varieties and shades of enjoyment—they had but a common name. What were those luxuries? *Solitude!*

My father died when I was eighteen; I was transferred to my uncle's protection, and I repaired to London. I arrived there, gaunt and stern, a giant in limbs and strength, and to the tastes of those about me, a savage in bearing and in mood. They would have laughed, but I awed them; they would have altered *me*, but I changed *them*; I threw a damp over their enjoyment and a cloud over their meetings. Though I said little, though I sat with them, estranged and silent, and passive, they seemed to wither beneath my presence. Nobody could live with me and be happy, or at ease! I felt it, and I hated them that they could love not me. Three years passed—I was of age—I demanded my fortune—and scorning social life, and pining once more for loneliness, I resolved to journey into those unpeopled and far lands, which if any have pierced, none have returned to describe. So I took my leave of them all, cousin and aunt—and when I came to my old uncle, who had liked me less than any, I grasped his hand with so friendly a gripe, that, well I ween, the dainty and nice member was but little inclined to its ordinary functions in future.

I commenced my pilgrimage—I pierced the burning sands—I traversed the vast deserts—I came into the enormous woods of Africa, where human step never trod, nor human voice ever startled the thrilling and intense solemnity that broods over the great solitudes, as it brooded over chaos before the world was! There the primeval nature springs and perishes; undisturbed and unvaried by the convulsions of the surrounding world; the seed becomes the tree, lives through its uncounted ages, falls and moulders, and rots and vanishes, unwitnessed in its mighty and mute changes, save by the wandering lion, or the wild ostrich, or that huge serpent—a hundred times more vast than the puny boa that the cold limners of Europe have painted, and whose bones the vain student has preserved, as a miracle and marvel. There, too, as beneath the heavy and dense shade I couched in the scorching noon I heard the trampling as of an army, and the crush and fall of the strong trees, and beheld through the matted boughs the behemoth pass on its terrible way, with its eyes burning as a sun, and its white teeth arched and glistening in the rabid jaw, as pillars of spar glitter in a cavern; the monster, to whom only those wastes are a home, and who never, since the waters rolled from the Daedal earth, has been given to human gaze and wonder but my own! Seasons glided on, but I counted them not; they were not doled to me by the tokens of man, nor made sick to me by the changes of his base life, and the evidence of his sordid labour. Seasons glided on, and my youth ripened into manhood, and manhood grew grey with the first frost of age; and then a vague and restless spirit fell upon me, and I said in my foolish heart, "I will look upon the countenances of my race once more!" I retraced my steps—I recrossed the wastes—I re-entered the cities—I took again the garb of man; for I had been hitherto naked in the wilderness, and hair had grown over me as a garment. I repaired to a sea-port, and took ship for England.

In the vessel there was one man, and only one, who neither avoided my companionship nor recoiled at my frown. He was an idle and curious being, full of the frivolities, and egotisms, and importance of them to whom towns are homes, and talk has become a mental aliment. He was one pervading, irritating, offensive tissue of little and low thoughts. The only meanness he had not was fear. It was impossible to awe, to silence, or to shun him. He sought me for ever; he was as a blister to me, which no force could tear away; my soul grew faint when my eyes met him. He was to my sight as those creatures which from their very loathsomeness are fearful as well as despicable to us. I longed and yearned to strangle him when he addressed me! Often I would have laid my hand on him, and hurled him into the sea to the sharks, which, lynx-eyed and eager-jawed, swam night and day around our ship; but the gaze of many was on us, and I curbed myself, and turned away, and shut my eyes in very sickness; and when I opened them again, lo! he was by my side, and his sharp quick voice grated, in its prying, and asking, and torturing accents, on my loathing and repugnant ear! One night I was roused from my sleep by the screams and oaths of men, and I hastened on deck: we had struck upon a rock. It was a ghastly, but, oh Christ! how glorious a sight! Moonlight still and calm—the sea sleeping in sapphires; and in the midst of the silent and soft repose of all things, three hundred and fifty souls were to perish from the world! I sat apart, and looked on, and aided not. A voice crept like an adder's hiss upon my ear; I turned, and saw my tormentor; the moonlight fell on his face, and it grinned with the maudlin grin of intoxication, and his pale blue eye glistened, and he said, "We will not part even here!" My blood ran coldly through my veins, and I would have thrown him into the sea, which now came fast and fast upon us; *but the moonlight was on him, and I did not dare to kill him.* But I would not stay to perish with the herd, and I threw myself alone from the vessel and swam towards a rock. I saw a shark dart after me, but I shunned him, and the moment after he had plenty to sate his maw. I heard a crash, and a mingled and wild burst of anguish, the anguish of three hundred and fifty hearts that a minute afterwards were stilled, and I said in my *own* heart, with a deep joy, "*His* voice is with the rest, and we *have* parted!" I gained the shore, and lay down to sleep.

The next morning my eyes opened upon a land more beautiful than a Grecian's dreams. The sun had just risen, and laughed over streams of silver, and trees bending with golden and purple fruits, and the diamond dew sparkled from a sod covered with flowers, whose faintest breath was a delight. Ten thousand birds, with all the hues of a northern rainbow blended in their glorious and glowing wings, rose from turf and tree, and loaded the air with melody and gladness; the sea, without a vestige of the past destruction upon its glassy brow, murmured at my feet; the heavens without a cloud, and bathed in a liquid and radiant light, sent their breezes as a blessing to my cheek. I rose with a refreshed and light heart; I traversed the new home I had found; I climbed upon a high mountain, and saw that I was in a small island—it had no trace of man—and my heart swelled as I gazed around and cried aloud in my exultation, "I shall be alone again!" I descended the hill: I had not yet reached its foot, when I saw the figure of a man approaching towards me. I looked at him, and my heart misgave me. He drew nearer, and I saw that my despicable persecutor had escaped the waters, and now stood before me. He came up with his hideous grin, and his twinkling eye; and he flung his arms round me,—I would sooner have felt the slimy folds of the serpent—and said, with his grating and harsh voice, "Ha! ha! my friend, we shall be together still!" I looked at him with a grim brow, but I said not a word. There was a great cave by the shore, and I walked down and entered it, and the man followed me. "We shall live so happily here," said he; "we will never separate!" And my lip trembled, and my hand clenched of its own accord. It was now noon, and hunger came upon me; I went forth and killed a deer, and I brought it home and broiled part of it on a fire of fragrant wood; and the man ate, and crunched, and laughed, and I wished that the bones had choked him; and he said, when we had done, "We shall have rare cheer here!" But I still held my peace. At last he stretched himself in a corner of the cave and slept. I looked at him, and saw that the slumber was heavy, and I went out and rolled a huge stone to the mouth of the cavern, and took my way to the opposite part of the island; it was my turn to laugh then! I found out another cavern; and I made a bed of moss and of leaves, and I wrought a table of wood, and I looked out from the mouth of the cavern and saw the wide seas before me, and I said, "Now I shall be alone!"

When the next day came, I again went out and caught a kid, and brought it in, and prepared it as before, but I was not hungered, and I could not eat, so I roamed forth and wandered over the island: the sun had nearly set when I returned. I entered the cavern, and sitting on my bed and by my table was that man whom I thought I had left buried alive in the other cave. He laughed when he saw me, and laid down the bone he was gnawing.

"Ha, ha!" said he, "you would have served me a rare trick, but there was a hole in the cave which you did not see, and I got out to seek you. It was not a difficult matter, for the island is so small; and now we *have* met, and we will part no more!"

I said to the man, "Rise, and follow me!" So he rose, and I saw that of all my food he had left only the bones. "Shall this thing reap and I sow?" thought I, and my heart felt to me like iron.

I ascended a tall cliff: "Look round," said I; "you see that stream which divides the island; you shall dwell on one side, and I on the other; but the same spot shall not hold us, nor the same feast supply!"

"That may never be!" quoth the man; "for I cannot catch the deer, not spring upon the mountain kid; and if you feed me not, I shall starve!"

"Are there not fruits," said I, "and birds that you may snare, and fishes which the sea throws up?"

"But I like them not," quoth the man, and laughed, "so well as the flesh of kids and deer!"

"Look, then," said I, "look: by that grey stone, upon the opposite side of the stream, I will lay a deer or a kid daily, so that you may have the food you covet; but if ever you cross the stream and come into my kingdom, so sure as the sea murmurs, and the bird flies, I will kill you!"

I descended the cliff, and led the man to the side of the stream. "I cannot swim," said he; so I took him on my shoulders and crossed the brook, and I found him out a cave, and I made him a bed and a table like my own, and left him. When I was on my own side of the stream again, I bounded with joy, and lifted up my voice; "I shall be alone now!" said I.

So two days passed, and I *was* alone. On the third I went after my prey; the noon was hot, and I was wearied when I returned. I entered my cavern, and behold the man lay stretched upon my bed. "Ha, ha!" said he, "here I am; I was so lonely at home that I have come to live with you again!"

I frowned on the man with a dark brow, and I said, "So sure as the sea murmurs, and the bird flies, I will kill you!" I seized him in my arms; I plucked him from my bed; I took him out into the open air, and we stood together on the smooth sand, and by the great sea. A fear came suddenly upon me; I was struck with the awe of the still Spirit which reigns over Solitude. Had a thousand been round us, I would have slain him before them all. I feared now because we were alone in the desert, with silence and GOD! I relaxed my hold. "Swear," I said, "never to molest me again: swear to preserve unpassed the boundary of our several homes, and I will *not* kill you!"

"I cannot swear," answered the man; "I would sooner die than forswear the blessed human face—even though that face be my enemy's!"

At these words my rage returned; I dashed the man to the ground, and

I put my foot upon his breast, and my hand upon his neck, and he struggled for a moment—and was dead! I was startled; and as I looked upon his face I thought it seemed to revive; I thought the cold blue eye fixed upon me, and the vile grin returned to the livid mouth, and the hands which in the death-pang had grasped the sand, stretched themselves out to me. So I stamped on the breast again, and I dug a hole in the shore, and I buried the body. "And now," said I, "I am alone at last!" And then *the sense of loneliness*, the vague, vast, comfortless, objectless sense of desolation passed into me. And I shook—shook in every limb of my giant frame, as if I had been a chill that trembles in the dark; and my hair rose, and my blood crept, and I would not have stayed in that spot a moment more if I had been made young again for it. I turned away and fled—fled round the whole island; and gnashed my teeth when I came to the sea, and longed to be cast into some illimitable desert, that I might flee on for ever. At sunset I returned to my cave—I sat myself down on one corner of the bed, and covered my face with my hands—I thought I heard a noise; I raised my eyes, and, as I live, I saw on the other end of the bed the man whom I had slain and buried. There he sat, six feet from me, and nodded to me, and looked at me with his wan eyes, and laughed. I rushed from the cave—I entered a wood—I threw myself down—there opposite to me, six feet from my face, was the face of that man again! And my courage rose, and I spoke, but he answered not. I attempted to seize him, he glided from my grasp, and was still opposite, six feet from me as before. I flung myself on the ground, and pressed my face to the sod, and would not look up till the night came on and darkness was over the earth. I then rose and returned to the cave; I lay down on my bed, and the man lay down by me; and I frowned and tried to seize him as before, but I could not, and I closed my eyes, *and the man lay by me.* Day passed on day and it was the same. At board, at bed, at home and abroad, in my uprising and my down-sitting, by day and at night, there, by my bed-side, six feet from me, and no more, was that ghastly and dead thing. And I said, as I looked upon the beautiful land and the still heavens, and then turned to that fearful comrade, "I shall never be alone again!" And the man laughed.

At last a ship came, and I hailed it—it took me up, and I thought, as I put my foot on the deck, "I shall escape from my tormentor!" As I thought so, I saw him climb the deck too, and I strove to push him down into the sea, but in vain; he was by my side, *and he fed and slept with me as before!* I came home to my native land! I forced myself into crowds—I went to the feast, and I heard music—and I made thirty men sit with me, and watch by day and by night. So I had thirty-one companions, and one was more social than all the rest.

At last I said to myself, "This is a delusion, and a cheat of the external senses, and the thing is not, save in my mind. I will consult those skilled in such disorders, and I will be *alone again!*"

I summoned one celebrated in purging from the mind's eye its films and deceits—I bound him by an oath to secrecy—and I told him my tale. He was a bold man and a learned, and he promised me relief and release.

"Where is the figure now?" said he, smiling; "I see it not."

And I answered, "It is six feet from us!"

"I see it not," said he again; "and if it were real, my senses would not receive the image less palpably than yours." And he spoke to me as schoolmen speak. I did not argue nor reply, but I ordered the servants to prepare a room, and to cover the floor with a thick layer of sand. When it was done, I had the Leech follow me into the room, and I barred the door.

"Where is the figure now?" repeated he; and I said, "Six feet from us as before!" And the Leech smiled.

"Look on the floor," said I, and I pointed to the spot; "what see you?"

And the Leech shuddered, and clung to me that he might not fall. "The sand," said he, "was smooth when we entered, and now I see on that spot the print of human feet!"

And I laughed, and dragged my *living* companion on; "See," said I, "where we move what follows us!"

The Leech gasped for breath; "The print," said he, "of those human feet!"

"Can you not minister to me then?" cried I, in a sudden and fierce agony, "and must I never be alone again?"

And I saw the feet of the dead thing trace one word upon the sand; and the word was—

NEVER.

Introduction to Hugenin's Wife

M. P. Shiel (1865-1947), a British author of West Indian and Irish descent, may not be particularly well known today except by dedicated fans of weird fiction. Nonetheless, he was a highly influential figure in the development of supernatural fiction and a prolific writer who contributed greatly to the advancement of the science fiction genre. Best known as the author of *The Purple Cloud* (1901), an acclaimed "last man on Earth" novel, Shiel often penned stories for *The Strand*, the publication in which Arthur Conan Doyle's Sherlock Holmes tales first appeared, as well as other similar publications. In his "Supernatural Horror in Literature," H. P. Lovecraft notably singled out Shiel's "The House of Sounds" as an example of supernatural fiction at its very finest.

Originally published in a collection of the author's short fiction entitled *The Pale Ape and Other Pulses* (1911), "Hugenin's Wife" takes place primarily on the Greek island of Delos. The site of archaeological excavations since the 1870s, Delos may be just a small bit of land, but it's a place where the classical past looms large and exerts an indelible impact upon the present. In this story, the narrator-protagonist recounts how, upon receiving an invitation to visit a friend residing on the Greek island, he gradually discovers that his friend is slowly going mad following the death of his wife.

With evocative prose, M. P. Shiel crafts a decadent tale in which ancient myth and prophecy collide with modernity. Altogether, "Hugenin's Wife" is a subtle, yet chilling tale about solitude as well as a timeless reminder of love's seemingly mystical hold upon human behavior. It is also an adventurous literary foray into the supernatural, a tale set betwixt the objective physical world and the subjective perceptions of the mind's eye. It is also, as the reader shall soon see, a tale in which the island setting truly comes to life.

HUGUENIN'S WIFE
M. P. Shiel

"Ah! bitter-sweet!" —Keats.

Huguenin, my friend—the man of Art and thrills and impulses—the *boulevardier*, the *persifleur*—must, I concluded with certainty, be frenzied. So, at last, I reasoned when, after years of silence, I received from him this letter:—

"'*Sdili*,' my friend; that is the name by which they now call this ancient Delos. Wherefore has it been written, 'so passeth the glory of the world.'

"Ah! but to me it is—as to *her* it was—still Delos, the Sacred Island, birthplace of Apollo, son of Leto! On the summit of Cynthus I look from my dwelling, and within the wild reach of the Cyclades perceive even yet the offerings of fruit arriving from Syria, from Sicily, from Egypt; to festival—I note the flutter of their holy robes—the breeze once more floats to me their 'Songs of Deliverance.'

"The island now belongs almost entirely to me. I am, too, almost its sole inhabitant. It is, you know, only four miles, long, and half as broad, and I have bought up every available foot of its face. On the flat top of the granite Cynthus I live, and here, my friend, I shall die. Fetters more inexorable and horrible than any that the limbs of Prometheus ever felt rivet me to this crag.

"A friend! That is the thing after which my sick spirit famishes. A *living man*: of the dead I have enough; of living monsters, ah, too much! and a servant or two, who seem persistently to shun me—this is all I possess of human fellowship. Yet I dare not implore you, my old companion, to come to the comfort of a sinking man in this place of desolation. . . ."

The epistle continued in this strain of mingled rhapsody and despair, containing, moreover, a long rigmarole on the Pythagorean dogma of the metempsychosis of the soul. Three times did the words "living monsters" occur. From London to Delos is a journey; yet, conquered during a long vacation by an irresistible impulse, and the fond memories of other days, I actually found myself, on a starry night, disembarking on the sands that bound the once renowned harbor of the tiny island, and my arrival may be dated by the fact that it took place just two months before the extraordinary phenomena of which Delos was the scene during the night of 13th August, 1890. I first crossed the ring of flat land that almost encircles the islet, and then commenced the ascent of the central rise, the air slumbrous with the breath of rose, jasmine, almond, with the call of the cicala, the shine of the firefly. In forty minutes I had walked into a tangled garden, and placed my hand on the back of a tall man, habited in Attic garments, who was pacing there.

With a start he faced me.

"Oh," he said, panting, and clapping his hands upon his chest, "I was awfully startled! My heart—"

It was Huguenin, and yet not he. The beard rolling over his snowy robes of wool was still ebon as ever; but the fluff of hair that floated with every zephyr over his face and neck was a lifeless fluff of wool white. He stared at me with the lifeless and cavernous eyes of a man long dead.

When we entered the dwelling together, the mere appearance of the building was enough to convince me that in some mysterious way, to some morbid degree, the past had fettered and darkened the intellect of my friend. The mansion was of Hellenic type, but nothing less than mad in extent— a desert more than a habitation, a Greek house multiplied many times over into a congeries of Greek houses, like objects seen through angular glasses. It consisted of a single storey, though here and there on the flat roof there rose a second layer of apartments, attained by ladders. We walked through a door—opening inwards into a passage, which took us to a courtyard, or *aule*, surrounded by Corinthian pillars, and having in the middle an altar of marble to *Zeus Herkeios*. Around this court were ranged chambers, *thalamoi*, hung with velvets; and the whole house—made up of a hundred and a hundred reproductions of such courtyards with their surrounding chambers—formed a trackless Sahara of halls through whose labyrinths the most crafty could not but fail to thread his way.

"This building," Huguenin said to me, somedays after my arrival, "this building—every stone, plank, drapery—was the creation of my wife's wild fancy."

I stared at him.

"You doubt that I have, or had, a wife? Come with me; you shall—see her face."

He now led the way through the windowless house, lighted throughout the day and night by the reddish ray shed from many little censer lamps of terra-cotta filled with *nardinum*, an oil pressed from the blossom of the fragrant grass *nardus* of the Arabs.

I followed Huguenin through a good number of the rooms, noticing that, as he moved slowly onward, he kept his body bent, seeming to seek for something; and this something I quickly found to be crimson thread, laid down on the floor to afford a clue for the foot through the mazes of the house. Suddenly he stopped before the door of one of the apartments called *amphithalamoi*, and, himself staying without, motioned me to enter.

Now I am hardly a man of what might be called a tremulous diathesis, yet it was not without a tremor that I looked round that room. At first I could discern nothing under the glimmer from a single *lampas* hanging in the middle, but presently a painting in oils, unframed, occupying nearly one side of the room, grew upon my sight: the painting of a woman: and my pulses underwent a strange agitation as I gazed on her face.

She stood robed in flowing ruby *peplos*, with her head thrown back, and one hand and arm pointing starkly outward and upward. The countenance was not merely Grecian antique Grecian, as distinct from modern—but Grecian in a highly exaggerated and unlife-like degree. Was the woman, I asked myself, more lovely than ever mortal was before—or loathsome? For Lamia stood there before me— "shape of gorgeous hue, vermilion-spotted, golden, green and blue" —and a kind of surprise held me fixed as the image slowly took possession of my vision. The Gorgon's head! whose hair was snakes; and as I thought of this I thought, too, of how from the guttering gore of the Gorgon's head monsters rose; and then, with abhorrence, I remember Huguenin's ravings as to "monsters." I stepped nearer, in order to analyze the impression almost of dread wrought upon me, and I quickly found—or thought that I found—the key: it lay in the lady's eyes: the very eyes of the tigress: greedy glories of green glaring with radii of gold. I hurried from her.

"You have seen her?" Huguenin asked me with an eager leer of cunning.

"Yes, Huguenin," I said, "she is very beautiful."

"She painted it herself," he said in a whisper.

"Really!"

"She considered herself—she *was*—the greatest painter since Apelles."

"But now—where is she?"

He brought his lips to my ear.

"Dead. *You*, at any rate, would say so."

Well, to words so apparently senseless I would pay no attention then; but they recurred to me when I unearthed the circumstance that it was his way, at certain intervals, to make furtive visits to distant districts of the dwelling. Our bed-chambers being close together I could not fail, as time passed, to notice that he would rise in the dead of night, when he supposed me drowsing, and gathering together the fragments of our last repast, depart rapidly and soundlessly with them through the vastness of the house, led always in one particular direction by the thread of silk whose crimson lay over the floor.

I now set myself strenuously to the study of Huguenin. The name and nature of his physical sickness, at least, was clear—the affection to which physicians have given the name Cheyne Stoke's Respiration, compelling him to lie back at times in an agony of inhalation, and groan for air. The

bones of his cheeks seemed to be near appearing through their sere
trumpery of mummyskin; the *alae* of his nose got no repose from their extravagance of expansion and retraction. But even this wreck of a body
might, I believe, be rescued, were it not that to assuage the rage and fever-
ishness of such a *mind* the spheres contained no thyme. For one thing, a
most queer belief in some unnamed fate hanging over the little land he lived
on haunted him. Again and again he recalled to me all that in the far past
had been written in regard to Delos: the strange notion contained both in
the Homeric and the Alexandrian hymns to the Delian Apollo that Delos
was *floating*; or that it was only held by chains; or that it had only been
thrown up from the ocean as a temporary resting-place for Ortygia in her
birth-giving; or that it might *sink* again before the spurning foot of the newborn god. He was never weary, through hours, of pursuing, as if in solil-
oquy, a species of sleepy exegesis of such scriptures as we read together. "Do
you know," he said to me, "that the Greeks really believed the streams of
Delos to rise and fall with the rise and fall of the Nile? Could anything point
more strongly to the extraordinary character of this land, its far-extend-
ing volcanic constructions, occult geologic eccentricities?" Then he might
recite the punning line of the very old Sibylling prophecy—

"*And Sumos shall be sand, and Delos (the far-seen) sink from sight;*" often, also, having recited it, he would strike from the repining chords of a
lyre the theme of a threnody which, as he told me, his wife had composed
to suit the line; and when to the funeral ruth of this tune—so wild with woe
and whining, that I could never listen to it without a thrill—Huguenin
added the sadness of his now so hollow voice, the intensity of effect upon
me got to the intolerable degree, and I was glad of that pallid gloaming of
the mansion, which partially hid my emotion.

"Remark, however," he said one day, "the meaning of the 'far-seen' as
regards Delos: it means 'glorious' 'illustrious'—far-seen to the spiritual
rather than to the physical eye, for the island is not very elevated. The words
'sink from sight' must, therefore, be supposed to have the corresponding
significance of an extinction of this glory. And now think whether or not
this prophecy has not been already fulfilled, when I tell you that this sacro-
sanct land, which no dog's foot was once permitted to touch, on which no
man was permitted to be born or be buried, bears at this moment on its
bosom a monster more loathsome than even a demon's brain, I believe, ever
conceived. A literal and physical fulfilment of the prophecy cannot, I consider, be always distant."

But all this esotericism was not native to Huguenin: his mind, I was convinced, had been ploughed into by some very potent energy, before ever
this growth had choked it. I enticed him, little by little, to speak of his wife.
She was, he told me, of a very antique Athenian family, which by constant

effort had preserved its purity of blood; and it was while moving through Greece in a world-weary mood that, on reaching one night the village of Castri, there, on the site of the ancient Delphi, in the center of an angry throng of Greeks and Turks, who threatened to rend her to fragments, he first saw Andromeda his wife. "This incredible courage," he said, "this vast originality was hers, to take upon herself the part of a modern Hypatia— to venture upon the task of the bringing back of the gods, in the midst of fanatics, at the latter end of a century like the present. The crowd from which I rescued her was howling round her in the vestibule of a just completed temple to Apollo, whose cult she was then and there attempting to set up."

The love of the woman fastened upon her preserver with passionate fervor, and Huguenin, constrained by the vigor of a will not to be resisted, came at her bidding to live in the gray building of her creation at Delos: in which solitude, under which shadow, the man and the woman faced each other. Ere many weeks it was revealed to the husband that he had married a seer of visions and a dreamer of dreams. And visions of what tinge! and dreams of what madness! He confessed to me that he was awed by her, and with his awe was blended a feeling which, if it was not fear, was akin to fear. That he loved her not at all he now knew, while the extravagance of her passion for him he grew to regard as gruesome. Yet his mind took on the hue of hers; he drank in her doctrines, followed her as a satellite. When for days she hid herself from him, he would wander desolate and full of search over his pathless home. Finding that she habitually yielded her body to the delights of certain seeds that grew on Delos, he found the courage to frown, but ended by himself becoming a bond-slave to the drowsy *ganja* of Hindustan. So, too, with the most strange fascination which she exercised over the animal world: he disliked it—dreaded it; regarded it as excessive and unnatural; but looked on only with the furtive eye of suspicion, and said nothing. When she walked she was accompanied by a magnetized *queue* of living things, felines in particular, and birds of large size; while dogs, on the contrary, shunned her, bristling. She had brought with her from the continent a throng of these followers, of which Huguenin had never beheld the half, since they were imprisoned in unknown nooks of the building; and anon she would vanish, to reappear with new companions. Her kindness to these creatures should, no doubt, have been sufficient to account for her power over them; but Huguenin's mind, already grown morbid, probed darkly after other explanation. The primary *motif* of this unquietness doubtless lay in his wife's fanaticism on the matter of the Pythagorean dogma of the transmigration of souls. On this theme Andromeda, it was clear, was outrageously deranged. She would stand, he declared, with her arm outstretched, her eyes wild-staring, her body rigid, and in a rapid recitative—like the rapt Pythoness—prophesy of the mutations prepared for the spirit of man, dwelling, above all, with contempt, on the paucity of animal forms in the world, and insisting that the spirit of an original man, disembodied, *should* and *must* re-embody itself in a correspondingly original form. "And," she would often add, "such forms exist, but the God, willing to save the race from frenzy, hides them from the eyes of common men."

It was long, however, before I could get Huguenin to describe the final catastrophe of his wedded life. He related it in these words:—

"You now know that Andromeda was among the great painters—you have gloated upon her portrait of herself. Well, one day, after dilating, as was her wont, on the paucity of forms, she said, 'But you, too, shall be of the initiated: come, you shall see *something*.' She then went swiftly, beckoning, looking back often to smile on me a fond patronage, and I followed, till she stopped before a lately finished painting, pointing. I will not attempt—the attempt would be folly—to tell you what thing I saw before me on the canvas; nor can I explain in words the tempest of anger, of loathing and disgust, that stirred within me at the sight; but at that blasphemy of her fancy, I raised my hand to strike her head; and to this moment I know not if I struck her. My hand, it is true, felt the sensation of contact with something soft; but the blow, if blow there was, was hardly hard enough to harm a creature far feebler than man. Yet she fell; the film of death spread over her upbraiding eye; one last thing only she spoke, pointing to the uncleanness: 'You may yet see it in the flesh'; and so, still pointing, sped away.

"I bore her body, embalmed in the Greek manner by an artist of Corinth, to one of the smaller apartments on the roof, and saw, as I moved to leave her in her gloom, the mortal smile on her lips within the open coffin. Two weeks later I went again to visit her. My friend, she had vanished—but for the bones; and from the coffin, above that skull, two eyes—living—the very eyes of Andromeda, but full of a newborn brightness—the eyes, too, of the horror she had painted, whose form I now made out in the darkness—looked out upon me. After I had slammed the door, I fainted on the stair."

"The suggestion," I said to him, "which you seem to wish to convey is that of a transition of forms, from man to animal; but, surely, the explanation that the monster, brought by your wife into the house, or born in it, imprisoned unawares by you with the dead, and maddened by famine, fed on the body, is, if not less horrible, yet less improbable."

He looked doubtingly at me a moment, and then coldly said: "There was no monster imprisoned with the dead."

But at least, I pleaded, he would see the necessity of flying from that place. He replied with the avowal that it was no longer doubtful to him, from the effect which any neglect to minister to the monster's wants had upon his own health, that his life was bound up with the life of the being he stayed to maintain; that with the *second* murder which he should perpetrate—nay, with the attempt to perpetrate it, as by flight from the island—his life would be forfeited.

I accordingly formed the idea to effect the deliverance of my friend in spite of himself. Two months had now passed; the end of my visit was drawing near; yet his maladies of brain and body were not relieved: and it pained me to think of leaving him once more alone, a prey to his manias. That very day, then, while he slept his damp trances, I started the tramp on the track of the scarlet thread. So far it hauled out its length, and the halls through which it passed were of such uniformity, and its path so wound about, that I could not doubt but that the clue once snapped at any point, the voyage along its route could be accomplished only by the most improbable chance. I followed the thread to its end, where it stopped at the foot of a ladder-stair. This I ascended to a door at its top, a door with a hole in it close to the bottom, big enough to admit a plate; but, as I placed my foot on the uppermost step, a whine, complaining low, with a wild likeness to a woman's wail, sent me skipping, sick, whence I came.

But, some little distance from the steps, I broke the thread, and, gathering it up in my hand as I ran, again broke it near the region of the mansion which we occupied.

"In this way," I said, as I held the mass of thread to the flame of a lamp, "shall a man be saved."

I watched him afterwards through my half-shut eyes, as he departed, haggard and shuddering, hugging himself, on his nightly errand; and my heart galloped in an agony of disquiet while I awaited his coming again.

He was long. But when he came, he came swiftly, softly into my chamber and shook me by the shoulder. On his face was a look of unusual coolness, of dignity, of mystery. "Wake up," he said: "I wish you to leave me tonight."

"But tell me—"

"I will take no refusal. Trust me this once, and go. There is a danger here. Two of the fisher-folk of the harbor will convey you over to Rhenea before the morning."

"But danger!" I said— "from what?"

"I cannot tell you: from the destiny, whatever it be, which awaits me. The thread on which my life depends is snapped."

"But suppose I tell you—"

"Ah! . . . you hear that?"

He held up his hand and hearkened: it was a sound of howling round the house. "

"It is the wind rising," I muttered, starting up.

"But that which followed: didn't you *feel* it?"

I made him no answer.

He now clasped with his arms a marble column upon which he rested his forehead, while with one foot he kept on patting the floor; in which posture, quite demoralized and craven, he remained for some time, while the wind continued to rise; and suddenly he span toward me with a scream in a rapture of fear.

"Now at least *you feel it!*"

I could not deny: it was as if the island had rocked a little to and fro on a pivot. Now thoroughly demoralized myself, I now caught Huguenin's arm, and sought to draw him from the column which, muttering low, he was again hugging. But he would not stir; and I, determined in any event to stay by him, stood hearing the earthquake's increase while he seemed to take no further note of anything, motionless but for the motion of his foot. In this way an hour went by: at the end of which interval the rocking had become strong, rapid and continuous.

There came a second, when captured by a new panic, I sprang to shake him, understanding that some lamp had been dashed down in that passion of the mansion's agitation.

"Why, man!" I cried, "have you parted with every sense? Can't you feel that the house is in flames?"

On this his eyes, which had become dazed and dull, blazed up with a new lunacy.

"Then," he suddenly shouted in a passion of loudness, "I say she *shall* be saved!"

Before I could lay hold of the now foaming maniac, he had dashed past me into a passage. I followed in hot pursuit through rooms and corridors that seemed to reel in a furious dream of heat and reek, hoping that he, weak of lung, would fall choked and exhausted. But some energy seemed to lend him strength—he rushed onward like the hurricane; some mysterious feeling seemed to lead him—never once did he hesitate.

And after all the long chase, which ever swayed at the rocking of the land, but never stopped, I saw that the intuitions of insanity had not failed the madman—he got to the goal he gasped after. I saw him fly up the ladder, whose foot was in a pool of fire, saw him fly to the door of the tomb of Andromeda, already flagrant, and drag it open. But as he dragged it, there broke out of the room—above the roaring of the conflagration, and of the gale, and of that thousandfold growling of the ground—a shriek, shrill yet ugly with gutturalness, which congealed me in that heat; and immediately I saw proceeding from the interior a creature whose obscenity and vileness language has no vocabulary to describe. For if I say that it was a cat—of

great size—its eyes glaring like a conflagration—its fat frame wrapped in
a mass of feathers, gray, vermilion-tipped—with a similitude of miniature
wings on it—with a width of tail vast, down-turned, like the tails of birds-
of-paradise—how by such words can I express half of all the retching of
my nausea, the shame, the hate . . . The fire had ere this reached the thing,
and on fire I could spy it fly rather than spring at Huguenin's heart; then
its fangs like grapnels buried in his breast, the gluttony of its gums that met
on his gullet, I saw through a fog of feathers raining, he tottering, tearing
at the feathery horror, as backward he toppled from the landing over the
spot where a moment before the ladder had stood.

By blessed luck, as I rapidly ran thence, I stumbled upon some exit, to
find outside the night quite cloudless, star-lit, though a whirl of all the winds
of the world were whistling within the vault of sky that night. In descending, too, to the level, I remarked a rather scorched aspect of some of
the leafage, and at one spot saw a series of conical openings in the ground
with greenish scoriae round their edges. Lower still, I stood on a bluff, and
looking over the sea, witnessed a sight sublime to wildness: for the sea, too
hurried to show billow, to show ripple, and lit up deep within its depth with
a sheen of phosphorescence, was speeding as if after the steeds of Diomedes
with the fleetest meaning towards Delos. Delos, indeed, seemed to "float,"
to be swimming like a little doomed fowl counter to the swoop of the
boundless. With the morning's light I passed away from this mysterious
shrine of Grecian piety, the final sight that greeted my gaze being the still
rising reek of Huguenin's grave.

Introduction to The Far Islands

John Buchan (1875-1940) was an author, an intelligence officer, and a politician. He attended both the University of Glasgow and Oxford University. His best-known fictional work, *The Thirty-Nine Steps* (1915) was adapted for both television and the big screen several times, most notably by Alfred Hitchcock. A prolific author, Buchan also wrote biographies, non-fiction, poetry, as well as novels and short stories.

Originally published in *Blackwood's Magazine* (1899) and republished in *The Watcher by the Threshold and Other Tales* (1902), "The Far Islands" is a both a supernatural tale and a ghost story. It reads less like a work of literary fiction and more like a work of folklore in which a mythical land plays a prominent thematic role. Indeed, "The Far Islands" is both an inquiry into Scottish national identity and a parable about death in which an unreachable island serves, in part, as a metaphor for the unknowable Great Beyond. Buchan makes skillful use of lyrical imagery to transport the reader to the ragged and remote northern Scottish coastline.

The story extends its narrative and its thematic reach far beyond the scope of the short story form. Buchan's tale about a man seemingly unable to outrun his tragic destiny traverses the limitations of time and space to create a multilayered, as opposed to a singular effect. On the surface, what initially reads as a story about one man's life turns out to be a more comprehensive exploration of the impossibility of detaching oneself from one's cultural heritage. More significantly, the story is an insightful meditation upon the enduring impact of childhood wonder on one man's inner life.

THE FAR ISLANDS
John Buchan

Lady Alice, Lady Louise,
Between the wash of the tumbling seas–

I

When Bran the Blessed, as the story goes, followed the white bird on the Last Questing, knowing that return was not for him, he gave gifts to his followers. To Heliodorus he gave the gift of winning speech, and straightway the man went south to the Italian seas, and, becoming a scholar, left many descendants who sat in the high places of the Church. To Raymond he gave his steel battle-axe, and bade him go out to the warrior's path and, hew his way to a throne; which the man forthwith accomplished, and became an ancestor in the fourth degree of the first king of Scots. But to Colin, the youngest and the dearest, he gave no gift, whispering only a word in his ear and laying a finger on his eyelids. Yet Colin was satisfied, and he alone of the three, after their master's going, remained on that coast of rock and heather.

In the third generation from Colin, as our elders counted years, came one Colin the Red, who built his keep on the cliffs of Acharra and was a mighty sea-rover in his day. Five times he sailed to the rich parts of France, and a good score of times he carried his flag of three stars against the easterly Vikings. A mere name in story, but a sounding piece of nomenclature well garnished with tales. A master-mind by all accounts, but cursed with a habit of fantasy; for, hearing in his old age of a land to the westward, he forthwith sailed into the sunset, and three days later was washed up, a twisted body, on one of the outer isles.

So far it is but legend, but with his grandson, Colin the Red, we fall into the safer hands of the chroniclers. To him God gave the unnumbered sorrows of story-telling, for he was a bard, cursed with a bard's fervours, and none the less a mighty warrior among his own folk. He it was who wrote the lament called "The White Waters of Usna," and the exquisite chain of romances, "Glede-Red Gold and Grey Silver." His tales were told by many fires, down to our grandfathers' time, and you will find them still pounded at by the folklorists. But his airs—they are eternal. On harp and pipe they have lived through the centuries; twisted and tortured, they survive in many songbooks; and I declare that the other day I heard the most beautiful of them all murdered by a band at a German watering-place. This Colin led the wanderer's life, for he disappeared at middle-age, no one knew whither, and his return was long looked for by his people. Some thought that he became a Christian monk, the holy man living in the seagirt isle of Cuna, who was found dead in extreme old age, kneeling on the beach, with his arms, contrary to the fashion of the Church, stretched to the westward.

As history narrowed into bonds and forms the descendants of Colin took Raden for their surname, and settled more firmly on their lands in the long peninsula of crag and inlets which runs west to the Atlantic. Under Donald of the Isles they harried the Kings of Scots, or, on their own authority, made war on Macleans and Macranalds, till their flag of the three stars, their badge of the grey-goose feather, and their on-cry of "Cuna" were feared from Lochalsh to Cantire. Later they made a truce with the King, and entered into the royal councils. For years they warded the western coast, and as king's lieutenants smoked out the inferior pirates of Eigg and Torosay. A Raden was made a Lord of Sleat, another was given lands in the low country and the name Baron of Strathyre, but their honours were transitory and short as their lives. Rarely one of the house saw middle age. A bold, handsome, and stirring race, it was their fate to be cut off in the rude warfare of the times, or, if peace had them in its clutches, to man vessel and set off once more on those mad western voyages which were the weird of the family. Three of the name were found drowned on the far shore of Cana; more than one sailed straight out of the ken of mortals. One rode with the Good Lord James on the pilgrimage of the Heart of Bruce, and died by his leader's side in the Saracen battle. Long afterwards a Raden led the western men against the Cheshire archers at Flodden, and was slain himself in the steel circle around the king.

But the years brought peace and a greater wealth, and soon the cold stone tower was left solitary on the headland, and the new house of Kinlochuna rose by the green links of the stream. The family changed its faith, and an Episcopal chaplain took the place of the old mass-priest in the tutoring of the sons. Radens were in the '15 and the '45. They rose with Bute to power, and they long disputed the pride of Dundas in the northern capital. They intermarried with great English houses till the sons of the family were Scots only in name, living much abroad or in London, many of them English landowners by virtue of a mother's blood. Soon the race was of the common over-civilised type, graceful, well-mannered, with abundant good looks, but only once in a generation reverting to the rugged northern strength. Eton and Oxford had in turn displaced the family chaplain, and the house by the windy headland grew emptier and emptier save when grouse and deer brought home its fickle masters.

II

A childish illness brought Colin to Kinlochuna when he had reached the mature age of five, and delicate health kept him there for the greater part of the next six years. During the winter he lived in London, but from the late northern spring through all the long bright summers he lived in the great tenantless place without company—for he was an only child. A French nurse had the charge of his doings, and when he had passed through the formality of lessons there were the long pinewoods at his disposal, the rough moor, the wonderful black holes with the rich black mud in them, and best of all the bay of Acharra, below the headland, with Cuna lying in the waves a mile to the west. At such times his father was busy elsewhere; his mother was dead; the family had few near relatives; so he passed a solitary childhood in the company of seagulls and the birds of the moor.

His time for the beach was the afternoon. On the left as you go down through the woods from the house there runs out the great headland of Acharra, red and grey with mosses, and with a nimbus always of screaming sea-fowl. To the right runs a low beach of sand, passing into rough limestone boulders and then into the heather of the wood. This in turn is bounded by a reef of low rocks falling by gentle breaks to the water's edge. It is crowned with a tangle of heath and fern, bright at most seasons with flowers, and dwarf pine-trees straggle on its crest till one sees the meaning of its Gaelic name, "The Ragged Cock's-Comb." This place was Colin's playground in fine weather. When it blew rain or snow from the north he dwelt indoors among dogs and books, puzzling his way through great volumes from his father's shelves. But when the mild west-wind weather fell on the sea, then he would lie on the hot sand—Amelie the nurse reading a novel on the nearest rock—and kick his small heels as he followed his fancy. He built great sand castles to the shape of Acharra old tower, and peopled them with preposterous knights and ladies; he drew great moats and rivers for the tide to fill; he fought battles innumerable with crackling seaweed, till Amelie, with her sharp cry of "Colin, Colin," would carry, him houseward for tea.

Two fancies remained in his mind through those boyish years. One was about the mysterious shining sea before him. In certain weathers it seemed to him a solid pathway. Cuna, the little ragged isle, ceased to block the horizon, and his own white road ran away down into the west, till suddenly it stopped and he saw no farther. He knew he ought to see more, but always at one place, just when his thoughts were pacing the white road most gallantly, there came a baffling mist to his sight, and he found himself looking at a commonplace sea with Cuna lying very real and palpable in the offing. It was a vexatious limitation, for all his dreams were about this pathway. One day in June, when the waters slept in a deep heat, he came down the sands barefoot, and lo! there was his pathway. For one moment things seemed clear, the mist had not gathered on the road, and with a cry he ran down to the tide's edge and waded in. The touch of water dispelled the illusion, and almost in tears he saw the cruel back of Cuna blotting out his own magic way.

The other fancy was about the low ridge of rocks which bounded the bay on the right. His walks had never extended beyond it, either on the sands or inland, for that way lay a steep hillside and a perilous bog. But often on the sands he had come to its foot and wondered what country lay beyond. He made many efforts to explore it, difficult efforts, for the vigilant Amelie had first to be avoided. Once he was almost at the top when some seaweed to which he clung gave way, and he rolled back again to the soft warm sand. By-and-by he found that he knew what was beyond. A clear picture had built itself up in his brain of a mile of reefs, with sand in bars between them, and beyond all a sea-wood of alders slipping from the hill's skirts to the water's edge. This was not what he wanted in his explorations, so he stopped till one day it struck him that the westward view might reveal something beyond the hog-backed Cuna. One day, pioneering alone, he scaled the steepest heights of the seaweed and pulled his chin over the crest of the ridge. There, sure enough, was his picture—a mile of reefs and the tattered sea-wood. He turned eagerly seawards. Cuna still lay humped on the waters, but beyond it he seemed to see his shining pathway running far to a speck which might be an island. Crazy with pleasure he stared at the vision, till slowly it melted into the waves, and Cuna the inexorable once more blocked the sky-line. He climbed down, his heart in a doubt between despondency and hope.

It was the last day of such fancies, for on the morrow he had to face the new world of school.

At Cecil's Colin found a new life and a thousand new interests. His early delicacy had been driven away by the sea-winds of Acharra, and he was rapidly growing up a tall, strong child, straight of limb like all his house, but sinewy and alert beyond his years. He learned new games with astonishing facility, became a fast bowler with a genius for twists, and a Rugby three-quarters full of pluck and cunning. He soon attained to the modified popularity of a private school, and, being essentially clean, strong, and healthy, found himself a mark for his juniors' worship and a favourite with masters. The homage did not spoil him, for no boy was ever less self-possessed. On the cricket-ground and the football-field he was a leader, but in private he had the nervous, sensitive manners of the would-be recluse. No one ever accused him of "side" —his polite, halting address was the same to junior and senior; and the result was that wild affection which simplicity in the great is wont to inspire. He spoke with a pure accent, in which lurked no northern trace; in a little he had forgotten all about his birthplace and his origin. His name had at first acquired for him the sobriquet of "Scottie," but the title was soon dropped from its manifest inaptness.

In his second year at Cecil's he caught a prevalent fever, and for days lay very near the brink of death. At his worst he was wildly delirious, crying ceaselessly for Acharra and the beach at Kinlochuna. But as he grew convalescent the absorption remained, and for the moment be seemed to have forgotten his southern life. He found himself playing on the sands, always with the boundary ridge before him, and the hump of Cuna rising in the sea. When dragged back to his environment by the inquiries of Bellew, his special friend, who came to sit with him, he was so abstracted and forgetful that the good Bellew was seriously grieved. "The chap's a bit cracked, you know," he announced in hall. "Didn't know me. Asked me what 'footer' meant when I told him about the Bayswick match, and talked about nothing but a lot of heathen Scotch names."

One dream haunted Colin throughout the days of his recovery. He was tormented with a furious thirst, poorly assuaged at long intervals by watered milk. So when he crossed the borders of dreamland his first search was always for a well. He tried the brushwood inland from the beach, but it was dry as stone. Then he climbed with difficulty the boundary ridge, and found little pools of salt water, while far on the other side gleamed the dark black bog-holes. Here was not what he sought, and he was in deep despair, till suddenly over the sea he caught a glimpse of his old path running beyond Cuna to a bank of mist. He rushed down to the tide's edge, and to his amazement found solid ground. Now was the chance for which he had long looked, and he ran happily westwards, till of a sudden the solid earth seemed to sink with him, and he was in the waters struggling. But two curious things he noted. One was that the far bank of mist seemed to open for a pinpoint of time, and he had a gleam of land. He saw nothing distinctly, only a line which was not mist and was not water. The second was that the water was fresh, and as he was drinking from this curious new fresh sea he awoke. The dream was repeated three times before he left the sick-room. Always he wakened at the same place, always he quenched his thirst in the fresh sea, but never again did the mist open for him, and show him the strange country.

From Cecil's he went to the famous school which was the tradition in his family. The head spoke to his house-master of his coming. "We are to have another Raden here," he said, "and I am glad of it, if the young one turns out to be anything like the others. There's a good deal of dry-rot among the boys just now. They are all too old for their years and too wise in the wrong way. They haven't anything like the enthusiasm in sports they had twenty years ago when I first came here. I hope this young Raden will stir them up." The house-master agreed, and when he first caught sight of Colin's slim, well-knit figure, looked into the handsome kindly eyes, and heard his curiously diffident speech, his doubts' vanished. "We have got the right stuff now," he told himself, and the senior for whom the new boy fagged made the same comment.

From the anomalous insignificance of fagdom Colin climbed up the school, leaving everywhere a record of honest good-nature. He was allowed to forget his cricket and football, but in return he was initiated into the mysteries of the river. Water had always been his delight, so he went through the dreary preliminaries of being coached in a tub-pair till he learned to swing steadily and get his arms quickly forward. Then came the stages of scratch fours and scratch eights, till after a long apprenticeship he was promoted to the dignity of a thwart in the Eight itself. In his last year he was Captain of Boats, a position which joins the responsibility of a Cabinet Minister to the rapturous popular applause of a successful warrior. Nor was he the least distinguished of a great band. With Colin at seven the School won the Ladies' after the closest race on record.

The Head's prophecy fell true, for Colin was a born leader. For all his good-humour and diffidence of speech, he had a trick of shutting his teeth which all respected. As captain he was the idol of the school, and he ruled it well and justly. For the rest, he was a curious boy with none of the ordinary young enthusiasms, reserved for all his kindliness. At house "shouters" his was not the voice which led the stirring strains of "Stroke out all you know," though his position demanded it. He cared little about work, and the Schoolhouse scholar, who fancied him from his manner a devotee of things intellectual, found in Colin but an affected interest. He read a certain amount of modern poetry with considerable boredom; fiction he never opened. The truth was that he had a romance in his own brain which, willy nilly, would play itself out, and which left him small relish for the pale second-hand inanities of art. Often, when with others he would lie in the deep meadows by the river on some hot summer's day, his fancies would take a curious colour. He adored the soft English landscape, the lush grasses, the slow streams, the ancient secular trees. But as he looked into the hazy green distance a colder air would blow on his cheek, a pungent smell of salt and pines would be for a moment in his nostrils, and he would be gazing at a line of waves on a beach, a ridge of low rocks, and a shining sea-path running out to—ah, that he could not tell! The envious Cuna would suddenly block all the vistas. He had constantly the vision before his eyes, and he strove to strain into the distance before Cuna should

intervene. Once or twice he seemed almost to achieve it. He found that by
keeping on the top of the low rock-ridge he could cheat Cuna by a second
or two, and get a glimpse of a misty something out in the west. The vision
took odd times for recurring—once or twice in lecture, once on the
cricket-ground, many times in the fields of a Sunday, and once while he
paddled down to the start in a Trials race. It gave him a keen pleasure: it
was his private domain, where at any moment he might make some enchanting discovery.

At this time he began to spend his vacations at Kinlochuna. His father,
an elderly ex-diplomat, had permanently taken up his abode there, and was
rapidly settling into the easy life of the Scotch laird. Colin returned to his
native place without enthusiasm. His childhood there had been full of
lonely hours, and he had come to like the warm south country. He found
the house full of people, for his father entertained hugely, and the talk was
of sport and sport alone. As a rule, your very great athlete is bored by
Scotch shooting. Long hours of tramping and crouching among heather
cramp without fully exercising the body; and unless he has the love of the
thing ingrained in him, the odds are that he will wish himself home. The
father, in his new-found admiration for his lot, was content to face all
weathers; the son found it an effort to keep pace with such vigour. He
thought upon the sunlit fields and reedy watercourses with regret, and saw
little in the hills but a rough waste scarred with rock and sour with
mosses.

He read widely throughout these days, for his father had a taste for modern letters, and new books lay littered about the rooms. He read queer
Celtic tales which he thought "sickening rot," and mild Celtic poetry which
he failed to understand. Among the guests was a noted manufacturer of
fiction, whom the elder Raden had met somewhere and bidden to Kinlochuna. He had heard the tale of Colin's ancestors and the sea headland
of Acharra, and one day he asked the boy to show him the place, as he
wished to make a story of it. Colin assented unwillingly, for he had been
slow to visit this place of memories, and he did not care to make his first
experiment in such company. But the gentleman would not be gainsaid,
so the two scrambled through the sea-wood and climbed the low ridge
which looked over the bay. The weather was mist and drizzle; Cuna had
wholly hidden herself, and the bluff Acharra loomed hazy and far. Colin
was oddly disappointed: this reality was a poor place compared with his
fancies. His companion stroked his peaked beard, talked nonsense about
Colin the Red and rhetoric about "the spirit of the misty grey, weather having entered into the old tale."

"Think," he cried; "to those old warriors beyond that bank of mist was
the whole desire of life, the Golden City, the Far Islands, whatever you care

to call it." Colin shivered, as if his holy places had been profaned, set down the man in his mind most unjustly as an "awful little cad," and hurried him back to the house.

Oxford received the boy with open arms, for his reputation had long preceded him. To the majority of men he was the one freshman of his year, and gossip was busy with his prospects. Nor was gossip disappointed. In his first year he rowed seven in the Eight. The next year he was captain of his college boats, and a year later the OUBC made him its president. For three years he rowed in the winning Eight, and old coaches agreed that in him the perfect seven had been found. It was he who in the famous race of 18—caught up in the last three hundred yards the quickened stroke which gave Oxford victory. As he grew to his full strength he became a splendid figure of a man—tall, supple, deep-chested for all his elegance. His quick dark eyes and his kindly hesitating manners made people think his face extraordinarily handsome, when really it was in no way above the common. But his whole figure, as he stood in his shorts and sweater on the raft at Putney, was so full of youth and strength that people involuntarily smiled when they saw him—a smile of pleasure in so proper a piece of manhood.

Colin enjoyed life hugely at Oxford, for to one so frank and well equipped the place gave of its best. He was the most distinguished personage of his day there, but, save to school friends and the men he met officially on the river, he was little known. His diffidence and his very real exclusiveness kept him from being the centre of a host of friends. His own countrymen in the place were utterly non-plussed by him. They claimed him, eagerly as a fellow, but he had none of the ordinary characteristics of the race. There were Scots of every description around him—pale-faced Scots who worked incessantly, metaphysical Scots who talked in the Union, industrious Scots who played football. They were all men of hearty manners and many enthusiasms—who quoted Burns and dined to the immortal bard's honour every 25th of January; who told interminable Scotch stories, and fell into fervours over national sports, dishes, drinks, and religions. To the poor Colin it was all inexplicable. At the remote house of Kinlochuna he had never heard of a Free Kirk, or a haggis. He had never read a line of Burns, Scott bored him exceedingly, and in all honesty he thought Scots games inferior to southern sports. He had no great love for the bleak country, he cared nothing for the traditions of his house, so he was promptly set down by his compatriots as "denationalised and degenerate."

He was idle, too, during these years as far as his "schools" were concerned, but he was always very intent upon his own private business. Whenever he sat down to read, when he sprawled on the grass at river picnics, in chapel, in lecture—in short, at any moment when his body was at rest and his mind at leisure—his fancies were off on the same old path. Things had changed, however, in that country. The boyish device of a hard road running over the waters had gone, and now it was invariably a boat which he saw beached on the shingle. It differed in shape. At first it was an ugly salmon-coble, such as the fishermen used for the nets at Kinlochuna. Then it passed, by rapid transitions, through a canvas skiff which it took good watermanship to sit, a whiff and an ordinary dinghy, till at last it settled itself into a long rough boat, pointed at both ends, with oar-holes in the sides instead of row-locks. It was the devil's own business to launch it, and launch it anew he was compelled to for every journey, for though he left it bound in a little rock hollow below the ridge after landing, yet when he returned, lo! there was the clumsy thing high and dry upon the beach.

The odd point about the new venture was that Cuna had ceased to trouble him. As soon as he had pulled his first stroke the island disappeared, and nothing lay before him but the sea-fog. Yet, try as he might, he could come little nearer. The shores behind him might sink and lessen, but the impenetrable mist was still miles to the westward. Sometimes he rowed so far that the shore was a thin line upon the horizon, but when he turned the boat it seemed to ground in a second on the beach. The long laboured journey out and the instantaneous return puzzled him at first, but soon he became used to them. His one grief was the mist, which seemed to grow denser as he neared it. The sudden glimpse of land which he had got from the ridge of rock in the old boyish days was now denied him, and with the denial came a keener exultation in the quest. Somewhere in the west, he knew, must be land, and in this land a well of sweet water—for so he had interpreted his feverish dream. Sometimes, when the wind blew against him, he caught scents from it—generally the scent of pines, as on the little ridge on the shore behind him.

One day on his college barge, while he was waiting for a picnic party to start, he seemed to get nearer than before. Out on that western sea, as he saw it, it was fresh, blowing weather, with a clear hot sky above. It was hard work rowing, for the wind was against him, and the sun scorched his forehead. The air seemed full of scents—and sounds, too, sounds of faraway surf and wind in trees. He rested for a moment on his oars and turned his head. His heart beat quickly, for there was a rift in the mist, and far through a line of sand ringed with snow-white foam.

Somebody shook him roughly; "Come on, Colin, old man. They're all waiting for you. Do you know you've been half asleep?"

Colin rose and followed silently, with drowsy eyes. His mind was curiously excited. He had looked inside the veil of mist. Now he knew what was the land he sought.

He made the voyage often, now that the spell was broken. It was short work to launch the boat, and, whereas it had been a long pull formerly, now it needed only a few strokes to bring him to the Rim of the Mist. There was no chance of getting farther, and he scarcely tried. He was content to rest there, in a world of curious scents and sounds, till the mist drew down and he was driven back to shore.

The change in his environment troubled him little. For a man who has been an idol at the University to fall suddenly into the comparative insignificance of town is often a bitter experience; but Colin, whose thoughts were not ambitious, scarcely noticed it. He found that he was less his own master than before, but he humbled himself to his new duties without complaint. Many of his old friends were about him; he had plenty of acquaintances; and, being "sufficient unto himself," he was unaccustomed to ennui. Invitations showered upon him thick and fast. Match-making mothers, knowing his birth and his father's income, and reflecting that he was the only child of his house, desired him as a son-in-law. He was bidden welcome everywhere, and the young girls, for whose sake he was thus courted, found in him an attractive mystery. The tall good-looking athlete, with the kind eyes and the preposterously nervous manner, wakened their maidenly sympathies. As they danced with him or sat next to him at dinner, they talked fervently of Oxford, of the north, of the army, of his friends. "Stupid, but nice, my dear," was Lady Afflint's comment; and Miss Clarissa Herapath, the beauty of the year, declared to her friends that he was a "dear boy, but so awkward." He was always forgetful, and ever apologetic; and when he forgot the Shandwicks' theatre-party, the Herapaths' dance, and at least a dozen minor matters, he began to acquire the reputation of a cynic and a recluse.

"You're a queer chap, Col," Lieutenant Bellew said in expostulation.

Colin shrugged his shoulders; he was used to the description.

"Do you know that Clara Herapath was trying all she knew to please you this afternoon, and you looked as if you weren't listening? Most men would have given their ears to be in your place."

"I'm awfully sorry, but I thought I was very polite to her."

"And why weren't you at the Marshams' garden-party?"

"Oh, I went to polo with Collinson and another man. And, I say, old chap, I'm not coming to the Logans tomorrow. I've got a fence on with Adair at the school."

Little Bellew, who was a tremendous mirror of fashion and chevalier in general, looked up curiously at his tall friend.

"Why don't you like the women, Col, when they're so fond of you?"

"They aren't," said Colin, hotly, "and I don't dislike 'em. But, Lord! they bore me. I might be doing twenty things when I talk nonsense to one of 'em for an hour. I come back as stupid as an owl, and besides there's heaps of things better sport."

The truth was that, while among men he was a leader and at his ease, among women his psychic balance was so oddly upset that he grew nervous and returned unhappy. The boat on the beach, ready in general to appear at the slightest call, would delay long after such experiences, and its place would be taken by some woman's face for which he cared not a straw. For the boat, on the other hand, he cared a very great deal. In all his frank wholesome existence there was this enchanting background, this pleasure-garden which he cherished more than anything in life. He had come of late to look at it with somewhat different eyes. The eager desire to search behind the mist was ever with him, but now he had also some curiosity about the details of the picture. As he pulled out to the Rim of the Mist sounds seemed to shape themselves on his lips, which by-and-by grew into actual words in his memory. He wrote them down in scraps, and after some sorting they seemed to him a kind of Latin. He remembered a college friend of his, one Medway, now reading for the Bar, who had been the foremost scholar of his acquaintance; so with the scrap of paper in his pocket he climbed one evening to Medway's rooms in the temple.

The man read the words curiously, and puzzled for a bit. "What's made you take to Latin comps so late in life, Colin? It's baddish, you know, even for you. I thought they'd have licked more into you at Eton."

Colin grinned with amusement "I'll tell you about it later," he said. "Can you make out what it means?"

"It seems to be a kind of dog-Latin or monkish Latin or something of the sort," said Medway. "It reads like this: '*Soles occidere solent*' (that's cribbed from Catullus, and besides it's the regular monkish pun) ... *qua* ... then *blandula* something. Then there's a lot of Choctaw, and then *illae insulae dilectae in quas festinant somnia animulae gaudia*. That's pretty fair rot. Hullo, by George! here's something better—*Insula pomorum insula vitae*. That's Geoffrey of Monmouth."

He made a dive to a bookcase and pulled out a battered little calf-bound duodecimo. "Here's all about your Isle of Apple Trees. Listen. 'Situate far out in the Western ocean, beyond the Utmost Islands, beyond even the little Isle of Sheep where the cairns of dead men are, lies the Island of Apple Trees where the heroes and princes of the nations live their second life.'" He closed the book and put it back. "It's the old ancient story, the Greek Hesperides, the British Avilion, and this Apple Tree Island is the northern equivalent."

Colin sat entranced, his memory busy with a problem. Could he distinguish the scents of apple trees among the perfumes of the Rim of the Mist.

For the moment he thought he could. He was roused by Medway's voice asking the story of the writing.

"Oh, it's just some nonsense that was running in my head, so I wrote it down to see what it was."

"But you must have been reading. A new exercise for you, Colin?"

"No, I wasn't reading. Look here. You know the sort of pictures you make for yourself of places you like."

"Rather! Mine is a Devon moor with a little red shooting-box in the heart of it."

"Well, mine is different. Mine is a sort of beach with a sea and a lot of islands somewhere far out. It is a jolly place, fresh, you know, and blowing, and smells good. 'Pon my word, now I think of it, there's always been a scent of apples."

"Sort of cider-press? Well, I must be off. You'd better come round to the club and see the telegrams about the war. You should be keen about it."

One evening, a week later, Medway met a friend called Tillotson at the club, and, being lonely, they dined together. Tillotson was a man of some note in science, a dabbler in psychology, an amateur historian, a ripe genealogist. They talked of politics and the war, of a new book, of Mrs. Runnymede, and finally of their hobbies.

"I am writing an article," said Tillotson. "Craikes asked me to do it for the *Monthly*. It's on a nice point in psychics. I call it "The Transmission of Fallacies," but I do not mean the logical kind. The question is, Can a particular form of hallucination run in a family for generations. The proof must, of course, come from my genealogical studies. I maintain it can. I instance the Douglas-Ernotts, not one of whom can see straight with the left eye. That is one side. In another class of examples I take the Drapiers, who hate salt water and never go on board ship if they can help it. Then you remember the Durwards? Old Lady Balcrynie used to tell me that no one of the lot could ever stand the sight of a green frock. There's a chance for the romancer. The Manorwaters have the same madness, only their colour is red."

A vague remembrance haunted Medway's brain.

"I know a man who might give you points from his own case. Did you ever meet a chap Raden—Colin Raden?" Tillotson nodded. "Long chap—in the Guards? 'Varsity oar, and used to be a crack bowler? No, I don't know him. I know him well by sight, and I should like to meet him tremendously—as a genealogist, of course."

"Why?" asked Medway.

"Why? Because the man's family is unique. You never hear much about them nowadays, but away up in that northwest corner of Scotland they have ruled since the days of Noah. Why, man, they were aristocrats when our Howards and Nevilles were green-grocers. I wish you would get this Raden to meet me some night."

"I am afraid there's no chance of it just at present," said Medway, taking up an evening paper. "I see that his regiment has been ordered to the front. But remind me when he comes back, and I'll be delighted."

III

And now there began for Colin a curious divided life: without, a constant shifting of scene, days of heat and bustle and toil; within, a slow, tantalising, yet exquisite adventure. The Rim of the Mist was now no more the goal of his journeys, but the starting-point. Lying there, amid cool, fragrant sea-winds, his fanciful ear was subtly alert for the sounds of the dim land before him. Sleeping and waking the quest haunted him. As he flung himself on his bed the kerosene-filled air would change to an ocean freshness, the old boat would rock beneath him, and with clear eye and a boyish hope he would be waiting and watching. And then suddenly he would be back on shore, Cuna and the Acharra headland shining grey in the morning light, and with gritty mouth and sand-filled eyes he would awaken to the heat of the desert camp.

He was kept busy, for his good-humour and energy made him a willing slave, and he was ready enough for volunteer work when others were weak with heat and despair. A thirty-mile ride left him unfired; more, he followed the campaign with a sharp intelligence and found a new enthusiasm for his profession. Discomforts there might be, but the days were happy; and then—the cool land, the bright land, which was his for the thinking of it.

Soon they gave him reconnoitring work to do, and his wits were put to the trial. He came well out of the thing; and earned golden praise from the silent colonel in command. He enjoyed it as he had enjoyed a hard race on the river or a good cricket match, and when his worried companions marvelled at his zeal he stammered and grew uncomfortable. "How the deuce do you keep it up, Colin?" the major asked him. "I'm an old hand at the job, and yet I've got a temper like devilled bones. You seem as chirpy as if you were going out to fish a chalk-stream on a June morning?'

"Well, the fact is—" and Colin pulled himself up short, knowing that he could never explain. He felt miserably that he had an unfair advantage of the others. Poor Bellew, who groaned and swore in the heat at his side, knew nothing of the Rim of the Mist. It was really rough luck on the poor beggars, and who but himself was the fortunate man?

As the days passed a curious thing happened. He found fragments of the other world straying into his common life. The barriers of the two domains were falling, and more than once he caught himself looking at a steel-blue sea when his eyes should have found a mustard-coloured desert. One day, on a reconnoitring expedition, they stopped for a little on a hillock above a jungle of scrub, and, being hot and tired, scanned listlessly the endless yellow distances.

"I suppose yon hill is about ten miles off," said Bellew with dry lips.

Colin looked vaguely. "I should say five?"

"And what's that below it—the black patch? Stones or scrub?"

Colin was in a day-dream. "Why do you call it black? It's blue, quite blue?"

"Rot," said the other. "It's grey-black."

"No, it's water with the sun shining on it. It's blue, but just at the edges it's very near sea-green."

Bellew rose excitedly. "Hullo, Col, you're seeing the mirage! And you the fittest of the lot of us! You've got the sun in your head, old man!"

"Mirage!" Colin cried in contempt. He was awake now, but the thought of confusing his own bright western sea with a mirage gave him a curious pain. For a moment he felt the gulf of separation between his two worlds, but only for a moment. As the party remounted he gave his fancies the rein, and ere he reached camp he had felt the oars in his hand and sniffed the apple-tree blossom from the distant beaches.

The major came to him after supper.

"Bellew told me you saw the mirage today, Colin," he said. "I expect your eyes are getting a bit bad. Better get your sand-spectacles out."

Colin laughed. "Thanks. It's awfully good of you to bother, but I think Bellew took me up wrong. I never was fitter in my life."

By-and-by the turn came for pride to be humbled. A low desert fever took him, and though he went through the day as usual, it was with dreary lassitude; and at night, with hot hands clasped above his damp hair, he found sleep a hard goddess to conquer.

It was the normal condition of the others, so he had small cause to complain, but it worked havoc with his fancies. He had never been ill since his childish days, and this little fever meant much to one whose nature was poised on a needlepoint. He found himself confronted with a hard bare world, with the gilt rubbed from its corners. The Rim of the Mist seemed a place of vague horrors; when he reached it his soul was consumed with terror; he struggled impotently to advance; behind him Cuna and the Acharra coast seemed a place of evil dreams. Again, as in his old fever, he was tormented with a devouring thirst, but the sea beside him was not fresh, but brackish as a rock-pool. He yearned for the apple-tree beaches in front; there, he knew, were cold springs of water, the fresh smell of it was blown towards him in his nightmare.

But as the days passed and the misery for all grew more intense, an odd hope began to rise in his mind. It could not last, coolness and health were waiting near, and his reason for the hope came from the odd events at the Rim of the Mist. The haze was clearing from the foreground, the surf-lined coast seemed nearer, and though all was obscure save the milk-white sand and the foam, yet here was earnest enough for him. Once more he became cheerful; weak and light-headed he rode out again; and the major, who was recovering from sunstroke, found envy take the place of pity in his soul.

The hope was near fulfilment. One evening when the heat was changing into the cooler twilight, Colin and Bellew were sent with a small picked body to scour the foothills above the river in case of a flank attack during the night-march. It was work they had done regularly for weeks, and it is possible that precautions were relaxed. At any rate, as they turned a corner of a hill, in a sandy pass where barren rocks looked down on more barren thorn thickets, a couple of rifle shots rang out from the scarp, and above them appeared a line of dark faces and white steel. A mere handful, taken at a disadvantage, they could not hope to disperse numbers, so Colin gave the word to wheel about and return. Again shots rang out, and little Bellew had only time to catch at his friend's arm to save him from falling from the saddle.

The word of command had scarcely left Colin's mouth when a sharp pain went through his chest, and his breath seemed to catch and stop. He felt as in a condensed moment of time the heat, the desert smell, the dust in his eyes and throat, while he leaned helplessly forward on his horse's mane. Then the world vanished for him.... The boat was rocking under him, the oars in his hand. He pulled and it moved, straight, arrow-like towards the forbidden shore. As if under a great wind the mist furled up and fled. Scents of pines, of apple-trees, of great fields of thyme and heather, hung about him; the sound of wind in a forest, of cool waters falling in showers, of old moorland music, came thin and faint with an exquisite clearness. A second and the boat was among the surf, its gunwale ringed with white foam, as it leaped to the still waters beyond. Clear and deep and still the water lay, and then the white beaches shelved downward, and the boat grated on the sand. He turned, every limb alert with a strange new life, crying out words which had shaped themselves on his lips and which an echo seemed to catch and answer. There was the green forest before him, the hills of peace, the cold white waters. With a passionate joy he leaped on the beach, his arms outstretched to this new earth, this light of the world, this old desire of the heart—youth, rapture, immortality.

Bellew brought the body back to camp, himself half-dead with fatigue and whimpering like a child. He almost fell from his horse, and when others took his burden from him and laid it reverently in his tent, he stood beside it, rubbing sand and sweat from his poor purblind eyes, his teeth chattering with fever. He was given something to drink, but he swallowed barely a mouthful.

"It was some d-d-damned sharpshooter," he said. "Right through the breast, and he never spoke to me again. My poor old Col! He was the best chap God ever created, and I do-don't care a dash what becomes of me now. I was at school with him, you know, you men."

"Was he killed outright?" asked the Major hoarsely.

"N-no. He lived for about five minutes. But I think the sun had got into his head or he was mad with pain, for he d-d-didn't know where he was. He kept crying out about the smell of pine-trees and heather and a lot of pure nonsense about water."

"*Et dulces reminiscitur Argos*," somebody quoted mournfully, as they went out to the desert evening.

Introduction to The Ship Who Saw a Ghost

Frank Norris (1870-1902) was a California-based journalist and novelist who worked in the American naturalist literary genre. Norris's most famous work was the novel, *The Octopus: A Story of California* (1901), the
first of a never finished trilogy about the wheat industry. He was also the
author of a posthumously published work of short stories entitled *A Deal
in Wheat and Other Stories of the New and Old West* (1903). It was in
this collection where the uncanny seafaring tale, "The Ship That Saw a
Ghost," initially appeared.

At once a ghost story and a superbly crafted work of adventure fiction,
"The Ship That Saw a Ghost" features a ship with a human personality,
a narrator psychically scarred by an encounter with a ghost ship, and a
quest for island treasure. Most significantly, the story works as a meditation on human solitude on the open sea and a metaphor for how a man
could find himself so very alone in the world.

Indeed, Norris's prose in "The Ship That Saw a Ghost" predates H. P.
Lovecraft's theme of mankind's relative insignificance in the universe.
Sentences such as the following aptly suggest that Norris had higher thematic ambitions and aimed to write more than just a fanciful ghost story:
"For we had come at last to that region of the Great Seas where no ship
goes, the silent sea of Coleridge and the Ancient One, the unplumbed, untracked, uncharted Dreadfulness, primordial, hushed, and we were as much
alone as a grain of star-dust whirling in the empty space beyond Uranus
and the ken of the greater telescopes."

With language such as this, it is difficult not to be enraptured by this little known, albeit chillingly effective supernatural tale.

THE SHIP THAT SAW A GHOST

Frank Norris

Very much of this story must remain untold, for the reason that if it were definitely known what business I had aboard the tramp steam-freighter *Glarus*, three hundred miles off the South American coast on a certain summer's day, some few years ago, I would very likely be obliged to answer a great many personal and direct questions put by fussy and impertinent experts in maritime law—who are paid to be inquisitive. Also, I would get "Ally Bazan", Strokher and Hardenberg into trouble.

Suppose on that certain summer's day, you had asked of Lloyds' agency where the *Glarus* was, and what was her destination and cargo. You would have been told that she was twenty days out from Callao, bound north to San Francisco in ballast; that she had been spoken by the bark *Medea* and the steamer *Benevento*; that she was reported to have blown out a cylinder head, but being manageable was proceeding on her way under sail.

That is what Lloyds would have answered.

If you know something of the ways of ships and what is expected of them, you will understand that the *Glarus*, to be some half a dozen hundred miles south of where Lloyds' would have her, and to be still going south, under full steam, was a scandal that would have made her brothers and sisters ostracize her finally and forever.

And that is curious, too. Humans may indulge in vagaries innumerable, and may go far afield in the way of lying; but a ship may not so much as quibble without suspicion. The least lapse of "regularity," the least difficulty in squaring performance with intuition, and behold she is on the black list, and her captain, owners, officers, agents and consignors, and even supercargoes, are asked to explain.

And the *Glarus* was already on the black list. From the beginning her stars had been malign. As the *Breda*, she had first lost her reputation, seduced into a filibustering escapade down the South American coast, where in the end a plain-clothes United States detective—that is to say, a revenue cutter—arrested her off Buenos Ayres and brought her home, a prodigal daughter, besmirched and disgraced.

After that she was in some dreadful black-birding business in a far quarter of the South Pacific; and after that—her name changed finally to the *Glarus*—poached seals for a syndicate of Dutchmen who lived in Tacoma, and who afterward built a club-house out of what she earned.

And after that we got her.

We got her, I say, through Ryder's South Pacific Exploitation Company. The "President" had picked out a lovely little deal for Hardenberg, Strokher and Ally Bazan (the Three Black Crows), which he swore would make them "independent rich" the rest of their respective lives. It is a promising deal (B. 300 it is on Ryder's map), and if you want to know more about it you may write to ask Ryder what B. 300 is. If he chooses to tell you, that is his affair.

For B. 300—let us confess it—is, as Hardenberg puts it, as crooked as a dog's hind leg. It is as risky as barratry. If you pull it off you may—after paying Ryder his share—divide sixty-five, or possibly sixty-seven, thousand dollars between you and your associates. If you fail, and you are perilously like to fail, you will be sure to have a man or two of your companions shot, maybe yourself obliged to pistol certain people, and in the end fetch up at Tahiti, prisoner in a French patrolboat.

Observe that B. 300 is spoken of as still open. It is so, for the reason that the Three Black Crows did not pull it off. It still stands marked up in red ink on the map that hangs over Ryder's desk in the San Francisco office; and any one can have a chance at it who will meet Cyrus Ryder's terms. Only he can't get the *Glarus* for the attempt.

For the trip to the island after B. 300 was the last occasion on which the *Glarus* will smell blue water or taste the trades. She will never clear again. She is lumber.

And yet the *Glarus* on this very blessed day of 1902 is riding to her buoys off Sausalito in San Francisco Bay, complete in every detail (bar a broken propeller shaft), not a rope missing, not a screw loose, not a plank started—a perfectly equipped steam-freighter.

But you may go along the "Front" in San Francisco from Fisherman's Wharf to the China steamships' docks and shake your dollars under the seamen's noses, and if you so much as whisper *Glarus* they will edge suddenly off and look at you with scared suspicion, and then, as like as not, walk away without another word. No pilot will take the *Glarus* out; no captain will navigate her; no stoker will feed her fires; no sailor will walk her decks. The *Glarus* is suspect. She has seen a ghost.

It happened on our voyage to the island after this same B. 300. We had stood well off from shore for day after day, and Hardenberg had shaped our course so far from the track of navigation that since the *Benevento* had hulled down and vanished over the horizon no stitch of canvas nor smudge of smoke had we seen. We had passed the equator long since, and would fetch a long circuit to the southard, and bear up against the island by a circuitous route. This to avoid being spoken. It was tremendously essential that the *Glarus* should not be spoken.

I suppose, no doubt, that it was the knowledge of our isolation that impressed me with the dreadful remoteness of our position. Certainly the sea in itself looks no different at a thousand than at a hundred miles from shore. But as day after day I came out on deck at noon, after ascertaining our position on the chart (a mere pin-point in a reach of empty paper), the sight of the ocean weighed down upon me with an infinitely great awesomeness—and I was no new hand to the high seas even then.

But at such times the *Glarus* seemed to me to be threading a loneliness beyond all worlds and beyond all conception desolate. Even in more populous waters, when no sail notches the line of the horizon, the propinquity of one's kind is nevertheless a thing understood, and to an unappreciated degree comforting. Here, however, I knew we were out, far out in the desert. Never a keel for years upon years before us had parted these waters; never a sail had bellied to these winds. Perfunctorily, day in and day out we turned our eyes through long habit toward the horizon. But we knew, before the look, that the searching would be bootless. Forever and forever, under the pitiless sun and cold blue sky stretched the indigo of the ocean floor. The ether between the planets can be no less empty, no less void.

I never, till that moment, could have so much as conceived the imagination of such loneliness, such utter stagnant abomination of desolation. In an open boat, bereft of comrades, I should have gone mad in thirty minutes.

I remember to have approximated the impression of such empty immensity only once before, in my younger days, when I lay on my back on a treeless, bushless mountainside and stared up into the sky for the better part of an hour.

You probably know the trick. If you do not, you must understand that if you look up at the blue long enough, the flatness of the thing begins little by little to expand, to give here and there; and the eye travels on and on and up and up, till at length (well for you that it lasts but the fraction of a second), you all at once see space. You generally stop there and cry out, and—your hands over your eyes—are only too glad to grovel close to the good old solid earth again. Just as I, so often on short voyage, was glad to wrench my eyes away from that horrid vacancy, to fasten them upon our sailless masts and stack, or to lay my grip upon the sooty smudged taffrail of the only thing that stood between me and the Outer Dark.

For we had come at last to that region of the Great Seas where no ship goes, the silent sea of Coleridge and the Ancient One, the unplumbed, untracked, uncharted Dreadfulness, primordial, hushed, and we were as much alone as a grain of star-dust whirling in the empty space beyond Uranus and the ken of the greater telescopes.

So the *Glarus* plodded and churned her way onward. Every day and all day the same pale-blue sky and the unwinking sun bent over that moving speck. Every day and all day the same black-blue water-world, untouched by any known wind, smooth as a slab of syenite, colourful as an opal, stretched out and around and beyond and before and behind us, forever, illimitable, empty. Every day the smoke of our fires veiled the streaked whiteness of our wake. Every day Hardenberg (our skipper) at noon pricked a pin-hole in the chart that hung in the wheel-house, and that showed we were so much farther into the wilderness. Every day the world of men, of civilization, of newspapers, policemen and street-railways receded, and we steamed on alone, lost and forgotten in that silent sea.

"Jolly lot o' room to turn raound in," observed Ally Bazan, the colonial, "withaout steppin' on y'r neighbour's toes."

"We're clean, clean out o' the track o' navigation," Hardenberg told him. "An' a blessed good thing for us, too. Nobody ever comes down into these waters. Ye couldn't pick no course here. Everything leads to nowhere."

"Might as well be in a bally balloon," said Strokher.

I shall not tell of the nature of the venture on which the *Glarus* was bound, further than to say it was not legitimate. It had to do with an ill thing done more than two centuries ago. There was money in the venture, but it was not to be gained by a violation of metes and bounds which are better left intact.

The island toward which we were heading is associated in the minds of men with a Horror.

A ship had called there once, two hundred years in advance of the *Glarus*—a ship not much unlike the crank high-prowed caravel of Hudson, and her company had landed, and having accomplished the evil they had set out to do, made shift to sail away. And then, just after the palms of the island had sunk from sight below the water's edge, the unspeakable had happened. The Death that was not Death had arisen from out the sea and stood before the ship, and over it, and the blight of the thing lay along the decks like mould, and the ship sweated in the terror of that which is yet without a name.

Twenty men died in the first week, all but six in the second. These six, with the shadow of insanity upon them, made out to launch a boat, returned to the island and died there, after leaving a record of what had happened.

The six left the ship exactly as she was, sails all set, lanterns all lit—left her in the shadow of the Death that was not Death.

She stood there, becalmed, and watched them go. She was never heard of again.

Or was she—well, that's as may be.

But the main point of the whole affair, to my notion, has always been this. The ship was the last friend of those six poor wretches who made back for the island with their poor chests of plunder. She was their guardian, as it were, would have defended and befriended them to the last; and also we, the Three Black Crows and myself, had no right under heaven, nor before the law of men, to come prying and peeping into this business—into this affair of the dead and buried past. There was sacrilege in it. We were no better than body-snatchers.

When I heard the others complaining of the loneliness of our surroundings, I said nothing at first. I was no sailor man, and I was on board only by tolerance. But I looked again at the maddening sameness of the horizon—the same vacant, void horizon that we had seen now for sixteen days on end, and felt in my wits and in my nerves that same formless rebellion and protest such as comes when the same note is reiterated over and over again.

It may seem a little thing that the mere fact of meeting with no other ship should have ground down the edge of the spirit. But let the incredulous—bound upon such a hazard as ours—sail straight into nothingness for sixteen days on end, seeing nothing but the sun, hearing nothing but the thresh of his own screw, and then put the question.

And yet, of all things, we desired no company. Stealth was our one great aim. But I think there were moments—toward the last—when the Three Crows would have welcomed even a cruiser.

Besides, there was more cause for depression, after all, than mere isolation.

On the seventh day Hardenberg and I were forward by the cat-head, adjusting the grain with some half-formed intent of spearing the porpoises that of late had begun to appear under our bows, and Hardenberg had been computing the number of days we were yet to run.

"We are some five hundred odd miles off that island by now," he said, "and she's doing her thirteen knots handsome. All's well so far—but do you know, I'd just as soon raise that point o' land as soon as convenient."

"How so?" said I, bending on the line. "Expect some weather?"

"Mr. Dixon," said he, giving me a curious glance, "the sea is a queer proposition, put it any ways. I've been a seafarin' man since I was big as a minute, and I know the sea, and what's more, the Feel o' the sea. Now, look out yonder. Nothin', hey? Nothin' but the same ol' skyline we've watched all the way out. The glass is as steady as a steeple, and this ol' hooker, I reckon, is as sound as the day she went off the ways. But just the same if I were to home now, a-foolin' about Gloucester way in my little dough-dish—d'ye know what? I'd put into port. I sure would. Because why? Because I got the Feel o' the Sea, Mr. Dixon. I got the Feel o' the Sea."

I had heard old skippers say something of this before, and I cited to Hardenberg the experience of a skipper captain I once knew who had turned turtle in a calm sea off Trincomalee. I ask him what this Feel of the Sea was warning him against just now (for on the high sea any premonition is a premonition of evil, not of good). But he was not explicit.

"I don't know," he answered moodily, and as if in great perplexity, coiling the rope as he spoke. "I don't know. There's some blame thing or other close to us, I'll bet a hat. I don't know the name of it, but there's a big Bird in the air, just out of sight som'eres, and," he suddenly exclaimed, smacking his knee and leaning forward, "I–don't–like–it–one–dam'–bit."

The same thing came up in our talk in the cabin that night, after the dinner was taken off and we settled down to tobacco. Only, at this time, Hardenberg was on duty on the bridge. It was Ally Bazan who spoke instead.

"Seems to me," he hazarded, "as haow they's somethin' or other a-goin' to bump up pretty blyme soon. I shouldn't be surprised, naow, y'know, if we piled her up on some bally uncharted reef along o' to-night and went strite daown afore we'd had a bloomin' charnce to s'y 'So long, gen'lemen all.'"

He laughed as he spoke, but when, just at that moment, a pan clattered in the galley, he jumped suddenly with an oath, and looked hard about the cabin.

Then Strokher confessed to a sense of distress also. He'd been having it since day before yesterday, it seemed.

"And I put it to you the glass is lovely," he said, "so it's no blow. I guess," he continued, "we're all a bit seedy and ship-sore."

And whether or not this talk worked upon my own nerves, or whether in very truth the Feel of the Sea had found me also, I do not know; but I do know that after dinner that night, just before going to bed, a queer sense of apprehension came upon me, and that when I had come to my stateroom, after my turn upon deck, I became furiously angry with nobody in particular, because I could not at once find the matches. But here was a difference. The other man had been merely vaguely uncomfortable.

I could put a name to my uneasiness. I felt that we were being watched.

It was a strange ship's company we made after that. I speak only of the Crows and myself. We carried a scant crew of stokers, and there was also a chief engineer. But we saw so little of him that he did not count. The Crows and I gloomed on the quarterdeck from dawn to dark, silent, irritable, working upon each other's nerves till the creak of a block would make a man jump like cold steel laid to his flesh. We quarreled over absolute nothings, glowered at each other for half a word, and each one of us, at different times, was at some pains to declare that never in the course of his career had he been associated with such a disagreeable trio of brutes. Yet we were always together, and sought each other's company with painful insistence.

Only once were we all agreed, and that was when the cook, a Chinaman, spoiled a certain batch of biscuits. Unanimously we fell foul of the creature with so much vociferation as fishwives till he fled the cabin in actual fear of mishandling, leaving us suddenly seized with noisy hilarity—for the first time in a week. Hardenberg proposed a round of drinks from our single remaining case of beer. We stood up and formed an Elk's chain and then drained our glasses to each other's health with profound seriousness.

That same evening, I remember, we all sat on the quarterdeck till late and—oddly enough—related each one his life's history up to date; and then went down to the cabin for a game of euchre before turning in.

We had left Strokher on the bridge—it was his watch—and had forgotten all about him in the interest of the game, when—I suppose it was about one in the morning—I heard him whistle long and shrill. I laid down my cards and said:

"Hark!"

In the silence that followed we heard at first only the muffled lope of our engines, the cadenced snorting of the exhaust, and the ticking of Hardenberg's big watch in his waistcoat that he had hung by the arm-hole to the back of his chair. Then from the bridge, above our deck, prolonged, intoned—a wailing cry in the night—came Strokher's voice:

"Sail oh-h-h."

And the cards fell from our hands, and, like men turned to stone, we sat looking at each other across the soiled red cloth for what seemed an immeasurably long minute.

Then stumbling and swearing, in a hysteria of hurry, we gained the deck.

There was a moon, very low and reddish, but no wind. The sea beyond the taffrail was as smooth as lava, and so still that the swells from the cutwater of the *Glarus* did not break as they rolled away from the bows.

I remember that I stood staring and blinking at the empty ocean—where the moonlight lay like a painted stripe reaching to the horizon—stupid and frowning, till Hardenberg, who had gone on ahead, cried:

"Not here—on the bridge!"

We joined Strokher, and as I came up the others were asking:

"Where? Where?"

And there, before he had pointed, I saw—we all of us saw— And I heard Hardenberg's teeth come together like a spring trap, while Ally Bazan ducked as though to a blow, muttering:

"Gord 'a' mercy, what nyme do ye put to' a ship like that?"

And after that no one spoke for a long minute, and we stood there, moveless black shadows, huddled together for the sake of the blessed elbow touch that means so incalculably much, looking off over our port quarter.

For the ship that we saw there—oh, she was not a half-mile distant—was unlike any ship known to present day construction.

She was short, and high-pooped, and her stern, which was turned a little toward us, we could see, was set with curious windows, not unlike a house. And on either side of this stern were two great iron cressets such as once were used to burn signal-fires in. She had three masts with mighty yards swung 'thwart ship, but bare of all sails save a few rotting streamers. Here and there about her a tangled mass of rigging drooped and sagged.

And there she lay, in the red eye of the setting moon, in that solitary ocean, shadowy, antique, forlorn, a thing the most abandoned, the most sinister I ever remember to have seen.

Then Strokher began to explain volubly and with many repetitions.

"A derelict, of course. I was asleep; yes, I was asleep. Gross neglect of duty. I say I was asleep—on watch. And we worked up to her. When I woke, why—you see, when I woke, there she was," he gave a weak little laugh, "and—and now, why, there she is, you see. I turned around and saw her sudden like—when I woke up, that is."

He laughed again, and as he laughed the engines far below our feet gave a sudden hiccough. Something crashed and struck the ship's sides till we lurched as we stood. There was a shriek of steam, a shout—and then silence.

The noise of the machinery ceased; the *Glarus* slid through the still water, moving only by her own decreasing momentum.

Hardenberg sang, "Stand by!" and called down the tube to the engine-room.

"What's up?"

I was standing close enough to him to hear the answer in a small, faint voice:

"Shaft gone, sir."

"Broke?"

"Yes, sir."

Hardenberg faced about.

"Come below. We must talk." I do not think any of us cast a glance at the Other Ship again. Certainly I kept my eyes away from her. But as we started down the companion-way I laid my hand on Strokher's shoulder. The rest were ahead. I looked him straight between the eyes as I asked:

"Were you asleep? Is that why you saw her so suddenly?"

It is now five years since I asked the question. I am still waiting for

Strokher's answer.

Well, our shaft was broken. That was flat. We went down into the engine-room and saw the jagged fracture that was the symbol of our broken hopes. And in the course of the next five minutes' conversation with the chief we found that, as we had not provided against such a contingency, there was to be no mending of it. We said nothing about the mishap coinciding with the appearance of the Other Ship. But I know we did not consider the break with any degree of surprise after a few moments.

We came up from the engine-room and sat down to the cabin table.

"Now what?" said Hardenberg, by way of beginning.

Nobody answered at first.

It was by now three in the morning. I recall it all perfectly. The ports opposite where I sat were open and I could see. The moon was all but full set. The dawn was coming up with a copper murkiness over the edge of the world. All the stars were yet out. The sea, for all the red moon and copper dawn, was gray, and there, less than half a mile away, still lay our consort. I could see her through the portholes with each slow careening of the *Glarus.*

"I vote for the island," cried Ally Bazan, "shaft or no shaft. We rigs a bit o' syle, y'know—" and thereat the discussion began.

For upward of two hours it raged, with loud words and shaken forefingers, and great noisy bangings of the table, and how it would have ended I do not know, but at last—it was then maybe five in the morning—the lookout passed word down to the cabin:

"Will you come on deck, gentlemen?" It was the mate who spoke, and the man was shaken—I could see that—to the very vitals of him. We started and stared at one another, and I watched little Ally Bazan go slowly white to the lips. And even then no word of the ship, except as it might be this from Hardenberg:

"What is it? Good God Almighty, I'm no coward, but this thing is getting one too many for me."

Then without further speech he went on deck.

The air was cool. The sun was not yet up. It was that strange, queer midperiod between dark and dawn, when the night is over and the day not yet come, just the gray that is neither light nor dark, the dim dead blink as of the refracted light from extinct worlds.

We stood at the rail. We did not speak; we stood watching. It was so still that the drip of steam from some loosened pipe far below was plainly audible, and it sounded in that lifeless, silent grayness like—God knows what—a death tick.

"You see," said the mate, speaking just above a whisper, "there's no mistake about it. She is moving—this way."

"Oh, a current, of course," Strokher tried to say cheerfully, "sets her toward us."

Would the morning never come?

Ally Bazan—his parents were Catholic—began to mutter to himself.

Then Hardenberg spoke aloud.

"I particularly don't want—that—out—there—to cross our bows. I don't want it to come to that. We must get some sails on her."

"And I put it to you as man to man," said Strokher, "where might be your wind."

He was right. The *Glarus* floated in absolute calm. On all that slab of ocean nothing moved but the Dead Ship.

She came on slowly; her bows, the high, clumsy bows pointed toward us, the water turning from her forefoot. She came on; she was near at hand. We saw her plainly—saw the rotted planks, the crumbling rigging, the rust-corroded metal-work, the broken rail, the gaping deck, and I could imagine that the clean water broke away from her sides in refluent wavelets as though in recoil from a thing unclean. She made no sound. No single thing stirred aboard the hulk of her—but she moved.

We were helpless. The *Glarus* could stir no boat in any direction; we were chained to the spot. Nobody had thought to put out our lights, and they still burned on through the dawn, strangely out of place in their red-and-green garishness, like maskers surprised by daylight.

And in the silence of that empty ocean, in that queer half-light between dawn and day, at six o'clock, silent as the settling of the dead to the bottomless bottom of the ocean, gray as fog, lonely, blind, soulless, voiceless, the Dead Ship crossed our bows.

I do not know how long after this the Ship disappeared, or what was the time of day when we at last pulled ourselves together. But we came to some sort of decision at last. This was to go on—under sail. We were too close to the island now to turn back for—for a broken shaft.

The afternoon was spent fitting on the sails to her, and when after nightfall the wind at length came up fresh and favourable, I believe we all felt heartened and a deal more hardy—until the last canvas went aloft, and Hardenberg took the wheel.

We had drifted a good deal since the morning, and the bows of the *Glarus* were pointed homeward, but as soon as the breeze blew strong enough to get steerageway Hardenberg put the wheel over and, as the booms swung across the deck, headed for the island again.

We had not gone on this course half an hour—no, not twenty minutes—before the wind shifted a whole quarter of the compass and took the *Glarus* square in the teeth, so that there was nothing for it but to tack. And then the strangest thing befell.

I will make allowance for the fact that there was no centre-board nor keel to speak of to the *Glarus*. I will admit that the sails upon a nine-hundred-ton freighter are not calculated to speed her, nor steady her. I will even admit the possibility of a current that set from the island toward us. All this may be true, yet the *Glarus* should have advanced. We should have made a wake.

And instead of this, our stolid, steady, trusty old boat was—what shall I say?

I will say that no man may thoroughly understand a ship—after all. I will say that new ships are cranky and unsteady; that old and seasoned ships have their little crochets, their little fussinesses that their skippers must learn and humour if they are to get anything out of them; that even the best ships may sulk at times, shirk their work, grow unstable, perverse, and refuse to answer helm and handling. And I will say that some ships that for years have sailed blue water as soberly and as docilely as a street-car horse has plodded the treadmill of the 'tween-tracks, have been known to balk, as stubbornly and as conclusively as any old Bay Billy that ever wore a bell. I know this has happened, because I have seen it. I saw, for instance, the *Glarus* do it.

Quite literally and truly we could do nothing with her. We will say, if you like, that that great jar and wrench when the shaft gave way shook her and crippled her. It is true, however, that whatever the cause may have been, we could not force her toward the island. Of course, we all said "current"; but why didn't the log-line trail?

For three days and three nights we tried it. And the *Glarus* heaved and plunged and shook herself just as you have seen a horse plunge and rear when his rider tries to force him at the steam-roller.

I tell you I could feel the fabric of her tremble and shudder from bow to stern-post, as though she were in a storm; I tell you she fell off from the wind, and broad-on drifted back from her course till the sensation of her shrinking was as plain as her own staring lights and a thing pitiful to see.

We roweled her, and we crowded sail upon her, and we coaxed and bullied and humoured her, till the Three Crows, their fortune only a plain sail two days ahead, raved and swore like insensate brutes, or shall we say like mahouts trying to drive their stricken elephant upon the tiger—and all to no purpose. "Damn the damned current and the damned luck and the damned shaft and all," Hardenberg would exclaim, as from the wheel he would catch the *Glarus* falling off. "Go on, you old hooker—you tub of junk! My God, you'd think she was scared!"

Perhaps the *Glarus* was scared, perhaps not; that point is debatable. But it was beyond doubt of debate that Hardenberg was scared.

A ship that will not obey is only one degree less terrible than a mutinous crew. And we were in a fair way to have both. The stokers, whom we had impressed into duty as A.B.'s, were of course superstitious; and they knew how the *Glarus* was acting, and it was only a question of time before they got out of hand.

That was the end. We held a final conference in the cabin and decided that there was no help for it—we must turn back.

And back we accordingly turned, and at once the wind followed us, and the "current" helped us, and the water churned under the forefoot of the *Glarus*, and the wake whitened under her stern, and the log-line ran out from the trail and strained back as the ship worked homeward.

We had never a mishap from the time we finally swung her about; and, considering the circumstances, the voyage back to San Francisco was propitious.

But an incident happened just after we had started back. We were perhaps some five miles on the homeward track. It was early evening and Strokher had the watch. At about seven o'clock he called me up on the bridge.

"See her?" he said.

And there, far behind us, in the shadow of the twilight, loomed the Other Ship again, desolate, lonely beyond words. We were leaving her rapidly astern. Strokher and I stood looking at her till she dwindled to a dot. Then Strokher said:

"She's on post again."

And when months afterward we limped into the Golden Gate and cast anchor off the "Front" our crew went ashore as soon as discharged, and in half a dozen hours the legend was in every sailors' boarding-house and in every seaman's dive, from Barbary Coast to Black Tom's.

It is still there, and that is why no pilot will take the *Glarus* out, no captain will navigate her, no stoker feed her fires, no sailor walk her decks. The *Glarus* is suspect. She will never smell blue water again, nor taste the trades. She has seen a Ghost.

Introduction to The Gray Wolf

Born in Scotland, George MacDonald (1824-1905) was raised in a
Calvinist household and after graduating from the University of Aberdeen
had a brief career as a pastor. It was, however, through his work as a Vic-
torian fantasy writer and as a mentor to Lewis Carroll that he gained his
prominence in British cultural life. Remembered primarily for his fairy tales
for children, MacDonald also wrote novels, including *Phantastes: A Faerie
Romance for Men and Women* (1858) and *The Princess and the Goblin*
(1872), non-fiction, poetry, and short stories.

Originally published in a collection entitled *Works of Fantasy and Imagination* (1871), "The Gray Wolf" is a short story that unfolds like a fairy
tale for adults. The three characters in the story do not have proper names
nor do they have any outwardly unique characteristics. This, along with
the isolated island setting, provides the story with a universal, ethereal sensibility, one in which the reader can thoroughly empathize with the protagonist's fright.

MacDonald sets his tale in the isolated, windswept Shetland Islands, thus
enhancing a hauntingly effective tale of lycanthropy. Indeed, the island setting in "The Gray Wolf" serves to highlight the sense of impending doom
that permeates the entire narrative. When the story's protagonist becomes
isolated from his companions on this remote Scottish island, he finds himself in a situation at once dangerous and stranger than anything he could
have possibly imagined. As the reader will soon learn, however, being cut
off from his mates will soon be the least of his concerns.

THE GRAY WOLF
George MacDonald

One evening-twilight in spring, a young English student, who had wandered northwards as far as the outlying fragments of Scotland called the Orkney and Shetland Islands, found himself on a small island of the latter group, caught in a storm of wind and hail, which had come on suddenly. It was in vain to look about for any shelter; for not only did the storm entirely obscure the landscape, but there was nothing around him save a desert moss.

At length, however, as he walked on for mere walking's sake, he found himself on the verge of a cliff, and saw, over the brow of it, a few feet below him, a ledge of rock, where he might find some shelter from the blast, which blew from behind. Letting himself down by his hands, he alighted upon something that crunched beneath his tread, and found the bones of many small animals scattered about in front of a little cave in the rock, offering the refuge he sought. He went in, and sat upon a stone. The storm increased in violence, and as the darkness grew he became uneasy, for he did not relish the thought of spending the night in the cave. He had parted from his companions on the opposite side of the island, and it added to his uneasiness that they must be full of apprehension about him. At last there came a lull in the storm, and the same instant he heard a footfall, stealthy and light as that of a wild beast, upon the bones at the mouth of the cave. He started up in some fear, though the least thought might have satisfied him that there could be no very dangerous animals upon the island. Before he had time to think, however, the face of a woman appeared in the opening. Eagerly the wanderer spoke. She started at the sound of his voice. He could not see her well, because she was turned towards the darkness of the cave.

"Will you tell me how to find my way across the moor to Shielness?" he asked.

"You cannot find it to-night," she answered, in a sweet tone, and with a smile that bewitched him, revealing the whitest of teeth.

"What am I to do, then?" he asked.

"My mother will give you shelter, but that is all she has to offer."

"And that is far more than I expected a minute ago," he replied. "I shall be most grateful."

She turned in silence and left the cave. The youth followed. She was barefooted, and her pretty brown feet went catlike over the sharp stones, as she led the way down a rocky path to the shore. Her garments were scanty and torn, and her hair blew tangled in the wind. She seemed about five and twenty, lithe and small. Her long fingers kept clutching and pulling nervously at her skirts as she went. Her face was very gray in complexion, and very worn, but delicately formed, and smooth-skinned. Her thin nostrils were tremulous as eyelids, and her lips, whose curves were faultless, had no colour to give sign of indwelling blood. What her eyes were like he could not see, for she had never lifted the delicate films of her eyelids.

At the foot of the cliff they came upon a little hut leaning against it, and having for its inner apartment a natural hollow within it. Smoke was spreading over the face of the rock, and the grateful odour of food gave hope to the hungry student. His guide opened the door of the cottage; he followed her in, and saw a woman bending over a fire in the middle of the floor. On the fire lay a large fish broiling. The daughter spoke a few words, and the mother turned and welcomed the stranger. She had an old and very wrinkled, but honest face, and looked troubled. She dusted the only chair in the cottage, and placed it for him by the side of the fire, opposite the one window, whence he saw a little patch of yellow sand over which the spent waves spread themselves out listlessly. Under this window there was a bench, upon which the daughter threw herself in an unusual posture, resting her chin upon her hand. A moment after the youth caught the first glimpse of her blue eyes. They were fixed upon him with a strange look of greed, amounting to craving, but as if aware that they belied or betrayed her, she dropped them instantly. The moment she veiled them, her face, notwithstanding its colourless complexion, was almost beautiful.

When the fish was ready, the old woman wiped the deal table, steadied it upon the uneven floor, and covered it with a piece of fine table-linen. She then laid the fish on a wooden platter, and invited the guest to help himself. Seeing no other provision, he pulled from his pocket a hunting knife, and divided a portion from the fish, offering it to the mother first.

"Come, my lamb," said the old woman; and the daughter approached the table. But her nostrils and mouth quivered with disgust.

The next moment she turned and hurried from the hut.

"She doesn't like fish," said the old woman, "and I haven't anything else to give her."

"She does not seem in good health," he rejoined.

The woman answered only with a sigh, and they ate their fish with the help of a little rye bread. As they finished their supper, the youth heard the sound as of the pattering of a dog's feet upon the sand close to the door; but ere he had time to look out of the window, the door opened and the young woman entered. She looked better, perhaps from having just washed her face. She drew a stool to the corner of the fire opposite him. But as she sat down, to his bewilderment, and even horror, the student spied a single drop of blood on her white skin within her torn dress. The woman brought out a jar of whisky, put a rusty old kettle on the fire, and took her place in front of it. As soon as the water boiled, she proceeded to make some toddy in a wooden bowl.

Meantime the youth could not take his eyes off the young woman, so that at length he found himself fascinated, or rather bewitched. She kept her eyes for the most part veiled with the loveliest eyelids fringed with darkest lashes, and he gazed entranced; for the red glow of the little oil-lamp covered all the strangeness of her complexion. But as soon as he met a stolen glance out of those eyes unveiled, his soul shuddered within him. Lovely face and craving eyes alternated fascination and repulsion.

The mother placed the bowl in his hands. He drank sparingly, and passed it to the girl. She lifted it to her lips, and as she tasted—only tasted it—looked at him. He thought the drink must have been drugged and have affected his brain. Her hair smoothed itself back, and drew her forehead backwards with it; while the lower part of her face projected towards the bowl, revealing, ere she sipped, her dazzling teeth in strange prominence. But the same moment the vision vanished; she returned the vessel to her mother, and rising, hurried out of the cottage.

Then the old woman pointed to a bed of heather in one corner with a murmured apology; and the student, wearied both with the fatigues of the day and the strangeness of the night, threw himself upon it, wrapped in his cloak. The moment he lay down, the storm began afresh, and the wind blew so keenly through the crannies of the hut, that it was only by drawing his cloak over his head that he could protect himself from its currents. Unable to sleep, he lay listening to the uproar which grew in violence, till the spray was dashing against the window. At length the door opened, and the young woman came in, made up the fire, drew the bench before it, and lay down in the same strange posture, with her chin propped on her hand and elbow, and her face turned towards the youth. He moved a little; she dropped her head, and lay on her face, with her arms crossed beneath her forehead. The mother had disappeared.

Drowsiness crept over him. A movement of the bench roused him, and he fancied he saw some four-footed creature as tall as a large dog trot quietly out of the door. He was sure he felt a rush of cold wind. Gazing fixedly through the darkness, he thought he saw the eyes of the damsel encountering his, but a glow from the falling together of the remnants of the fire, revealed clearly enough that the bench was vacant. Wondering what could have made her go out in such a storm, he fell fast asleep.

In the middle of the night he felt a pain in his shoulder, came broad awake, and saw the gleaming eyes and grinning teeth of some animal close to his face. Its claws were in his shoulder, and its mouth in the act of seeking his throat. Before it had fixed its fangs, however, he had its throat in one hand, and sought his knife with the other. A terrible struggle followed; but regardless of the tearing claws, he found and opened his knife. He had made one futile stab, and was drawing it for a surer, when, with a spring of the whole body, and one wildly-contorted effort, the creature twisted its neck from his hold, and with something betwixt a scream and a howl, darted from him. Again he heard the door open; again the wind blew in upon him, and it continued blowing; a sheet of spray dashed across the floor, and over his face. He sprung from his couch and bounded to the door.

It was a wild night—dark, but for the flash of whiteness from the waves as they broke within a few yards of the cottage; the wind was raving, and the rain pouring down the air. A gruesome sound as of mingled weeping and howling came from somewhere in the dark. He turned again into the hut and closed the door, but could find no way of securing it.

The lamp was nearly out, and he could not be certain whether the form of the young woman was upon the bench or not. Overcoming a strong repugnance, he approached it, and put out his hands—there was nothing there. He sat down and waited for the daylight: he dared not sleep any more.

When the day dawned at length, he went out yet again, and looked around. The morning was dim and gusty and gray. The wind had fallen, but the waves were tossing wildly. He wandered up and down the little strand, longing for more light.

At length he heard a movement in the cottage. By and by the voice of the old woman called to him from the door.

"You're up early, sir. I doubt you didn't sleep well."

"Not very well," he answered. "But where is your daughter?"

"She's not awake yet," said the mother. "I'm afraid I have but a poor breakfast for you. But you'll take a dram and a bit of fish. It's all I've got."

Unwilling to hurt her, though hardly in good appetite, he sat down at the table. While they were eating, the daughter came in, but turned her face away and went to the further end of the hut. When she came forward after a minute or two, the youth saw that her hair was drenched, and her face whiter than before. She looked ill and faint, and when she raised her eyes, all their fierceness had vanished, and sadness had taken its place. Her neck was now covered with a cotton handkerchief. She was modestly attentive to him, and no longer shunned his gaze. He was gradually yielding to the temptation of braving another night in the hut, and seeing what would follow, when the old woman spoke.

"The weather will be broken all day, sir," she said. "You had better be going, or your friends will leave without you."

Ere he could answer, he saw such a beseeching glance on the face of the girl, that he hesitated, confused. Glancing at the mother, he saw the flash of wrath in her face. She rose and approached her daughter, with her hand lifted to strike her. The young woman stooped her head with a cry. He darted round the table to interpose between them. But the mother had caught hold of her; the handkerchief had fallen from her neck; and the youth saw five blue bruises on her lovely throat—the marks of the four fingers and the thumb of a left hand. With a cry of horror he darted from the house, but as he reached the door he turned. His hostess was lying motionless on the floor, and a huge gray wolf came bounding after him.

There was no weapon at hand; and if there had been, his inborn chivalry would never have allowed him to harm a woman even under the guise of a wolf. Instinctively, he set himself firm, leaning a little forward, with half outstretched arms, and hands curved ready to clutch again at the throat upon which he had left those pitiful marks. But the creature as she sprung eluded his grasp, and just as he expected to feel her fangs, he found a woman weeping on his bosom, with her arms around his neck. The next instant, the gray wolf broke from him, and bounded howling up the cliff. Recovering himself as he best might, the youth followed, for it was the only way to the moor above, across which he must now make his way to find his companions.

All at once he heard the sound of a crunching of bones—not as if a creature was eating them, but as if they were ground by the teeth of rage and disappointment; looking up, he saw close above him the mouth of the little cavern which he had taken refuge the day before. Summoning all his resolution, he passed it slowly and softly. From within came the sounds of a mingled moaning and growling.

Having reached the top, he ran at full speed for some distance across the moor before venturing to look behind him. When at length he did so, he saw, against the sky, the girl standing on the edge of the cliff, wringing her hands. One solitary wail crossed the space between. She made no attempt to follow him, and he reached the opposite shore in safety.

Introduction to The Camp of the Dog

Algernon Blackwood (1869-1951) is a name surely familiar to those immersed in Anglo-American horror fiction. Highly prolific and with an acute attention to detail, Blackwood wrote numerous ghost stories and other tales of the occult, many of them inspired by his prodigious foreign travels. Born in London, he worked as a journalist in New York City, vacationed in the rustic Canadian backwoods, and traveled in the exotic Near East.

As the creator of the psychic sleuth, John Silence, Blackwood skillfully blended the detective genre with the tropes of what would soon called "weird fiction." His collection of original stories, *John Silence: Physician Extraordinary* (1908) not only was a breakout commercial success, but it also remains an important milestone in the development of supernatural fiction. It was in that work that the "The Camp of the Dog" first appeared. This tale of lycanthropy unfolds on a remote Swedish island providing it with an aura of both mystery and suspense. Mike Ashley, author of the biography, *Algernon Blackwood: An Extraordinary Life* (Carroll & Graf, 2001), has contended that this "The Camp of the Dog" is almost certainly based on Blackwood's 1908 sojourn to Ängsholmen, an island forty miles north of Stockholm.

The story begins with a fairly lengthy and vivid portrait of rural Sweden, further indicating the author's closeness to the subject matter. Like a campfire tale, this John Silence story unfolds slowly, with hints of danger to come. Blackwood sets his tale on a remote island to better contrast the shackles of civilization with the liberating power of Nature. As the reader shall soon discover, however, sometimes too much freedom to be one's truest self may end up costing a steep price.

THE CAMP OF THE DOG
Algernon Blackwood

I

Islands of all shapes and sizes troop northward from Stockholm by the hundred, and the little steamer that threads their intricate mazes in summer leaves the traveller in a somewhat bewildered state as regards the points of the compass when it reaches the end of its journey at Waxholm. But it is only after Waxholm that the true islands begin, so to speak, to run wild, and start up the coast on their tangled course of a hundred miles of deserted loveliness, and it was in the very heart of this delightful confusion that we pitched our tents for a summer holiday. A veritable wilderness of islands lay about us: from the mere round button of a rock that bore a single fir, to the mountainous stretch of a square mile, densely wooded, and bounded by precipitous cliffs; so close together often that a strip of water ran between no wider than a country lane, or, again, so far that an expanse stretched like the open sea for miles.

Although the larger islands boasted farms and fishing stations, the majority were uninhabited. Carpeted with moss and heather, their coast-lines showed a series of ravines and clefts and little sandy bays, with a growth of splendid pine-woods that came down to the water's edge and led the eye through unknown depths of shadow and mystery into the very heart of primitive forest.

The particular islands to which we had camping rights by virtue of paying a nominal sum to a Stockholm merchant lay together in a picturesque group far beyond the reach of the steamer, one being a mere reef with a fringe of fairy-like birches, and two others, cliff-bound monsters rising with wooded heads out of the sea. The fourth, which we selected because it enclosed a little lagoon suitable for anchorage, bathing, night-lines, and whatnot, shall have what description is necessary as the story proceeds; but, so far as paying rent was concerned, we might equally well have pitched our tents on any one of a hundred others that clustered about us as thickly as a swarm of bees.

It was in the blaze of an evening in July, the air clear as crystal, the sea a cobalt blue, when we left the steamer on the borders of civilisation and sailed away with maps, compasses, and provisions for the little group of dots in the Skägård that were to be our home for the next two months. The dinghy and my Canadian canoe trailed behind us, with tents and dunnage carefully piled aboard, and when the point of cliff intervened to hide the steamer and the Waxholm hotel we realised for the first time that the horror of trains and houses was far behind us, the fever of men and cities, the weariness of streets and confined spaces. The wilderness opened up on all sides into endless blue reaches, and the map and compasses were so frequently called into requisition that we went astray more often than not and progress was enchantingly slow. It took us, for instance, two whole days to find our crescent-shaped home, and the camps we made on the way were so fascinating that we left them with difficulty and regret, for each island seemed more desirable than the one before it, and over all lay the spell of haunting peace, remoteness from the turmoil of the world, and the freedom of open and desolate spaces.

And so many of these spots of world-beauty have I sought out and dwelt in, that in my mind remains only a composite memory of their faces, a true map of heaven, as it were, from which this particular one stands forth with unusual sharpness because of the strange things that happened there, and also, I think, because anything in which John Silence played a part has a habit of fixing itself in the mind with a living and lasting quality of vividness.

For the moment, however, Dr. Silence was not of the party. Some private case in the interior of Hungary claimed his attention, and it was not till later—the 15th of August, to be exact—that I had arranged to meet him in Berlin and then return to London together for our harvest of winter work. All the members of our party, however, were known to him more or less well, and on this third day as we sailed through the narrow opening into the lagoon and saw the circular ridge of trees in a gold and crimson sunset before us, his last words to me when we parted in London for some unaccountable reason came back very sharply to my memory, and recalled the curious impression of prophecy with which I had first heard them:

"Enjoy your holiday and store up all the force you can," he had said as the train slipped out of Victoria; "and we will meet in Berlin on the 15th—unless you should send for me sooner."

And now suddenly the words returned to me so clearly that it seemed I almost heard his voice in my ear: "Unless you should send for me sooner"; and returned, moreover, with a significance I was wholly at a loss to understand that touched somewhere in the depths of my mind a vague sense of apprehension that they had all along been intended in the nature of a prophecy.

In the lagoon, then, the wind failed us this July evening, as was only natural behind the shelter of the belt of woods, and we took to the oars, all breathless with the beauty of this first sight of our island home, yet all talking in somewhat hushed voices of the best place to land, the depth of water, the safest place to anchor, to put up the tents in, the most sheltered spot for the camp-fires, and a dozen things of importance that crop up when a home in the wilderness has actually to be made.

And during this busy sunset hour of unloading before the dark, the souls of my companions adopted the trick of presenting themselves very vividly anew before my mind, and introducing themselves afresh.

In reality, I suppose, our party was in no sense singular. In the conventional life at home they certainly seemed ordinary enough, but suddenly, as we passed through these gates of the wilderness, I saw them more sharply than before, with characters stripped of the atmosphere of men and cities. A complete change of setting often furnishes a startlingly new view of people hitherto held for well-known; they present another facet of their personalities. I seemed to see my own party almost as new people—people I had not known properly hitherto, people who would drop all disguises and henceforth reveal themselves as they really were. And each one seemed to say: "Now you will see me as I am. You will see me here in this primitive life of the wilderness without clothes. All my masks and veils I have left behind in the abodes of men. So, look out for surprises!"

The Reverend Timothy Maloney helped me to put up the tents, long practice making the process easy, and while he drove in pegs and tightened ropes, his coat off, his flannel collar flying open without a tie, it was impossible to avoid the conclusion that he was cut out for the life of a pioneer rather than the church. He was fifty years of age, muscular, blue-eyed and hearty, and he took his share of the work, and more, without shirking. The way he handled the axe in cutting down saplings for the tent-poles was a delight to see, and his eye in judging the level was unfailing.

Bullied as a young man into a lucrative family living, he had in turn bullied his mind into some semblance of orthodox beliefs, doing the honours of the little country church with an energy that made one think of a coal-heaver tending china; and it was only in the past few years that he had resigned the living and taken instead to cramming young men for their examinations. This suited him better. It enabled him, too, to indulge his passion for spells of "wild life," and to spend the summer months of most years under canvas in one part of the world or another where he could take his young men with him and combine "reading" with open air.

His wife usually accompanied him, and there was no doubt she enjoyed the trips, for she possessed, though in less degree, the same joy of the wilderness that was his own distinguishing characteristic. The only difference was that while he regarded it as the real life, she regarded it as an interlude. While he camped out with his heart and mind, she played at camping out with her clothes and body. None the less, she made a splendid companion, and to watch her busy cooking dinner over the fire we had built among the stones was to understand that her heart was in the business for the moment and that she was happy even with the detail.

Mrs. Maloney at home, knitting in the sun and believing that the world was made in six days, was one woman; but Mrs. Maloney, standing with bare arms over the smoke of a wood fire under the pine trees, was another; and Peter Sangree, the Canadian pupil, with his pale skin, and his loose, though not ungainly figure, stood beside her in very unfavourable contrast as he scraped potatoes and sliced bacon with slender white fingers that seemed better suited to hold a pen than a knife. She ordered him about like a slave, and he obeyed, too, with willing pleasure, for in spite of his general appearance of debility he was as happy to be in camp as any of them.

But more than any other member of the party, Joan Maloney, the daughter, was the one who seemed a natural and genuine part of the landscape, who belonged to it all just in the same way that the trees and the moss and the grey rocks running out into the water belonged to it. For she was obviously in her right and natural setting, a creature of the wilds, a gipsy in her own home.

To any one with a discerning eye this would have been more or less apparent, but to me, who had known her during all the twenty-two years of her life and was familiar with the ins and outs of her primitive, utterly unmodern type, it was strikingly clear. To see her there made it impossible to imagine her again in civilisation. I lost all recollection of how she looked in a town. The memory somehow evaporated. This slim creature before me, flitting to and fro with the grace of the woodland life, swift, supple, adroit, on her knees blowing the fire, or stirring the frying-pan through a veil of smoke, suddenly seemed the only way I had ever really seen her. Here she was at home; in London she became some one concealed by clothes, an artificial doll overdressed and moving by clockwork, only a portion of her alive. Here she was alive all over.

I forget altogether how she was dressed, just as I forget how any particular tree was dressed, or how the markings ran on any one of the boulders that lay about the Camp. She looked just as wild and natural and untamed as everything else that went to make up the scene, and more than that I cannot say.

Pretty, she was decidedly not. She was thin, skinny, dark-haired, and possessed of great physical strength in the form of endurance. She had, too, something of the force and vigorous purpose of a man, tempestuous sometimes and wild to passionate, frightening her mother, and puzzling her easy-going father with her storms of waywardness, while at the same time she stirred his admiration by her violence. A pagan of the pagans she was besides, and with some haunting suggestion of old-world pagan beauty about her dark face and eyes. Altogether an odd and difficult character, but with a generosity and high courage that made her very lovable.

In town life she always seemed to me to feel cramped, bored, a devil in a cage, in her eyes a hunted expression as though any moment she dreaded to be caught. But up in these spacious solitudes all this disappeared. Away from the limitations that plagued and stung her, she would show at her best, and as I watched her moving about the Camp I repeatedly found myself thinking of a wild creature that had just obtained its freedom and was trying its muscles.

Peter Sangree, of course, at once went down before her. But she was so obviously beyond his reach, and besides so well able to take care of herself, that I think her parents gave the matter but little thought, and he himself worshipped at a respectful distance, keeping admirable control of his passion in all respects save one; for at his age the eyes are difficult to master, and the yearning, almost the devouring, expression often visible in them was probably there unknown even to himself. He, better than any one else, understood that he had fallen in love with something most hard of attainment, something that drew him to the very edge of life, and almost beyond it. It, no doubt, was a secret and terrible joy to him, this passionate worship from afar; only I think he suffered more than any one guessed, and that his want of vitality was due in large measure to the constant stream of unsatisfied yearning that poured for ever from his soul and body. Moreover, it seemed to me, who now saw them for the first time together, that there was an unnamable something—an elusive quality of some kind—that marked them as belonging to the same world, and that although the girl ignored him she was secretly, and perhaps unknown to herself, drawn by some attribute very deep in her own nature to some quality equally deep in his.

This, then, was the party when we first settled down into our two months' camp on the island in the Baltic Sea. Other figures flitted from time to time across the scene, and sometimes one reading man, sometimes another, came to join us and spend his four hours a day in the clergyman's tent, but they came for short periods only, and they went without leaving much trace in my memory, and certainly they played no important part in what subsequently happened.

The weather favoured us that night, so that by sunset the tents were up, the boats unloaded, a store of wood collected and chopped into lengths, and the candle-lanterns hung round ready for lighting on the trees. Sangree, too, had picked deep mattresses of balsam boughs for the women's beds, and had cleared little paths of brushwood from their tents to the central fireplace. All was prepared for bad weather. It was a cosy supper and a well-cooked one that we sat down to and ate under the stars, and, according to the clergyman, the only meal fit to eat we had seen since we left London a week before.

The deep stillness, after that roar of steamers, trains, and tourists, held something that thrilled, for as we lay round the fire there was no sound but the faint sighing of the pines and the soft lapping of the waves along the shore and against the sides of the boat in the lagoon. The ghostly outline of her white sails was just visible through the trees, idly rocking to and fro in her calm anchorage, her sheets flapping gently against the mast. Beyond lay the dim blue shapes of other islands floating in the night, and from all the great spaces about us came the murmur of the sea and the soft breathing of great woods. The odours of the wilderness—smells of wind and earth, of trees and water, clean, vigorous, and mighty—were the true odours of a virgin world unspoilt by men, more penetrating and more subtly intoxicating than any other perfume in the whole world. Oh!—and dangerously strong, too, no doubt, for some natures!

"Ahhh!" breathed out the clergyman after supper, with an indescribable gesture of satisfaction and relief. "Here there is freedom, and room for body and mind to turn in. Here one can work and rest and play. Here one can be alive and absorb something of the earth-forces that never get within touching distance in the cities. By George, I shall make a permanent camp here and come when it is time to die!"

The good man was merely giving vent to his delight at being under canvas. He said the same thing every year, and he said it often. But it more or less expressed the superficial feelings of us all. And when, a little later, he turned to compliment his wife on the fried potatoes, and discovered that she was snoring, with her back against a tree, he grunted with content at the sight and put a ground-sheet over her feet, as if it were the most natural thing in the world for her to fall asleep after dinner, and then moved back to his own corner, smoking his pipe with great satisfaction.

And I, smoking mine too, lay and fought against the most delicious sleep imaginable, while my eyes wandered from the fire to the stars peeping through the branches, and then back again to the group about me. The Rev. Timothy soon let his pipe go out, and succumbed as his wife had done, for he had worked hard and eaten well. Sangree, also smoking, leaned against a tree with his gaze fixed on the girl, a depth of yearning in his face that he could not hide, and that really distressed me for him. And Joan herself, with wide staring eyes, alert, full of the new forces of the place, evidently keyed up by the magic of finding herself among all the things her soul recognised as "home," sat rigid by the fire, her thoughts roaming through the spaces, the blood stirring about her heart. She was as unconscious of the Canadian's gaze as she was that her parents both slept. She looked to me more like a tree, or something that had grown out of the island, than a living girl of the century; and when I spoke across to her in a whisper and suggested a tour of investigation, she started and looked up at me as though she heard a voice in her dreams.

Sangree leaped up and joined us, and without waking the others we three went over the ridge of the island and made our way down to the shore behind. The water lay like a lake before us still coloured by the sunset. The air was keen and scented, wafting the smell of the wooded islands that hung about us in the darkening air. Very small waves tumbled softly on the sand. The sea was sown with stars, and everywhere breathed and pulsed the beauty of the northern summer night. I confess I speedily lost consciousness of the human presences beside me, and I have little doubt Joan did too. Only Sangree felt otherwise, I suppose, for presently we heard him sighing; and I can well imagine that he absorbed the whole wonder and passion of the scene into his aching heart, to swell the pain there that was more searching even than the pain at the sight of such matchless and incomprehensible beauty.

The splash of a fish jumping broke the spell.

"I wish we had the canoe now," remarked Joan; "we could paddle out to the other islands."

"Of course," I said; "wait here and I'll go across for it," and was turning to feel my way back through the darkness when she stopped me in a voice that meant what it said.

"No; Mr. Sangree will get it. We will wait here and cooee to guide him."

The Canadian was off in a moment, for she had only to hint her wishes and he obeyed.

"Keep out from shore in case of rocks," I cried out as he went, "and turn to the right out of the lagoon. That's the shortest way round by the map."

My voice travelled across the still waters and woke echoes in the distant islands that came back to us like people calling out of space. It was only thirty or forty yards over the ridge and down the other side to the lagoon where the boats lay, but it was a good mile to coast round the shore in the dark to where we stood and waited. We heard him stumbling away among the boulders, and then the sounds suddenly ceased as he topped the ridge and went down past the fire on the other side.

"I didn't want to be left alone with him," the girl said presently in a low voice. "I'm always afraid he's going to say or do something—" She hesitated a moment, looking quickly over her shoulder towards the ridge where he had just disappeared— "something that might lead to unpleasantness."

She stopped abruptly.

"*You* frightened, Joan!" I exclaimed, with genuine surprise. "This is a new light on your wicked character. I thought the human being who could frighten you did not exist." Then I suddenly realised she was talking seriously—looking to me for help of some kind—and at once I dropped the teasing attitude.

"He's very far gone, I think, Joan," I added gravely. "You must be kind to him, whatever else you may feel. He's exceedingly fond of you."

"I know, but I can't help it," she whispered, lest her voice should carry in the stillness; "there's something about him that—that makes me feel creepy and half afraid."

"But, poor man, it's not his fault if he is delicate and sometimes looks like death," I laughed gently, by way of defending what I felt to be a very innocent member of my sex.

"Oh, but it's not that I mean," she answered quickly; "it's something I feel about him, something in his soul, something he hardly knows himself, but that may come out if we are much together. It draws me, I feel, tremendously. It stirs what is wild in me—deep down—oh, very deep down,—yet at the same time makes me feel afraid."

"I suppose his thoughts are always playing about you," I said, "but he's nice-minded and—"

"Yes, yes," she interrupted impatiently, "I can trust myself absolutely with him. He's gentle and singularly pure-minded. But there's something else that—" She stopped again sharply to listen. Then she came up close beside me in the darkness, whispering—

"You know, Mr. Hubbard, sometimes my intuitions warn me a little too strongly to be ignored. Oh, yes, you needn't tell me again that it's difficult to distinguish between fancy and intuition. I know all that. But I also know that there's something deep down in that man's soul that calls to something deep down in mine. And at present it frightens me. Because I cannot make out what it is; and I know, I *know*, he'll do something some day that—that will shake my life to the very bottom." She laughed a little at the strangeness of her own description.

I turned to look at her more closely, but the darkness was too great to show her face. There was an intensity, almost of suppressed passion, in her voice that took me completely by surprise.

"Nonsense, Joan," I said, a little severely; "you know him well. He's been with your father for months now."

"But that was in London; and up here it's different—I mean, I feel that it may be different. Life in a place like this blows away the restraints of the artificial life at home. I know, oh, I know what I'm saying. I feel all untied in a place like this; the rigidity of one's nature begins to melt and flow. Surely *you* must understand what I mean!"

"Of course I understand," I replied, yet not wishing to encourage her in her present line of thought, "and it's a grand experience—for a short time. But you're overtired to-night, Joan, like the rest of us. A few days in this air will set you above all fears of the kind you mention."

Then, after a moment's silence, I added, feeling I should estrange her confidence altogether if I blundered any more and treated her like a child—

"I think, perhaps, the true explanation is that you pity him for loving you, and at the same time you feel the repulsion of the healthy, vigorous animal for what is weak and timid. If he came up boldly and took you by the throat and shouted that he would force you to love him—well, then you would feel no fear at all. You would know exactly how to deal with him. Isn't it, perhaps, something of that kind?"

The girl made no reply, and when I took her hand I felt that it trembled a little and was cold.

"It's not his love that I'm afraid of," she said hurriedly, for at this moment we heard the dip of a paddle in the water, "it's something in his very soul that terrifies me in a way I have never been terrified before,—yet fascinates me. In town I was hardly conscious of his presence. But the moment we got away from civilisation, it began to come. He seems so—so *real* up here. I dread being alone with him. It makes me feel that something must burst and tear its way out—that he would do something—or I should do something—I don't know exactly what I mean, probably,—but that I should let myself go and scream—"

"Joan!"

"Don't be alarmed," she laughed shortly; "I shan't do anything silly, but I wanted to tell you my feelings in case I needed your help. When I have intuitions as strong as this they are never wrong, only I don't know yet what it means exactly."

"You must hold out for the month, at any rate," I said in as matter-of-fact a voice as I could manage, for her manner had somehow changed my surprise to a subtle sense of alarm. "Sangree only stays the month, you know. And, anyhow, you are such an odd creature yourself that you should feel generously towards other odd creatures," I ended lamely, with a forced laugh.

She gave my hand a sudden pressure. "I'm glad I've told you at any rate," she said quickly under her breath, for the canoe was now gliding up silently like a ghost to our feet, "and I'm glad you're here, too," she added as we moved down towards the water to meet it.

I made Sangree change into the bows and got into the steering seat myself, putting the girl between us so that I could watch them both by keeping their outlines against the sea and stars. For the intuitions of certain folk—women and children usually, I confess—I have always felt a great respect that has more often than not been justified by experience; and now the curious emotion stirred in me by the girl's words remained somewhat vividly in my consciousness. I explained it in some measure by the fact that the girl, tired out by the fatigue of many days' travel, had suffered a vigorous reaction of some kind from the strong, desolate scenery, and further, perhaps, that she had been treated to my own experience of seeing the members of the party in a new light—the Canadian, being partly a stranger, more vividly than the rest of us. But, at the same time, I felt it was quite possible that she had sensed some subtle link between his personality and her own, some quality that she had hitherto ignored and that the routine of town life had kept buried out of sight. The only thing that seemed difficult to explain was the fear she had spoken of, and this I hoped the wholesome effects of camp-life and exercise would sweep away naturally in the course of time.

We made the tour of the island without speaking. It was all too beautiful for speech. The trees crowded down to the shore to hear us pass. We saw their fine dark heads, bowed low with splendid dignity to watch us, forgetting for a moment that the stars were caught in the needled network of their hair. Against the sky in the west, where still lingered the sunset gold, we saw the wild toss of the horizon, shaggy with forest and cliff, gripping the heart like the motive in a symphony, and sending the sense of beauty all a-shiver through the mind—all these surrounding islands standing above the water like low clouds, and like them seeming to post along silently into the engulfing night. We heard the musical drip-drip of the paddle, and the little wash of our waves on the shore, and then suddenly we found ourselves at the opening of the lagoon again, having made the complete circuit of our home.

The Reverend Timothy had awakened from sleep and was singing to himself; and the sound of his voice as we glided down the fifty yards of enclosed water was pleasant to hear and undeniably wholesome. We saw the glow of the fire up among the trees on the ridge, and his shadow moving about as he threw on more wood.

"There you are!" he called aloud. "Good again! Been setting the nightlines, eh? Capital! And your mother's still fast asleep, Joan."

His cheery laugh floated across the water; he had not been in the least disturbed by our absence, for old campers are not easily alarmed.

"Now, remember," he went on, after we had told our little tale of travel by the fire, and Mrs. Maloney had asked for the fourth time exactly where her tent was and whether the door faced east or south, "every one takes their turn at cooking breakfast, and one of the men is always out at sunrise to catch it first. Hubbard, I'll toss you which you do in the morning and which I do!" He lost the toss. "Then I'll catch it," I said, laughing at his discomfiture, for I knew he loathed stirring porridge. "And mind you don't burn it as you did every blessed time last year on the Volga," I added by way of reminder.

Mrs. Maloney's fifth interruption about the door of her tent, and her further pointed observation that it was past nine o'clock, set us lighting lanterns and putting the fire out for safety.

But before we separated for the night the clergyman had a time-honoured little ritual of his own to go through that no one had the heart to deny him. He always did this. It was a relic of his pulpit habits. He glanced briefly from one to the other of us, his face grave and earnest, his hands lifted to the stars and his eyes all closed and puckered up beneath a momentary frown. Then he offered up a short, almost inaudible prayer, thanking Heaven for our safe arrival, begging for good weather, no illness or accidents, plenty of fish, and strong sailing winds.

And then, unexpectedly—no one knew why exactly—he ended up with an abrupt request that nothing from the kingdom of darkness should be allowed to afflict our peace, and no evil thing come near to disturb us in the night-time.

And while he uttered these last surprising words, so strangely unlike his usual ending, it chanced that I looked up and let my eyes wander round the group assembled about the dying fire. And it certainly seemed to me that Sangree's face underwent a sudden and visible alteration. He was staring at Joan, and as he stared the change ran over it like a shadow and was gone. I started in spite of myself, for something oddly concentrated, potent, collected, had come into the expression usually so scattered and feeble. But it was all swift as a passing meteor, and when I looked a second time his face was normal and he was looking among the trees.

And Joan, luckily, had not observed him, her head being bowed and her eyes tightly closed while her father prayed.

"The girl has a vivid imagination indeed," I thought, half laughing, as I lit the lanterns, "if her thoughts can put a glamour upon mine in this way"; and yet somehow, when we said good-night, I took occasion to give her a few vigorous words of encouragement, and went to her tent to make sure I could find it quickly in the night in case anything happened. In her quick way the girl understood and thanked me, and the last thing I heard as I moved off to the men's quarters was Mrs. Maloney crying that there were beetles in her tent, and Joan's laughter as she went to help her turn them out.

Half an hour later the island was silent as the grave, but for the mournful voices of the wind as it sighed up from the sea. Like white sentries stood the three tents of the men on one side of the ridge, and on the other side, half hidden by some birches, whose leaves just shivered as the breeze caught them, the women's tents, patches of ghostly grey, gathered more closely together for mutual shelter and protection. Something like fifty yards of broken ground, grey rock, moss and lichen, lay between, and over all lay the curtain of the night and the great whispering winds from the forests of Scandinavia.

And the very last thing, just before floating away on that mighty wave that carries one so softly off into the deeps of forgetfulness, I again heard the voice of John Silence as the train moved out of Victoria Station; and by some subtle connection that met me on the very threshold of consciousness there rose in my mind simultaneously the memory of the girl's half-given confidence, and of her distress. As by some wizardry of approaching dreams they seemed in that instant to be related; but before I could analyse the why and the wherefore, both sank away out of sight again, and I was off beyond recall.

"Unless you should send for me sooner."

II

Whether Mrs. Maloney's tent door opened south or east I think she never discovered, for it is quite certain she always slept with the flap tightly fastened; I only know that my own little "five by seven, all silk" faced due east, because next morning the sun, pouring in as only the wilderness sun knows how to pour, woke me early, and a moment later, with a short run over soft moss and a flying dive from the granite ledge, I was swimming in the most sparkling water imaginable.

It was barely four o'clock, and the sun came down a long vista of blue islands that led out to the open sea and Finland. Nearer by rose the wooded domes of our own property, still capped and wreathed with smoky trails of fast-melting mist, and looking as fresh as though it was the morning of Mrs. Maloney's Sixth Day and they had just issued, clean and brilliant, from the hands of the great Architect.

In the open spaces the ground was drenched with dew, and from the sea a cool salt wind stole in among the trees and set the branches trembling in an atmosphere of shimmering silver. The tents shone white where the sun caught them in patches. Below lay the lagoon, still dreaming of the summer night; in the open the fish were jumping busily, sending musical ripples towards the shore; and in the air hung the magic of dawn—silent, incommunicable.

I lit the fire, so that an hour later the clergyman should find good ashes to stir his porridge over, and then set forth upon an examination of the island, but hardly had I gone a dozen yards when I saw a figure standing a little in front of me where the sunlight fell in a pool among the trees.

It was Joan. She had already been up an hour, she told me, and had bathed before the last stars had left the sky. I saw at once that the new spirit of this solitary region had entered into her, banishing the fears of the night, for her face was like the face of a happy denizen of the wilderness, and her eyes stainless and shining. Her feet were bare, and drops of dew she had shaken from the branches hung in her loose-flying hair. Obviously she had come into her own.

"I've been all over the island," she announced laughingly, "and there are two things wanting."

"You're a good judge, Joan. What are they?"

"There's no animal life, and there's no—water."

"They go together," I said. "Animals don't bother with a rock like this unless there's a spring on it."

And as she led me from place to place, happy and excited, leaping adroitly from rock to rock, I was glad to note that my first impressions were correct. She made no reference to our conversation of the night before. The new spirit had driven out the old. There was no room in her heart for fear or anxiety, and Nature had everything her own way.

The island, we found, was some three-quarters of a mile from point to point, built in a circle, or wide horseshoe, with an opening of twenty feet at the mouth of the lagoon. Pine-trees grew thickly all over, but here and there were patches of silver birch, scrub oak, and considerable colonies of wild raspberry and gooseberry bushes. The two ends of the horseshoe formed bare slabs of smooth granite running into the sea and forming dangerous reefs just below the surface, but the rest of the island rose in a forty-foot ridge and sloped down steeply to the sea on either side, being nowhere more than a hundred yards wide.

The outer shore-line was much indented with numberless coves and bays and sandy beaches, with here and there caves and precipitous little cliffs against which the sea broke in spray and thunder. But the inner shore, the shore of the lagoon, was low and regular, and so well protected by the wall of trees along the ridge that no storm could ever send more than a passing ripple along its sandy marges. Eternal shelter reigned there.

On one of the other islands, a few hundred yards away—for the rest of the party slept late this first morning, and we took to the canoe—we discovered a spring of fresh water untainted by the brackish flavour of the Baltic, and having thus solved the most important problem of the Camp, we next proceeded to deal with the second—fish. And in half an hour we reeled in and turned homewards, for we had no means of storage, and to clean more fish than may be stored or eaten in a day is no wise occupation for experienced campers.

And as we landed towards six o'clock we heard the clergyman singing as usual and saw his wife and Sangree shaking out their blankets in the sun, and dressed in a fashion that finally dispelled all memories of streets and civilisation.

"The Little People lit the fire for me," cried Maloney, looking natural and at home in his ancient flannel suit and breaking off in the middle of his singing, "so I've got the porridge going—and this time it's *not* burnt."

We reported the discovery of water and held up the fish.

"Good! Good again!" he cried. "We'll have the first decent breakfast we've had this year. Sangree'll clean 'em in no time, and the Bo'sun's Mate—"

"Will fry them to a turn," laughed the voice of Mrs. Maloney, appearing on the scene in a tight blue jersey and sandals, and catching up the frying-pan. Her husband always called her the Bo'sun's Mate in Camp, because it was her duty, among others, to pipe all hands to meals.

"And as for you, Joan," went on the happy man, "you look like the spirit of the island, with moss in your hair and wind in your eyes, and sun and stars mixed in your face." He looked at her with delighted admiration. "Here, Sangree, take these twelve, there's a good fellow, they're the biggest; and we'll have 'em in butter in less time than you can say Baltic island!"

I watched the Canadian as he slowly moved off to the cleaning pail. His eyes were drinking in the girl's beauty, and a wave of passionate, almost feverish, joy passed over his face, expressive of the ecstasy of true worship more than anything else. Perhaps he was thinking that he still had three weeks to come with that vision always before his eyes; perhaps he was thinking of his dreams in the night. I cannot say. But I noticed the curious mingling of yearning and happiness in his eyes, and the strength of the impression touched my curiosity. Something in his face held my gaze for a second, something to do with its intensity. That so timid, so gentle a personality should conceal so virile a passion almost seemed to require explanation.

But the impression was momentary, for that first breakfast in Camp permitted no divided attentions, and I dare swear that the porridge, the tea, the Swedish "flatbread," and the fried fish flavoured with points of frizzled bacon, were better than any meal eaten elsewhere that day in the whole world.

The first clear day in a new camp is always a furiously busy one, and we soon dropped into the routine upon which in large measure the real comfort of every one depends. About the cooking-fire, greatly improved with stones from the shore, we built a high stockade consisting of upright poles thickly twined with branches, the roof lined with moss and lichen and weighted with rocks, and round the interior we made low wooden seats so that we could lie round the fire even in rain and eat our meals in peace. Paths, too, outlined themselves from tent to tent, from the bathing places and the landing stage, and a fair division of the island was decided upon between the quarters of the men and the women. Wood was stacked, awkward trees and boulders removed, hammocks slung, and tents strengthened. In a word, Camp was established, and duties were assigned and accepted as though we expected to live on this Baltic island for years to come and the smallest detail of the Community life was important.

Moreover, as the Camp came into being, this sense of a community developed, proving that we were a definite whole, and not merely separate human beings living for a while in tents upon a desert island. Each fell willingly into the routine. Sangree, as by natural selection, took upon himself the cleaning of the fish and the cutting of the wood into lengths sufficient for a day's use. And he did it well. The pan of water was never without a fish, cleaned and scaled, ready to fry for whoever was hungry; the nightly fire never died down for lack of material to throw on without going farther afield to search.

And Timothy, once reverend, caught the fish and chopped down the trees. He also assumed responsibility for the condition of the boat, and did it so thoroughly that nothing in the little cutter was ever found wanting. And when, for any reason, his presence was in demand, the first place to look for him was—in the boat, and there, too, he was usually found, tinkering away with sheets, sails, or rudder and singing as he tinkered.

Nor was the "reading" neglected; for most mornings there came a sound of droning voices from the white tent by the raspberry bushes, which signified that Sangree, the tutor, and whatever other man chanced to be in the party at the time, were hard at it with history or the classics.

And while Mrs. Maloney, also by natural selection, took charge of the larder and the kitchen, the mending and general supervision of the rough comforts, she also made herself peculiarly mistress of the megaphone which summoned to meals and carried her voice easily from one end of the island to the other; and in her hours of leisure she daubed the surrounding scenery on to a sketching block with all the honesty and devotion of her determined but unreceptive soul.

Joan, meanwhile, Joan, elusive creature of the wilds, became I know not exactly what. She did plenty of work in the Camp, yet seemed to have no very precise duties. She was everywhere and anywhere. Sometimes she slept in her tent, sometimes under the stars with a blanket. She knew every inch of the island and kept turning up in places where she was least expected—for ever wandering about, reading her books in sheltered corners, making little fires on sunless days to "worship by to the gods," as she put it, ever finding new pools to dive and bathe in, and swimming day and night in the warm and waveless lagoon like a fish in a huge tank. She went barelegged and bare-footed, with her hair down and her skirts caught up to the knees, and if ever a human being turned into a jolly savage within the compass of a single week, Joan Maloney was certainly that human being. She ran wild.

So completely, too, was she possessed by the strong spirit of the place that the little human fear she had yielded to so strangely on our arrival seemed to have been utterly dispossessed. As I hoped and expected, she made no reference to our conversation of the first evening. Sangree bothered her with no special attentions, and after all they were very little together. His behaviour was perfect in that respect, and I, for my part, hardly gave the matter another thought. Joan was ever a prey to vivid fancies of one kind or another, and this was one of them. Mercifully for the happiness of all concerned, it had melted away before the spirit of busy, active life and deep content that reigned over the island. Every one was intensely alive, and peace was upon all.

Meanwhile the effect of the camp-life began to tell. Always a searching test of character, its results, sooner or later, are infallible, for it acts upon the soul as swiftly and surely as the hypo bath upon the negative of a photograph. A readjustment of the personal forces takes place quickly; some parts of the personality go to sleep, others wake up: but the first sweeping change that the primitive life brings about is that the artificial portions of the character shed themselves one after another like dead skins. Attitudes and poses that seemed genuine in the city drop away. The mind, like the body, grows quickly hard, simple, uncomplex. And in a camp as primitive and close to nature as ours was, these effects became speedily visible.

Some folk, of course, who talk glibly about the simple life when it is safely out of reach, betray themselves in camp by for ever peering about for the artificial excitements of civilisation which they miss. Some get bored at once; some grow slovenly; some reveal the animal in most unexpected fashion; and some, the select few, find themselves in very short order and are happy.

And, in our little party, we could flatter ourselves that we all belonged to the last category, so far as the general effect was concerned. Only there were certain other changes as well, varying with each individual, and all interesting to note.

It was only after the first week or two that these changes became marked, although this is the proper place, I think, to speak of them. For, having myself no other duty than to enjoy a well-earned holiday, I used to load my canoe with blankets and provisions and journey forth on exploration trips among the islands of several days together; and it was on my return from the first of these—when I rediscovered the party, so to speak— that these changes first presented themselves vividly to me, and in one particular instance produced a rather curious impression.

In a word, then, while every one had grown wilder, naturally wilder, Sangree, it seemed to me, had grown much wilder, and what I can only call unnaturally wilder. He made me think of a savage.

To begin with, he had changed immensely in mere physical appearance, and the full brown cheeks, the brighter eyes of absolute health, and the general air of vigour and robustness that had come to replace his customary lassitude and timidity, had worked such an improvement that I hardly knew him for the same man. His voice, too, was deeper and his manner bespoke for the first time a greater measure of confidence in himself. He now had some claims to be called nice-looking, or at least to a certain air of virility that would not lessen his value in the eyes of the opposite sex.

All this, of course, was natural enough, and most welcome. But, altogether apart from this physical change, which no doubt had also been going forward in the rest of us, there was a subtle note in his personality that came to me with a degree of surprise that almost amounted to shock.

And two things—as he came down to welcome me and pull up the canoe—leaped up in my mind unbidden, as though connected in some way I could not at the moment divine—first, the curious judgment formed of him by Joan; and secondly, that fugitive expression I had caught in his face while Maloney was offering up his strange prayer for special protection from Heaven.

The delicacy of manner and feature—to call it by no milder term—which had always been a distinguishing characteristic of the man, had been replaced by something far more vigorous and decided, that yet utterly eluded analysis. The change which impressed me so oddly was not easy to name. The others—singing Maloney, the bustling Bo'sun's Mate, and Joan, that fascinating half-breed of undine and salamander—all showed the effects of a life so close to nature; but in their case the change was perfectly natural and what was to be expected, whereas with Peter Sangree, the Canadian, it was something unusual and unexpected.

It is impossible to explain how he managed gradually to convey to my mind the impression that something in him had turned savage, yet this, more or less, is the impression that he did convey. It was not that he seemed really less civilised, or that his character had undergone any definite alteration, but rather that something in him, hitherto dormant, had awakened to life. Some quality, latent till now—so far, at least, as we were concerned, who, after all, knew him but slightly—had stirred into activity and risen to the surface of his being.

And while, for the moment, this seemed as far as I could get, it was but natural that my mind should continue the intuitive process and acknowledge that John Silence, owing to his peculiar faculties, and the girl, owing to her singularly receptive temperament, might each in a different way have divined this latent quality in his soul, and feared its manifestation later.

On looking back to this painful adventure, too, it now seems equally natural that the same process, carried to its logical conclusion, should have wakened some deep instinct in me that, wholly without direction from my will, set itself sharply and persistently upon the watch from that very moment. Thenceforward the personality of Sangree was never far from my thoughts, and I was for ever analysing and searching for the explanation that took so long in coming.

"I declare, Hubbard, you're tanned like an aboriginal, and you look like one, too," laughed Maloney.

"And I can return the compliment," was my reply, as we all gathered round a brew of tea to exchange news and compare notes.

And later, at supper, it amused me to observe that the distinguished tutor, once clergyman, did not eat his food quite as "nicely" as he did at home—he devoured it; that Mrs. Maloney ate more, and, to say the least, with less delay, than was her custom in the select atmosphere of her English dining-room; and that while Joan attacked her tin plateful with genuine avidity, Sangree, the Canadian, bit and gnawed at his, laughing and talking and complimenting the cook all the while, and making me think with secret amusement of a starved animal at its first meal. While, from their remarks about myself, I judged that I had changed and grown wild as much as the rest of them.

In this and in a hundred other little ways the change showed, ways difficult to define in detail, but all proving—not the coarsening effect of leading the primitive life, but, let us say, the more direct and unvarnished methods that became prevalent. For all day long we were in the bath of the elements—wind, water, sun—and just as the body became insensible to cold and shed unnecessary clothing, the mind grew straightforward and shed many of the disguises required by the conventions of civilisation.

And in each, according to temperament and character, there stirred the life-instincts that were natural, untamed, and, in a sense—savage.

III

So it came about that I stayed with our island party, putting off my second exploring trip from day to day, and I think that this far-fetched instinct to watch Sangree was really the cause of my postponement.

For another ten days the life of the Camp pursued its even and delightful way, blessed by perfect summer weather, a good harvest of fish, fine winds for sailing, and calm, starry nights. Maloney's selfish prayer had been favourably received. Nothing came to disturb or perplex. There was not even the prowling of night animals to vex the rest of Mrs. Maloney; for in previous camps it had often been her peculiar affliction that she heard the porcupines scratching against the canvas, or the squirrels dropping fir-cones in the early morning with a sound of miniature thunder upon the roof of her tent. But on this island there was not even a squirrel or a mouse. I think two toads and a small and harmless snake were the only living creatures that had been discovered during the whole of the first fortnight. And these two toads in all probability were not two toads, but one toad.

Then, suddenly, came the terror that changed the whole aspect of the place—the devastating terror.

It came, at first, gently, but from the very start it made me realise the unpleasant loneliness of our situation, our remote isolation in this wilderness of sea and rock, and how the islands in this tideless Baltic ocean lay about us like the advance guard of a vast besieging army. Its entry, as I say, was gentle, hardly noticeable, in fact, to most of us: singularly undramatic it certainly was. But, then, in actual life this is often the way the dreadful climaxes move upon us, leaving the heart undisturbed almost to the last minute, and then overwhelming it with a sudden rush of horror. For it was the custom at breakfast to listen patiently while each in turn related the trivial adventures of the night—how they slept, whether the wind shook their tent, whether the spider on the ridge pole had moved, whether they had heard the toad, and so forth—and on this particular morning Joan, in the middle of a little pause, made a truly novel announcement:

"In the night I heard the howling of a dog," she said, and then flushed up to the roots of her hair when we burst out laughing. For the idea of there being a dog on this forsaken island that was only able to support a snake and two toads was distinctly ludicrous, and I remember Maloney, half-way through his burnt porridge, capping the announcement by declaring that he had heard a "Baltic turtle" in the lagoon, and his wife's expression of frantic alarm before the laughter undeceived her.

But the next morning Joan repeated the story with additional and convincing detail.

"Sounds of whining and growling woke me," she said, "and I distinctly heard sniffing under my tent, and the scratching of paws."

"Oh, Timothy! Can it be a porcupine?" exclaimed the Bo'sun's Mate with distress, forgetting that Sweden was not Canada.

But the girl's voice had sounded to me in quite another key, and looking up I saw that her father and Sangree were staring at her hard. They, too, understood that she was in earnest, and had been struck by the serious note in her voice.

"Rubbish, Joan! You are always dreaming something or other wild," her father said a little impatiently.

"There's not an animal of any size on the whole island," added Sangree with a puzzled expression. He never took his eyes from her face.

"But there's nothing to prevent one swimming over," I put in briskly, for somehow a sense of uneasiness that was not pleasant had woven itself into the talk and pauses. "A deer, for instance, might easily land in the night and take a look round—"

"Or a bear!" gasped the Bo'sun's Mate, with a look so portentous that we all welcomed the laugh.

But Joan did not laugh. Instead, she sprang up and called to us to follow.

"There," she said, pointing to the ground by her tent on the side farthest from her mother's; "there are the marks close to my head. You can see for yourselves."

We saw plainly. The moss and lichen—for earth there was hardly any— had been scratched up by paws. An animal about the size of a large dog it must have been, to judge by the marks. We stood and stared in a row.

"Close to my head," repeated the girl, looking round at us. Her face, I noticed, was very pale, and her lip seemed to quiver for an instant. Then she gave a sudden gulp—and burst into a flood of tears.

The whole thing had come about in the brief space of a few minutes, and with a curious sense of inevitableness, moreover, as though it had all been carefully planned from all time and nothing could have stopped it. It had all been rehearsed before—had actually happened before, as the strange feeling sometimes has it; it seemed like the opening movement in some ominous drama, and that I knew exactly what would happen next. Something of great moment was impending.

For this sinister sensation of coming disaster made itself felt from the very beginning, and an atmosphere of gloom and dismay pervaded the entire Camp from that moment forward.

I drew Sangree to one side and moved away, while Maloney took the distressed girl into her tent, and his wife followed them, energetic and greatly flustered.

For thus, in undramatic fashion, it was that the terror I have spoken of first attempted the invasion of our Camp, and, trivial and unimportant though it seemed, every little detail of this opening scene is photographed upon my mind with merciless accuracy and precision. It happened exactly as described. This was exactly the language used. I see it written before me in black and white. I see, too, the faces of all concerned with the sudden ugly signature of alarm where before had been peace. The terror had stretched out, so to speak, a first tentative feeler toward us and had touched the hearts of each with a horrid directness. And from this moment the Camp changed.

Sangree in particular was visibly upset. He could not bear to see the girl distressed, and to hear her actually cry was almost more than he could stand. The feeling that he had no right to protect her hurt him keenly, and

I could see that he was itching to do something to help, and liked him for it. His expression said plainly that he would tear in a thousand pieces anything that dared to injure a hair of her head.

We lit our pipes and strolled over in silence to the men's quarters, and it was his odd Canadian expression "Gee whiz!" that drew my attention to a further discovery.

"The brute's been scratching round my tent too," he cried, as he pointed to similar marks by the door and I stooped down to examine them. We both stared in amazement for several minutes without speaking.

"Only I sleep like the dead," he added, straightening up again, "and so heard nothing, I suppose."

We traced the paw-marks from the mouth of his tent in a direct line across to the girl's, but nowhere else about the Camp was there a sign of the strange visitor. The deer, dog, or whatever it was that had twice favoured us with a visit in the night, had confined its attentions to these two tents. And, after all, there was really nothing out of the way about these visits of an unknown animal, for although our own island was destitute of life, we were in the heart of a wilderness, and the mainland and larger islands must be swarming with all kinds of four-footed creatures, and no very prolonged swimming was necessary to reach us. In any other country it would not have caused a moment's interest—interest of the kind we felt, that is. In our Canadian camps the bears were for ever grunting about among the provision bags at night, porcupines scratching unceasingly, and chipmunks scuttling over everything.

"My daughter is overtired, and that's the truth of it," explained Maloney presently when he rejoined us and had examined in turn the other paw-marks. "She's been overdoing it lately, and camp-life, you know, always means a great excitement to her. It's natural enough. If we take no notice she'll be all right." He paused to borrow my tobacco pouch and fill his pipe, and the blundering way he filled it and spilled the precious weed on the ground visibly belied the calm of his easy language. "You might take her out for a bit of fishing, Hubbard, like a good chap; she's hardly up to the long day in the cutter. Show her some of the other islands in your canoe, perhaps. Eh?"

And by lunch-time the cloud had passed away as suddenly, and as suspiciously, as it had come.

But in the canoe, on our way home, having till then purposely ignored the subject uppermost in our minds, she suddenly spoke to me in a way that again touched the note of sinister alarm—the note that kept on sounding and sounding until finally John Silence came with his great vibrating presence and relieved it; yes, and even after he came, too, for a while.

"I'm ashamed to ask it," she said abruptly, as she steered me home, her sleeves rolled up, her hair blowing in the wind, "and ashamed of my silly tears too, because I really can't make out what caused them; but, Mr. Hubbard, I want you to promise me not to go off for your long expeditions—just yet. I beg it of you." She was so in earnest that she forgot the canoe, and the wind caught it sideways and made us roll dangerously. "I have tried hard not to ask this," she added, bringing the canoe round again, "but I simply can't help myself."

It was a good deal to ask, and I suppose my hesitation was plain; for she went on before I could reply, and her beseeching expression and intensity of manner impressed me very forcibly.

"For another two weeks only—"

"Mr. Sangree leaves in a fortnight," I said, seeing at once what she was driving at, but wondering if it was best to encourage her or not.

"If I knew you were to be on the island till then," she said, her face alternately pale and blushing, and her voice trembling a little, "I should feel so much happier."

I looked at her steadily, waiting for her to finish.

"And safer," she added almost in a whisper; "especially—at night, I mean."

"Safer, Joan?" I repeated, thinking I had never seen her eyes so soft and tender. She nodded her head, keeping her gaze fixed on my face.

It was really difficult to refuse, whatever my thoughts and judgment may have been, and somehow I understood that she spoke with good reason, though for the life of me I could not have put it into words.

"Happier—and safer," she said gravely, the canoe giving a dangerous lurch as she leaned forward in her seat to catch my answer. Perhaps, after all, the wisest way was to grant her request and make light of it, easing her anxiety without too much encouraging its cause.

"All right, Joan, you queer creature; I promise," and the instant look of relief in her face, and the smile that came back like sunlight to her eyes, made me feel that, unknown to myself and the world, I was capable of considerable sacrifice after all.

"But, you know, there's nothing to be afraid of," I added sharply; and she looked up in my face with the smile women use when they know we are talking idly, yet do not wish to tell us so.

"*You* don't feel afraid, I know," she observed quietly.

"Of course not; why should I?"

"So, if you will just humour me this once I—I will never ask anything foolish of you again as long as I live," she said gratefully.

"You have my promise," was all I could find to say.

She headed the nose of the canoe for the lagoon lying a quarter of a mile ahead, and paddled swiftly; but a minute or two later she paused again and stared hard at me with the dripping paddle across the thwarts.

"You've not heard anything at night yourself, have you?" she asked.

"I never hear anything at night," I replied shortly, "from the moment I lie down till the moment I get up."

"That dismal howling, for instance," she went on, determined to get it out, "far away at first and then getting closer, and stopping just outside the Camp?"

"Certainly not."

"Because, sometimes I think I almost dreamed it."

"Most likely you did," was my unsympathetic response.

"And you don't think father has heard it either, then?"

"No. He would have told me if he had."

This seemed to relieve her mind a little. "I know mother hasn't," she added, as if speaking to herself, "for she hears nothing— ever."

It was two nights after this conversation that I woke out of deep sleep and heard sounds of screaming. The voice was really horrible, breaking the peace and silence with its shrill clamour. In less than ten seconds I was half dressed and out of my tent. The screaming had stopped abruptly, but I knew the general direction, and ran as fast as the darkness would allow over to the women's quarters, and on getting close I heard sounds of suppressed weeping. It was Joan's voice. And just as I came up I saw Mrs. Maloney, marvellously attired, fumbling with a lantern. Other voices became audible in the same moment behind me, and Timothy Maloney arrived, breathless, less than half dressed, and carrying another lantern that had gone out on the way from being banged against a tree. Dawn was just breaking, and a chill wind blew in from the sea. Heavy black clouds drove low overhead.

The scene of confusion may be better imagined than described. Questions in frightened voices filled the air against this background of suppressed weeping. Briefly—Joan's silk tent had been torn, and the girl was in a state bordering upon hysterics. Somewhat reassured by our noisy presence, however,—for she was plucky at heart,—she pulled herself together and tried to explain what had happened; and her broken words, told there on the edge of night and morning upon this wild island ridge, were oddly thrilling and distressingly convincing.

"Something touched me and I woke," she said simply, but in a voice still hushed and broken with the terror of it, "something pushing against the tent; I felt it through the canvas. There was the same sniffing and scratching as before, and I felt the tent give a little as when wind shakes it. I heard breathing—very loud, very heavy breathing—and then came a sudden great tearing blow, and the canvas ripped open close to my face."

She had instantly dashed out through the open flap and screamed at the top of her voice, thinking the creature had actually got into the tent. But nothing was visible, she declared, and she heard not the faintest sound of an animal making off under cover of the darkness. The brief account seemed to exercise a paralysing effect upon us all as we listened to it. I can see the dishevelled group to this day, the wind blowing the women's hair, and Maloney craning his head forward to listen, and his wife, open-mouthed and gasping, leaning against a pine tree.

"Come over to the stockade and we'll get the fire going," I said; "that's the first thing," for we were all shaking with the cold in our scanty garments. And at that moment Sangree arrived wrapped in a blanket and carrying his gun; he was still drunken with sleep.

"The dog again," Maloney explained briefly, forestalling his questions; "been at Joan's tent. Torn it, by Gad! this time. It's time we did something." He went on mumbling confusedly to himself.

Sangree gripped his gun and looked about swiftly in the darkness. I saw his eyes aflame in the glare of the flickering lanterns. He made a movement as though to start out and hunt—and kill. Then his glance fell on the girl crouching on the ground, her face hidden in her hands, and there leaped into his features an expression of savage anger that transformed them. He could have faced a dozen lions with a walking-stick at that moment, and again I liked him for the strength of his anger, his self-control, and his hopeless devotion.

But I stopped him going off on a blind and useless chase.

"Come and help me start the fire, Sangree," I said, anxious also to relieve the girl of our presence; and a few minutes later the ashes, still growing from the night's fire, had kindled the fresh wood, and there was a blaze that warmed us well while it also lit up the surrounding trees within a radius of twenty yards.

"I heard nothing," he whispered; "what in the world do you think it is? It surely can't be only a dog!"

"We'll find that out later," I said, as the others came up to the grateful warmth; "the first thing is to make as big a fire as we can."

Joan was calmer now, and her mother had put on some warmer, and less miraculous, garments. And while they stood talking in low voices Maloney and I slipped off to examine the tent. There was little enough to see, but that little was unmistakable. Some animal had scratched up the ground at the head of the tent, and with a great blow of a powerful paw—a paw clearly provided with good claws—had struck the silk and torn it open. There was a hole large enough to pass a fist and arm through.

"It can't be far away," Maloney said excitedly. "We'll organise a hunt at once; this very minute."

We hurried back to the fire, Maloney talking boisterously about his proposed hunt. "There's nothing like prompt action to dispel alarm," he whispered in my ear; and then turned to the rest of us.

"We'll hunt the island from end to end at once," he said, with excitement; "that's what we'll do. The beast can't be far away. And the Bo'sun's Mate and Joan must come too, because they can't be left alone. Hubbard, you take the right shore, and you, Sangree, the left, and I'll go in the middle with the women. In this way we can stretch clean across the ridge, and nothing bigger than a rabbit can possibly escape us." He was extraordinarily excited, I thought. Anything affecting Joan, of course, stirred him prodigiously. "Get your guns and we'll start the drive at once," he cried. He lit another lantern and handed one each to his wife and Joan, and while I ran to fetch my gun I heard him singing to himself with the excitement of it all.

Meanwhile the dawn had come on quickly. It made the flickering lanterns look pale. The wind, too, was rising, and I heard the trees moaning overhead and the waves breaking with increasing clamour on the shore. In the lagoon the boat dipped and splashed, and the sparks from the fire were carried aloft in a stream and scattered far and wide.

We made our way to the extreme end of the island, measured our distances carefully, and then began to advance. None of us spoke. Sangree and I, with cocked guns, watched the shore lines, and all within easy touch and speaking distance. It was a slow and blundering drive, and there were many false alarms, but after the best part of half an hour we stood on the farther end, having made the complete tour, and without putting up so much as a squirrel. Certainly there was no living creature on that island but ourselves.

"*I* know what it is!" cried Maloney, looking out over the dim expanse of grey sea, and speaking with the air of a man making a discovery; "it's a dog from one of the farms on the larger islands" —he pointed seawards where the archipelago thickened—" and it's escaped and turned wild. Our fires and voices attracted it, and it's probably half starved as well as savage, poor brute!"

No one said anything in reply, and he began to sing again very low to himself.

The point where we stood—a huddled, shivering group—faced the wider channels that led to the open sea and Finland. The grey dawn had broken in earnest at last, and we could see the racing waves with their angry crests of white. The surrounding islands showed up as dark masses in the distance, and in the east, almost as Maloney spoke, the sun came up with a rush in a stormy and magnificent sky of red and gold. Against this splashed and gorgeous background black clouds, shaped like fantastic and

legendary animals, filed past swiftly in a tearing stream, and to this day I
have only to close my eyes to see again that vivid and hurrying procession
in the air. All about us the pines made black splashes against the sky. It was
an angry sunrise. Rain, indeed, had already begun to fall in big drops.

We turned, as by a common instinct, and, without speech, made our way
back slowly to the stockade, Maloney humming snatches of his songs, Sangree in front with his gun, prepared to shoot at a moment's notice, and the
women floundering in the rear with myself and the extinguished lanterns.

Yet it was only a dog!

Really, it was most singular when one came to reflect soberly upon it all.
Events, say the occultists, have souls, or at least that agglomerate life due
to the emotions and thoughts of all concerned in them, so that cities, and
even whole countries, have great astral shapes which may become visible
to the eye of vision; and certainly here, the soul of this drive—this vain,
blundering, futile drive—stood somewhere between ourselves and—
laughed.

All of us heard that laugh, and all of us tried hard to smother the sound,
or at least to ignore it. Every one talked at once, loudly, and with exaggerated decision, obviously trying to say something plausible against
heavy odds, striving to explain naturally that an animal might so easily conceal itself from us, or swim away before we had time to light upon its trail.
For we all spoke of that "trail" as though it really existed, and we had more
to go upon than the mere marks of paws about the tents of Joan and the
Canadian. Indeed, but for these, and the torn tent, I think it would, of
course, have been possible to ignore the existence of this beast intruder altogether.

And it was here, under this angry dawn, as we stood in the shelter of the
stockade from the pouring rain, weary yet so strangely excited—it was here,
out of this confusion of voices and explanations, that—very stealthily—
the ghost of something horrible slipped in and stood among us. It made
all our explanations seem childish and untrue; the false relation was instantly exposed. Eyes exchanged quick, anxious glances, questioning, expressive of dismay. There was a sense of wonder, of poignant distress, and
of trepidation. Alarm stood waiting at our elbows. We shivered.

Then, suddenly, as we looked into each other's faces, came the long, unwelcome pause in which this new arrival established itself in our hearts.

And, without further speech, or attempt at explanation, Maloney moved
off abruptly to mix the porridge for an early breakfast; Sangree to clean
the fish; myself to chop wood and tend the fire; Joan and her mother to
change their wet garments; and, most significant of all, to prepare her
mother's tent for its future complement of two.

Each went to his duty, but hurriedly, awkwardly, silently; and this new arrival, this shape of terror and distress stalked, viewless, by the side of each.

"If only I could have traced that dog," I think was the thought in the minds of all.

But in Camp, where every one realises how important the individual contribution is to the comfort and well-being of all, the mind speedily recovers tone and pulls itself together.

During the day, a day of heavy and ceaseless rain, we kept more or less to our tents, and though there were signs of mysterious conferences between the three members of the Maloney family, I think that most of us slept a good deal and stayed alone with his thoughts. Certainly, I did, because when Maloney came to say that his wife invited us all to a special "tea" in her tent, he had to shake me awake before I realised that he was there at all.

And by supper-time we were more or less even-minded again, and almost jolly. I only noticed that there was an undercurrent of what is best described as "jumpiness," and that the merest snapping of a twig, or plop of a fish in the lagoon, was sufficient to make us start and look over our shoulders. Pauses were rare in our talk, and the fire was never for one instant allowed to get low. The wind and rain had ceased, but the dripping of the branches still kept up an excellent imitation of a downpour. In particular, Maloney was vigilant and alert, telling us a series of tales in which the wholesome humorous element was especially strong. He lingered, too, behind with me after Sangree had gone to bed, and while I mixed myself a glass of hot Swedish punch, he did a thing I had never known him do before—he mixed one for himself, and then asked me to light him over to his tent. We said nothing on the way, but I felt that he was glad of my companionship.

I returned alone to the stockade, and for a long time after that kept the fire blazing, and sat up smoking and thinking. I hardly knew why; but sleep was far from me for one thing, and for another, an idea was taking form in my mind that required the comfort of tobacco and a bright fire for its growth. I lay against a corner of the stockade seat, listening to the wind whispering and to the ceaseless drip-drip of the trees. The night, otherwise, was very still, and the sea quiet as a lake. I remember that I was conscious, peculiarly conscious, of this host of desolate islands crowding about us in the darkness, and that we were the one little spot of humanity in a rather wonderful kind of wilderness.

But this, I think, was the only symptom that came to warn me of highly strung nerves, and it certainly was not sufficiently alarming to destroy my peace of mind. One thing, however, did come to disturb my peace, for just as I finally made ready to go, and had kicked the embers of the fire into a last effort, I fancied I saw, peering at me round the farther end of the stockade wall, a dark and shadowy mass that might have been—that strongly resembled, in fact—the body of a large animal. Two glowing eyes shone for an instant in the middle of it. But the next second I saw that it was merely a projecting mass of moss and lichen in the wall of our stockade, and the eyes were a couple of wandering sparks from the dying ashes I had kicked. It was easy enough, too, to imagine I saw an animal moving here and there between the trees, as I picked my way stealthily to my tent. Of course, the shadows tricked me.

And though it was after one o'clock, Maloney's light was still burning, for I saw his tent shining white among the pines.

It was, however, in the short space between consciousness and sleep— that time when the body is low and the voices of the submerged region tell sometimes true—that the idea which had been all this while maturing reached the point of an actual decision, and I suddenly realised that I had resolved to send word to Dr. Silence. For, with a sudden wonder that I had hitherto been so blind, the unwelcome conviction dawned upon me all at once that some dreadful thing was lurking about us on this island, and that the safety of at least one of us was threatened by something monstrous and unclean that was too horrible to contemplate. And, again remembering those last words of his as the train moved out of the platform, I understood that Dr. Silence would hold himself in readiness to come.

"Unless you should send for me sooner," he had said.

I found myself suddenly wide awake. It is impossible to say what woke me, but it was no gradual process, seeing that I jumped from deep sleep to absolute alertness in a single instant. I had evidently slept for an hour and more, for the night had cleared, stars crowded the sky, and a pallid half-moon just sinking into the sea threw a spectral light between the trees.

I went outside to sniff the air, and stood upright. A curious impression that something was astir in the Camp came over me, and when I glanced across at Sangree's tent, some twenty feet away, I saw that it was moving. He too, then, was awake and restless, for I saw the canvas sides bulge this way and that as he moved within.

Then the flap pushed forward. He was coming out, like myself, to sniff the air; and I was not surprised, for its sweetness after the rain was intoxicating. And he came on all fours, just as I had done. I saw a head thrust round the edge of the tent.

And then I saw that it was not Sangree at all. It was an animal. And the same instant I realised something else too—it was *the* animal; and its whole presentment for some unaccountable reason was unutterably malefic.

A cry I was quite unable to suppress escaped me, and the creature turned on the instant and stared at me with baleful eyes. I could have dropped on the spot, for the strength all ran out of my body with a rush. Something about it touched in me the living terror that grips and paralyses.

If the mind requires but the tenth of a second to form an impression, I must have stood there stockstill for several seconds while I seized the ropes for support and stared. Many and vivid impressions flashed through my mind, but not one of them resulted in action, because I was in instant dread that the beast any moment would leap in my direction and be upon me. Instead, however, after what seemed a vast period, it slowly turned its eyes from my face, uttered a low whining sound, and came out altogether into the open.

Then, for the first time, I saw it in its entirety and noted two things: it was about the size of a large dog, but at the same time it was utterly unlike any animal that I had ever seen. Also, that the quality that had impressed me first as being malefic was really only its singular and original strangeness. Foolish as it may sound, and impossible as it is for me to adduce proof, I can only say that the animal seemed to me then to be—not real.

But all this passed through my mind in a flash, almost subconsciously, and before I had time to check my impressions, or even properly verify them, I made an involuntary movement, catching the tight rope in my hand so that it twanged like a banjo string, and in that instant the creature turned the corner of Sangree's tent and was gone into the darkness.

Then, of course, my senses in some measure returned to me, and I realised only one thing: it had been inside his tent!

I dashed out, reached the door in half a dozen strides, and looked in. The Canadian, thank God! lay upon his bed of branches. His arm was stretched outside, across the blankets, the fist tightly clenched, and the body had an appearance of unusual rigidity that was alarming. On his face there was an expression of effort, almost of painful effort, so far as the uncertain light permitted me to see, and his sleep seemed to be very profound. He looked, I thought, so stiff, so unnaturally stiff, and in some indefinable way, too, he looked smaller—shrunken.

I called to him to wake, but called many times in vain. Then I decided to shake him, and had already moved forward to do so vigorously when there came a sound of footsteps padding softly behind me, and I felt a stream of hot breath burn my neck as I stooped. I turned sharply. The tent door was darkened and something silently swept in. I felt a rough and shaggy body push past me, and knew that the animal had returned. It seemed to leap forward between me and Sangree—in fact, to leap upon Sangree, for its dark body hid him momentarily from view, and in that moment my soul turned sick and coward with a horror that rose from the very dregs and depths of life, and gripped my existence at its central source.

The creature seemed somehow to melt away into him, almost as though it belonged to him and were a part of himself, but in the same instant—

that instant of extraordinary confusion and terror in my mind—it seemed to pass over and behind him, and, in some utterly unaccountable fashion, it was gone. And the Canadian woke and sat up with a start.

"Quick! You fool!" I cried, in my excitement, "the beast has been in your tent, here at your very throat while you sleep like the dead. Up, man! Get your gun! Only this second it disappeared over there behind your head. Quick! or Joan—!"

And somehow the fact that he was there, wide-awake now, to corroborate me, brought the additional conviction to my own mind that this was no animal, but some perplexing and dreadful form of life that drew upon my deeper knowledge, that much reading had perhaps assented to, but that had never yet come within actual range of my senses.

He was up in a flash, and out. He was trembling, and very white. We searched hurriedly, feverishly, but found only the traces of paw-marks passing from the door of his own tent across the moss to the women's. And the sight of the tracks about Mrs. Maloney's tent, where Joan now slept, set him in a perfect fury.

"Do you know what it is, Hubbard, this beast?" he hissed under his breath at me; "it's a damned wolf, that's what it is—a wolf lost among the islands, and starving to death—desperate. So help me God, I believe it's that!"

He talked a lot of rubbish in his excitement. He declared he would sleep by day and sit up every night until he killed it. Again his rage touched my admiration; but I got him away before he made enough noise to wake the whole Camp.

"I have a better plan than that," I said, watching his face closely. "I don't think this is anything we can deal with. I'm going to send for the only man I know who can help. We'll go to Waxholm this very morning and get a telegram through."

Sangree stared at me with a curious expression as the fury died out of his face and a new look of alarm took its place.

"John Silence," I said, "will know—"

"You think it's something—of that sort?" he stammered.

"I am sure of it."

There was a moment's pause. "That's worse, far worse than anything material," he said, turning visibly paler. He looked from my face to the sky, and then added with sudden resolution, "Come; the wind's rising. Let's get off at once. From there you can telephone to Stockholm and get a telegram sent without delay."

I sent him down to get the boat ready, and seized the opportunity myself to run and wake Maloney. He was sleeping very lightly, and sprang up the moment I put my head inside his tent. I told him briefly what I had seen, and he showed so little surprise that I caught myself wondering for the first time whether he himself had seen more going on than he had deemed wise to communicate to the rest of us.

He agreed to my plan without a moment's hesitation, and my last words to him were to let his wife and daughter think that the great psychic doctor was coming merely as a chance visitor, and not with any professional interest.

So, with frying-pan, provisions, and blankets aboard, Sangree and I sailed out of the lagoon fifteen minutes later, and headed with a good breeze for the direction of Waxholm and the borders of civilisation.

IV

Although nothing John Silence did ever took me, properly speaking, by surprise, it was certainly unexpected to find a letter from Stockholm waiting for me. "I have finished my Hungary business," he wrote, "and am here for ten days. Do not hesitate to send if you need me. If you telephone any morning from Waxholm I can catch the afternoon steamer."

My years of intercourse with him were full of "coincidences" of this description, and although he never sought to explain them by claiming any magical system of communication with my mind, I have never doubted that there actually existed some secret telepathic method by which he knew my circumstances and gauged the degree of my need. And that this power was independent of time in the sense that it saw into the future, always seemed to me equally apparent.

Sangree was as much relieved as I was, and within an hour of sunset that very evening we met him on the arrival of the little coasting steamer, and carried him off in the dinghy to the camp we had prepared on a neighbouring island, meaning to start for home early next morning.

"Now," he said, when supper was over and we were smoking round the fire, "let me hear your story." He glanced from one to the other, smiling.

"You tell it, Mr. Hubbard," Sangree interrupted abruptly, and went off a little way to wash the dishes, yet not so far as to be out of earshot. And while he splashed with the hot water, and scraped the tin plates with sand and moss, my voice, unbroken by a single question from Dr. Silence, ran on for the next half-hour with the best account I could give of what had happened.

My listener lay on the other side of the fire, his face half hidden by a big sombrero; sometimes he glanced up questioningly when a point needed elaboration, but he uttered no single word till I had reached the end, and his manner all through the recital was grave and attentive. Overhead, the wash of the wind in the pine branches filled in the pauses; the darkness settled down over the sea, and the stars came out in thousands, and by the time I finished the moon had risen to flood the scene with silver. Yet, by his face and eyes, I knew quite well that the doctor was listening to something he had expected to hear, even if he had not actually anticipated all the details.

"You did well to send for me," he said very low, with a significant glance at me when I finished; "very well," —and for one swift second his eye took in Sangree,—" for what we have to deal with here is nothing more than a werewolf—rare enough, I am glad to say, but often very sad, and sometimes very terrible."

I jumped as though I had been shot, but the next second was heartily ashamed of my want of control; for this brief remark, confirming as it did my own worst suspicions, did more to convince me of the gravity of the adventure than any number of questions or explanations. It seemed to draw close the circle about us, shutting a door somewhere that locked us in with the animal and the horror, and turning the key. Whatever it was had now to be faced and dealt with.

"No one has been actually injured so far?" he asked aloud, but in a matter-of-fact tone that lent reality to grim possibilities.

"Good heavens, no!" cried the Canadian, throwing down his dish-cloths and coming forward into the circle of firelight. "Surely there can be no question of this poor starved beast injuring anybody, can there?"

His hair straggled untidily over his forehead, and there was a gleam in his eyes that was not all reflection from the fire. His words made me turn sharply. We all laughed a little short, forced laugh.

"I trust not, indeed," Dr. Silence said quietly. "But what makes you think the creature is starved?" He asked the question with his eyes straight on the other's face. The prompt question explained to me why I had started, and I waited with just a tremor of excitement for the reply.

Sangree hesitated a moment, as though the question took him by surprise. But he met the doctor's gaze unflinchingly across the fire, and with complete honesty.

"Really," he faltered, with a little shrug of the shoulders, "I can hardly tell you. The phrase seemed to come out of its own accord. I have felt from the beginning that it was in pain and—starved, though why I felt this never occurred to me till you asked."

"You really know very little about it, then?" said the other, with a sudden gentleness in his voice.

"No more than that," Sangree replied, looking at him with a puzzled expression that was unmistakably genuine. "In fact, nothing at all, really," he added, by way of further explanation.

"I am glad of that," I heard the doctor murmur under his breath, but so low that I only just caught the words, and Sangree missed them altogether, as evidently he was meant to do.

"And now," he cried, getting on his feet and shaking himself with a characteristic gesture, as though to shake out the horror and the mystery, "let us leave the problem till to-morrow and enjoy this wind and sea and stars. I've been living lately in the atmosphere of many people, and feel that I want to wash and be clean. I propose a swim and then bed. Who'll second me?" And two minutes later we were all diving from the boat into cool, deep water, that reflected a thousand moons as the waves broke away from us in countless ripples.

We slept in blankets under the open sky, Sangree and I taking the outside places, and were up before sunrise to catch the dawn wind. Helped by this early start we were half-way home by noon, and then the wind shifted to a few points behind us so that we fairly ran. In and out among a thousand islands, down narrow channels where we lost the wind, out into open spaces where we had to take in a reef, racing along under a hot and cloudless sky, we flew through the very heart of the bewildering and lonely scenery.

"A real wilderness," cried Dr. Silence from his seat in the bows where he held the jib sheet. His hat was off, his hair tumbled in the wind, and his lean brown face gave him the touch of an Oriental. Presently he changed places with Sangree, and came down to talk with me by the tiller.

"A wonderful region, all this world of islands," he said, waving his hand to the scenery rushing past us, "but doesn't it strike you there's something lacking?"

"It's—hard," I answered, after a moment's reflection. "It has a superficial, glittering prettiness, without—" I hesitated to find the word I wanted.

John Silence nodded his head with approval.

"Exactly," he said. "The picturesqueness of stage scenery that is not real, not alive. It's like a landscape by a clever painter, yet without true imagination. Soulless—that's the word you wanted."

"Something like that," I answered, watching the gusts of wind on the sails. "Not dead so much, as without soul. That's it."

"Of course," he went on, in a voice calculated, it seemed to me, not to reach our companion in the bows, "to live long in a place like this—long and alone—might bring about a strange result in some men."

I suddenly realised he was talking with a purpose and pricked up my ears.

"There's no life here. These islands are mere dead rocks pushed up from below the sea—not living land; and there's nothing really alive on them. Even the sea, this tideless, brackish sea, neither salt water nor fresh, is dead. It's all a pretty image of life without the real heart and soul of life. To a man with too strong desires who came here and lived close to nature, strange things might happen."

"Let her out a bit," I shouted to Sangree, who was coming aft. "The wind's gusty and we've got hardly any ballast."

He went back to the bows, and Dr. Silence continued

"Here, I mean, a long sojourn would lead to deterioration, to degeneration. The place is utterly unsoftened by human influences, by any humanising associations of history, good or had. This landscape has never awakened into life; it's still dreaming in its primitive sleep."

"In time," I put in, "you mean a man living here might become brutal?"

"The passions would run wild, selfishness become supreme, the instincts coarsen and turn savage probably."

"But—"

"In other places just as wild, parts of Italy for instance, where there are other moderating influences, it could not happen. The character might grow wild, savage too in a sense, but with a human wildness one could understand and deal with. But here, in a hard place like this, it might be otherwise." He spoke slowly, weighing his words carefully.

I looked at him with many questions in my eyes, and a precautionary cry to Sangree to stay in the fore part of the boat, out of earshot.

"First of all there would come callousness to pain, and indifference to the rights of others. Then the soul would turn savage, not from passionate human causes, or with enthusiasm, but by deadening down into a kind of cold, primitive, emotionless savagery—by turning, like the landscape, soulless."

"And a man with strong desires, you say, might change?"

"Without being aware of it, yes; he might turn savage, his instincts and desires turn animal. And if" —he lowered his voice and turned for a moment towards the bows, and then continued in his most weighty manner— "owing to delicate health or other predisposing causes, his Double—you know what I mean, of course—his etheric Body of Desire, or astral body, as some term it—that part in which the emotions, passions and desires reside—if this, I say, were for some constitutional reason loosely joined to his physical organism, there might well take place an occasional projection—"

Sangree came aft with a sudden rush, his face aflame, but whether with wind or sun, or with what he had heard, I cannot say. In my surprise I let the tiller slip and the cutter gave a great plunge as she came sharply into the wind and flung us all together in a heap on the bottom. Sangree said nothing, but while he scrambled up and made the jib sheet fast my companion found a moment to add to his unfinished sentence the words, too low for any ear but mine—

"Entirely unknown to himself, however."

We righted the boat and laughed, and then Sangree produced the map and explained exactly where we were. Far away on the horizon, across an open stretch of water, lay a blue cluster of islands with our crescent-shaped home among them and the safe anchorage of the lagoon. An hour with this wind would get us there comfortably, and while Dr. Silence and Sangree fell into conversation, I sat and pondered over the strange suggestions that had just been put into my mind concerning the "Double," and the possible form it might assume when dissociated temporarily from the physical body.

The whole way home these two chatted, and John Silence was as gentle and sympathetic as a woman. I did not hear much of their talk, for the wind grew occasionally to the force of a hurricane and the sails and tiller absorbed my attention; but I could see that Sangree was pleased and happy, and was pouring out intimate revelations to his companion in the way that most people did—when John Silence wished them to do so.

But it was quite suddenly, while I sat all intent upon wind and sails, that the true meaning of Sangree's remark about the animal flared up in me with its full import. For his admission that he knew it was in pain and starved was in reality nothing more or less than a revelation of his deeper self. It was in the nature of a confession. He was speaking of something that he knew positively, something that was beyond question or argument, something that had to do directly with himself. "Poor starved beast" he had called it in words that had "come out of their own accord," and there had not been the slightest evidence of any desire to conceal or explain away. He had spoken instinctively—from his heart, and as though about his own self.

And half an hour before sunset we raced through the narrow opening of the lagoon and saw the smoke of the dinner-fire blowing here and there among the trees, and the figures of Joan and the Bo'sun's Mate running down to meet us at the landing-stage.

V

Everything changed from the moment John Silence set foot on that island; it was like the effect produced by calling in some big doctor, some great arbiter of life and death, for consultation. The sense of gravity increased a hundredfold. Even inanimate objects took upon themselves a subtle alteration, for the setting of the adventure—this deserted bit of sea with its hundreds of uninhabited islands—somehow turned sombre. An element that was mysterious, and in a sense disheartening, crept unbidden into the severity of grey rock and dark pine forest and took the sparkle from the sunshine and the sea.

I, at least, was keenly aware of the change, for my whole being shifted, as it were, a degree higher, becoming keyed up and alert. The figures from the background of the stage moved forward a little into the light—nearer to the inevitable action. In a word this man's arrival intensified the whole affair.

And, looking back down the years to the time when all this happened, it is clear to me that he had a pretty sharp idea of the meaning of it from the very beginning. How much he knew beforehand by his strange divining powers, it is impossible to say, but from the moment he came upon the scene and caught within himself the note of what was going on amongst us, he undoubtedly held the true solution of the puzzle and had no need to ask questions. And this certitude it was that set him in such an atmosphere of power and made us all look to him instinctively; for he took no tentative steps, made no false moves, and while the rest of us floundered he moved straight to the climax. He was indeed a true diviner of souls.

I can now read into his behaviour a good deal that puzzled me at the time, for though I had dimly guessed the solution, I had no idea how he would deal with it. And the conversations I can reproduce almost verbatim, for, according to my invariable habit, I kept full notes of all he said.

To Mrs. Maloney, foolish and dazed; to Joan, alarmed, yet plucky; and to the clergyman, moved by his daughter's distress below his usual shallow emotions, he gave the best possible treatment in the best possible way, yet all so easily and simply as to make it appear naturally spontaneous. For he dominated the Bo'sun's Mate, taking the measure of her ignorance with infinite patience; he keyed up Joan, stirring her courage and interest to the highest point for her own safety; and the Reverend Timothy he soothed and comforted, while obtaining his implicit obedience, by taking him into his confidence, and leading him gradually to a comprehension of the issue that was bound to follow.

And Sangree—here his wisdom was most wisely calculated—he neglected outwardly because inwardly he was the object of his unceasing and most concentrated attention. Under the guise of apparent indifference his mind kept the Canadian under constant observation.

There was a restless feeling in the Camp that evening and none of us lingered round the fire after supper as usual. Sangree and I busied ourselves with patching up the torn tent for our guest and with finding heavy stones to hold the ropes, for Dr. Silence insisted on having it pitched on the highest point of the island ridge, just where it was most rocky and there was no earth for pegs. The place, moreover, was midway between the men's and women's tents, and, of course, commanded the most comprehensive view of the Camp.

"So that if your dog comes," he said simply, "I may be able to catch him as he passes across."

The wind had gone down with the sun and an unusual warmth lay over the island that made sleep heavy, and in the morning we assembled at a late breakfast, rubbing our eyes and yawning. The cool north wind had given way to the warm southern air that sometimes came up with haze and moisture across the Baltic, bringing with it the relaxing sensations that produced enervation and listlessness.

And this may have been the reason why at first I failed to notice that anything unusual was about, and why I was less alert than normally; for it was not till after breakfast that the silence of our little party struck me and I discovered that Joan had not yet put in an appearance. And then, in a flash, the last heaviness of sleep vanished and I saw that Maloney was white and troubled and his wife could not hold a plate without trembling.

A desire to ask questions was stopped in me by a swift glance from Dr. Silence, and I suddenly understood in some vague way that they were waiting till Sangree should have gone. How this idea came to me I cannot determine, but the soundness of the intuition was soon proved, for the moment he moved off to his tent, Maloney looked up at me and began to speak in a low voice.

"You slept through it all," he half whispered.

"Through what?" I asked, suddenly thrilled with the knowledge that something dreadful had happened.

"We didn't wake you for fear of getting the whole Camp up," he went on, meaning, by the Camp, I supposed, Sangree. "It was just before dawn when the screams woke me."

"The dog again?" I asked, with a curious sinking of the heart.

"Got right into the tent," he went on, speaking passionately but very low, "and woke my wife by scrambling all over her. Then she realised that Joan was struggling beside her. And, by God! the beast had torn her arm; scratched all down the arm she was, and bleeding."

"Joan injured?" I gasped.

"Merely scratched—this time," put in John Silence, speaking for the first time; "suffering more from shock and fright than actual wounds."

"Isn't it a mercy the doctor was here?" said Mrs. Maloney, looking as if she would never know calmness again. "I think we should both have been killed."

"It has been a most merciful escape," Maloney said, his pulpit voice struggling with his emotion. "But, of course, we cannot risk another—we must strike Camp and get away at once—"

"Only poor Mr. Sangree must not know what has happened. He is so attached to Joan and would he so terribly upset," added the Bo'sun's Mate distractedly, looking all about in her terror.

"It is perhaps advisable that Mr. Sangree should not know what has occurred," Dr. Silence said with quiet authority, "but I think, for the safety of all concerned, it will be better not to leave the island just now." He spoke with great decision and Maloney looked up and followed his words closely.

"If you will agree to stay here a few days longer, I have no doubt we can put an end to the attentions of your strange visitor, and incidentally have the opportunity of observing a most singular and interesting phenomenon—"

"What!" gasped Mrs. Maloney, "a phenomenon?—you mean that you know what it is?"

"I am quite certain I know what it is," he replied very low, for we heard the footsteps of Sangree approaching, "though I am not so certain yet as to the best means of dealing with it. But in any case it is not wise to leave precipitately—"

"Oh, Timothy, does he think it's a devil—?" cried the Bo'sun's Mate in a voice that even the Canadian must have heard.

"In my opinion," continued John Silence, looking across at me and the clergyman, "it is a case of modern lycanthropy with other complications that may—" He left the sentence unfinished, for Mrs. Maloney got up with a jump and fled to her tent fearful she might hear a worse thing, and at that moment Sangree turned the corner of the stockade and came into view.

"There are footmarks all round the mouth of my tent," he said with excitement. "The animal has been here again in the night. Dr. Silence, you really must come and see them for yourself. They're as plain on the moss as tracks in snow."

But later in the day, while Sangree went off in the canoe to fish the pools near the larger islands, and Joan still lay, bandaged and resting, in her tent, Dr. Silence called me and the tutor and proposed a walk to the granite slabs at the far end. Mrs. Maloney sat on a stump near her daughter, and busied herself energetically with alternate nursing and painting.

"We'll leave you in charge," the doctor said with a smile that was meant to be encouraging, "and when you want us for lunch, or anything, the megaphone will always bring us back in time."

For, though the very air was charged with strange emotions, every one talked quietly and naturally as with a definite desire to counteract unnecessary excitement.

"I'll keep watch," said the plucky Bo'sun's Mate, "and meanwhile I find comfort in my work." She was busy with the sketch she had begun on the day after our arrival. "For even a tree," she added proudly, pointing to her little easel, "is a symbol of the divine, and the thought makes me feel safer."

We glanced for a moment at a daub which was more like the symptom of a disease than a symbol of the divine—and then took the path round the lagoon.

At the far end we made a little fire and lay round it in the shadow of a big boulder. Maloney stopped his humming suddenly and turned to his companion.

"And what do you make of it all?" he asked abruptly.

"In the first place," replied John Silence, making himself comfortable against the rock, "it is of human origin, this animal; it is undoubtedly lycanthropy."

His words had the effect precisely of a bombshell. Maloney listened as though he had been struck.

"You puzzle me utterly," he said, sitting up closer and staring at him.

"Perhaps," replied the other, "but if you'll listen to me for a few moments you may be less puzzled at the end—or more. It depends how much you know. Let me go further and say that you have underestimated, or miscalculated, the effect of this primitive wild life upon all of you."

"In what way?" asked the clergyman, bristling a trifle.

"It is strong medicine for any town-dweller, and for some of you it has been too strong. One of you has gone wild." He uttered these last words with great emphasis.

"Gone savage," he added, looking from one to the other. Neither of us found anything to reply.

"To say that the brute has awakened in a man is not a mere metaphor always," he went on presently.

"Of course not!"

"But, in the sense I mean, may have a very literal and terrible significance," pursued Dr. Silence. "Ancient instincts that no one dreamed of, least of all their possessor, may leap forth—"

"Atavism can hardly explain a roaming animal with teeth and claws and sanguinary instincts," interrupted Maloney with impatience.

"The term is of your own choice," continued the doctor equably, "not mine, and it is a good example of a word that indicates a result while it conceals the process; but the explanation of this beast that haunts your island and attacks your daughter is of far deeper significance than mere atavistic tendencies, or throwing back to animal origin, which I suppose is the thought in your mind."

"You spoke just now of lycanthropy," said Maloney, looking bewildered and anxious to keep to plain facts evidently; "I think I have come across the word, but really—really—it can have no actual significance today, can it? These superstitions of mediæval times can hardly—"

He looked round at me with his jolly red face, and the expression of astonishment and dismay on it would have made me shout with laughter at any other time. Laughter, however, was never farther from my mind than at this moment when I listened to Dr. Silence as he carefully suggested to the clergyman the very explanation that had gradually been forcing itself upon my own mind.

"However mediæval ideas may have exaggerated the idea is not of much importance to us now," he said quietly, "when we are face to face with a modern example of what, I take it, has always been a profound fact. For the moment let us leave the name of any one in particular out of the matter and consider certain possibilities."

We all agreed with that at any rate. There was no need to speak of Sangree, or of any one else, until we knew a little more.

"The fundamental fact in this most curious case," he went on, "is that the 'Double' of a man—"

"You mean the astral body? I've heard of that, of course," broke in Maloney with a snort of triumph.

"No doubt," said the other, smiling, "no doubt you have;—that this Double, or fluidic body of a man, as I was saying, has the power under certain conditions of projecting itself and becoming visible to others. Certain training will accomplish this, and certain drugs likewise; illnesses, too, that ravage the body may produce temporarily the result that death produces permanently, and let loose this counterpart of a human being and render it visible to the sight of others.

"Every one, of course, knows this more or less today; but it is not so generally known, and probably believed by none who have not witnessed it, that this fluidic body can, under certain conditions, assume other forms than human, and that such other forms may be determined by the dominating thought and wish of the owner. For this Double, or astral body as you call it, is really the seat of the passions, emotions and desires in the psychical economy. It is the Passion Body; and, in projecting itself, it can often assume a form that gives expression to the overmastering desire that moulds it; for it is composed of such tenuous matter that it lends itself readily to the moulding by thought and wish."

"I follow you perfectly," said Maloney, looking as if he would much rather be chopping firewood elsewhere and singing.

"And there are some persons so constituted," the doctor went on with increasing seriousness, "that the fluid body in them is but loosely associated with the physical, persons of poor health as a rule, yet often of strong desires and passions; and in these persons it is easy for the Double to dissociate itself during deep sleep from their system, and, driven forth by some consuming desire, to assume an animal form and seek the fulfilment of that desire."

There, in broad daylight, I saw Maloney deliberately creep closer to the fire and heap the wood on. We gathered in to the heat, and to each other, and listened to Dr. Silence's voice as it mingled with the swish and whirr of the wind about us, and the falling of the little waves.

"For instance, to take a concrete example," he resumed; "suppose some young man, with the delicate constitution I have spoken of, forms an overpowering attachment to a young woman, yet perceives that it is not welcomed, and is man enough to repress its outward manifestations. In such a case, supposing his Double be easily projected, the very repression of his love in the daytime would add to the intense force of his desire when released in deep sleep from the control of his will, and his fluidic body might issue forth in monstrous or animal shape and become actually visible to others. And, if his devotion were dog-like in its fidelity, yet concealing the fires of a fierce passion beneath, it might well assume the form of a creature that seemed to be half dog, half wolf—"

"A werewolf, you mean?" cried Maloney, pale to the lips as he listened.

John Silence held up a restraining hand. "A werewolf," he said, "is a true psychical fact of profound significance, however absurdly it may have been exaggerated by the imaginations of a superstitious peasantry in the days of unenlightenment, for a werewolf is nothing but the savage, and possibly sanguinary, instincts of a passionate man scouring the world in his fluidic body, his passion body, his body of desire. As in the case at hand, he may not know it—"

"It is not necessarily deliberate, then?" Maloney put in quickly, with relief.

"It is hardly ever deliberate. It is the desires released in sleep from the control of the will finding a vent. In all savage races it has been recognised and dreaded, this phenomenon styled 'Wehr Wolf,' but today it is rare. And it is becoming rarer still, for the world grows tame and civilised, emotions have become refined, desires lukewarm, and few men have savagery enough left in them to generate impulses of such intense force, and certainly not to project them in animal form."

"By Gad!" exclaimed the clergyman breathlessly, and with increasing excitement, "then I feel I must tell you—what has been given to me in confidence—that Sangree has in him an admixture of savage blood—of Red Indian ancestry—"

"Let us stick to our supposition of a man as described," the doctor stopped him calmly, "and let us imagine that he has in him this admixture of savage blood; and further, that he is wholly unaware of his dreadful physical and psychical infirmity; and that he suddenly finds himself leading the primitive life together with the object of his desires; with the result that the strain of the untamed wild-man in his blood—"

"Red Indian, for instance," from Maloney.

"Red Indian, perfectly," agreed the doctor; "the result, I say, that this savage strain in him is awakened and leaps into passionate life. What then?"

He looked hard at Timothy Maloney, and the clergyman looked hard at him.

"The wild life such as you lead here on this island, for instance, might quickly awaken his savage instincts—his buried instincts—and with profoundly disquieting results."

"You mean his Subtle Body, as you call it, might issue forth automatically in deep sleep and seek the object of its desire?" I said, corning to Maloney's aid, who was finding it more and more difficult to get words.

"Precisely;—yet the desire of the man remaining utterly unmalefic—pure and wholesome in every sense—"

"Ah!" I heard the clergyman gasp.

"The lover's desire for union run wild, run savage, tearing its way out in primitive, untamed fashion, I mean," continued the doctor, striving to make himself clear to a mind bounded by conventional thought and knowledge; "for the desire to possess, remember, may easily become importunate, and, embodied in this animal form of the Subtle Body which acts as its vehicle, may go forth to tear in pieces all that obstructs, to reach to the very heart of the loved object and seize it. *Au fond,* it is nothing more than the aspiration for union, as I said—the splendid and perfectly clean desire to absorb utterly into itself—"

He paused a moment and looked into Maloney's eyes.

"To bathe in the very heart's blood of the one desired," he added with grave emphasis.

The fire spurted and crackled and made me start, but Maloney found relief in a genuine shudder, and I saw him turn his head and look about him from the sea to the trees. The wind dropped just at that moment and the doctor's words rang sharply through the stillness.

"Then it might even kill?" stammered the clergyman presently in a hushed voice, and with a little forced laugh by way of protest that sounded quite ghastly.

"In the last resort it might kill," repeated Dr. Silence. Then, after another pause, during which he was clearly debating how much or how little it was wise to give to his audience, he continued: "And if the Double does not succeed in getting back to its physical body, that physical body would wake an imbecile—an idiot—or perhaps never wake at all."

Maloney sat up and found his tongue.

"You mean that if this fluid animal thing, or whatever it is, should be prevented getting back, the man might never wake again?" he asked, with shaking voice.

"He might be dead," replied the other calmly. The tremor of a positive sensation shivered in the air about us.

"Then isn't that the best way to cure the fool—the brute—?" thundered the clergyman, half rising to his feet.

"Certainly it would be an easy and undiscoverable form of murder," was the stern reply, spoken as calmly as though it were a remark about the weather.

Maloney collapsed visibly, and I gathered the wood over the fire and coaxed up a blaze.

"The greater part of the man's life—of his vital forces—goes out with this Double," Dr. Silence resumed, after a moment's consideration, "and a considerable portion of the actual material of his physical body. So the physical body that remains behind is depleted, not only of force, but of matter. You would see it small, shrunken, dropped together, just like the body of a materialising medium at a séance. Moreover, any mark or injury inflicted upon this Double will be found exactly reproduced by the phenomenon of repercussion upon the shrunken physical body lying in its trance—"

"An injury inflicted upon the one you say would be reproduced also on the other?" repeated Maloney, his excitement growing again.

"Undoubtedly," replied the other quietly; "for there exists all the time a continuous connection between the physical body and the Double—a connection of matter, though of exceedingly attenuated, possibly of etheric, matter. The wound *travels*, so to speak, from one to the other, and if this connection were broken the result would be death."

"Death," repeated Maloney to himself, "death!" He looked anxiously at our faces, his thoughts evidently beginning to clear.

"And this solidity?" he asked presently, after a general pause; "this tearing of tents and flesh; this howling, and the marks of paws? You mean that the Double—?"

"Has sufficient material drawn from the depleted body to produce physical results? Certainly!" the doctor took him up. "Although to explain at this moment such problems as the passage of matter through matter would be as difficult as to explain how the thought of a mother can actually break the bones of the child unborn."

Dr. Silence pointed out to sea, and Maloney, looking wildly about him, turned with a violent start. I saw a canoe, with Sangree in the stern-seat, slowly coming into view round the farther point. His hat was off, and his tanned face for the first time appeared to me—to us all, I think—as though it were the face of some one else. He looked like a wild man. Then he stood up in the canoe to make a cast with the rod, and he looked for all the world like an Indian. I recalled the expression of his face as I had seen it once or twice, notably on that occasion of the evening prayer, and an involuntary shudder ran down my spine.

At that very instant he turned and saw us where we lay, and his face broke into a smile, so that his teeth showed white in the sun. He looked in his element, and exceedingly attractive. He called out something about his fish, and soon after passed out of sight into the lagoon.

For a time none of us said a word.

"And the cure?" ventured Maloney at length.

"Is not to quench this savage force," replied Dr. Silence, "but to steer it better, and to provide other outlets. This is the solution of all these problems of accumulated force, for this force is the raw material of usefulness, and should be increased and cherished, not by separating it from the body by death, but by raising it to higher channels. The best and quickest cure of all," he went on, speaking very gently and with a hand upon the clergyman's arm, "is to lead it towards its object, provided that object is not unalterably hostile—to let it find rest where—"

He stopped abruptly, and the eyes of the two men met in a single glance of comprehension.

"Joan?" Maloney exclaimed, under his breath.

"Joan!" replied John Silence.

We all went to bed early. The day had been unusually warm, and after sunset a curious hush descended on the island. Nothing was audible but that faint, ghostly singing which is inseparable from a pinewood even on the stillest day—a low, searching sound, as though the wind had hair and trailed it o'er the world.

With the sudden cooling of the atmosphere a sea fog began to form. It appeared in isolated patches over the water, and then these patches slid together and a white wall advanced upon us. Not a breath of air stirred; the firs stood like flat metal outlines; the sea became as oil. The whole scene lay as though held motionless by some huge weight in the air; and the flames from our fire—the largest we had ever made—rose upwards, straight as a church steeple.

As I followed the rest of our party tent-wards, having kicked the embers of the fire into safety, the advance guard of the fog was creeping slowly among the trees, like white arms feeling their way. Mingled with the smoke was the odour of moss and soil and bark, and the peculiar flavour of the Baltic, half salt, half brackish, like the smell of an estuary at low water.

It is difficult to say why it seemed to me that this deep stillness masked an intense activity; perhaps in every mood lies the suggestion of its opposite, so that I became aware of the contrast of furious energy, for it was like moving through the deep pause before a thunderstorm, and I trod gently lest by breaking a twig or moving a stone I might set the whole scene into some sort of tumultuous movement. Actually, no doubt, it was nothing more than a result of overstrung nerves.

There was no more question of undressing and going to bed than there was of undressing and going to bathe. Some sense in me was alert and expectant. I sat in my tent and waited. And at the end of half an hour or so my waiting was justified, for the canvas suddenly shivered, and some one tripped over the ropes that held it to the earth. John Silence came in.

The effect of his quiet entry was singular and prophetic: it was just as though the energy lying behind all this stillness had pressed forward to the edge of action. This, no doubt, was merely the quickening of my own mind, and had no other justification; for the presence of John Silence always suggested the near possibility of vigorous action, and as a matter of fact, he came in with nothing more than a nod and a significant gesture.

He sat down on a corner of my ground-sheet, and I pushed the blanket over so that he could cover his legs. He drew the flap of the tent after him and settled down, but hardly had he done so when the canvas shook a second time, and in blundered Maloney.

"Sitting in the dark?" he said self-consciously, pushing his head inside, and hanging up his lantern on the ridge-pole nail. "I just looked in for a smoke. I suppose—"

He glanced round, caught the eye of Dr. Silence, and stopped. He put his pipe back into his pocket and began to hum softly—that under-breath humming of a nondescript melody I knew so well and had come to hate.

Dr. Silence leaned forward, opened the lantern and blew the light out. "Speak low," he said, "and don't strike matches. Listen for sounds and movements about the Camp, and be ready to follow me at a moment's notice." There was light enough to distinguish our faces easily, and I saw Maloney glance again hurriedly at both of us.

"Is the Camp asleep?" the doctor asked presently, whispering. "Sangree is," replied the clergyman, in a voice equally low. "I can't answer for the women; I think they're sitting up."

"That's for the best." And then he added: "I wish the fog would thin a bit and let the moon through; later—we may want it."

"It is lifting now, I think," Maloney whispered back. "It's over the tops of the trees already."

I cannot say what it was in this commonplace exchange of remarks that thrilled. Probably Maloney's swift acquiescence in the doctor's mood had something to do with it; for his quick obedience certainly impressed me a good deal. But, even without that slight evidence, it was clear that each recognised the gravity of the occasion, and understood that sleep was impossible and sentry duty was the order of the night.

"Report to me," repeated John Silence once again, "the least sound, and do nothing precipitately."

He shifted across to the mouth of the tent and raised the flap, fastening it against the pole so that he could see out. Maloney stopped humming and began to force the breath through his teeth with a kind of faint hissing, treating us to a medley of church hymns and popular songs of the day.

Then the tent trembled as though some one had touched it.

"That's the wind rising," whispered the clergyman, and pulled the flap open as far as it would go. A waft of cold damp air entered and made us shiver, and with it came a sound of the sea as the first wave washed its way softly along the shores.

"It's got round to the north," he added, and following his voice came a long-drawn whisper that rose from the whole island as the trees sent forth a sighing response. "The fog'll move a bit now. I can make out a lane across the sea already."

"Hush!" said Dr. Silence, for Maloney's voice had risen above a whisper, and we settled down again to another long period of watching and waiting, broken only by the occasional rubbing of shoulders against the canvas as we shifted our positions, and the increasing noise of waves on the outer coast-line of the island. And over all whirred the murmur of wind sweeping the tops of the trees like a great harp, and the faint tapping on the tent as drops fell from the branches with a sharp pinging sound.

We had sat for something over an hour in this way, and Maloney and I were finding it increasingly hard to keep awake, when suddenly Dr. Silence rose to his feet and peered out. The next minute he was gone.

Relieved of the dominating presence, the clergyman thrust his face close into mine. "I don't much care for this waiting game," he whispered, "but Silence wouldn't hear of my sitting up with the others; he said it would prevent anything happening if I did."

"He knows," I answered shortly.

"No doubt in the world about that," he whispered back; "it's this 'Double' business, as he calls it, or else it's obsession as the Bible describes it. But it's bad, whichever it is, and I've got my Winchester outside ready cocked, and I brought this too." He shoved a pocket Bible under my nose. At one time in his life it had been his inseparable companion.

"One's useless and the other's dangerous," I replied under my breath, conscious of a keen desire to laugh, and leaving him to choose. "Safety lies in following our leader—"

"I'm not thinking of myself," he interrupted sharply; "only, if anything happens to Joan tonight I'm going to shoot first—and pray afterwards!"

Maloney put the book back into his hip-pocket, and peered out of the doorway. "What is he up to now, in the devil's name, I wonder!" he added; "going round Sangree's tent and making gestures. How weird he looks disappearing in and out of the fog."

"Just trust him and wait," I said quickly, for the doctor was already on his way back. "Remember, he has the knowledge, and knows what he's about. I've been with him through worse cases than this."

Maloney moved back as Dr. Silence darkened the doorway and stooped to enter.

"His sleep is very deep," he whispered, seating himself by the door again. "He's in a cataleptic condition, and the Double may be released any minute now. But I've taken steps to imprison it in the tent, and it can't get out till I permit it. Be on the watch for signs of movement." Then he looked hard at Maloney. "But no violence, or shooting, remember, Mr. Maloney, unless you want a murder on your hands. Anything done to the Double acts by repercussion upon the physical body. You had better take out the cartridges at once."

His voice was stern. The clergyman went out, and I heard him emptying the magazine of his rifle. When he returned he sat nearer the door than before, and from that moment until we left the tent he never once took his eyes from the figure of Dr. Silence, silhouetted there against sky and canvas.

And, meanwhile, the wind came steadily over the sea and opened the mist into lanes and clearings, driving it about like a living thing.

It must have been well after midnight when a low booming sound drew my attention; but at first the sense of hearing was so strained that it was impossible exactly to locate it, and I imagined it was the thunder of big guns far out at sea carried to us by the rising wind. Then Maloney, catching hold of my arm and leaning forward, somehow brought the true relation, and I realised the next second that it was only a few feet away.

"Sangree's tent," he exclaimed in a loud and startled whisper.

I craned my head round the corner, but at first the effect of the fog was so confusing that every patch of white driving about before the wind looked like a moving tent and it was some seconds before I discovered the one patch that held steady. Then I saw that it was shaking all over, and the sides, flapping as much as the tightness of the ropes allowed, were the cause of the booming sound we had heard. Something alive was tearing frantically about inside, banging against the stretched canvas in a way that made me think of a great moth dashing against the walls and ceiling of a room. The tent bulged and rocked.

"It's trying to get out, by Jupiter!" muttered the clergyman, rising to his feet and turning to the side where the unloaded rifle lay. I sprang up too, hardly knowing what purpose was in my mind, but anxious to be prepared for anything. John Silence, however, was before us both, and his figure slipped past and blocked the doorway of the tent. And there was some quality in his voice next minute when he began to speak that brought our minds instantly to a state of calm obedience.

"First—the women's tent," he said low, looking sharply at Maloney, "and if I need your help, I'll call."

The clergyman needed no second bidding. He dived past me and was out in a moment. He was labouring evidently under intense excitement. I watched him picking his way silently over the slippery ground, giving the moving tent a wide berth, and presently disappearing among the floating shapes of fog.

Dr. Silence turned to me. "You heard those footsteps about half an hour ago?" he asked significantly.

"I heard nothing."

"They were extraordinarily soft—almost the soundless tread of a wild creature. But now, follow me closely," he added, "for we must waste no time if I am to save this poor man from his affliction and lead his were-wolf Double to its rest. And, unless I am much mistaken" —he peered at me through the darkness, whispering with the utmost distinctness— "Joan and Sangree are absolutely made for one another. And I think she knows it too—just as well as he does."

My head swam a little as I listened, but at the same time something cleared in my brain and I saw that he was right. Yet it was all so weird and incredible, so remote from the commonplace facts of life as commonplace people know them; and more than once it flashed upon me that the whole scene—people, words, tents, and all the rest of it—were delusions created by the intense excitement of my own mind somehow, and that suddenly the sea-fog would clear off and the world become normal again.

The cold air from the sea stung our cheeks sharply as we left the close atmosphere of the little crowded tent. The sighing of the trees, the waves breaking below on the rocks, and the lines and patches of mist driving about us seemed to create the momentary illusion that the whole island had broken loose and was floating out to sea like a mighty raft.

The doctor moved just ahead of me, quickly and silently; he was making straight for the Canadian's tent where the sides still boomed and shook as the creature of sinister life raced and tore about impatiently within. A little distance from the door he paused and held up a hand to stop me. We were, perhaps, a dozen feet away.

"Before I release it, you shall see for yourself," he said, "that the reality of the werewolf is beyond all question. The matter of which it is composed is, of course, exceedingly attenuated, but you are partially clairvoyant—and even if it is not dense enough for normal sight you will see something."

He added a little more I could not catch. The fact was that the curiously strong vibrating atmosphere surrounding his person somewhat confused my senses. It was the result, of course, of his intense concentration of mind and forces, and pervaded the entire Camp and all the persons in it. And as I watched the canvas shake and heard it boom and flap I heartily welcomed it. For it was also protective.

At the back of Sangree's tent stood a thin group of pine trees, but in front and at the sides the ground was comparatively clear. The flap was wide open and any ordinary animal would have been out and away without the least trouble. Dr. Silence led me up to within a few feet, evidently careful not to advance beyond a certain limit, and then stooped down and signalled to me to do the same. And looking over his shoulder I saw the interior lit faintly by the spectral light reflected from the fog, and the dim blot upon the balsam boughs and blankets signifying Sangree; while over him, and round him, and up and down him, flew the dark mass of "something" on four legs, with pointed muzzle and sharp ears plainly visible against the tent sides, and the occasional gleam of fiery eyes and white fangs.

I held my breath and kept utterly still, inwardly and outwardly, for fear, I suppose, that the creature would become conscious of my presence; but the distress I felt went far deeper than the mere sense of personal safety, or the fact of watching something so incredibly active and real. I became keenly aware of the dreadful psychic calamity it involved. The realisation that Sangree lay confined in that narrow space with this species of monstrous projection of himself—that he was wrapped there in the cataleptic sleep, all unconscious that this thing was masquerading with his own life and energies—added a distressing touch of horror to the scene. In all the cases of John Silence—and they were many and often terrible—no other psychic affliction has ever, before or since, impressed me so convincingly with the pathetic impermanence of the human personality, with its fluid nature, and with the alarming possibilities of its transformations.

"Come," he whispered, after we had watched for some minutes the frantic efforts to escape from the circle of thought and will that held it prisoner, "come a little farther away while I release it."

We moved back a dozen yards or so. It was like a scene in some impossible play, or in some ghastly and oppressive nightmare from which I should presently awake to find the blankets all heaped up upon my chest.

By some method undoubtedly mental, but which, in my confusion and excitement, I failed to understand, the doctor accomplished his purpose, and the next minute I heard him say sharply under his breath, "It's out! Now watch!"

At this very moment a sudden gust from the sea blew aside the mist, so that a lane opened to the sky, and the moon, ghastly and unnatural as the effect of stage limelight, dropped down in a momentary gleam upon the door of Sangree's tent, and I perceived that something had moved forward from the interior darkness and stood clearly defined upon the threshold. And, at the same moment, the tent ceased its shuddering and held still.

There, in the doorway, stood an animal, with neck and muzzle thrust forward, its head poking into the night, its whole body poised in that attitude of intense rigidity that precedes the spring into freedom, the running leap of attack. It seemed to be about the size of a calf, leaner than a mastiff, yet more squat than a wolf, and I can swear that I saw the fur ridged sharply upon its back. Then its upper lip slowly lifted, and I saw the whiteness of its teeth.

Surely no human being ever stared as hard as I did in those next few minutes. Yet, the harder I stared the clearer appeared the amazing and monstrous apparition. For, after all, it was Sangree—and yet it was not Sangree. It was the head and face of an animal, and yet it was the face of Sangree: the face of a wild dog, a wolf, and yet his face. The eyes were sharper, narrower, more fiery, yet they were his eyes—his eyes run wild; the teeth were longer, whiter, more pointed—yet they were his teeth, his teeth grown cruel; the expression was flaming, terrible, exultant—yet it was his expression carried to the border of savagery—his expression as I had already surprised it more than once, only dominant now, fully released from human constraint, with the mad yearning of a hungry and importunate soul. It was the soul of Sangree, the long suppressed, deeply loving Sangree, expressed in its single and intense desire—pure utterly and utterly wonderful.

Yet, at the same time, came the feeling that it was all an illusion. I suddenly remembered the extraordinary changes the human face can undergo in circular insanity, when it changes from melancholia to elation; and I recalled the effect of hascheesh, which shows the human countenance in the form of the bird or animal to which in character it most approximates; and for a moment I attributed this mingling of Sangree's face with a wolf to some kind of similar delusion of the senses. I was mad, deluded, dreaming! The excitement of the day, and this dim light of stars and bewildering mist combined to trick me. I had been amazingly imposed upon by some false wizardry of the senses. It was all absurd and fantastic; it would pass.

And then, sounding across this sea of mental confusion like a bell through a fog, came the voice of John Silence bringing me back to a consciousness of the reality of it all—

"Sangree—in his Double!"

And when I looked again more calmly, I plainly saw that it was indeed the face of the Canadian, but his face turned animal, yet mingled with the brute expression a curiously pathetic look like the soul seen sometimes in the yearning eyes of a dog,—the face of an animal shot with vivid streaks of the human.

The doctor called to him softly under his breath—

"Sangree! Sangree, you poor afflicted creature! Do you know me? Can you understand what it is you're doing in your 'Body of Desire'?"

For the first time since its appearance the creature moved. Its ears twitched and it shifted the weight of its body on to the hind legs. Then, lifting its head and muzzle to the sky, it opened its long jaws and gave vent to a dismal and prolonged howling.

But, when I heard that howling rise to heaven, the breath caught and strangled in my throat and it seemed that my heart missed a beat; for, though the sound was entirely animal, it was at the same time entirely human. But, more than that, it was the cry I had so often heard in the Western States of America where the Indians still fight and hunt and struggle— it was the cry of the Redskin!

"The Indian blood!" whispered John Silence, when I caught his arm for support; "the ancestral cry."

And that poignant, beseeching cry, that broken human voice, mingling with the savage howl of the brute beast, pierced straight to my very heart and touched there something that no music, no voice, passionate or tender, of man, woman or child has ever stirred before or since for one second into life. It echoed away among the fog and the trees and lost itself somewhere out over the hidden sea. And some part of myself—something that was far more than the mere act of intense listening—went out with it, and for several minutes I lost consciousness of my surroundings and felt utterly absorbed in the pain of another stricken fellow-creature.

Again the voice of John Silence recalled me to myself.

"Hark!" he said aloud. "Hark!"

His tone galvanised me afresh. We stood listening side by side.

Far across the island, faintly sounding through the trees and brushwood, came a similar, answering cry. Shrill, yet wonderfully musical, shaking the heart with a singular wild sweetness that defies description, we heard it rise and fall upon the night air.

"It's across the lagoon," Dr. Silence cried, but this time in full tones that paid no tribute to caution. "It's Joan! She's answering him!"

Again the wonderful cry rose and fell, and that same instant the animal lowered its head, and, muzzle to earth, set off on a swift easy canter that took it off into the mist and out of our sight like a thing of wind and vision.

The doctor made a quick dash to the door of Sangree's tent, and, following close at his heels, I peered in and caught a momentary glimpse of the small, shrunken body lying upon the branches but half covered by the blankets—the cage from which most of the life, and not a little of the actual corporeal substance, had escaped into that other form of life and energy, the body of passion and desire.

By another of those swift, incalculable processes which at this stage of my apprenticeship I failed often to grasp, Dr. Silence reclosed the circle about the tent and body.

"Now it cannot return till I permit it," he said, and the next second was off at full speed into the woods, with myself close behind him. I had already had some experience of my companion's ability to run swiftly through a dense wood, and I now had the further proof of his power almost to see in the dark. For, once we left the open space about the tents, the trees seemed to absorb all the remaining vestiges of light, and I understood that special sensibility that is said to develop in the blind—the sense of obstacles.

And twice as we ran we heard the sound of that dismal howling drawing nearer and nearer to the answering faint cry from the point of the island whither we were going.

Then, suddenly, the trees fell away, and we emerged, hot and breathless, upon the rocky point where the granite slabs ran bare into the sea. It was like passing into the clearness of open day. And there, sharply defined against sea and sky, stood the figure of a human being. It was Joan.

I at once saw that there was something about her appearance that was singular and unusual, but it was only when we had moved quite close that I recognised what caused it. For while the lips wore a smile that lit the whole face with a happiness I had never seen there before, the eyes themselves were fixed in a steady, sightless stare as though they were lifeless and made of glass.

I made an impulsive forward movement, but Dr. Silence instantly dragged me back.

"No," he cried, "don't wake her!"

"What do you mean?" I replied aloud, struggling in his grasp. "She's asleep. It's somnambulistic. The shock might injure her permanently."

I turned and peered closely into his face. He was absolutely calm. I began to understand a little more, catching, I suppose, something of his strong thinking.

"Walking in her sleep, you mean?"

He nodded. "She's on her way to meet him. From the very beginning he must have drawn her—irresistibly."

"But the torn tent and the wounded flesh?"

"When she did not sleep deep enough to enter the somnambulistic trance he missed her—he went instinctively and in all innocence to seek her out—with the result, of course, that she woke and was terrified—"

"Then in their heart of hearts they love?" I asked finally.

John Silence smiled his inscrutable smile. "Profoundly," he answered, "and as simply as only primitive souls can love. If only they both come to realise it in their normal waking states his Double will cease these nocturnal excursions. He will be cured, and at rest."

The words had hardly left his lips when there was a sound of rustling branches on our left, and the very next instant the dense brushwood parted where it was darkest and out rushed the swift form of an animal at full gallop. The noise of feet was scarcely audible, but in that utter stillness I heard the heavy panting breath and caught the swish of the low bushes against its sides. It went straight towards Joan—and as it went the girl lifted her head and turned to meet it. And the same instant a canoe that had been creeping silently and unobserved round the inner shore of the lagoon, emerged from the shadows and defined itself upon the water with a figure at the middle thwart. It was Maloney.

It was only afterwards I realised that we were invisible to him where we stood against the dark background of trees; the figures of Joan and the animal he saw plainly, but not Dr. Silence and myself standing just beyond them. He stood up in the canoe and pointed with his right arm. I saw something gleam in his hand.

"Stand aside, Joan girl, or you'll get hit," he shouted, his voice ringing horribly through the deep stillness, and the same instant a pistol-shot cracked out with a burst of flame and smoke, and the figure of the animal, with one tremendous leap into the air, fell back in the shadows and disappeared like a shape of night and fog. Instantly, then, Joan opened her eyes, looked in a dazed fashion about her, and pressing both hands against her heart, fell with a sharp cry into my arms that were just in time to catch her.

And an answering cry sounded across the lagoon—thin, wailing, piteous. It came from Sangree's tent.

"Fool!" cried Dr. Silence, "you've wounded him!" and before we could move or realise quite what it meant, he was in the canoe and half-way across the lagoon.

Some kind of similar abuse came in a torrent from my lips, too—though I cannot remember the actual words—as I cursed the man for his disobedience and tried to make the girl comfortable on the ground. But the clergyman was more practical. He was spreading his coat over her and dashing water on her face.

"It's not Joan I've killed at any rate," I heard him mutter as she turned and opened her eyes and smiled faintly up in his face. "I swear the bullet went straight."

Joan stared at him; she was still dazed and bewildered, and still imagined herself with the companion of her trance. The strange lucidity of the somnambulist still hung over her brain and mind, though outwardly she appeared troubled and confused.

"Where has he gone to? He disappeared so suddenly, crying that he was hurt," she asked, looking at her father as though she did not recognise him. "And if they've done anything to him—they have done it to me too—for he is more to me than—"

Her words grew vaguer and vaguer as she returned slowly to her normal waking state, and now she stopped altogether, as though suddenly aware that she had been surprised into telling secrets. But all the way back, as we carried her carefully through the trees, the girl smiled and murmured Sangree's name and asked if he was injured, until it finally became clear to me that the wild soul of the one had called to the wild soul of the other and in the secret depths of their beings the call had been heard and understood. John Silence was right. In the abyss of her heart, too deep at first for recognition, the girl loved him, and had loved him from the very beginning. Once her normal waking consciousness recognised the fact they would leap together like twin flames, and his affliction would be at an end; his intense desire would be satisfied; he would be cured.

And in Sangree's tent Dr. Silence and I sat up for the remainder of the night—this wonderful and haunted night that had shown us such strange glimpses of a new heaven and a new hell—for the Canadian tossed upon his balsam boughs with high fever in his blood, and upon each cheek a dark and curious contusion showed, throbbing with severe pain although the skin was not broken and there was no outward and visible sign of blood.

"Maloney shot straight, you see," whispered Dr. Silence to me after the clergyman had gone to his tent, and had put Joan to sleep beside her mother, who, by the way, had never once awakened. "The bullet must have passed clean through the face, for both cheeks are stained. He'll wear these marks all his life—smaller, but always there. They're the most curious scars in the world, these scars transferred by repercussion from an injured Double. They'll remain visible until just before his death, and then with the withdrawal of the subtle body they will disappear finally."

His words mingled in my dazed mind with the sighs of the troubled sleeper and the crying of the wind about the tent. Nothing seemed to paralyse my powers of realisation so much as these twin stains of mysterious significance upon the face before me.

It was odd, too, how speedily and easily the Camp resigned itself again to sleep and quietness, as though a stage curtain had suddenly dropped down upon the action and concealed it; and nothing contributed so vividly to the feeling that I had been a spectator of some kind of visionary drama as the dramatic nature of the change in the girl's attitude.

Yet, as a matter of fact, the change had not been so sudden and revolutionary as appeared. Underneath, in those remoter regions of consciousness where the emotions, unknown to their owners, do secretly mature, and owe thence their abrupt revelation to some abrupt psychological climax, there can be no doubt that Joan's love for the Canadian had been growing steadily and irresistibly all the time. It had now rushed to the surface so that she recognised it; that was all.

And it has always seemed to me that the presence of John Silence, so potent, so quietly efficacious, produced an effect, if one may say so, of a psychic forcing-house, and hastened incalculably the bringing together of these two "wild" lovers. In that sudden awakening had occurred the very psychological climax required to reveal the passionate emotion accumulated below. The deeper knowledge had leaped across and transferred itself to her ordinary consciousness, and in that shock the collision of the personalities had shaken them to the depths and shown her the truth beyond all possibility of doubt.

"He's sleeping quietly now," the doctor said, interrupting my reflections. "If you will watch alone for a bit I'll go to Maloney's tent and help him to arrange his thoughts." He smiled in anticipation of that "arrangement." "He'll never quite understand how a wound on the Double can transfer itself to the physical body, but at least I can persuade him that the less he talks and 'explains' tomorrow, the sooner the forces will run their natural course now to peace and quietness."

He went away softly, and with the removal of his presence Sangree, sleeping heavily, turned over and groaned with the pain of his broken head.

And it was in the still hour just before the dawn, when all the islands were hushed, the wind and sea still dreaming, and the stars visible through clearing mists, that a figure crept silently over the ridge and reached the door of the tent where I dozed beside the sufferer, before I was aware of its presence. The flap was cautiously lifted a few inches and in looked—Joan.

That same instant Sangree woke and sat up on his bed of branches. He recognised her before I could say a word, and uttered a low cry. It was pain and joy mingled, and this time all human. And the girl too was no longer walking in her sleep, but fully aware of what she was doing. I was only just able to prevent him springing from his blankets.

"Joan, Joan!" he cried, and in a flash she answered him, "I'm here—I'm with you always now," and had pushed past me into the tent and flung herself upon his breast.

"I knew you would come to me in the end," I heard him whisper. "It was all too big for me to understand at first," she murmured, "and for a long time I was frightened—"

"But not now!" he cried louder; "you don't feel afraid now of—of anything that's in me—"

"I fear nothing," she cried, "nothing, nothing!"

I led her outside again. She looked steadily into my face with eyes shining and her whole being transformed. In some intuitive way, surviving probably from the somnambulism, she knew or guessed as much as I knew.

"You must talk tomorrow with John Silence," I said gently, leading her towards her own tent. "He understands everything."

I left her at the door, and as I went back softly to take up my place of sentry again with the Canadian, I saw the first streaks of dawn lighting up the far rim of the sea behind the distant islands.

And, as though to emphasise the eternal closeness of comedy to tragedy, two small details rose out of the scene and impressed me so vividly that I remember them to this very day. For in the tent where I had just left Joan, all aquiver with her new happiness, there rose plainly to my ears the grotesque sounds of the Bo'sun's Mate heavily snoring, oblivious of all things in heaven or hell; and from Maloney's tent, so still was the night, where I looked across and saw the lantern's glow, there came to me, through the trees, the monotonous rising and falling of a human voice that was beyond question the sound of a man praying to his God.

Introduction to Island of Ghosts

As the son of one of America's most famous writers, Julian Hawthorne (1846-1934) lived and worked in his father Nathaniel's proverbial shadow. That is not to say, however, that he wasn't a prolific writer himself. Over the course of his lifetime, the younger Hawthorne wrote numerous poems, short stories, and works of non-fiction.

This story was published first in the American pulp magazine *All Story Weekly*, April 13, 1918, as "Absolute Evil," and reprinted as "Island of Ghosts" in *The Premier Magazine*, a British periodical, in June 1919. It is the latter version that appears here below.

"Island of Ghosts" is a werewolf story written in the first person from the perspective of a strong-willed female protagonist. This tale of lycanthropy is set on an island just off the Virginia and North Carolina coasts. Hawthorne's story appears to suggest that it is through solitude on an island that one begins to finally discover one's true identity, even if that identity is that of a werewolf.

Although Hawthorne's protagonist is not the most compelling of characters, she does allow the author to explore themes such as what it means to escape urban life for a more natural setting. "Island of Ghosts" also contains occasional moments of deep psychological insight, particularly with regard to the nature of people who thrive in comparative solitude.

As in other stories included in this anthology, "Island of Ghosts" utilizes an island setting both for atmosphere and as a means of telling a particular kind of story wherein a protagonist, isolated from both the comforts and norms of civilization, is thrust into a world that defies conventional understanding and is forced to confront evil in her midst.

ISLAND OF GHOSTS
Julian Hawthorne

I

I was halfway between twenty and thirty when I joined the Pleasances'
houseboat party on their adventure to Thirteen-Mile Beach. Nobody—no
society women, at any rate—had been there before, and we called ourselves
pioneers.

What made it our objective was the tale of its being haunted. Haunted
houses were a fashionable subject of polite investigation at that period; and
to test a haunted island was an enterprise even more engaging.

Our route lay along that chain of sounds, or inland seas, which extend
from Chesapeake to below Hatteras. The island was one of those long, narrow sand-bars that form outlying buttresses against Atlantic storms. That,
apart from legend, was all that any of us knew about it at starting. And
even legend did not inform us by whom it was haunted, or why.

Two years after our expedition I was led by circumstances, chiefly subjective, to repeat the trip; this time alone. It is of this last occasion that I
am to tell you; but first I must say a little more about our pioneering.

The houseboat belonged to the Pleasances, very nice, middle-aged people, of Quaker stock, but reconciled to the world, while still retaining between each other their thee-and-thy locution. They were rich, of course,
and childless; but they brought along their ward, Ann Marlowe, a pretty
girl of demure bearing, but with fire in her eye.

To amuse her came Jack Peters, a gilded youth of that epoch, with many
suits of wonderful clothes, including two yachting-suits, in anticipation of
maritime vicissitudes. Of somewhat older years than Jack was Topham
Brent, an old friend of my own, already a distinguished surgeon. Topham
ought not to have come, for I had refused his offer of marriage not long
before; but he was of the persistent sort, and, I admit, the finest sort of fellow.

Then there was Professor Nathaniel Tyler, high-bred and learned, with
a fine reputation, but suffering from nervous breakdown, owing to too as-
siduous study, no doubt. This did not prevent him from being very seriously interested in me, and we spent much of our time in intimate conversations about original sin and esoteric philosophy, with sentiment
never far off; while Topham rambled about the craft, smoking cigars and
trying to look indifferent.

Finally, there was myself, Martha Klemm, a handsome spinster. After this rather long interval I am a spinster still.

The houseboat was sixty or seventy feet long and more than half as wide, luxuriously decorated and furnished, with a chef and two other servants, and an inexhaustible supply of good things to eat and drink. Quakers know how to live.

II

I was interested in original sin, and had dabbled in esoteric philosophy; my ancestors had been, according to tradition, Salem witches. So, on these grounds, at least, I was ready to meet the Professor Nat Tyler halfway.

He was magnetic, fine-looking, and anything but a fool. He was tall, spare, dark-browed, with deep-set, grey eyes rather near together. His long hands were very sensitive and expressive. His lips were thin, but sharply curved, implying eloquence and with a suggestion of voluptuousness. There was a conspicuous black mole on his left cheek, close to the furrow that went from the arched nostril to the corner of the mouth. His voice was a deep baritone, agreeably modulated, with reserves of power. I had heard him lecture.

Every once in a while something peeped forth from the shadows of those eyes of his that made me jump—interiorly, of course; I was woman of the world enough to betray nothing. It was as if somebody I knew very well had suddenly peeped out at me from a window in a strange place, where that face was the last I should have expected to see.

It seemed to have nothing to do with the personality of Nat Tyler himself. It conveyed a profound, fascinating wickedness. It was as old as the pyramids, yet riotous with vitality. Perhaps I ought not to speak in this way of a thing which belonged to imagination; this young professor's life had always been open as daylight, and more than blameless. His family was as old—established as my own, and I had known of him long, though our first personal meeting was recent.

Nothing diabolic, therefore, could justly be inferred from what I have mentioned. Call it just a grotesque notion of mine. I'm sure nobody but I had noticed it, not even Topham Brent, who might have been not unwilling to detect anything objectionable in my learned crony.

Topham was not so wise then as he is now, and may not have known that women are often attracted by what ought to repel them—some women! I confess I was on the look-out for that satanic drama in Tyler's eyes, and enjoyed the little fillip it gave me. By no word or gesture did Tyler himself betray consciousness of his peculiarity.

We discovered that we both had queer books—antique lore about witchcraft and the like. This gave us common ground, and, what was more to the point, uncommon, too.

Imagine us side by side in our low deckchairs on a moonlight evening, with the calm, watery expanse far and near, and a dark line of low shore on the horizon. Yonder the red, reflected light of a fisherman's dory; around one corner of the deck-house the giggle and babble of Jack Peters entertaining Ann, and her brief rejoinders; round the other occasional smoke drifts from the excellent cigar Topham was smoking; inside the houseboat was the placid silence of the benign old Pleasances, reading magazines to themselves.

Tyler, in his agreeable murmur, was speculating in my ear on the origin of evil.

"Thomas Aquinas says that angels, white and black, can change men into beasts permanently; enchanters could do it, too, but not for long. Seventeenth century witchcraft affirmed that certain natural objects and rites could produce strange effects without aid of God or devil. But the operator must renounce God, and be marked in a certain way—a symbolic transaction. The person could then do only evil—good was forbidden to him, or her!"

"Do you believe people can be changed into beasts?" I inquired, as if we were talking of the weather tomorrow.

"Spiritually, I know they can be, and we often notice the resemblance of someone to an animal. Well, if, as the poet Spencer says, 'Soul is form and doth the body make,' why mightn't the body of a man with the soul of a hog assume, under favourable conditions, hoggish lineaments?"

"I wonder. But what are the favourable conditions?"

"His own persistent will, or dominating suggestion from another."

Here there was the creaking of a chair, and Jack came grinning round the corner. "I say, professor, here's Ann says there are ghosts, and I'll leave it to you. Are there?"

Ann, with her inscrutable smile, appeared in the background. "Ghosts, yes; but can we see them?" returned Tyler. "Ask Dr Brent."

"How about it, doc?" Jack called out.

"We're on our way to Thirteen-Mile Beach to find out," answered Topham's voice, with a whiff of cigar smoke.

"I'll bet a dozen pairs of gloves to a cigarette we don't see one." Mr Pleasance put his head out of the window.

"Quarter to twelve, folks; wife and I are going to bed."

"Run along, Mr Peters," said Ann.

The currents were mixed, and we all stood up. Tyler and I, however, found ourselves leaning over the taffrail at the front of our old boat, as it slowly pushed its way through the liquid wilderness. The moonlight fell upon his aquiline features as he faced towards me, and I involuntarily watched for Satan.

"I wish we could have met sooner," he remarked. "I have longed for stimulus and companionship in my researches; such things are perilous when one goes alone. The absolute evil—is there such a thing? Until we know, how can we understand and combat it?"

"The difficulty seems to be," I said, "that those who know it don't care to combat it. We'll assume, for the sake of argument, that witches really existed as well as ghosts. But, for my part, I don't feel sure that we ought to combat it that is, if we felt any assurance of extirpating it. Evil is as necessary an ingredient of life as red pepper is of an epicure's menu; it stimulates one to enjoy the banquet of life."

Out peeped Beelzebub for a moment.

"You are incomparable!" murmured the professor.

"It's a fine night for a broomstick ride," I said. "But we'd better go in."

"'The bridal of the earth and sky!'" he quoted, from Herbert, I think, looking round admiringly on the tranquil prospect.

When he turned back the devil had vanished, and we went inside like two Christians.

III

No place to compare with a houseboat for being bored, or for a flirtation, has been invented; and when the youth of one flirtation is complicated by the animated corpse of a former one, the resources of the situation might keep anyone awake. But I shall not adduce further illustrations; and I am free to confess that, although I afforded my reverend friend adequate opportunities, he did not come to a technical issue. Something kept him back at the critical juncture; whether it was Satan, or whether Satan lacked power to bring on the avowal, I won't decide.

Or maybe that the fatuity of poor Jack being slowly eviscerated by that demure little devil of an Ann Marlowe deterred me from putting forth all my spells; or, possibly, it may have been a stroke of altruistic conscience about Topham Brent, who vainly and intemperately sought an anodyne in tobacco.

Howbeit, neither Ann nor I was engaged when we arrived at Thirteen-Mile Beach and set forth in quest of the ghost.

All we found there was endless prolongation of sand, with a low backbone of tussocks tufted with beach-grass, and a few groups of storm-stunted cedars. Nothing seemed farther from any taint of the supernatural as we four young people tramped here and there, and our hosts sat in their deckchairs and contemplated the incoming or withdrawing tides.

The place was not wholly destitute of incarnate human beings, however. I must give a word to the Duckworths.

What a spot for a man to bring his bride to! Old Tom Duckworth had been a sailor originally, and after giving up the Seven Seas had become a sort of beach-comber. He had put together a hut on the highest part of the beach, at its far end; had fished the Sound and the ocean, and had salvaged flotsam and jetsam from wrecks, of which there was always a tolerable supply after a gale. He had a little garden, and kept goats, pigs, and poultry. And there he dwelt in a solitude more unmitigated than Robinson Crusoe's.

One or twice a year, though, he rowed across the ten miles of Sound, and made his way to a neighbouring town for provisions.

And it chanced, on an excursion of this kind, that he encountered an elderly female.

Jane—I never learned her maiden name—had been a schoolteacher in the vicinity for half a lifetime, but had been recently retired by the school board in favour of some younger and postdiluvian rival. She was thrown upon her own resources, which amounted to nothing, for, either from inability or from moral principle, she had contracted no debts.

Tom proposed marriage, she accepted him; and here they were, and for the past ten years had been, contented with their environment and each other.

Tom had added to his mansion—made of old ships' timbers—two more rooms, and a fence circumventing the building, five feet high, and sunk at least as far into the sand as a protection against storm-tides. The enclosure was about forty feet square; the pigs had their sty, and the goats and the hens wandered at will.

I once spent a summer at Étretat, on the Normandy coast, where the old sailors' huts are made of overturned boats with windows cut in the sides, a flue sticking up at one end, and a hole at the other by way of a door. They have been painted by a thousand artists, but were less picturesque than Tom Duckworth's contrivance. Within, the rooms were kept scrupulously neat by Jane, and she did much useful domestic knitting in addition to her other household duties.

They were a healthy, wholesome old couple, and may have been more than a hundred and twenty years old, combined. They had no children, and both seemed to be sorry for it.

After a first shyness they allowed us to become well acquainted with them. You might think there wasn't much of them or theirs for us to get acquainted with; but the natures of solitary people are apt to have more unmapped country in them than worldly folk imagine. They see and think and do things peculiar to themselves, and one may turn up buried treasure in them at any moment.

Our houseboat was moored off their garden for three days while we explored the island. Sea, sand, and sky—that was all, a portentous, desolate monotony. But I began to feel the spell of it, and so, I think, did Tyler.

On our last day he and I, both good walkers, tramped to the other end of the island and back, a long twenty-five miles. We had gone pretty deep into each other's minds before we returned; but, as I said, nothing ever took place. Our only substantial discovery was another hut, or shack, perched on a hummock in a kind of marsh near the southern extremity of the beach. It was uninhabited.

Tyler observed: "What a chance for a hermit!"

The Duckworths told us on our return that legend said it had been occupied many years before by a fugitive negro murderer, and was supposed to be haunted. So here was what we had come for, after all!

But Mr and Mrs Pleasance wanted to be heading for Philadelphia, and it was agreed that Jack had won his cigarettes by default. A twenty-five-mile journey and a night in the shack was voted to be too high a price to pay to decide the problem of the supernatural. We left the ghost to its own devices.

At Beaufort, on our way back, we met our forwarded letters, and Tyler, after reading his, said he would have to leave us there and get home by rail.

"I hope, Martha," he said, as he held my hand at parting—we had got as far as first names— "that we may soon meet again, and arrive at more definite conclusions."

"As to the origin of evil?" I inquired with simplicity.

I felt his eyes for a moment, but I happened to be facing the sun, and could not be sure whether or not that interesting look of his made its appearance.

"So far as I am concerned," he replied after a little, "friendship with you could be only a source of good."

It was a clever turn, and now I saw that his glance was as innocent as a child's. Topham, with his broad shoulders and square face, was puffing his cigar near by, leaning back against the rail and looking quite happy. He was to stick to the ship until the last. Jack, who was dejected, suddenly resolved to accompany Tyler, and his two big trunks and four suitcases went over the side, Ann Marlowe looking serenely on. She afterwards married Philip Bramwell, a banker of fifty.

Between Topham and me during the rest of the voyage nothing important transpired. I learned later that Nathaniel Tyler had resigned his college appointment, and would spend some years in Europe, especially Palestine.

I had meditations over that news, but could make nothing of it. I dreamed of him several times vividly, a most unusual thing for me. In these dreams we were always travelling somewhere at great speed, I reluctantly, he with eagerness. We never arrived

I will end this prologue, as I might term it, here. After two years I went back to Thirteen-Mile Beach alone, and making no one privy to my destination.

IV

Not only did I tell no one, not even Topham, where I was going, but I could not myself reasonably account for my escapade. If you are indulging the notion that some hypnotic influence was involved, dismiss it immediately.

I have said that I am supposed to be a descendant of witches. My exterior motive was an intense craving for solitude. Many good-looking and affluent young women in society might feel the same, after too much social dissipation. I thought of that endless, desolate beach with a longing which at last became irresistible.

It did not occur to me that absence of human companionship does not assure solitude. It may, on the contrary, plunge one into an environment compared with which New York or London would appear deserts. For we take memory and imagination with us. The seabirds that scream overhead or waddle along the margins of the surf; the grotesque forms of twisted cedars; the rustle of sea-grass in the wind; the interminable percussion of the breakers; the dead infinity of the sand itself—there can be no solitude, in the sense of freedom from disturbances of thought, in the presence of such things. They draw us back into the maelstrom.

I meant to spend a month on Thirteen-Mile Beach, and sent a message to the Duckworths asking shelter with them, and naming the date of my arrival. Should they refuse it—which I was confident they would not—I was prepared to camp out on the sands; the weather was warm and I was hardy.

I remitted money to cover extra expenses for board and lodging. I took with me a trunk full of necessities, my bicycle—a chainless one—and a revolver; not for self-defence, but I am a good shot, and might amuse myself by practising at the gulls.

After leaving the train I had to drive forty miles in an open wagon over the preposterous roads, and then, not finding Duckworth, as I had expected, was obliged to hunt up a local fisherman and get him to row me across. He explained Duckworth's failure to appear. The poor fellow had been drowned in a great storm that winter. But Jane, he said, was still there, and he believed there was 'a little gal' with her.

It was near sunset when the dory stuck its nose in the mud at the end of the Duckworths' thin-legged little pier. Jane was waiting there; she had seen our approach from afar. She greeted me with a sober countenance and words, but the grip of her lean old hand was expressive of a dreary kind of satisfaction. I asked if the young woman could help us up with the trunk. She stared. Young woman?

Just then the gate of the fence was pushed open, and a child of four came toddling down the path. I understood.

My fisherman got his bony back under the trunk and plodded up with it. Jane had made ready my room for me; she gave the man a slice of pork and some baked beans as refreshment after his trip. I glanced at myself in the crooked bit of looking-glass, and shook down my hair and combed it out, and changed my travelling-dress for a jersey and a pair of loose knee-breeches, which was to be my costume in this retirement, and then came into the combination kitchen and sitting-room to drink a dish of tea, as Jane called it.

The 'little gal' stood between my knees all the while and stared up in my face. She had taken to me at first sight, and was interested in my black stream of hair. When I asked her name she puffed out her mouth and said something like "Puhd!" Jane explained:

"I named her Perdita; she was lost, you see, and my Tom he was lost getting her ashore."

The child was sturdy, and had thick, yellow hair, cut square off at the back, like a fourteenth century page's.

My room being on the side of the sea, I had already seen through the window the ribs of the wrecked vessel—a schooner—sticking up outside the breakers and deeply embedded in the sand. Jane told me the story, not consecutively, but a little now and then, day after day. The gale— "Tom called it a hurricane, and I reckon he knew" —had blown two days, and the evening of the third was approaching when the vessel was sighted, driving straight on the beach, only the stumps of the masts left, and nobody, as it turned out, on board.

When she struck, the wind stopped, as if it had done its job and left. The surf was too high to go out to her, however; the clouds broke away overhead, and the full moon shone down, it being then midnight.

As the two old people stood watching, Jane had fancied she heard a sound of crying from the wreck—the crying of a child. Tom had finally agreed he heard something, too, in the intervals of the breakers. He got out his old binoculars, but could make out nothing on the deck; but the name of the vessel, painted in white letters on her bows, was discernible: *Jane—New Orleans.*

"Tom looks at me," said the old woman, "and says he: 'Jane—and a child crying! Looks like the Lord sent us a baby after all!' And when that idea struck him, Miss Klemm, there was nothing could hold him. 'Tide's goin' out,' says he, 'and sea calmin' down; I got to get that kid!'"

The stout old mariner had brought out the life-belt and line, hitched one end of the line to the post, and had gone in. Jane stood by the post and watched. Tom passed the breakers safely and struck out for the ship. He would disappear in the trough of the seas and then reappear when she thought him lost.

But as he approached the side of the vessel, which lay broadside-on, a big comber lapped over her from seaward and came on, bearing something with it from the deck. It was an impromptu raft, made of heavy timbers, and the child had been made fast to it. A corner of the structure, carried on the crest of the wave, was dashed against Tom Duckworth's head. Jane ran down into the froth of the breakers and received the raft, with the little child upon it, still living, and her husband's dead body.

I suppose such things are not uncommon on this treacherous coast. But what a simple, appalling drama! There was nothing dramatic in Jane's temperament, and no gift of expression but might have been beggared in portraying such a catastrophe. She told me the thing without emphasis or gesture—doing her knitting or stirring the contents of the saucepan on the kitchen stove. There had been no one present to sympathise with her agony—only the thunder of the waves upon the sand, the screaming seagulls, the moon staring down from the cloud rifts.

She drew the body up beyond the reach of the waves, and took the child into the cabin, fed it, and warmed it. The next day men came over from the mainland.

"It wasn't any use hating the child; it wasn't to blame, so I got fond of it," she remarked. The Lord had sent it to her, a substitute for what He had taken away! That was her interpretation. Perdita was not a marvel of beauty, but she was an active, smiling, affectionate little thing, and kept Jane busy looking after her.

"She keeps the loneliness off," Jane observed.

V

I took up my regimen of life immediately. The sand was hard and elastic, just the consistency for bicycle-riding. It was September, and warm for the season. I had the freedom of the island—nobody ever visited it. I would ride out before breakfast eight or ten miles down the beach, and then take a surf bath, unimpeded by a bathing-dress. Coming out, I would get on my cycle again and enjoy a wild witch-ride to and fro till my skin was dry and glowing.

What a tonic for body and mind! No born savage could have had a tithe my delight in it. The sun, the sea, the sand, the gulls were my sole play-mates. I would throw a long wreath of kelp over my shoulder and race till it flew out behind me, mingling with the fluttering flag of my hair. Nature seems to welcome defiance of conventions, and to say, with a smile, "So, the truant has come back again!"

How men and women interfere with and imprison one another!

After breakfast and washing up the things, in which I collaborated with Jane, though she didn't wish it, I would go out and sprawl in the sun and play with Perdita and feed the pigs and chickens and have fun with the goat. An hour or two of this, and then, with a little bundle of lunch at my belt, I would jump on the cycle again and be off till late afternoon. Dismount-ing, I would make ready for another bath of sun and air, if not of sea, and seldom resumed my riding-dress till it was time to go home. It was not many days before I might have been taken for a wild Indian. I was golden brown from head to feet.

Why not live this way always? The thought of going back to civilisation was intolerable! Nature and I were one thing.

One evening, after Perdita had been got to her crib and was asleep, and Jane and I were sitting beside the driftwood fire, and all was still except the deep, soft rhythm of the surf, a strange, remote sound came vibrating to my ears. Jane gave a slight movement, but did not look up from her knit-ting. The sound came again.

"Are there dogs on the island?" I asked.

"Best not notice it, Miss Klemm," said Jane; she seemed embarrassed. "Gulls, maybe."

This evasion roused my curiosity. No seabird could emit a sound like that. It had reminded me of the coyotes, as I had heard them on the western deserts at night; but, of course, it couldn't be that. It must be a dog, run-ning wild. But how had a dog got over here? Some man must have brought it, but the idea of a man coming to the island was disquieting. It would be an invasion of my liberties!

The sound came once more—now further off.

"Just not mind it—that's my plan," repeated Jane. "My mother she was born in Ireland, and used to tell us about the banshee. I reckon this is some-thing in that way. Nothing there—only the sound. I heard it first after Tom died."

"Never before that?"

"No, miss; and, if you're agreeable, I'd sooner not talk of it. Things like that comes oftener if you worry about 'em."

"I thought you had more sense, Jane," I said. "I know all about banshees, but we're not children—we're two women out here alone. A wild dog like that might kill one of your pigs or chickens. Besides, where there's a dog a man is apt to be not far off. The creature ought to be hunted down and killed, and I'll do it tomorrow," I added, remembering my revolver at the bottom of my trunk. "Its howling is disagreeable, and its being here interferes with my privacy."

Jane heaved a sigh, and went on with her knitting in silence, and there was no further disturbance that night. Next morning there was a northerly wind, with gusts of rain, and I omitted my early ride. But going out, during an intermission of the showers, I met Perdita at the seaward gate of the palisade, crying lustily.

In explanation she pointed over to Tom Duckworth's grave, which had been made about thirty yards south of the enclosure; it was surrounded with a little picket, and Jane had planted flowers on it.

But mischief had been at work there the night before. The flowers had been violently dug up and scattered about, and a hole of some depth hollowed out, as if to get at what lay beneath. There were no marks of spade or pickaxe, but there were other traces that left no doubt as to the perpetrator—it was the howling beast of the foregoing evening. Perdita, going out to pluck a flower, and finding the destruction, had been smitten with indignation and grief.

I would have kept knowledge of it from Jane, but the child's lamentations had drawn her out of the kitchen—she came, wiping her hands on her apron, and beheld the desecration. She stood rigid a minute, her meagre old face twisted with horror. Then her lips trembled, and she said: "I didn't know I'd an enemy in the world!"

"Enemy? It's that hound!" I answered in wrath. "Clear your imagination of enemies and banshees, woman. The plundering beast has lived too long."

But Jane's reticence being thus broken, she became almost voluble, and her supernatural fears came out. The howling, she told me, had begun soon after Tom's death—it was an evil spirit! The physical attack upon the grave seemed to confirm her in that conviction. Once, she declared, she had gone out at night to bring in a skirt that had been blown over the fence, and the thing had made a swoop at her through the air. No, not a gull, not a hawk—no mortal creature went on such wings.

She didn't know whether the things were the souls of the folks that had been swept off the ship before she struck, and had been carried away in the sea and never had burial; or whether the persecution was aimed at poor Tom for something he might have done when he was a sailor before the mast; or whether it was something about Perdita, who had appeared miraculously, as one might say, or whether, finally, she herself were the person concerned.

In short, to my surprise, the old schoolmistress confessed herself a prey to the rankest superstition, and reason and ridicule were alike wasted on her. The only thing to do was to kill the dog and show her its body.

The rain-clouds drifted away during the night, and the sun rose clear for a day of perfect beauty and radiance. I awoke betimes and hastened to get abroad, not delaying to delve into my trunk for the revolver; neither concrete dogs nor ghosts were likely to be out so early. I swept down the beach as swiftly as I could ride, reached the point where I was accustomed to take my dip, threw off my clothes, and ran in, eager to feel the thrill of the breakers on my body.

I came out breathing hard and tingling with joy of life. I had been carried down some distance by the set of the current, and as I debouched beyond the reach of the sliding surf I saw something which startled me not a little—a man's bare footprint in the sand!

VI

Without staying to examine it, I scuttled to my jersey and breeches and huddled them on in a jiffy. Then my panic changed to anger; I regretted not having brought my revolver, and went back to investigate.

There were several of them; they emerged from below the surf line and proceeded diagonally inland till they were lost in the loose, grass-grown sand. The tide was ebbing; they might be two or three hours old. They were long and narrow.

Where was the man?

From the little elevation, where I now stood, the surface of the island was visible for miles in all directions; but no living creature was in sight. My eyes are good, and I could have seen any moving object at a great distance in that clear atmosphere, with the sun standing an hour high above the sea. Of course, the fellow might be hiding behind one of the little clumps of cedars that dotted the expanse.

A man and a dog on my island! Howlings by night and footprints in the morning! There were no dog footprints, to be sure, but it was inevitable to associate the evidences to ear and eye. They must have a habitation—where was it?

I recalled, for the first time, the little abandoned shack at the further end of the island, said to have been the refuge of the negro murderer of old times. I had never yet ridden more than ten or twelve miles from the Duckworth cabin. Had the shack a new tenant? If so, he could hardly be a desirable neighbour. Thirteen miles was, indeed, a considerable distance to go and return, for a man, if not for a dog. But, if the man were a 'wild man', distance might be no hindrance to him. There had been no indications, however, that he had accompanied his dog on the nocturnal excursions.

I was now much nearer his abode than the Duckworths.

I took another look at the footprints and noticed their great distance apart—more than five feet. Thirty inches is a good average stride for a man, walking on sand. The sixty-inch intervals showed that he must have been running. Perhaps there was nothing singular in that; but it gave me an unpleasant sensation—a naked man running insanely along the beach! But I laughed at myself—I was giving imagination too much rein. The tracks could not be traced more than thirty or forty yards, and a barefoot man is not necessarily devoid of clothing. Possibly he had been taking a bath, like myself, and had run out of the water, as I had, under a natural stimulus.

After all, too, he had as much ostensible right to be on the island as I had.

Nevertheless—and I am sensitive to such impressions—there was an evil 'vibration', as the saying is, from the footprints. And, at any rate, their presence destroyed my freedom. I determined to get my revolver and explore. Meanwhile I would say nothing to Jane. She had enough to tax her nerves as it was!

As I rode home my fancy pictured a big, shambling negro, with an ugly dog, roaming about the place; an outlaw, doubtless, subsisting on fish what else was there for him to eat? He must be ripe for robbery and violence. And to oppose him, two lone women and a child, forty miles from help! I was glad as I thought of my revolver.

On my arrival back at the cabin I took a look at the place as a post of defence. The palisade completely surrounded it, and was five feet in height; made of massive pieces of ship-timber, planted deep and firm in the sand. The strength had been designed to resist the onset of the waves in case they should come up so far; but, of course, an athletic man could easily vault over it—unless he was shot down in the act!

The cabin itself was also very strongly constructed, as strong as an ordinary blockhouse. I was confident I could defend it against any single assailant, especially were he unarmed, as the negro would most likely be. A surprise assault was the thing to be guarded against. A small dog of our own would have been useful—to give the alarm at night. Perhaps we could procure one.

After breakfast I spent an hour cleaning my revolver and trying my skill at a target. Jane shook her head, probably thinking that bullets were vain against demonic powers. But Perdita was hugely delighted with the shining little instrument, and wanted it for a plaything; women of all ages will play with death! When I fired it the explosion didn't frighten her; her little heart had never learned to tremble, but she couldn't grasp the connection between the sharp, sudden noise and the hole in the plank thirty yards distant. I took a shot at a gull on the wing, and by chance cut a piece of a feather from its tail. Perdita shouted with astonishment and delight; it was wondrous magic to her.

About ten o'clock I mounted my bicycle and set off down the beach— the revolver in my belt. In the sunshine, beside the sparkling sea, I felt secure and adventurous; after all, there was good fighting blood in my veins!

It was my purpose to ride to the end of the beach and take a look at the negro's shack. My apprehensions might prove groundless. The owner of the footprints might be a harmless hunter in quest of ducks, or even a wandering tourist on a holiday. Old Jane's supernatural gossip had perhaps caused me to take too romantic a view of the situation. I would solve the problem forthwith.

The tide, since my early excursion, had passed its low mark, and was now coming in. But when I got to the place where I had bathed the footprints were still uncovered. They were three inches longer than my own beside them. The fellow must be immense.

I rode on slowly, pondering, but, under the genial moisture of exercise on my body, neither uneasy nor as much irritated as before. The Atlantic coast of the United States was long enough to accommodate two persons without crowding. Very likely this was the first, and would be the last time the invader would leave his trail on this part of it!

But a mile or so beyond I halted sharply. The trail again—and something more!

I dismounted. The footsteps, still indicating a running gait, came down towards the sea again; but after going parallel with the surf line for a little began circling around, as if the crazy negro—such I now imagined him—were in a fit. Some of the prints were deep driven. At first I thought there were two sets of prints. But, no! All were made by the same pair of feet. The circuits they traced were narrow and irregular; the marks often crossed one another—a sort of insane dance.

But there was something else, and it turned me cold when I realised what it meant.

The footprints didn't go on beyond the general circle in any direction! Where, then, was the man—unless an aeroplane had swooped down and borne him away?

That was one bad thing; the other was quite as bad.

The human footprints were intermingled with others, not human— the marks of the four paws of an enormous dog! But this beast had not entered the circle from any point outside of it—at least, if he had, the man must have carried him in his arms. But this was unthinkable; and if the man had carried him in the beast had left the circle on its own feet, continuing at full speed down the beach, leaving behind it—what? Nothing at all!

I was armed, and am far from being a timorous person. But this weird thing crawled into my nerves with a sensation, compared with which the threat of impending death would have seemed trivial.

A man had entered that circle and had vanished there. A beast had run out of that circle without having entered it.

As I rode slowly homeward, beside the sparkling sea, under the cloudless sky, that was all I could make of it; and I didn't like it.

VII

But the creeping paralysis of helpless dismay—helpless against I knew not what—presently changed into a passion of black anger. I would have it out with this thing and be done with it—one way or another. To flinch from it would be to lose nerve and self-respect for ever.

At the cabin I was monosyllabic with Jane, and in no mood to respond to Perdita's invitations to play with her. I wanted to take counsel with myself—by myself. I would have dismissed even Topham Brent, though I was used to think of him as a counsellor. I would rather have discussed the matter with that very different person, Nathaniel Tyler, with whom, as I have said, I had interests in common.

Upon second thought, however, I dismissed him, too; he would be too refined and fastidious to cope with this brutal event efficiently. I must deal with it alone!

But thinking about it only made it worse. I must act. I must hunt the enigma down, solve it, and destroy it, or be destroyed by it. Still I stayed in my room, unable to decide how to go about the adventure. I sat listening to the surf and to the gulls and to the occasional voices of the child and Jane; once or twice the rap of soft little knuckles came on my door, but I kept silence.

When, later, Jane summoned me to dinner, I declined to come out. I wasn't hungry, I told her; had a headache.

Through my uneasy preoccupation I was sensible by familiar sounds that Perdita was being put to bed. I had usually helped at this ceremony, and the child asked after me. "I want Aunt Martha" —such was my title in her list of friends. Jane and I were the only persons represented there. I had an impulse to go to her, but resisted it. After she had gone to sleep the silence in the cabin was complete; there was only the heavy chanting of the surf coming through my open window.

A couple of hours passed and it was now dark—the moon had not yet risen. Jane's voice at my door; she hoped I was feeling better; she had put a dish of food on the stove for me, in case I got an appetite; she was going to bed.

"Goodnight, Jane; I'll be all right tomorrow!" I said. Should I, too, turn in? What was the use of sitting up?

But I was in no condition to sleep, and it was better to be awake standing than lying down. I leaned out of the window and breathed in the soft air from the sea; there was a light breeze from the south. I could see the long, level line of the horizon, and part of the black ribs of the wrecked schooner, thrusting up against the sky.

All at once, between the ribs, appeared a pyramid of bright red light, the gibbous moon rising in the east. A moment after I thought I heard, very far away, a long howl, which crisped my nerves.

The dog was abroad.

Since childhood I have always been affected by the changes of the moon, sometimes very much so. As the light of the satellite fell on my face my mind cleared, and I knew what was to be done. I had partly undressed; I pulled on my sweater again and buckled on the revolver. I had left my bicycle under the shed outside; to avoid disturbing Jane I slipped out of the window. One of the hens uttered an interrogative croak as I passed the coop.

I got my bicycle, opened the gate of the palisade, closed it behind me, and ran the machine down the firm sand of the beach, where I mounted; it was just past eleven o'clock. I set off in the old direction, glad to be in action and strung up to meet anything.

The horizon line had been clear a few minutes before; but now I observed a low, grey fog moving in towards the coast, with the mysteriously slow yet swift movement characteristic of sea fogs. It had seemed distant, yet now it had reached out a long, silent arm, and had touched the beach ahead. The moon hung a little way above it. The fog clung close to the surface of the scene—seemed hardly more than a man's height in thickness.

In another minute it had swathed me in grey impalpability; and at the same time I heard again the howl of the dog, much more distinct than at first. My pedals revolved more swiftly, and the revolver thumped against my hip; I hoped the negro was with his dog. My only fear was lest they should pass me in the obscurity of the flowing mist.

The line of the beach was not straight; there were wide, shallow bays and projections, and the mist confused me, so that occasionally I found myself running close to the surf, or away from it. But the sea was a safeguard against losing my direction entirely, and I kept on at a fast pace. But was that which I sought coming towards me, or fleeing before me? If the latter, my best speed would be needed to catch up with it. I bent over the handlebars; speed in either case!

Three short barks, followed by a long howl, sounded not fifty yards away. In the few seconds that followed I halted, leaped off the cycle, snatched the revolver from my belt, and held it ready in my right hand, standing behind the wheel. I could not risk a shot while mounted; but afoot I was confident of my aim, and could use the saddle as a rest.

Then, at last, the beast disclosed itself. It was alone. Itself grey, it seemed formed out of the fog. The cantering movement was what I first discerned; but when within a dozen yards it stopped, plunging its forepaws in the sand, its head extended forward.

Shreds of mist drifted past it, and perhaps exaggerated its apparent size, but it seemed much bigger than I had anticipated. And the long, dripping jaws, the short, thick ears, the build of the chest and shoulders, and the shaggy tail flung out behind, showed me at a glance that this was no dog of any breed; it was a wolf!

Unaccountable though its presence in this region might be, there could be no doubt of that. I had to deal with a savage wild beast—a giant of its kind.

For an instant a perplexing thought of its association with a human being, even a crazy negro, flashed across my brain; but the present emergency was enough, and I gripped myself to meet it.

"*The absolute evil—is there such a thing?*" This saying of Tyler's recurred to my mind as I faced the creature, challenging the glare of its close-set eyes down the barrel of my weapon. The aspect of the monster answered the question. Hell could engender nothing more diabolical than this!

My hand did not tremble as I sighted to a point between the glaring eyes and touched the trigger. The detonation sounded flat in the boundless grey expanse that surrounded us.

The beast gave a lurch of the head, uttered a harsh bark, swung round in its tracks, and was out of sight in a moment. I had missed it clean!

I sent a second bullet after it at hazard. Another long howl was the answer, and already it seemed to be a mile away.

The fog thickened and now obscured the moon. I had sprung to my saddle, but almost immediately gave up the pursuit. There wasn't a chance in a million that I would set eyes upon the creature again that night.

I turned and rode back, feeling upon the whole glad of the encounter. I had met the thing and knew what it was; and though I had incredibly missed killing it, I had put it to flight, and perhaps driven it off the island entirely.

But there was a feeling in me that I should meet it again. I didn't believe that an incident so out of the ordinary would have no sequel.

VIII

Time passed on, however, and there was no more baying at the moon or alarms in our household, nor did I find any more tracks on the beach.

The weather was the most exhilarating I had ever known, and Diana, the goddess—to whom fanciful admirers had often compared me—couldn't have felt more of the elixir of immortality in her than I did.

The moon, after her brief retirement, appeared once more, a lovely crescent, in the west, and, gradually attaining her full splendour, shone at last transcendent in the pallid sky. I was in the pink of condition, as the young fellows in training for a race say. I had ceased thinking of the wolf, and had never told Jane of my meeting with it. Either she had forgotten her misgivings, or some odd reluctance prevented her mentioning them. Perdita and I had become sworn playfellows—her innocence and confidence had made me love her.

'Absolute evil' seemed a grotesque hallucination. Absolute good was more real and near.

One thing only marred my tranquility—though the wolf never occurred to my mind in waking hours, I dreamed of it several times at night. I was alone in some desolate place, deeply preoccupied, and suddenly felt that I had lost my way. Looking up, I saw the wolf before me. Nothing but its head was clearly visible, however. And in this head the terrible, glaring, close-set eyes drew mine irresistibly till, after a moment, the eyes alone seemed there. Behind them spread a region of darkness, out of which the beast had emerged, and into which it seemed striving to entice me, as a snake fascinates a bird.

I struggled against the hideous lure, but felt I was yielding—at which juncture I awoke.

This dream, almost the same in details, visited me three or four times. In sleep only the nature of the sleeper is active; what belongs to acquired character no longer exists. And the nature possesses impulse, but not will. My resistance could never have been overcome in my waking state.

There was one other feature of this experience to which I will merely allude; I didn't understand it at the time. It was the most revolting of all. The eyes of the beast reminded me of eyes that I had seen before. Not the eyes themselves, either, but the look that came from them. I could not trace this impression back to its source, though that seemed only just beyond my reach. It disturbed me.

But by the time the moon had filled her circle, this obsession, too, left me, and there was no cloud on my sky except regret at my approaching departure from the beach. When I spoke of it to Jane, her face fell.

"I'd be thankful if you'd stay longer, miss," she said. "And the child—what'll she do?" She pressed her lips together, as if trying to keep something back; but it came. She bent forward and whispered, "I'm afeared of the dog!"

I laughed with ruddy-cheeked assurance.

"I think the dog, as you call it, won't trouble you again." Then I told her my story. "I fancied I must have wounded it," I said; "it's either dead or gone for good. I've been down and back scores of times since, and seen no trace of it. Put it out of your mind."

I did not tell her of that insoluble enigma of the mingled tracks of the beast and the man. In truth, I preferred to keep away from it. There must have been some error in my observation; impossibilities don't happen.

Jane said no more, and after sitting in a brown study for a while, got up and went about her domestic affairs. Perdita, from outside, called me to come and have a romp with the goat. But the goat was perverse that day, and I, being in my bathing-dress—it was the forenoon—proposed to take the child in with me for a bath.

The sea was as smooth as a pond and the sun warm. Perdita was fearless, and could swim well. The tide was low, and we managed to get out to the wreck, where we amused ourselves with the sea anemones and shells sticking to the old timbers.

Children, brought up naturally and in freedom, not only have imagination, but live in a world of imagination more real to them than our reality. Perdita, perched on one of the crosspieces, with her small feet dabbling in the water, and a ribbon of green seaweed twisted round her head for a crown, said: "This ship mine. By-'n'-by, when I'm big, I make it all new and sail away, and get away from naughty dog."

I hadn't supposed that she knew anything about the dog. "There is no dog," I said; "and dogs don't hurt little children."

She looked at me, rounding her blue eyes, and then her mood changed, and she burst into uproarious laughter. I caught her up in my arms and kissed her.

The weather changed that afternoon, with the abruptness peculiar to this coast; a wind began blowing from the south, the temperature rose and became sticky and uncomfortable, and the sea 'got up', as Jane expressed it.

States of the atmosphere pass into us as water through the meshes of a sieve, and storms occur in us before they break upon the world without, creating restless sensations. The cabin became oppressive, and we opened the doors and windows to let the air through. Perdita was so uneasy, after being put into her crib, that we drew the crib to the seaward door to give her the benefit of the draught.

Jane went to bed about nine o'clock as usual; but I remained sitting in the doorway beside Perdita, who now seemed to sleep quietly. The moon, now riding high, broke through the hurrying clouds once in a while, and sent broad rays across the rough backs of the seas. The wind was not violent, except in gusts, but the heat of it was extraordinary—it seemed to come out of an oven.

I stood up at last out of patience, and, going to my room, took off my skirt and blouse, and put on my pyjamas, in which I returned to the doorway. It was some relief, but now, as I looked over to the breaking surf, an impulse came upon me to go down and take one dip in the cool waves and out again.

I didn't pause to debate the matter, but with a glance at the child, peaceful on her little pillow, I crossed the yard quickly and out of the gate of the palisade, which I left open behind me. I would let the sea just wet me as I was, and return; by the time the wind had dried my pyjamas I should be cool enough to sleep.

As I stood upon the margin, the on-driving waves loomed gigantic, and the force of them appeared so great that I wouldn't venture far in. I stepped into the sliding tongues of water, and threw myself down at full length where the depth was not above my knees. Even there the drag of the withdrawing wave was very strong. But the coolness was delicious, and I may have lain wallowing there as long as five minutes. The thunder and rush of sound filled my ears. What an incomparable creature is the sea!

I got to my feet, thoroughly revived, and turned towards the cabin.

As I did so a shrill scream, which was more like a squeal, pierced my brain like a needle. It defined itself against the surf-roar like a slender stab of light against the dark. Almost simultaneously, out through the gate of the palisade, which my neglect had left open, plunged the grey shape of the wolf, bearing in its jaws a bundle of whiteness, partly trailing on the ground. He headed down the beach in a long, swinging canter, his pace hardly impeded by the weight he carried.

My knees weakened for an instant as if from a violent blow in the breast. An instant more I wavered, prompted to pursue on foot. That folly forced back, I leaped towards the cabin for my cycle and revolver.

I rushed against something in the doorway—Jane distracted, frantically moaning—and we stumbled together over the overturned crib. In another breath I was in my room, had snatched the revolver from the dressing-table, was out again, and on my wheel. After a fierce interval of ploughing through heavy sand, I felt the firm beach under my tyres, and was off.

Beneath this frenzy of physical effort, some region far within me seemed to remain cold and unflurried, calculating chances, foreseeing obstacles, measuring advantages.

Be the strength of the beast what it might and it appeared supernatural— I knew that I should overtake it. There was supernatural vigour in my limbs, too, and my heart was firm as granite and hot as fire. I would not miss my aim this time, but I clearly perceived the danger of sending a bullet through Perdita as well as through the beast.

There was another possibility—the child might be already dead. I must accept these risks; get her alive or dead, and deal out vengeance.

The wind, meanwhile, had backed to the north and blew much harder, but being more behind me than in front, aided rather than hindered my speed. There was great darkness, so that I could see nothing except the relative blanching of the breakers as they foamed up to me on my left hand. The temperature fell headlong, and I felt the sting of hail on the thin wet silk of my pyjamas. But I was warm, and my body exulted, in spite of the wrath of my soul.

I was steering with my left hand only on the handlebars, my right being occupied with the revolver, but my arm felt as strong as a steel bar. No sound reached me from ahead; the beast could not bark, and Perdita had not screamed after the first. How far had I ridden? Miles probably, but distance seemed nothing, and I felt that Nature, to which I so loved to give myself, was on my side. Absolute evil could not prevail.

The crisis came unawares, yet found me ready.

There—almost under my wheel!—the beast, with its burden, was revealed suddenly in the darkness, huddled back upon its haunches, snarling, dripping froth, at bay. Before it lay the child on the wet sand, her arms tossed up beyond her head, her cheek resting on a roll of brown seaweed, as if asleep, swathed in her torn white wrappings. Gale, sea, and sky drove upon us.

The beast seemed to tower up, huge, hideous, and fatal; it hurtled at me, snarling, and I fired.

I think I laughed aloud as I saw the bullet strike its left shoulder. The coarse, grey hair was dabbled with spurting blood. I leaped from my cycle, which fell to the left, and stepped forward to complete my work.

But the beast had vanished. The gale shrieked; in the blackness the grey form of a wave surged almost to my feet—grey and writhing like the beast itself. But the wind swept the spume away, and there was nothing visible but the white, precious bundle that was Perdita. From somewhere far off, against the gale, came faintly back the long-drawn howl. It sounded to my fancy like the despairing call of a damned soul.

I lifted the child from the sand, and, holding her on my left arm, regained my seat and began to fight my way back to the cabin.

IX

Perdita was alive. Hardly a scratch marred her little body, there were only a few bruises on her head and shoulder, which, combined with the shock of fear, had made her unconscious. She had stirred and whimpered before we reached home, and Jane and I ministered to her, and before morning she slept in comfort. Marvellous beings are little children!

These things went by like the figures of a magic-lantern to which one pays but dim attention. I was reliving that wild hour, and answered Jane at random. I was content; the beast had not died on the spot, but I knew it must die. The corpse could be found later.

I felt no curiosity about it. I had done my part—saved Perdita and freed Jane from the forebodings that had haunted her. The rest would take care of itself. Nature, through my agency, had been relieved of an ulcer that had been festering in her breast, and her wholesome law had been re-established. I felt like a soldier returned from an honourable campaign, conscious of duty done, and indifferent to what fame rumoured of the battle. Enough for him that the enemy was defeated, for me that the beast was no more.

I don't deny that this has a mystical sound. Probably our lives are full of symbols which only an unacknowledged sense perceives. Spiritual events assume a material guise, in accordance with some creative principle, but do not insist on recognition. The soul is wounded, or is healed, as the case may be, and the effect, echoed upon the mortal plane, exercises in silence its benign office as penalty or reward.

The storm continued for three days; it has happened twice or thrice to me that memorable events in my life have been ushered in or accompanied by great storms. When the turmoil and darkness passed away, a new, crisp brightness began, as of approaching winter. The black bones of the wreck upon the beach had been broken up by the waves, and lay scattered for miles along the shore. Jane congratulated herself on the supply of firewood, but Perdita was displeased. How was she to build her ship and sail away?

That problem has since been solved in a less magical manner than her fancy had provided. I kept alive the link between myself and these two. Jane died after a few years; Perdita, after adventures not to be told here, is a fortunate and happy woman.

But why do I dilly-dally and gossip and procrastinate? I must tell the end of this story, great as is my unwillingness to do it. It is inhuman and incredible, but the truth has no concern with such adjectives. And you may give it credence according to the character of your philosophy, you have your choice and opportunity.

But perhaps you know the end already. I thought afterwards that I had known it. No secrets are better hidden than are those that we hide from ourselves.

X

I got back home about the middle of November of that year, and was enjoying, I must admit, the various luxuries abounding in that most respectable old house of mine, which I had so well dispensed with, and with such a glow of fresh life, in the primitive cabin on Thirteen-Mile Beach. My friends in society had also returned from their holidays, and we were practising upon one another our old urbane amenities.

One of the first to call on me was, of course, Topham Brent. I flirted artistically with him, as it is my fate to do with some men. He told me I looked tremendously fit, and wanted to know what adventures I had had. I answered "None," and inquired whether he had heard anything of Professor Tyler. "That man interested me," I remarked.

"Not really? Never should have imagined it!" was his ironic rejoinder. "Why, seems to me I heard somewhere that he was back from the Orient, or some such place. They said he was in bad health, too; worse than when we had the benefit of his company on the Pleasances' houseboat two years ago. But he hasn't called me in, so I'm unable to present any pathological details."

"I must drop him a line, I'd like to see him," said I.

But the next day I received a note from him. He wrote:

I've dwelt in the desert since we met, and while there sustained an injury which confines me to my house. I can never expect to appear in a pulpit again. It would afford me great pleasure if you would come to see me. I have never forgotten our talks on the houseboat, and I have reached some conclusions on the subjects we discussed which I would like to submit to you.

I had accepted an invitation to a lunch next day, Tuesday, and to a reception the same evening. On Wednesday I had tickets for an afternoon concert, and a dinner later. On Thursday I was particularly desired to attend the meeting of the Ladies' Club, and on Friday—No matter what; I made up my mind to give my Friday to the afflicted Professor.

I found him in his study, which apparently adjoined his bedroom; a soothing brown effect of furniture and decoration, steel engravings of classical subjects on the walls, shelves of books, old quartos, volumes of recent philosophical and scientific essays; on the table a portfolio of designs of 'The Dance of Death', and several French and Russian novels; on the mantelpiece a bronze replica of the Venus Kallipygos, of Naples.

These things reported themselves to the corners of my eyes, the direct look of which, of course, was fixed upon Tyler. He reclined in an invalid's chair, fronting an open coal grate fire; his attitude reminded me of how he and I used to recline side by side in our deckchairs on the houseboat.

Otherwise he was strangely altered. His hair was grey and thin, and hung down to his neck. A thin grey beard was on his cheeks and chin and upper lip. His former spareness had become mere boniness; the sutures of his head, his cheek-bones, the angles of the jaw might have been a skull's, and his body, as indicated beneath the wrappings over him, was but a skeleton.

His eyes, sunken deep under the tufted eyebrows, appeared almost black in the subdued light of the room; they seemed to draw inward towards the narrow dividing ridge of his high nose, giving his gaze an intense concentration. His long hands rested on the arms of his chair; they were like talons, with prominent knuckles, and narrow, polished nails of a purplish hue. But his mouth had still its sharp, voluptuous curves, and smiled as he greeted me, though the eyes had no part in the smile. There was a sort of bunch over his left shoulder which the drapery didn't wholly conceal.

I said to myself, "The man will be dead in a few days." I felt this, quite as much as I inferred it from his aspect.

But the tones of his voice were firm and cheerful, with even a half-laughing accent of raillery in them.

"If you were a pupil of mine, Miss Klemm, summoned here for ghostly counsel, you'd need no better symbol of *memento mori* than myself, I fancy. But it is I who am under obligation to you—for this and other favours. I won't keep you long. I'm mortified at not being able to get up and fetch you a chair; will you pardon me, and be seated?"

As I sat down beside him he made a movement of the head, upon which the young woman in the attires of a professional nurse, who had been standing near his chair, silently withdrew into the bedroom and softly closed the door.

"As you've surmised," he then said, "I shall shortly lay aside this muddy vesture of decay; but I thought, in deference to your feelings and many social engagements, that it would be more considerate to arrange our interview before than after that event; it was bound to take place one way or the other. You—er—enjoyed yourself last summer?"

"I'm feeling the better for it," I replied.

"You have the goddess-like quality of sweeping obstacles from your path, and punishing interlopers," he rejoined; and as he spoke that satanic presence sparkled in the depths of his eyes. "When Diana, your prototype, was surprised at her bath by Actaeon, she didn't suffer him to live to boast of his enjoyment of her perfections."

"I hear you've been abroad," said I, not ready to understand him.

"Oh, that is for the vulgar ear. You and I have no subterfuges. Perhaps, in the good old days, we may have bestridden a broomstick together. I've always had a notion that our acquaintance is of long standing."

I kept silence, instinctively shutting my mind.

"Abroad, yes; far abroad!—and in the desert, to which the Sahara or the plain of Nineveh would be populous." He pointed to his own breast with a light laugh. "There, as the poet says, I invited my soul, and we had it out *à outrance*—thanks to my friend, Miss Martha Klemm."

"What do you expect me to say, Mr Tyler?"

"My dear young lady, you are voluble! From the moment of your entrance—if not before—you and I have been conversing like babbling brooks, though even had my clinical attendant not so discreetly retired, she couldn't have heard a syllable of it. The footprints perplexed you, possibly; but that first moonlight tryst, which ended so explosively—surely you've had no doubts since then?"

The sensation was as if he were throwing invisible nets around me. I stood up, with angry eyes. "Shall I call the nurse?"

"Ah, have a little patience! Give a poor moribund wretch the consolation of shriving himself. Don't let me perish quite alone in this world—alone—*with the beast!*"

At that word, and at that thought, I sat down again. I put out all my self-command to keep from trembling. He nodded thankfully, but for some moments, contending against the exhaustion which his assumption of mockery had, as I now perceived, cost him, he could not speak. When he did, it was in another vein.

"It needed a man like me—if I am a man—to conceive it and to do it. Learning, culture, the cloistered training and atmosphere, personal sanctity, aesthetic sensitiveness, a heredity without blemish—I abounded in all that. To descend deep, you must first go high—touch the halo before polluting it. I can say that I went deep at least. None has been lower. Yes, I went into the desert but not to pray. It was a wonderful journey! Not for the elixir of life, not for gold, not for holiness. And, oh, if I could have gone with your hand in mine! It might have been, Martha, that if we'd gone on the quest together, we might not only have found what we sought, but have returned alive!"

"Am I a part of your confession, Mr Tyler?" I said, with a coldness which was partly designed to chill him back to earth from this feverish flight.

"Ah, well, I ask your pardon!" he returned, his smile ghastly. "I shouldn't have ventured on the liberty if I hadn't thought my condition might excuse it. Really, though, as a rank outsider, which I certainly am now, I may say that you are the only woman I could ever have loved.

"Possibly I led you to suspect as much on the boat; and I will add that I was withheld from proposing—as they say—by the very strength of the sentiment; that is, the risk of the enterprise I had undertaken. Had you happened to accept me, you see, and braved the desert with me, we might, so far from getting back alive, have shared in the disaster—made it even worse, if possible!"

"Put what you have to say in plain words," I said, not trusting myself to a longer speech.

"Thank you! Yes, it's a vice—phrases, circumlocutions! Thank you! The quest of the absolute evil—that's a phrase, too." He set his teeth, and partly rose on his right elbow. "I went to find the devil, and I found him! He's all they say of him and more. I looked down—down; I put away everything human, sacred, innocent, pure; I worshipped the black he-goat with the flame between his horns—ha, ha, ha!—and at last the beast was there! Squatting there in the little shack in the marsh, I felt the transformation—oh, the agony and triumph of it! The big, grizzled, shaggy body—the crooked thighs and sharp, pointed hocks—the clawed forepaws, the long, slavering grin, thick ears, and those eyes—those eyes! You recognised them, my dear Miss Klemm—yes, you did! And the odour—pah!"

"Stop!" I whispered.

But he had gone too far.

"Then out I galloped into the moonlight, and howled—how I howled! You heard me; not quite the popular preacher's voice, but you recognised it! Fancy the Professor Tyler cantering down the street, howling—howling!"

I leaned forward and put my hand resolutely on his, bending my will to check his hysteria. He panted, gurgled in his throat, and presently expressed his gratitude in a look once more human. I didn't like to think what might have come to pass in another moment! Indeed, the next thing he said, speaking now very faintly, with closed eyes, "There was no telling when—where!" confirmed my misgiving.

The flicker of life almost failed in him, but he feebly resisted my attempt to remove my hand.

"You know," he said with trembling eyelids, "persons fed on poisons are poisoned by the antidote. Your touch would have saved me at first—now it brings a delicious death! It finishes what your bullet began. I'm glad to die a—man!"

The words were low, but distinct.

At last he lifted himself and gathered energy. "The—child lived?"

"She was not hurt."

He relaxed, a convulsion that I couldn't interpret passed over his face. But I knew this was the end, and called sharply to the nurse. His grip on my hand had not loosened.

The nurse bent over him, and turned back the wrap on his left shoulder, and then loosened the bandage beneath. A puncture, not large, but with inflamed edges, was revealed; my bullet must have passed just above the heart.

"An odd case," said the woman. "He'd been away on a trip for several weeks, and came back wounded; wouldn't have a doctor, and acted strange about it. When he got weak, they had a surgeon in to examine him.

Not a mortal wound at all, but his neglect of it, or something, gave it a bad turn; likely his vitality was low, too."

After death his lips gradually drew back in a sort of grimace, disclosing both the upper and lower teeth, which were remarkably perfect and white. Efforts to correct the contraction of the facial muscles were futile. It gave the narrow, lean face a sort of wolfish look.

Sometimes, even after so many years, I feel the grip of his fingers on my arm.

BIZARRE CREATURES AND FANTASTIC REALMS

Introduction to The Fiend of the Cooperage

Although Arthur Conan Doyle (1859-1930) is best known as the creator of the legendary fictional sleuth Sherlock Holmes, he also wrote numerous historical novels and supernatural tales. Born in Edinburgh, Scotland, Doyle is, along with John Buchan, George MacDonald, and Robert Louis Stevenson, one of a solid group of Scottish-born authors whose work appears in this collection. In the latter part of his life, Doyle also wrote extensively on spiritualism, a subject that had interested him for many years.

Doyle's "The Fiend of the Cooperage" (1897), a tale of a strikingly decadent sensibility, takes place in a land both culturally and geographically far removed from the author's native city. The mystery of "The Fiend of the Cooperage" unfolds in present day Gabon wherein the story's protagonist, a butterfly collector by the name of Meldrum, recounts a bizarre and terrifying ordeal on a remote African island. Doyle skillfully utilizes the island setting to craft a chilling tale in which entrapment, fear, and superstition loom large over an inscrutable murder mystery.

At once both an unnerving horror story and a work of crypto-zoological fiction, "The Fiend of the Cooperage" may not have the most intricate of plots. Yet, it more than makes up for this in its steamy, jungle setting in which the reader can all but feel the heat and the impending peril all around him.

THE FIEND OF THE COOPERAGE
Sir Arthur Conan Doyle

It was no easy matter to bring the *Gamecock* up to the island, for the river had swept down so much silt that the banks extended for many miles out into the Atlantic. The coast was hardly to be seen when the first white curl of the breakers warned us of our danger, and from there onwards we made our way very carefully under mainsail and jib, keeping the broken water well to the left, as is indicated on the chart. More than once her bottom touched the sand (we were drawing something under six feet at the time), but we had always way enough and luck enough to carry us through. Finally, the water shoaled, very rapidly, but they had sent a canoe from the factory, and the Krooboy pilot brought us within two hundred yards of the island. Here we dropped our anchor, for the gestures of the negro indicated that we could not hope to get any farther. The blue of the sea had changed to the brown of the river, and, even under the shelter of the island, the current was singing and swirling round our bows. The stream appeared to be in spate, for it was over the roots of the palm trees, and everywhere upon its muddy, greasy surface we could see logs of wood and debris of all sorts which had been carried down by the flood.

When I had assured myself that we swung securely at our moorings, I thought it best to begin watering at once, for the place looked as if it reeked with fever. The heavy river, the muddy, shining banks, the bright poisonous green of the jungle, the moist steam in the air, they were all so many danger signals to one who could read them. I sent the longboat off, therefore, with two large hogsheads, which should be sufficient to last us until we made St. Paul de Loanda. For my own part I took the dinghy and rowed for the island, for I could see the Union Jack fluttering above the palms to mark the position of Armitage and Wilson's trading station.

When I had cleared the grove, I could see the place, a long, low, whitewashed building, with a deep veranda in front, and an immense pile of palm-oil barrels heaped upon either flank of it. A row of surfboats and canoes lay along the beach, and a single small jetty projected into the river. Two men in white suits with red cummerbunds round their waists were waiting upon the end of it to receive me. One was a large portly fellow with a greyish beard. The other was slender and tall, with a pale pinched face, which was half concealed by a great mushroom-shaped hat.

"Very glad to see you," said the latter, cordially. "I am Walker, the agent of Armitage and Wilson. Let me introduce Dr. Severall of the same company. It is not often we see a private yacht in these parts."

"She's the *Gamecock*," I explained. "I'm owner and captain—Meldrum is the name."

"Exploring?" he asked.

"I'm a lepidopterist—a butterfly-catcher. I've been doing the west coast from Senegal downwards."

"Good sport?" asked the Doctor, turning a slow yellow-shot eye upon me.

"I have forty cases full. We came in here to water, and also to see what you have in my line."

These introductions and explanations had filled up the time whilst my two Krooboys were making the dinghy fast. Then I walked down the jetty with one of my new acquaintances upon either side, each plying me with questions, for they had seen no white man for months.

"What do we do?" said the Doctor, when I had begun asking questions in my turn. "Our business keeps us pretty busy, and in our leisure time we talk politics."

"Yes, by the special mercy of Providence Severall is a rank Radical, and I am a good stiff Unionist, and we talk Home Rule for two solid hours every evening."

"And drink quinine cocktails," said the Doctor. "We're both pretty well salted now, but our normal temperature was about 103 last year. I shouldn't, as an impartial adviser, recommend you to stay here very long unless you are collecting bacilli as well as butterflies. The mouth of the Ogowai River will never develop into a health resort."

There is nothing finer than the way in which these outlying pickets of civilization distil a grim humour out of their desolate situation, and turn not only a bold, but a laughing face upon the chances which their lives may bring. Everywhere from Sierra Leone downwards I had found the same reeking swamps, the same isolated fever-racked communities and the same bad jokes. There is something approaching to the divine in that power of man to rise above his conditions and to use his mind for the purpose of mocking at the miseries of his body.

"Dinner will be ready in about half an hour, Captain Meldrum," said the Doctor. "Walker has gone in to see about it; he's the housekeeper this week. Meanwhile, if you like, we'll stroll round and I'll show you the sights of the island."

The sun had already sunk beneath the line of palm trees, and the great arch of the heaven above our head was like the inside of a huge shell, shimmering with dainty pinks and delicate iridescence. No one who has not lived in a land where the weight and heat of a napkin become intolerable upon the knees can imagine the blessed relief which the coolness of evening brings along with it. In this sweeter and purer air the Doctor and I walked round the little island, he pointing out the stores, and explaining the routine of his work.

"There's a certain romance about the place," said he, in answer to some remark of mine about the dullness of their lives. "We are living here just upon the edge of the great unknown. Up there," he continued, pointing to the north-east, "Du Chaillu penetrated, and found the home of the gorilla. That is the Gaboon country—the land of the great apes. In this direction," pointing to the south-east, "no one has been very far. The land which is drained by this river is practically unknown to Europeans. Every log which is carried past us by the current has come from an undiscovered country. I've often wished that I was a better botanist when I have seen the singular orchids and curious-looking plants which have been cast up on the eastern end of the island."

The place which the Doctor indicated was a sloping brown beach, freely littered with the flotsam of the stream. At each end was a curved point, like a little natural breakwater, so that a small shallow bay was left between. This was full of floating vegetation, with a single huge splintered tree lying stranded in the middle of it, the current rippling against its high black side.

"These are all from up country," said the Doctor. "They get caught in our little bay, and then when some extra freshet comes they are washed out again and carried out to sea."

"What is the tree?" I asked.

"Oh, some kind of teak, I should imagine, but pretty rotten by the look of it. We get all sorts of big hardwood trees floating past here, to say nothing of the palms. Just come in here, will you?"

He led the way into a long building with an immense quantity of barrel staves and iron hoops littered about in it.

"This is our cooperage," said he. "We have the staves sent out in bundles, and we put them together ourselves. Now, you don't see anything particularly sinister about this building, do you?"

I looked round at the high corrugated iron roof, the white wooden walls, and the earthen floor. In one corner lay a mattress and a blanket.

"I see nothing very alarming," said I.

"And yet there's something out of the common, too," he remarked. "You see that bed? Well, I intend to sleep there tonight. I don't want to buck, but I think it's a bit of a test for nerve."

"Why?"

"Oh, there have been some funny goings on. You were talking about the monotony of our lives, but I assure you that they are sometimes quite as exciting as we wish them to be. You'd better come back to the house now, for after sundown we begin to get the fever-fog up from the marshes. There, you can see it coming across the river."

I looked and saw long tentacles of white vapour writhing out from among the thick green underwood and crawling at us over the broad swirling surface of the brown river. At the same time the air turned suddenly dank and cold.

"There's the dinner gong," said the Doctor. "If this matter interests you I'll tell you about it afterwards."

It did interest me very much, for there was something earnest and subdued in his manner as he stood in the empty cooperage, which appealed very forcibly to my imagination. He was a big, bluff, hearty man, this Doctor, and yet I had detected a curious expression in his eyes as he glanced about him—an expression which I would not describe as one of fear, but rather of a man who is alert and on his guard.

"By the way," said I, as we returned to the house, "you have shown me the huts of a good many of your native assistants, but I have not seen any of the natives themselves."

"They sleep in the hulk over yonder," the Doctor answered, pointing over to one of the banks.

"Indeed. I should not have thought in that case that they would need the huts."

"Oh, they used the huts until quite recently. We've put them on the hulk until they recover their confidence a little. They were all half mad with fright, so we let them go, and nobody sleeps on the island except Walker and myself."

"What frightened them?" I asked.

"Well, that brings us back to the same story. I suppose Walker has no objection to your hearing all about it. I don't know why we should make any secret about it, though it is certainly a pretty bad business."

He made no further allusion to it during the excellent dinner which had been prepared in my honour. It appeared that no sooner had the little white topsail of the *Gamecock* shown round Cape Lopez than these kind fellows had begun to prepare their famous pepper-pot—which is the pungent stew peculiar to the West Coast—and to boil their yams and sweet potatoes. We sat down to as good a native dinner as one could wish, served by a smart Sierra Leone waiting boy. I was just remarking to myself that he at least had not shared in the general fright when, having laid the dessert and wine upon the table, he raised his hand to his turban.

"Anything else I do, Massa Walker?" he asked.

"No, I think that is all right, Moussa," my host answered. "I am not feeling very well to-night, though, and I should much prefer if you would stay on the island."

I saw a struggle between his fears and his duty upon the swarthy face of the African. His skin had turned of that livid purplish tint which stands for pallor in a negro, and his eyes looked furtively about him.

"No, no, Massa Walker," he cried, at last, "you better come to the hulk with me, sah. Look after you much better in the hulk, sah!"

"That won't do, Moussa. White men don't run away from the posts where they are placed."

Again I saw the passionate struggle in the negro's face, and again his fears prevailed.

"No use, Massa Walker, sah!" he cried. "S'elp me, I can't do it. If it was yesterday or if it was to-morrow, but this is the third night, sah, an' it's more than I can face."

Walker shrugged his shoulders.

"Off with you then!" said he. "When the mail-boat comes you can get back to Sierra Leone, for I'll have no servant who deserts me when I need him most. I suppose this is all mystery to you, or has the Doctor told you, Captain Meldrum?"

"I showed Captain Meldrum the cooperage, but I did not tell him anything," said Dr. Severall. "You're looking bad, Walker," he added, glancing at his companion. "You have a strong touch coming on you."

"Yes, I've had the shivers all day, and now my head is like a cannon-ball. I took ten grains of quinine, and my ears are singing like a kettle. But I want to sleep with you in the cooperage to-night."

"No, no, my dear chap. I won't hear of such a thing. You must get to bed at once, and I am sure Meldrum will excuse you. I shall sleep in the cooperage, and I promise you that I'll be round with your medicine before breakfast."

It was evident that Walker had been struck by one of those sudden and violent attacks of remittent fever which are the curse of the West Coast. His sallow cheeks were flushed and his eyes shining with fever, and suddenly as he sat there he began to croon out a song in the high-pitched voice of delirium.

"Come, come, we must get you to bed, old chap," said the Doctor, and with my aid he led his friend into his bedroom. There we undressed him and presently, after taking a strong sedative, he settled down into a deep slumber.

"He's right for the night," said the Doctor, as we sat down and filled our glasses once more. "Sometimes it is my turn and sometimes his, but, fortunately, we have never been down together. I should have been sorry to be out of it to-night, for I have a little mystery to unravel. I told you that I intended to sleep in the cooperage."

"Yes, you said so."

"When I said sleep I meant watch, for there will be no sleep for me. We've had such a scare here that no native will stay after sundown, and I mean to find out to-night what the cause of it all may be. It has always been the custom for a native watchman to sleep in the cooperage, to prevent the barrel hoops being stolen. Well, six days ago the fellow who slept there disappeared, and we have never seen a trace of him since. It was certainly singular, for no canoe had been taken, and these waters are too full of crocodiles for any man to swim to shore. What became of the fellow, or how he could have left the island is a complete mystery. Walker and I were merely surprised, but the blacks were badly scared and queer Voodoo tales began to get about amongst them. But the real stampede broke out three nights ago, when the new watchman in the cooperage also disappeared."

"What became of him?" I asked.

"Well, we not only don't know, but we can't even give a guess which would fit the facts. The niggers swear there is a fiend in the cooperage who claims a man every third night. They wouldn't stay in the island—nothing could persuade them. Even Moussa, who is a faithful boy enough, would, as you have seen, leave his master in a fever rather than remain for the night. If we are to continue to run this place we must reassure our niggers, and I don't know any better way of doing it than by putting in a night there myself. This is the third night, you see, so I suppose the thing is due, whatever it may be."

"Have you no clue?" I asked. "Was there no mark of violence, no blood-stain, no foot-prints, nothing to give you a hint as to what kind of danger you may have to meet?"

"Absolutely nothing. The man was gone and that was all. Last time it was old Ali, who has been wharf-tender here since the place was started. He was always as steady as a rock, and nothing but foul play would take him from his work."

"Well," said I, "I really don't think that this is a one-man job. Your friend is full of laudanum, and come what might he can be of no assistance to you. You must let me stay and put in a night with you at the cooperage."

"Well, now, that's very good of you, Meldrum," said he heartily, shaking my hand across the table. "It's not a thing that I should have ventured to propose, for it is asking a good deal of a casual visitor, but if you really mean it —"

"Certainly I mean it. If you will excuse me a moment, I will hail the *Gamecock* and let them know that they need not expect me."

As we came back from the other end of the little jetty we were both struck by the appearance of the night. A huge blue-black pile of clouds had built itself up upon the landward side, and the wind came from it in little hot pants, which beat upon our faces like the draught from a blast furnace. Under the jetty the river was swirling and hissing, tossing little white spurts of spray over the planking.

"Confound it!" said Doctor Severall. "We are likely to have a flood on the top of all our troubles. That rise in the river means heavy rain up-country, and when it once begins you never know how far it will go. We've had the island nearly covered before now. Well, we'll just go and see that Walker is comfortable, and then if you like we'll settle down in our quarters."

The sick man was sunk in a profound slumber, and we left him with some crushed limes in a glass beside him in case he should awake with the thirst of fever upon him. Then we made our way through the unnatural gloom thrown by that menacing cloud. The river had risen so high that the little bay which I have described at the end of the island had become almost obliterated through the submerging of its flanking peninsula. The great raft of driftwood, with the huge black tree in the middle, was swaying up and down in the swollen current.

"That's one good thing a flood will do for us," said the Doctor. "It carries away all the vegetable stuff which is brought down on to the east end of the island. It came down with the freshet the other day, and here it will stay until a flood sweeps it out into the main stream. Well, here's our room, and here are some books and here is my tobacco pouch, and we must try and put in the night as best we may."

By the light of our single lantern the great lonely room looked very gaunt and dreary. Save for the piles of staves and heaps of hoops there was absolutely nothing in it, with the exception of the mattress for the Doctor, which had been laid in the corner. We made a couple of seats and a table out of the staves, and settled down together for a long vigil. Severall had brought a revolver for me and was himself armed with a double-barrelled shot-gun. We loaded our weapons and laid them cocked within reach of our hands. The little circle of light and the black shadows arching over us were so melancholy that he went off to the house, and returned with two candles. One side of the cooperage was pierced, however, by several open windows, and it was only by screening our lights behind staves that we could prevent them from being extinguished.

The Doctor, who appeared to be a man of iron nerves, had settled down to a book, but I observed that every now and then he laid it upon his knee, and took an earnest look all round him. For my part, although I tried once or twice to read, I found it impossible to concentrate my thoughts upon the book. They would always wander back to this great empty silent room, and to the sinister mystery which overshadowed it. I racked my brains for some possible theory which would explain the disappearance of these two men. There was the black fact that they were gone, and not the least tittle of evidence as to why or whither. And here we were waiting in the same place—waiting without an idea as to what we were waiting for. I was right in saying that it was not a one-man job. It was trying enough as it was, but no force upon earth would have kept me there without a comrade.

What an endless, tedious night it was! Outside we heard the lapping and gurgling of the great river, and the soughing of the rising wind. Within, save for our breathing, the turning of the Doctor's pages, and the high, shrill ping of an occasional mosquito, there was a heavy silence. Once my heart sprang into my mouth as Severall's book suddenly fell to the ground and he sprang to his feet with his eyes on one of the windows.

"Did you see anything, Meldrum?"

"No. Did you?"

"Well, I had a vague sense of movement outside that window." He caught up his gun and approached it. "No, there's nothing to be seen, and yet I could have sworn that something passed slowly across it."

"A palm leaf, perhaps," said I, for the wind was growing stronger every instant.

"Very likely," said he, and settled down to his book again, but his eyes were for ever darting little suspicious glances up at the window. I watched it also, but all was quiet outside.

And then suddenly our thoughts were turned into a new direction by the bursting of the storm. A blinding flash was followed by a clap which shook the building. Again and again came the vivid white glare with thunder at the same instant, like the flash and roar of a monstrous piece of artillery. And then down came the tropical rain, crashing and rattling on the corrugated iron roofing of the cooperage. The big hollow room boomed like a drum. From the darkness arose a strange mixture of noises, a gurgling, splashing, tinkling, bubbling, washing, dripping—every liquid sound that nature can produce from the thrashing and swishing of the rain to the deep steady boom of the river. Hour after hour the uproar grew louder and more sustained.

"My word," said Severall, "we are going to have the father of all the floods this time. Well, here's the dawn coming at last and that is a blessing. We've about exploded the third night superstition anyhow."

A grey light was stealing through the room, and there was the day upon us in an instant. The rain had eased off, but the coffee-coloured river was roaring past like a waterfall. Its power made me fear for the anchor of the *Gamecock*.

"I must get aboard," said I. "If she drags she'll never be able to beat up the river again."

"The island is as good as a breakwater," the Doctor answered. "I can give you a cup of coffee if you will come up to the house."

I was chilled and miserable, so the suggestion was a welcome one. We left the ill-omened cooperage with its mystery still unsolved, and we splashed our way up to the house.

"There's the spirit lamp," said Severall. "If you would just put a light to it, I will see how Walker feels this morning."

He left me, but was back in an instant with a dreadful face.

"He's gone!" he cried hoarsely.

The words sent a thrill of horror through me. I stood with the lamp in my hand, glaring at him.

"Yes, he's gone!" he repeated. "Come and look!"

I followed him without a word, and the first thing that I saw as I entered the bedroom was Walker himself lying huddled on his bed in the grey flannel sleeping suit in which I had helped to dress him on the night before.

"Not dead, surely!" I gasped.

The Doctor was terribly agitated. His hands were shaking like leaves in the wind.

"He's been dead some hours."

"Was it fever?"

"Fever! Look at his foot!"

I glanced down and a cry of horror burst from my lips. One foot was not merely dislocated, but was turned completely round in a most grotesque contortion.

"Good God!" I cried. "What can have done this?"

Severall had laid his hand upon the dead man's chest.

"Feel here," he whispered.

I placed my hand at the same spot. There was no resistance. The body was absolutely soft and limp. It was like pressing a sawdust doll.

"The breast-bone is gone," said Severall in the same awed whisper. "He's broken to bits. Thank God that he had the laudanum. You can see by his face that he died in his sleep."

"But who can have done this?"

"I've had about as much as I can stand," said the Doctor, wiping his forehead. "I don't know that I'm a greater coward than my neighbors, but this gets beyond me. If you're going out to the *Gamecock*—"

"Come on!" said I, and off we started. If we did not run it was because each of us wished to keep up the last shadow of his self-respect before the other. It was dangerous in a light canoe on that swollen river, but we never paused to give the matter a thought. He bailing and I paddling we kept her above water, and gained the deck of the yacht. There, with two hundred yards of water between us and this cursed island we felt that we were our own men once more.

"We'll go back in an hour or so," said he. "But we need a little time to steady ourselves. I wouldn't have had the niggers see me as I was just now for a year's salary."

"I've told the steward to prepare breakfast. Then we shall go back," said I. "But in God's name, Doctor Severall, what do you make of it all?"

"It beats me—beats me clean. I've heard of Voodoo deviltry, and I've laughed at it with the others. But that poor old Walker, a decent, God-fearing, nineteenth-century, Primrose-League Englishman should go under like this without a whole bone in his body—it's given me a shake, I won't deny it. But look there, Meldrum, is that hand of yours mad or drunk, or what is it?"

Old Patterson, the oldest man of my crew, and as steady as the Pyramids, had been stationed in the bows with a boat-hook to fend off the drifting logs which came sweeping down with the current. Now he stood with crooked knees, glaring out in front of him, and one forefinger stabbing furiously at the air.

"Look at it!" he yelled. "Look at it!"

And at the same instant we saw it.

A huge black trunk was coming down the river, its broad glistening back just lapped by the water. And in front of it—about three feet in front—arching upwards like the figure-head of a ship, there hung a dreadful face, swaying slowly from side to side. It was flattened, malignant, as large as a small beer-barrel, of a faded fungoid colour, but the neck which supported it was mottled with a dull yellow and black. As it flew past the *Gamecock* in the swirl of the waters I saw two immense coils roll up out of some great hollow in the tree, and the villainous head rose suddenly to the height of eight or ten feet, looking with dull, skin-covered eyes at the yacht. An instant later the tree had shot past us and was plunging with its horrible passenger towards the Atlantic.

"What was it?" I cried.

"It is our fiend of the cooperage," said Dr. Severall, and he had become in an instant the same bluff, self-confident man that he had been before. "Yes, that is the devil who has been haunting our island. It is the great python of the Gaboon."

I thought of the stories which I had heard all down the coast of the monstrous constrictors of the interior, of their periodical appetite, and of the murderous effects of their deadly squeeze. Then it all took shape in my mind. There had been a freshet the week before. It had brought down this huge hollow tree with its hideous occupant. Who knows from what far distant tropical forest it may have come! It had been stranded on the little east bay of the island. The cooperage had been the nearest house. Twice with the return of its appetite it had carried off the watchman. Last night it had doubtless come again, when Severall had thought he saw something move at the window, but our lights had driven it away. It had writhed onwards and had slain poor Walker in his sleep.

"Why did it not carry him off?" I asked.

"The thunder and lightning must have scared the brute away. There's your steward, Meldrum. The sooner we have breakfast and get back to the island the better, or some of those niggers might think that we had been frightened."

Introduction to Spirit Island

Henry Toke Munn (1864-1952) led an adventurous life, one that took him from his native Great Britain all the way to the Canadian Arctic, South Africa, and the Seychelles. He served as a storekeeper during the Yukon gold rush, prospected for gold in Canada, founded the Gold Exploration Syndicate, and spent two years on Southampton Island in the Canadian Arctic living with the Eskimos. His novel *Home is the Hunter* (1930) draws upon his familiarity with Eskimo culture.

"Spirit Island" likewise demonstrates the author's knowledge of Eskimo customs and legends. Published in *Chambers Journal* (November 1922), Munn's story straddles the divide between the adventure tale and weird fiction. As a work of cryptozoology, "Spirit Island" seamlessly blends the genres of exploration literature with that of supernatural fiction. With a reluctant narrator afraid that no one will believe what horrors he has experienced, the story will be of great interest to H. P. Lovecraft fans.

Much as in Henry S. Whitehead's "The People of Pan," also in this anthology, this story involves a protagonist who, when searching for natural resources, comes face to face with something else entirely—something fantastic and terrifying. Unlike "The People of Pan" and H. P. Lovecraft's "Dagon," however, "Spirit Island" takes place neither in the Caribbean, nor in the South Pacific. Rather, this uncanny tale unfolds in and on an island in the frigid lands of the Canadian Arctic, a remote land traversed by few and distantly removed from the confines of modern civilization.

SPIRIT ISLAND
Henry Toke Munn

I have told this story to only a few people, and my attempt to get a hearing before the Natural History authorities, both in New York and in London, completely failed, the secretaries treating me in pretty much the same manner. "Oh yes," they said indulgently, looking at my card, "that's all right. We have heard about it, and we'll take the matter up sometime. But don't call again; wait till we write you." Then they rang, and one of the attendants was told to show me round, if I cared to see the place, and put me on the way to where I was staying. Of course, they thought I was a crank.

I publish the narrative, therefore, rather reluctantly, accepting the fact that it will not be believed, but with a hope that it may inspire some credulous and courageous naturalist, with a taste for adventure, to visit Spirit Island, and return with a live or a dead specimen of what I saw there. If he can do this, his name will go down in history, and the museums—and the circuses—of the world will grovel at his feet for its possession. But he needn't ask me to accompany him.

In 1914 I was sent to the Arctic by my employers (a London firm well known in the mining world) to investigate certain localities for alluvial gold, and others for tin ore. In 1914-15 I wintered at Ponds Inlet, the north-east end of Baffin Land—lat. 72.48° N., long. 76.10° W. I made the investigations according to my instructions, and in August 1915 returned to the depot to await the arrival of my ship. By 15th October no ship had appeared, and I knew I was in for another winter. I had with me a Scottish lad to look after the depot in my absence—for the Eskimo will steal if no white man is about, and we were not short of supplies.

In the event of the non-arrival of my ship, and a second winter being enforced, I had been asked to try to investigate a certain locality on the north coast of a large island, known as Prince of Wales Land, about five hundred miles west of my depot. This island lies at the southwest end of Barrow Strait, and between Peel Sound and Franklin Strait to the east and M'-Clintock Channel and M'Clure Strait to the west. It can be seen on any Arctic map.

I set out from the depot in February, with seven natives and three dog-sleds, leaving orders for the ship to come for me to Leopold Island in Lancaster Sound if I did not return before the ice broke up. My party were Panne-lou, my head man, who drove my sled with ten dogs; Akko-molee, who had his own sled and team of nine dogs; and Now-yea, who also had his own sled and eleven dogs, four of which were only three-quarter-grown puppies. Each man had his wife, without whom no native will make a prolonged journey, and Akko-molee had the only child in the party, a lad of about eleven years old, named Kyak-jua.

A word as to my natives. Panne-lou was a steady, reliable fellow, a good seal-hunter and dog-driver. His wife, Sal-pinna, was a disagreeable, cross-grained—and cross-eyed woman, but capable and a good worker. Akko-molee was taken mainly because he was a native of Admiralty Inlet, two hundred miles west of my depot, and had hunted bear on the North Somerset coast. He was only moderately useful, and very inclined to sulk on any provocation. His boy, Kyak-jua, was a capital little fellow, the life of our party, full of energy, and a great favorite with all of us. I had given him a .22 rifle, and he was constantly getting me ptarmigan and Arctic hares with it when we were on the land. His mother, Anno-rito, was a quiet, pleasant woman, and entirely devoted to her boy.

Now-yea, my third native, was an active merry little man, willing and tireless, but irresponsible and very excitable. His number two wife (he had a couple), In-noya, was the best woman, and eventually proved to be the best man, in the party. I shall have more to say about her later on. Now-yea had left his number one wife and four children, all of whom were hers, at my depot, and I had agreed to provide for them till our return.

The pay, arranged before starting, consisted of tobacco, sugar, tea, and biscuit for the trip—or as long as our supplies lasted—and to each man, on our return to the depot, a new rifle, ammunition, a box (twenty-two pounds) of tobacco, a barrel of biscuit, some tea, coffee, and molasses, and a spy-glass, or some equivalent if they already had one; also some oddments, such as cooking-utensils, day-clocks, needles, braid, scented soap, &c., for the women, and ten pounds of tobacco to each one. These were regarded as high wages by the other natives, of whom I could have had my pick, but they were fully earned, and many extras I threw in, as the sequel will show.

My outfit—besides the supplies already mentioned—consisted of twenty pounds of dynamite, some caps and fuse, also one of these new, very small, 'Ubique' batteries, six short drills, and a two and a half pound hammer. We had a rifle per man, and one spare one—all single shot .303 carbines, except mine, which was an ordinary English service magazine-rifle; plenty of ammunition; a complete sailing-gear for each man, and two spare harpoons and lances; a hand-axe for each sled; native lamps for cooking and heating, and cooking-utensils. We had ogjuke (bearded seal) skins, for boot-soles later on, and seal-skins and deer-skin legs for cold-weather foot-wear, plenty of dressed deer-skin for stockings and socks, deer-skin blankets and heavy winter-killed hides to sleep on. We all had new deer-skin clothes, and expected to get young seal 'white coats' for wear on the return journey, when the others would be too warm.

My medicines were a flask of brandy, some tabloid drugs and antiseptics, a few bandages, and some surgical needles and thread. My personal luxury was a few dozen of the excellent 'Cambridge' soup-powders. I took a small kayak (skin canoe) as far as Leopold Island for sealing later, if we had to wait there, and also a tent.

One item of my outfit, a small Kodak camera, I was unfortunate enough to smash hopelessly a few days before starting. I shall for ever regret this disaster—for such it proved to be—and the irremediable loss it occasioned me.

This is not a story of Arctic travel, so I will omit the details of the journey. My route lay through Navy Board Inlet, and thence west along Lancaster Sound to Prince Regent Inlet, crossing to Leopold Island, and over the North Somerset Land—which is a flat tableland in from the coast—to Peel Sound and Prince of Wales Land. We had to make about six hundred and twenty-five miles of travelling, though, as I have said, it was only five hundred miles as the crow flies, and, of course, we had to depend on sea and land animals for ourselves and our dogs to live on, and for blubber for light, cooking, and warmth. Such journeys are made every winter by some of the Eskimo, either when visiting other parties or on hunting-trips, and are by no means unusual. The main, indeed the indispensable, thing being to find seals, halts of a day or two are made for the purpose.

Now, I want to emphasise the fact that Prince of Wales Land is by no means what literary people call a *terra incognita*, at least so far as the coast-line is concerned. Parry discovered it a hundred years ago, and Roald Amundsen sailed his famous little ship the *Gjøa* down Peel Sound and Franklin Strait when he made the North-West Passage.

No natives have been found on North Somerset or on Prince of Wales Land, though hunting-parties visit North Somerset occasionally.

I had not told my destination to the natives beyond North Somerset, and when we arrived at Leopold Island, and I unfolded my plans in the igloo that night, there was great consternation. We should starve; the ice would go out and leave us stranded there; and, lastly—here was the real hitch—it was a "bad" country.

"Why bad," I asked, "when you say none of you have been there?"

There was a pause before Panne-lou said reluctantly, "It is full of *Tornga* [bad spirits]; we are afraid of them."

It took me half the night, talking and cajoling, before I overcame this absurd objection. Finally they consented to go on, but stipulated that we should travel close to the shore at Prince of Wales Land, to which I, of course, willingly agreed.

A small building, once full of stores, stands on Leopold Island. Naturally, it had been completely looted by the natives, but it served excellently to store our kayak and tent in, out of the weather.

I will relate one incident of the journey, as it shows the stuff one member of our party was made of. The day after we left Leopold Island we camped on the tableland of North Somerset, and I decided to stay a day there, and try for some deer, both as a change from seal-meat, of which we were all tired, and also to provide a 'cache,' or store of meat against our return.

I sent the three men off with all the dogs early in the morning; not feeling very well, I remained at the igloo. I had taken my rifle to pieces to clean it, and had all the parts in my lap, when I heard a cry outside, and Sal-pinna said, "Quick! He says a bear." My rifle was, for the moment, useless, so I plunged out of the igloo to get the spare rifle, which was always in In-noya's care in the other igloo. Outside I saw little Kyak-jua, about a hundred yards away, running for his life towards the igloos with a very large bear within fifteen or twenty paces of him. In-noya was out of the igloo, with the rifle, running towards them. I did not think the boy had a chance, for he was directly between the rifle and the bear, and one blow of those formidable paws would have brained him, but suddenly In-noya called sharply, "*Tella-peea-nin; tella-peea-nin*" ("To the right; to the right"). The boy, instantly divining he was in the line of fire, doubled to the right like a hare. A shot rang out, and the bear roared with pain, then turned and savagely bit his hind-quarter, which had been hit. The next instant he was charging full tilt at In-noya. She had dropped on one knee to shoot, and, without moving, coolly levelled her rifle again. So close was the bear when she shot, and laid him dead with a bullet in his brain, that as she sprang on one side the impetus of his charge carried him half his length over where she had knelt; the record was written plainly on the snow.

I asked In-noya later why she did not fire sooner. "I had only taken two cartridges, when I ran out of the igloo," she said indifferently, "and I had to make sure of him." It was as fine an exhibition of coolness and steady nerve as I have ever seen.

We reached my objective on 25th March, crossing Peel Sound from North Somerset in one day's travel of about forty-five miles. We kept very close to the Prince of Wales Land shore, and I noticed we always built our igloos now on the land, even if suitable snow was not so handy as on the ice, though we often had to negotiate some rough ground-ice before getting to shore.

A very disastrous mishap occurred the day after we arrived. Seven of our dogs, divided amongst the three teams, ate something poisonous they found along the shore, and died the same night; three more were very bad, but recovered. I cannot imagine what an Eskimo dog could find to poison him in his own country, but this was certainly the cause of death. The natives, of course, blamed the *Torn-ga*, and were greatly disturbed.

By 27th March I had seen all I needed to. The reported tin-vein was a vein of iron pyrite ore. I do not know who started this yarn about tin, but the description and locality of the vein agreed so closely with the data given me that I have always concluded the information was found in one of the private logs of the old Arctic voyagers, perhaps one of Parry's or Ross's crews.

Seals had been very hard to find since we crossed Peel Sound, and our dogs were getting hungry, so, after wasting the 28th looking for seals, which refused to come to the breathing-holes we found, we started the return journey on the 29th, and reached the north-east end of Prince of Wales Land on the 31st, only getting one small seal in that time.

About fifteen miles north of Prince of Wales Land lies a large island, and Panne-lou volunteered the information that the Eskimo name of it was "Spirit Island"; but he could not, or would not, tell me anything more, the subject being strictly taboo by him, and also by the others.

When we left the next morning early, a south-east breeze was blowing up Peel Sound, and it looked as if it would be a fine day for the crossing. We had made only about half-way over when one of those sudden Arctic storms swept down on us, shutting out all sight of land at once. The natives had a discussion whether to go ahead or return, and decided to push on. Panne-lou complained he was feeling ill, and was on the sled all day. Soon after the storm broke, the wind must suddenly have changed, for by five o'clock no land came in sight, and the storm was increasing in violence every minute. Panne-lou became very ill, so there was no alternative but to camp where we were.

Next morning it was blowing a blizzard, and Panne-lou was delirious and in a high fever. Even if it had been fit weather, it would have killed him to move him.

This part of the Arctic lies north of the Magnetic Pole, and the compass variation is nearly one hundred degrees; it is so sluggish and unreliable that it is quite useless for making a course in thick weather. We did not know, therefore, if we were north or south of our course.

That night—1st April—the first two dogs disappeared. My log says: "At 11 P.M. dogs suddenly started howling; thought it was a bear, but dogs stampeded to igloo door much afraid. Suddenly one gave a queer stifled yap, and about same time door broke and dogs tumbled pell-mell into igloo..." The 'door' is a block of snow set up on the inside of the igloo. Now-yea and In-noya were sleeping in my igloo, to help nurse Panne-lou—

for he had to be constantly watched—and as soon as the row started Now-yea, at In-noya's instigation, jumped up, and throwing his *kouletang* (deer-skin jumper) on the floor of the igloo from the snow sleeping-bench, stood on it naked—Eskimo always turn in thus—and held the snow 'door' till it broke in his hands, letting the dogs in.

Meantime I had slipped on my *kouletang* and some deer-skin stockings, and, as soon as the door was clear of dogs, cautiously crawled out with my rifle, expecting to find an unusually bold and hungry bear at our 'store-house,' a small snow-house built against the side of the igloo, containing the meat, blubber, harness, &c., which the dogs might damage or eat. As a rule rifles are kept outside, to prevent the frost coming out of them; but the natives insisted that they must all be taken inside that night.

I saw or heard nothing; it was a very dark night, and the drifting snow was blinding, stinging the eyes like sand. I crawled back, half-frozen, and we put up another snow door. The other igloo, fifteen or twenty yards away, had the same experience, so there must have been two visitors, as we each lost a dog at the same time.

The blizzard lasted three days, and though we built porches for the dogs in front of igloo doors and shut them in, we lost two dogs each night in the same mysterious manner. The 'doors' were always broken inwards, and a dog quickly and neatly snatched away. Obviously no bear was doing this, for his methods would have been more clumsy.

On the third night I made a hole in the igloo over the 'door,' and as soon as the dogs yelped put my rifle through and fired three or four shots into the porch. Next morning Akko-molee's dog was gone, but outside our porch our dog lay dead. His neck was broken and his throat torn out.

By this time the natives were completely demoralised, with the exception of In-noya. Now-yea sat shivering, as if with ague, the whole night, and Sal-pinna was little better. She had trodden on a knife-blade in the igloo, and cut her foot so badly that I had to put seven stitches in it. In Akko-molee's igloo they remained in their blankets all the time, and he would hardly answer me when I called to him.

Meanwhile Panne-lou improved but little, and I kept him alive on a few spoonfuls of brandy-and-water every hour. On the third day the fever had abated, but he was still wandering and semi-conscious.

There was good excuse for the natives. An igloo is not the slightest pro-tection against an attack; an arrow or a lance would go through it like pa-per. It was a trying job, therefore, to sit inside expecting something—one could not tell what—to happen. For the natives, who believed implicitly it was the *Torn-ga*, it was worse than for me. In-noya, however, never lost her self-control, and she and I fed and watched Panne-lou in turn.

On the morning of the fourth day—3rd April—the storm had blown itself out, but there was a dense fog, and we could not see more than a hundred yards or so. The natives would have harnessed the dogs and left at once, in spite of my urging that it would certainly kill Panne-lou to do so, but until it cleared they did not know which way to go, for till we saw some land, or even the stars to steer by, we were completely lost.

Akko-molee said the fog showed there was open water not far away, and vaguely opined it was a bad sign. A pressure-ridge was behind the igloos; in fact, it was at this we found snow suitable for building. I asked Akko-molee to walk in one direction along it for a short distance with a sealing-dog to try to find a breathing-hole, as we were completely out of feed, and the poor brutes were starving. I would walk down the pressure-ridge in the opposite direction for the same purpose. I arranged we should both return the moment the fog cleared. Now-yea, who was much too shaky to go away alone, was to remain at the igloo on guard.

Akko-molee demurred at first, but finally consented to go, adding, "Only a very little way, though." In-noya looked after Panne-lou, who was now sleeping quietly and in a profuse perspiration. I made some soup for him, gave her a few instructions, then left with my sealing-gear and rifle, leading a dog.

It was nine o'clock in the morning. I walked along the pressure-ridge for eight or ten minutes, when, to my surprise, I came to open water. The tide ran strongly in Barrow Strait, I knew, and the gale must have opened the ice up. We had, therefore, got far to the north of our course to reach the floe-edge, as the ice fast to the land is called. The water seemed to be of some extent, but the fog made it impossible to see how large it was. As the floe-edge is generally very irregular, deep bights forming in it where the moving pack exercises pressure, it would be very dangerous to move before we saw where we were.

It was a mere chance that we had not driven into the water or on to the moving ice in the blizzard. Seeing a seal in the water a short distance from the pressure-ridge, I let the dog go, as I did not need him, and he ran back to the igloo; I then sat down and waited for the seal to appear. Presently I shot one, but found the tide was running away from the floe, and I lost him, so I waited till it turned, which it did in about three hours. I then shot two seals; though I had to wait another hour before they came in to the floe. By this time a fairly strong tide was running under it.

As I was tying the seals together to drag them back to the igloo, I caught through the fog, in the direction of the pressure-ridge, a glimpse of a man walking down to the water's edge. It was only an uncertain impression, for the fog shut him out immediately. I rather wondered why Akko-molee had followed me, but remembering I had sent the dog back, supposed that had to do with it.

When I arrived at the pressure-ridge, I saw nothing of Akko-molee, but leading down to the water were large drops of blood, and at the floe-edge lay a little deer-skin mitten; it could only have been Kyak-jua's. The snow was packed as hard as a pavement by the gale, so it was no use to look for tracks on it, but right at the water's edge, where it was softer and wet, was an odd-looking track, rather as if it had been made by some gigantic bird with webbed feet. The claw-marks did not show, as the toes overlapped the edge of the ice.

What did the blood mean? How came little Kyak-jua's mitten to be there? I felt sick at heart as I quickly thought it over. A tragedy had happened, I was sure. I ran back to where I had left the seals, about sixty yards from the water's edge; hastily buried one in the snow to keep it thawed, cutting a hole with my sheath-knife for the purpose; threw the other on my shoulder—they were both small seals—and ran towards the igloo. The tell-tale drops of blood stopped about three hundred yards from the floe-edge.

At the igloo I found Now-yea pacing back and forth before the door, shouting 'spirit-talk,' and nearly crazy; Anno-rito, the boy's mother, inside unconscious; and In-noya gray-faced and crying quietly, but faithfully tending Panne-lou as I had told her. My arrival upset her for a moment, however, as she cried out, "I thought you had gone too." I shut up Now-yea by cuffing him, and sent him into the igloo, where he sat and shivered.

In-noya told me the story succinctly. Kyak-jua had left his mother's igloo to come and see In-noya, for they were great friends. Now-yea was inside, warming himself, at the time; by-and-by Anno-rito called out, and In-noya replied the boy was not there. The poor mother rushed out shrieking for the boy, and on entering our igloo fell unconscious. In-noya did not dare to leave Panne-lou, who was very restless—Sal-pinna was useless—but she made Now-yea go out and look about. The tears streamed down her face, for she loved the little lad dearly. "It is no good to look," she sobbed; "the *Torn-ga* have taken him." Akko-molee's dog had returned, and In-noya said she feared for poor little Kyak-jua's father. "I am going to fetch Akko-molee," I declared; "he is not far away."

As I left the igloo I realised what had happened. Something had been lying hidden behind the pressure-ridge, and had crept close to the igloo. It had swiftly and silently seized Kyak-jua, and as swiftly and silently departed. The dogs, all asleep inside the porch, had given no alarm, the lad himself not made a sound. What manner of beast was this to do such a daring deed? It explained those drops of blood near the water. I at least, knew where the boy had gone, and a fierce anger surged over me when I thought of his merry face, and the happy smile with which he would bring me a ptarmigan, saying, "For you, *kabloona* [white man]."

I thought of all this as I ran along the pressure-ridge through the fog, when suddenly I nearly fell over Akko-molee's body. He was lying on his face, dead, with a hole in the back of his skull, from which the brain was oozing. He had evidently been sitting at a seal-hole, and his assailant had crept up behind him. His right sleeve was torn open, and the artery under the arm had been ripped up, *but there was no blood on the snow from it.*

I felt sick when I realised what this ghoulish murderer had done; he had sucked the blood from the artery till it was dry. The sealing-spear, harpoon, seal-line, and lance were gone, but the rifle rested against a block of snow where Akko-molee had placed it. I left him lying there on the snow; my business was with the living.

I returned to the igloo, to find Anno-rito had been persuaded by In-noya to turn in under her blanket, which she had done, native fashion, with nothing on. She looked up when I took off my mitts and *kouletang*, and said dully, "Akko-molee is dead. I have seen him. Is it not so?"

Then I did a fool thing, but I was overstrung and rattled. I nodded "Yes," and said, "He is dead." There was a silence while you might have counted ten; then, without any warning, Anno-rito sprang up, dived under the low exit of the igloo, and fled shrieking, "*Oo-wonga ky-it; oo-wonga ky-it*" ("I come; I come").

I was into my *kouletang* in a few seconds, grabbed my rifle (without which I would not have gone ten yards), and was after her, but, stripped naked as she was, she could keep her lead. She ran along the pressure-ridge, where I had gone in the morning, and I shouted when I realised a few minutes would take her to the water's edge. I was near enough to see her fling up her arms and spring into the water, and her despairing cry, "*Oo-wonga ky-it,*" was borne faintly back to me through the fog. Unhappy Anno-rito had joined her boy and her man.

It was now about four o'clock, and, live or die, Panne-lou must be moved in the morning. I would have left at once, but it was impossible to travel in the fog after dark. If it did not lift, I would try a compass course, uncertain as it was, in the morning, or steer by the breeze, if there was one, away from the open water. If the fog lifted, I would steer by the stars that night.

Meantime the dogs might as well be fed, and, with this in my mind, I pulled out the seal I had left in the snow. The fog was for a moment thinner than it had been, and I had just done this when I saw another seal in the water on the far side of the pressure-ridge. Running to the floe edge, I sat down beside an up-ended piece of ice about ten yards from the water to wait for him to come up again. After a few minutes I leaned forward to look along the floe-edge, peering round the piece of ice. About sixty or seventy yards from me, standing on the ice, close to the water and looking intently at the seal lying near the pressure-ridge, I saw a man—or, rather, a two-footed beast in a man's shape.

He was but that moment out of the water, for it was dripping off him, and even as I looked his body began to turn white, as if the drops had been frozen on him in glistening little nodules. His head was thrown back and he was sniffing the air, as if using his scenting-powers. Suddenly he ran— rather clumsily, I thought, but swiftly and with unusually long strides—towards the dead seal. My brain started working again, and I knew I had him; I was between him and the water.

As he stopped and picked up the seal, throwing it over his shoulder very easily, I sprang out from behind the slab of ice, and he saw me. Without a second's hesitation, and before the seal fell from his shoulder on to the ice with a thud, he was running swiftly and silently at me, a short throwing-lance poised in his right hand. I covered him without haste, and pulled the trigger, but the cartridge missed fire. I jerked in another cartridge, and as I threw my rifle to my shoulder his arm shot forward like a piston-stroke, and I dropped quickly on one knee. As I did so, the hood of my *kouletang* was thrown back from my head and—it seemed to me at the same instant—I fired.

I suppose the lance, which had struck my hood, threw my aim off, for the shot went high, and broke my assailant's left shoulder, causing him to drop a second lance he held in his hand. But it did not stop him, and before I could jerk in another cartridge he was on me. Dodging the muzzle of my rifle, he seized my left arm above the elbow with incredible strength, for I felt the nails or claws sink deeply into my flesh through my thick deerskin clothes. At the same time he pulled me towards him and tried to get at my throat with his teeth. I seized his neck with my free hand, and for some seconds we swayed back and forward thus, the blood from his wound drenching me. Flecks of bloody foam ran down from his mouth, and as we tussled he made a snarling growl, as a dog does when at grips with his foe. This was the only sound I heard from him.

We were unpleasantly near the water, so I bent my energies on working back from it, and was able to make some yards farther in on the ice. I soon found it quite beyond my strength to squeeze his windpipe and choke him, the neck being very strong and thick; and although I had the advantage of at least five inches in height, and am over the average of my size in strength, it was all I could do to hold him off me. Had his other arm been whole, he would have torn my throat out with his claws.

We twisted and turned, struggling desperately, when suddenly he relinquished his grasp of my left arm, I suppose for a hold at my throat. As I felt him do so, I pushed him violently away and sprang back. He came at me again like a wildcat, snarling savagely; but I was readier now, and beating down his outstretched hand with my left fist, I landed him on the point of the jaw with all the weight and strength I could put into an upper-cut. It lifted him clean off his feet, and he fell backwards. As he dazedly and unsteadily recovered his feet again, I snatched up the lance he had dropped—for we had reached the place in our struggle—and rushing on him, drove it with both hands and all my might at his heart. He fell dead at my feet.

For a few minutes I sat down, feeling sick and giddy. I was blood from head to foot, and I saw for the first time some of it was my own, for my arm was bleeding freely enough for it to run down inside my sleeve over my hand. The indescribable horror of the Thing's appearance, the smell of his breath, and the ferocity and courage of his attack, badly wounded as he was, all affected me strongly. More and more I realised that I could have done nothing against him had he been unwounded.

Pulling myself together, I turned the *Torn-ga* over—so I call him, from this date, in my log, and the name will serve. Sticking out under his left shoulder-blade was a harpoon-head, lashed to the point of an ivory lance with sinew. I set my foot on the body and drew the lance out at his back, and, after cleaning it in the snow, examined it. The harpoon-head was Akko-molee's! I knew it instantly, for I had seen him filing it a few days before. I felt better, somehow, when I had seen this, and turned to examine more fully the body of my grim foe.

He was perhaps an inch over five feet in height, and was covered, except the palms of his hands and the soles of his feet, with short, fine seal-hair of a grayish-brown colour. The eyes were enormous, with no eyelashes, very like a seal's, the hips tremendously developed, and the legs disproportionately long; the instep was very broad and flat, and both the toes and the fingers very long, webbed, and ending in thick nails like claws. It struck me he would have been a truly formidable antagonist in the water. The face was hideous; it had a wide receding jaw, with very prominent eyebrows overhanging the huge eyes, a low forehead, and small furry ears. I noticed, too, the teeth were sharp, the dog-teeth much developed, and the front-teeth of the lower jaw noticeably longer than the others. He had died with his lips drawn back in a savage snarl. Jets of very dark blood were flowing from his breast. The limbs and the body had a smooth roundness that could mean only one thing, but to satisfy myself I drew my knife and cut a gash in the thigh. As I expected, there was over an inch of blubber under the skin, exactly as a seal has.

Behind where I had knelt and fired, an ivory lance was sticking deeply in the hard snow. I looked at my hood—the lance had torn the top off it.

Acting on some impulse, I dragged the body to the floe-edge, and shot it into the water. It floated buoyantly, but the strong tide soon swept it out of sight under the ice; and as its blood-smeared, snarling face disappeared, I thought of little Kyak-jua, and felt glad that some, at least, of the account was paid.

Throwing the seal on my shoulder, I returned to the igloo. There was no one now to take counsel with but In-noya, for the other two only sat huddled up and moaning. Calling her outside, I assured her I was not hurt—she was horrified at the mess I was in—and related what I had done, and how I planned to leave the moment the fog permitted.

These Eskimo know more about this mystery than they will tell, because In-noya shook her head, saying "Many will come to-night and kill us, *kabloona*." She told me she had put my revolver beside her, adding very quietly she wanted it to shoot Panne-lou and herself with it if the *Torn-ga* broke into the igloo. "They suck your blood when you are alive," she said calmly. I had not mentioned what I had seen on Akko-molee's body. How did she know this was their ghoulish habit?

I patted the plucky girl on the back, and told her we should come through the night all right as I had a plan. Fortunately, there was a spare *kouletang* in my kit-bag. Before I went inside the igloo I took off my blood-soaked garment and threw it away behind the pressure-ridge, explaining to the others that the blood on my foot-gear and deer-skin outer trousers was from the seal. These garments I took off, and started Sal-pinna thawing and cleaning them. My arm pained me, and was still bleeding. Examining it in the unoccupied igloo, I found five claw-like incisions, which had cut deeply into the flesh. I washed them with antiseptic, and In-noya bound them up.

I then shook up Now-yea, made him come out and feed the two seals—saving a meal for ourselves—to the dogs, and carefully ice the sledrunners and get all the harness ready. The dogs would need five or six hours after feeding, but I hoped that by midnight we should have the stars to steer by, and could make a start.

I thawed ten pounds of dynamite, wrapped it up in several pieces of deer-skin, and as soon as it was dusk laid it the full length of my wires along the pressure-ridge, making a track for the wires, and carefully covering it all over with snow. I brought the wires into the igloo through the wall, and connected them up with the battery. Then, shutting the dogs into the porch, I ran a reel of strong thread I happened to have with me round the igloo and porch about ten paces away, setting up blocks of snow some two and a half feet high, and driving into them bits of stick, to which I fastened the thread. As I was short of sticks, I used one of the two lances I had brought from the scene of the fight; the other I put away in a dunnage-bag. Midway between each of the blocks, I ran pieces of thread fastened to the thread circling us, and led them into the igloo through paper tubes, to keep them from freezing to the wall. I then pulled them gently taut, and fastened them to small strips of wood, so that when they were struck into the igloo wall they were bent by the pull of the line; there were five of them. In-noya helped me deftly and intelligently, asking no questions, except what I wanted done. When back in the igloo, I insisted on their finishing the seal meal, and we made a brew of strong tea. Panne-lou was now conscious and free from fever, but utterly prostrated.

It was a nerve-racking watch. I am not sure if I would come through another like it. I had seen now what we were waiting for, and if—as In-noya said they would—many came, if indeed only a few attacked us, I knew now we should have no chance at all, penned up inside the igloo. Yet we should be worse off freezing outside in the gray fog and darkness. I had seen their swiftness and savage determination. How many could we account for before the end came?

Suddenly I remembered there would be a young moon up about one o'-clock, and I decided to start then and steer by it, if the weather was clear enough to locate it.

The hours dragged on till nearly midnight. Now-yea and Sal-pinna dozed fitfully, and awoke shivering.

Panne-lou slept; In-noya sat beside him, gray-faced and self-possessed, occasionally trimming the native lamp, but with my revolver ever ready at her hand. We whispered once or twice, and listened, straining our ears for some sound outside, till every minute seemed an hour, watching the little bent sticks, and waiting.

I kept my hand on the battery-handle, and my rifle across my knees. Suddenly a stick straightened with a faint click, and I nodded to In-noya, who touched the other two natives. I lifted the handle and pressed it down smartly. The roar of the explosion tore the silence of the night. The ice shook, threatening to demolish the igloo, and snow fell down on us inside. The dogs yelped with fear once or twice; then came silence. Presently an inarticulate, eerie, wailing cry rang out, distinct and very high-pitched; then silence once more, and we listened, listened. And then I knew how it is men go mad with the strain of waiting for some unseen danger to strike them.

At one o'clock we had some more tea, and I crept outside to see the weather. The fog was thinning fast, and I could see the young moon faintly, low down towards the open water. I knew it rose in the north-east, and gave the word to hitch up the dogs and start. It seemed certain I was giving Panne-lou his death-sentence, but there was probably a more terrible death for him, and all of us, if we delayed. Now-yea worked feverishly; the dogs were divided between two sleds; Panne-lou was rolled like a mummy in deer-skin blankets and lashed on; and we started.

With a match I hastily examined the snow outside the circle of thread, where I had purposely scraped it soft, and could see that only one track had been made. The lance to which the thread had been fastened was gone. The last thing I took out of the igloo was a deer-skin parcel containing the rest of the dynamite, thawed and ready for the fuse and cap, and the six drill-steels and the hammer-head. I put the dynamite between Panne-lou's blankets to keep it thawed. The fuse was marked in half-minutes. Panne-lou knew everything we were doing, and whispered to me, "The land, *kabloona*; get the land. *Torn-ga* will not come there."

Now-yea drove one sled with Sal-pinna on it. She walked with great pain, the cut on her foot being a deep one. Till daylight I led with the other sled, which In-noya drove. Now-yea had nine and I had eight dogs, but three on my sled were very weak from the poison they had eaten a few days before, and four of Now-yea's were puppies. In-noya handled the mixed team of dogs with wonderful skill.

By three o'clock it was light, and at half-past four the blessed sun rose, dispersing the last of the fog—never did I welcome him more—and there to the south-east of us was the bold coast-line of North Somerset, some twenty-five miles or so away. Behind us lay the north-east end of Spirit Island, and near it, extending far to the eastward, a curtain of mist rose in the still, cold air from the floe-edge, a dark patch of water-sky behind it denoting a large hole of water. Our igloos were not visible, but they must have been very close to the north-eastern end of Spirit Island.

With the bright morning sun shining in our faces; our hearts rose to cheerfulness, and the horrors of a few hours before seemed like some bad dream, till I thought of merry little Kyak-jua, and how I had left his father lying out there on the ice. That was no dream, but a grim reality.

I told Now-yea to take the lead, warning him I would shoot him if he did not stick to his sled, but tried to run away. In-noya also shouted out the message to him, and added on her own account, "And you know the *kabloona* does not often miss." We walked and trotted alongside the sleds, not sparing the whip. In-noya handled it and its twenty-seven-foot lash as skilfully as any native I have ever seen.

Soon after sunrise we came to rather rough ice, which, though not bad enough to delay us seriously, quickly took the ice-shoeing off the runners of the sleds, so that they pulled heavily. The walking was hard and good, and by skilful handling the sleds were steered clear of any large rough hummocks; but this all helped to retard our progress.

By half-past six we were apparently fifteen or sixteen miles from the land and making a good five miles an hour, but some of our dogs were flagging, and presently one lay down, and had to be taken out of the team. Soon after this two of Now-yea's puppies were turned loose, but they followed on, and eventually made the land, unlike our dog, who did not rise again.

At seven o'clock I climbed a piece of ice and had a look back with the telescope. I speedily made out a number of black dots coming in an irregular line along our track; they were about five or six miles away. I ran after the sled and told In-noya quietly—it was no use frightening the others yet. She only glanced at the revolver lying in its case under the lashing, and applied herself to the sled and team. She was the bravest person (man or woman) I have ever met. We halted for two or three minutes to clear the traces, and while this was being done I took the dynamite parcel out, rolled it and the drill-steels and hammer-head into one parcel with deer-skin, and adjusted the cap and fuse, slipping it all under the lashing, ready instantly to be taken out.

As we drew nearer the land I saw the cliffs ran sheerly down to the ice, and thought for a minute or two we were going to be trapped, for the only man who had known the coast was dead—Akko-molee. After a while, however, I picked up a little bay with my telescope, perhaps three-quarters of a mile wide and rather deeper, from the head of which the land sloped steeply back, so I ran forward and pointed out to Now-yea where to steer for. He seemed to have his nerves under better control now, for he answered "All right" quite cheerfully. Perhaps he thought he could make a race for it, and reach the land alone, if the pinch came, though I may be doing him an injustice. The fact that the natives had dared to come to this region at all, knowing what they did, lent some colour to their reiterated assertion that we should be safe on the land. My reason rebelled, nevertheless, at the seeming absurdity of the idea. If our pursuers could travel on the snow of the ice, of course they could do the same on the land. Yet, somehow, among them the natives had imbued me with a quite unreasonable but firm faith in our salvation could we win *terra firma*.

At half-past eight the *Torn-ga* were about a mile away, and coming up on us fast. They were spread in an irregular line extending across our track, but I was glad to see a number of them were straggling badly. The pace was telling on them, for we must have had a long start. There seemed to be at least a hundred of them.

Presently we came to a small pressure-ridge, and as soon as we had passed it I took the time very carefully; to when the first of our pursuers appeared on our side, it was exactly six and a half minutes. I cut the fuse and lighted it, and laid the smoking parcel down on the ice, running on with my watch in my hand. Ten seconds or so before the charge was due to explode, I stopped and looked back with the telescope. The nearest *Torn-ga* had reached the parcel and were standing round it, more coming up every second. Those on the flanks had also stopped, and they all seemed to be waiting for one of their number, as they were looking back. Even as I took this scene in, a *Torn-ga*, fully a head taller than the rest, burst through the knot standing irresolutely about, and gesticulated violently in our direction. As he did so the charge exploded.

When the snow and smoke cleared, I counted six bodies prone on the snow, and saw several more limping away or sitting down, evidently badly hurt. I turned and raced after the sled.

When I told In-noya what I had seen, she pressed her lips grimly together, saying, "It pays a little of the debt for Kyak-jua and Akko-molee." I inquired if she had looked at Panne-lou lately. I had not thought about him for some time, and it occurred to me that, if he were dead, we would cut the lashings and leave him. She nodded, saying, "He sleeps," then went to urging the dogs forward. I noticed the revolver was now taken out of its case and ready for instant action. We pushed steadily on for some time, improving our pace, as the dogs began to smell the land, and when next I looked back I saw about twenty of the *Torn-ga* five hundred yards or so in advance of the rest.

The dynamite had answered its purpose, and if it came to a fight close in on the land, I at first hoped we could handle these, for I knew I could depend on In-noya. But they drew up on us so steadily I saw this hope was vain, and, with a sinking feeling at my heart, thought of the savage determination the day before of only one of them—and he badly wounded.

Something must be done, however, and thinking it rapidly over, I decided to let the sled go on, and make a stand at a suitable hummock, with my magazine-rifle and the revolver, when they were about three hundred yards away. It sounds self-sacrificing, and all that sort of nonsense, but as a matter of fact it was only plain common-sense; it would be absurd to lose the advantage the firearms gave me by letting them get to close quarters before turning at bay. I should not have mentioned it, however, but for the part In-noya played. I told her my intention, whereon she said, "Yes, *kabloona*, but we will take all the rifles, and I will stay and reload for you. The dogs see the land now, and will not stop." I refused to allow this; but she was quietly obstinate, pointing out that she could do some shooting on her own account, and then reload my rifle while I used the others.

She took the revolver up and put the cord over her head, saying calmly, "It is settled. Do not speak any more about it. I will take two rifles off the sled when you say the word; do you take the others and the cartridge-bag." Suddenly she cried quickly, "Where is the thing which smokes [the fuse]? It will delay them a little." Fool! I had not thought of it. In half-a-minute I had wrapped the rest of the coil in deer-skin, lighted it at both ends to make more smoke—there was plenty of it—and laid it on the snow. It was quite harmless, but the bluff might go.

The nearest *Torn-ga* were about four hundred yards away from us, and when they saw the smoking parcel they halted a few seconds, and then made a wide detour on either side of it, allowing us to increase our lead considerably. About this time another of our dogs staggered and fell, but In-noya had been watching him, and whipping a knife from the sled, severed his trace without stopping the others.

Then Now-yea, who was about one hundred yards ahead, called out something, and In-noya said, "He says he can see the snow in the bay has been flooded—by the late spring-tide, of course—and it is all smooth ice." She cast a glance back. "We shall make the land, *kabloona*," she said quietly. "*Koya-nimik*" ("I am glad"). Glad! Blown as I was, I shouted for joy. "Hurrah! Hurrah, In-noya!" I said; but she only smiled back, and plied her skilful whip, and cheered on the weary dogs. We were running on either side of our sleds now, even lame Sal-pinna holding on to a lashing and limping gamely along.

I looked back, and could plainly see in the frosty air the smoking breath of the nearest *Torn-ga*, and got a glimpse of his savage face. He was obviously tired, and, I noticed, ran 'flat-footedly' and ungracefully, but with long jumping strides, which took him over the ground at a great pace. Some of his companions were lame.

When Now-yea reached the smooth ice he ran ahead of his dogs to encourage them—for a moment I thought he was deserting his sled—and they, knowing the land meant rest for them, broke into a tired gallop. Sal-pinna was able to ride on the sled.

Just before we reached the ice I took a snapshot at the crowd, and by a fluke hit one in the leg, and he sprawled over. The others did not stop or take the slightest notice of him, but came doggedly on. In-noya called on the team with voice and whip, and once on the smooth, almost 'glare' ice— save for a few frost-crystals which gave the dogs footing—they wearily galloped, and we could sit on the sled without slowing it down, so easily did it run.

We looked at each other; the hoods and breasts of our *kouletangs* were white with our frosted breath, and the perspiration was streaming off us. I was pretty well 'all in,' for I had not ridden on the sled since starting; In-noya, whom during the whole journey I saw on the sled only for a moment occasionally when looking at Panne-lou, seemed active and tireless yet.

She woke Panne-lou, and told him we should win the land, and the poor fellow's thin face lit up as he said, "That is good." I did not know till later how fully he realised our race from death—and what a death for him!

For the last mile over the smooth ice, which was also slippery going for our pursuers, we almost held our own, though at the ground-ice the nearest *Torn-ga* was not more than two hundred yards away. Those behind him had stopped and were looking at us! A wave of thankfulness swept over me, for I realised now the truth of the Eskimo's assertion: They would not come on the land.

We were too busy steadying and guiding the sled through the ground-ice to bother about the nearest *Torn-ga* then, but at the shore, as he still urged doggedly on, I took my rifle and turned. He was only fifty or sixty yards away, and I couldn't miss him. He pitched forward on his face—the same sort of savage, snarling face I had seen at the floe-edge—and lay still. As I live, his waiting companions turned, and trotted leisurely back the way we had come!

As soon as the panting, worn-out dogs had been urged over the shore and a few hundred yards up the rising ground, I stopped and looked back. Every *Torn-ga* in sight was lying prone. Those on the snow beyond the smooth ice were eating mouthfuls of it, as a dog does when thirsty in winter. A little cloud of steam rose in the air from their bodies. 1 called out, and both sleds stopped, the dogs flinging themselves down in utter exhaustion.

One more amazing incident occurred before we saw the last of the *Torn-ga*. As we started across the bay, a large bear came ambling round the southern point and headed for the opposite one. Instantly every *Torn-ga* was lying motionless, except that they raised their heads occasionally, and looked about as a seal does when out on the ice in spring for sleep. I could not have told the nearest of them from a seal without a telescope. A light land-breeze was quartering from the bear to the *Torn-ga*, and when he saw the—to him—welcome and, so early in the year, unusual sight, he evidently thought the supposed seals would soon wind him, so charged down at the nearest group, hoping to flurry one and catch him before he slipped down his hole through the ice.

Ten paces away from the bear the nearest *Torn-ga* sprang to his feet, and the next instant a dozen of them were at him, hurling their short ivory lances at his side, and leaping back with amazing activity. Each lance brought forth a roar of pain and anger. One of the *Torn-ga*, who slipped as he sprang away, came within reach of the bear's mighty paws, and was instantly killed by a blow which tore his head half off.

This did not check the others in the least, and in three minutes it was all over. One of them ripped the bear up from throat to tail with a knife, whether of flint, ivory, or steel I could not see, but the next second they were tearing the smoking flesh with their teeth and drinking the blood. I could plainly see with the telescope their fierce blood-stained faces, like a pack of human wolves; it was a sickening sight.

I might have made some long-range practice on them with the rifle, but, to tell the truth, I had had enough of them; I only wanted to get away. They did not take the least interest in our movements now, though they had chased us relentlessly for forty miles or so. I can offer no conjecture why, but they dared not come on the land. Repulsive travesties of human beings though they were, they possessed courage of a very high order; some mysterious law of their being ordained they must live and murder only on the salt sea.

Turning my attention to the sleds, 1 found In-noya giving Panne-lou some weak brandy-and-water we had placed in a flask in his blankets. She was self-possessed enough, but a few tears stole down her cheeks as she replaced the revolver in its case and fastened the strap. That she would have turned it on herself at the last, when all chance was gone, I have not the slightest doubt. Lion-hearted In-noya, may you get a mate more worthy of you, and some day be the mother of many children filled with your own heroic courage, and cool, resourceful mind; it will be a great thing for your tribe and race.

We pushed on up the rise of the tableland, travelled over it for an hour, built an igloo, and turned in. We were foodless, exhausted, and our eyes bloodshot and red-lidded for want of sleep—but we were safe.

My narrative has already extended in length far beyond my anticipation, and to detail our return is unnecessary. We found deer plentiful, nursed Panne-lou back to life, and reached Leopold Island on 15th April. I might have gone on to the depot, short as we were of dogs, but Sal-pinna's foot required constant dressing, for the stitches had all burst, and neither she nor, of course, Panne-lou could walk. My arm, too, had become badly swollen, and gave me some trouble, the slight wounds I received in the fight at the floe-edge festering and causing me a lot of pain. It was fortunate I had attended to them promptly, as they were undoubtedly very poisonous.

I therefore decided to wait at Leopold Island for my ship. The kayak—In-noya's suggestion, by-the-bye—was most useful, and we were not short of food during our nearly four months' detention there. Personally, I felt I had had enough of the floe-edge, and hunted deer on the mainland; but the natives were unafraid, asserting positively that nothing was ever seen of the *Torn-ga* east of North Somerset.

It was almost impossible to get the natives to talk about them at all, but during my stay at Leopold Island I dragged a little information out of Panne-lou.

The *Torn-ga* have been seen lying on the rocks off-shore, but never on the land. He said they bred on Spirit Island, which was 'their land,' but was very vague about it, and stated that no natives had ever come from there who had seen them ashore.

"Have any ever gone there?" I asked.

"*Ar-my*" ("I don't know"), he replied evasively, adding that they (the *Torn-ga*) were "all the same as seals, and lived in the water."

"Why don't they come here, or to Ponds Bay, if they live in the water?" I asked.

"I don't know," he replied. "No one knows about them but the Spirits of the Dead, and it is not good to talk about them at all, lest evil befall you."

This was all I could get out of him, and I found it just as unsatisfactory an explanation of the mystery as, no doubt, the reader will; but it is all I have to offer from the natives.

On 2nd August my ship hove in sight, and I heard that the Great War had been raging for a year. A few days later we were back at the depot. It was sad news I brought for the Eskimos gathered to welcome their friends home. I do not know if Panne-lou told them the true story. I mentioned it to no one, white man or Eskimo.

I have tried to write this narrative as plainly and as straight-forwardly as I could, always remembering it will be read by people most of whom are unfamiliar with Arctic conditions, and the mode of life and travel there. This must be my excuse for often being prolix. I might have added some more pages of details of my journey, but these had nothing to do with the main object—namely, making public the existence of a hitherto unheard and undreamt of animal in the Far North.

A scientific friend of mine returned me the MS. of this narrative with the following pithy comment: "Liven it up a bit; it's dull enough to be true." Had I the gift of imagination, and some literary skill, I have no doubt I could improve the story and 'liven it up a bit' with some touches of thrilling incidents to make it far more sensational and exciting—and far less truthful.

Later the same friend commenced to demonstrate to me the absurdity of the idea that the human organism could exist in the water as its habitat. I do not claim the *Torn-ga* are human, and I know nothing of their organism. Eons ago, before life existed on the land of this planet, it was, we now know, in full swing in its waters, and the lineal descendants of the animals of those unknown ages are the seals, walruses, and whales, which in countless numbers make their home in the icy waters of the Arctic Seas.

I once read in some magazine an account of a fossil skeleton found in Java which was neither ape nor man. Pithecanthropus, they called him. Why may not the seas, where life first began, have some yet undiscovered secrets of primeval life hidden in these lonely Arctic waters, teeming as they are with warm-blooded life? Why! ... Pah! what's the use? I am no scientist. I cannot prove my assertion with long words; but I know what I have seen, and fought, and killed. I know what gave me the five odd-looking little scars I carry on my left arm, and where I got the small ivory lance of narwhal horn which hangs on my wall. These are enough for me. And I know, too, what the terror of the hunted animal is when Death is following swiftly on its trail.

Let some naturalist winter where I have been, and bring home his specimens—dead or alive. But he will not get an Eskimo from Hudson Bay to Lancaster Sound to stay there with him; and for me—well there is not enough money in America and Europe together to tempt me to visit Spirit Island again.

Introduction to The Purple Terror

All but unknown today, Fred M. White (1859-1935), a British author and a contemporary of H. G. Wells, is perhaps best known for writing science fiction stories in which London is faced with numerous catastrophes. Aside from his work in the science fiction genre, White also wrote numerous spy stories. His work appeared in such publications as *Pearson's Magazine* and *The Strand Magazine*, the latter being the periodical in which Arthur Conan Doyle's Sherlock Holmes stories were first published.

Originally appearing in the September 1899 issue of *The Strand Magazine*, "The Purple Terror" is a strange island story that takes place during a time of great political upheaval. Set to the backdrop of the Spanish-American War in the Caribbean, this unsettling tale evokes an aura of both wonder and *fin de siècle* decadence. Consider this passage from the text in which orchids, meant to symbolize both exoticism and rot, play a prominent role: "Most orchids have a kind of face of their own; the purple blooms had a positive expression of ferocity and cunning. They exhumed too, a queer, sickly fragrance."

Unlike other stories in this anthology that involve unnatural forms of animal life, "The Purple Terror" is distinguished by its singular gaze on bizarre forms of plant life, a stark reminder that no matter how many hothouse flowers a man seeks to nurture in an artificial, controlled environment, nature may have its own way of doing things, and the results may not always be so pretty.

THE PURPLE TERROR
Fred M. White

I

Lieutenant Will Scarlett's instructions were devoid of problems, physical or otherwise. To convey a letter from Captain Driver of the *Yankee Doodle*, in Porto Rico Bay, to Admiral Lake on the other side of the isthmus, was an apparently simple matter.

"All you have to do," the captain remarked, "is to take three or four men with you in case of accidents, cross the isthmus on foot, and simply give this letter into the hands of Admiral Lake. By so doing we shall save at least four days, and the aborigines are presumedly friendly."

The aborigines aforesaid were Cuban insurgents. Little or no strife had taken place along the neck lying between Porto Rico and the north bay where Lake's flagship lay, though the belt was known to be given over to the disaffected Cubans.

"It is a matter of fifty miles through practically unexplored country," Scarlett replied; "and there's a good deal of the family quarrel in this business, sir. If the Spaniards hate us, the Cubans are not exactly enamored of our flag."

Captain Driver roundly denounced the whole pack of them.

"Treacherous thieves to a man," he said. "I don't suppose your progress will have any brass bands and floral arches to it. And they tell me the forest is pretty thick. But you'll get there all the same. There is the letter, and you can start as soon as you like."

"I may pick my own men, sir?"

"My dear fellow, take whom you please. Take the mastiff, if you like."

"I'd like the mastiff," Scarlett replied; "as he is practically my own, I thought you would not object."

Will Scarlett began to glow as the prospect of adventure stimulated his imagination. He was rather a good specimen of West Point naval dandyism. He had brains at the back of his smartness, and his geological and botanical knowledge were going to prove of considerable service to a grateful country when said grateful country should have passed beyond the rudimentary stages of colonization. And there was some disposition to envy Scarlett on the part of others floating for the past month on the liquid prison of the sapphire sea.

A warrant officer, Tarrer by name, *plus* two A.B.'s of thews and sinews, to say nothing of the dog, completed the exploring party. By the time that the sun kissed the tip of the feathery hills they had covered some six miles of their journey. From the first Scarlett had been struck by the absolute absence of the desolation and horror of civil strife. Evidently the fiery cross had not been carried here; huts and houses were intact; the villagers stood under sloping eaves, and regarded the Americans with a certain sullen curiosity.

"We'd better stop for the night here," said Scarlett.

They had come at length to a village that boasted some pretensions. An adobe chapel at one end of the straggling street was faced by a wine-house at the other. A padre, with hands folded over a bulbous, greasy gabardine, bowed gravely to Scarlett's salutation. The latter had what Tarrer called "considerable Spanish."

"We seek quarters for the night," said Scarlett. "Of course, we are prepared to pay for them."

The sleepy padre nodded towards the wine-house.

"You will find fair accommodations there," he said. "We are friends of the Americanos."

Scarlett doubted the fact, and passed on with florid thanks. So far, little signs of friendliness had been encountered on the march. Coldness, suspicion, a suggestion of fear, but no friendliness to be embarrassing.

The keeper of the wine-shop had his doubts. He feared his poor accommodation for guests so distinguished. A score or more of picturesque, cut-throat-looking rascals with cigarettes in their mouths lounged sullenly in the bar. The display of a brace of gold dollars enlarged mine host's opinion of his household capacity.

"I will do my best, señors," he said. "Come this way."

So it came to pass that an hour after twilight Tarrer and Scarlett were seated in the open amongst the oleanders and the trailing gleam of the fireflies, discussing cigars of average merit and a native wine that was not without virtues. The long bar of the wine-house was brilliantly illuminated; from within came shouts of laughter mingled with the ting, tang of the guitar and the rollicking clack of the castanets.

"They seem to be happy in there," Tarrer remarked. "It isn't all daggers and ball in this distressful country."

A certain curiosity came over Scarlett.

"It is the duty of a good officer," he said, "to lose no opportunity of acquiring useful information. Let us join the giddy throng, Tarrer."

Tarrer expressed himself with enthusiasm in favor of any amusement that might be going. A month's idleness on shipboard increases the appetite for that kind of thing wonderfully. The long bar was comfortable, and filled with Cubans who took absolutely no notice of the intruders. Their eyes were turned towards a rude stage at the far end of the bar, whereon a girl was gyrating in a dance with a celerity and grace that caused the wreath of flowers around her shoulders to resemble a trembling zone of purple flame.

"A wonderfully pretty girl and a wonderfully pretty dance," Scarlett murmured, when the motions ceased and the girl leapt gracefully to the ground. "Largesse, I expect. I thought so. Well, I'm good for a quarter."

The girl came forward, extending a shell prettily. She curtsied before Scarlett and fixed her dark, liquid eyes on his. As he smiled and dropped his quarter-dollar into the shell a coquettish gleam came into the velvety eyes. An ominous growl came from the lips of a bearded ruffian close by.

"Othello's jealous," said Tarrer. "Look at his face."

"I am better employed," Scarlett laughed. "That was a graceful dance, pretty one. I hope you are going to give us another one presently—"

Scarlett paused suddenly. His eyes had fallen on the purple band of flowers the girl had twined round her shoulder. Scarlett was an enthusiastic botanist; he knew most of the gems in Flora's crown, but he had never looked upon such a vivid wealth of blossom before.

The flowers were orchids, and orchids of a kind unknown to collectors anywhere. On this point Scarlett felt certain. And yet this part of the world was by no means a difficult one to explore in comparison with New Guinea and Sumatra, where the rarer varieties had their homes.

The blooms were immensely large, far larger than any flower of the kind known to Europe or America, of a deep pure purple, with a blood-red center. As Scarlett gazed upon them he noticed a certain cruel expression on the flower. Most orchids have a kind of face of their own; the purple blooms had a positive expression of ferocity and cunning. They exhumed, too, a queer, sickly fragrance. Scarlett had smelt something like it before, after the Battle of Manila. The perfume was the perfume of a corpse.

"And yet they are magnificent flowers," said Scarlett. "Won't you tell me where you got them from, pretty one?"

The girl was evidently flattered by the attention bestowed upon her by the smart young American. The bearded Othello alluded to edged up to her side.

"The señor had best leave the girl alone," he said, insolently.

Scarlett's fist clenched as he measured the Cuban with his eyes. The Admiral's letter crackled in his breast pocket, and discretion got the best of valor.

"You are paying yourself a poor compliment, my good fellow," he said, "though I certainly admire your good taste. Those flowers interested me."

The man appeared to be mollified. His features corrugated in a smile.

"The señor would like some of those blooms?" he asked. "It was I who procured them for little Zara here. I can show you where they grow."

Every eye in the room was turned in Scarlett's direction. It seemed to him that a kind of diabolical malice glistened on every dark face there, save that of the girl, whose features paled under her healthy tan.

"If the señor is wise," she began, "he will not—"

"Listen to the tales of a silly girl," Othello put in menacingly. He grasped the girl by the arm, and she winced in positive pain. "Pshaw, there is no harm where the flowers grow, if one is only careful. I will take you there, and I will be your guide to Port Anna, where you are going, for a gold dollar."

All Scarlett's scientific enthusiasm was aroused. It is not given to every man to present a new orchid to the horticultural world. And this one would dwarf the finest plant hitherto discovered.

"Done with you," he said; "we start at daybreak. I shall look to you to be ready. Your name is Tito? Well, good-night, Tito."

As Scarlett and Tarrer withdrew the girl suddenly darted forward. A wild word or two fluttered from her lips. Then there was a sound as of a blow, followed by a little stifled cry of pain.

"No, no," Tarrer urged, as Scarlett half turned. "Better not. They are ten to one, and they are no friends of ours. It never pays to interfere in these family quarrels. I daresay, if you interfered, the girl would be just as ready to knife you as her jealous lover."

"But a blow like that, Tarrer!"

"It's a pity, but I don't see how we can help it. Your business is the quick dispatch of the Admiral's letter, not the squiring of dames." Scarlett owned with a sigh that Tarrer was right.

II

It was quite a different Tito who presented himself at daybreak the following morning. His insolent manner had disappeared. He was cheerful, alert, and he had a manner full of the most winning politeness.

"You quite understand what we want," Scarlett said. "My desire is to reach Port Anna as soon as possible. You know the way?"

"Every inch of it, señor. I have made the journey scores of times. And I shall have the felicity of getting you there early on the third day from now."

"Is it so far as that?"

"The distance is not great, señor. It is the passage through the woods. There are parts where no white man has been before."

"And you will not forget the purple orchids?"

A queer gleam trembled like summer lightning in Tito's eyes. The next instant it had gone. A time was to come when Scarlett was to recall that look, but for the moment it was allowed to pass.

"The señor shall see the purple orchid," he said; "thousands of them. They have a bad name amongst our people, but that is nonsense. They grow in the high trees, and their blossoms cling to long, green tendrils. These tendrils are poisonous to the flesh, and great care should be taken in handling them. And the flowers are quite harmless, though we call them the devil's poppies."

To all of this Scarlett listened eagerly. He was all-impatient to see and handle the mysterious flower for himself. The whole excursion was going to prove a wonderful piece of luck. At the same time he had to curb his impatience. There would be no chance of seeing the purple orchid today.

For hours they fought their way along through the dense tangle. A heat seemed to lie over all the land like a curse—a blistering sweltering, moist heat with no puff of wind to temper its breathlessness. By the time that the sun was sliding down, most of the party had had enough of it.

They passed out of the underwood at length, and, striking upwards, approached a clump of huge forest trees on the brow of a ridge. All kinds of parasites hung from the branches; there were ropes and bands of green, and high up a fringe of purple glory that caused Scarlett's pulses to leap a little faster.

"Surely that is the purple orchid?" he cried.

Tito shrugged his shoulders contemptuously.

"A mere straggler or two," he said, "and out of reach in any case. The señor will have all he wants and more tomorrow."

"But it seems to me," said Scarlett, "that I could—"

Then he paused. The sun like a great glowing shield was shining full behind the tree with its crown of purple, and showing up every green rope and thread clinging to the branches with the clearness of liquid crystal. Scarlett saw a network of green cords like a huge spider's web, and in the center of it was not a fly, but a human skeleton!

The arms and legs were stretched apart as if the victim had been crucified. The wrists and ankles were bound in the cruel web. Fragments of tattered clothing fluttered in the faint breath of the evening breeze.

"Horrible," Scarlett cried, "absolutely horrible!"

"You may well say that," Tarrer exclaimed, with a shudder. "Like the fly in the amber or the apple in the dumpling, the mystery is how he got there."

"Perhaps Tito can explain the mystery," Scarlett suggested.

Tito appeared to be uneasy and disturbed. He looked furtively from one to the other of his employers as a culprit might who feels he has been found out. But his courage returned as he noted the absence of suspicion in the faces turned upon him.

"I can explain," he exclaimed, with teeth that chattered from some unknown terror or guilt. "It is not the first time that I have seen the skeleton. Some plant-hunter doubtless who came here alone. He climbed into the tree without a knife, and those green ropes got twisted round his limbs, as a swimmer gets entangled in the weeds. The more he struggled, the more the cords bound him. He would call in vain for anyone to assist him here. And so he must have died."

The explanation was a plausible one, but by no means detracted from the horror of the discovery. For some time the party pushed their way on in the twilight, till the darkness descended suddenly like a curtain.

"We will camp here," Tito said; "it is high, dry ground, and we have this belt of trees above us. There is no better place than this for miles around. In the valley the miasma is dangerous."

As Tito spoke he struck a match, and soon a torch flamed up. The little party were on a small plateau, fringed by trees. The ground was dry and hard, and, as Scarlett and his party saw to their astonishment, littered with bones. There were skulls of animals and skulls of human beings, the skeletons of birds, the frames of beasts both great and small. It was a weird, shuddering sight.

"We can't possibly stay here," Scarlett exclaimed.

Tito shrugged his shoulders.

"There is nowhere else," he replied. "Down in the valley there are many dangers. Further in the woods are the snakes and jaguars. Bones are nothing. Peuf, they can be easily cleared away."

They had to be cleared away, and there was an end of the matter. For the most part the skeletons were white and dry as air and sun could make them. Over the dry, calcined mass the huge fringe of trees nodded mournfully. With the rest, Scarlett was busy scattering the mocking frames aside. A perfect human skeleton lay at his feet. On one finger something glittered—a signet ring. As Scarlett took it in his hand he started.

"I know this ring!" he exclaimed; "it belonged to Pierre Anton, perhaps the most skilled and intrepid plant-hunter the *Jardin des Plantes* ever employed. The poor fellow was by way of being a friend of mine. He met the fate that he always anticipated."

"There must have been a rare holocaust here," said Tarrer.

"It beats me," Scarlett responded. By this time a large circle had been shifted clear of human and other remains. By the light of the fire loathsome insects could be seen scudding and straddling away. "It beats me entirely. Tito, can you offer any explanation? If the bones were all human I could get some grip of the problem. But when one comes to birds and animals as well! Do you see that the skeletons lie in a perfect circle, starting from the center of the clump of trees above us? What does it mean?"

Tito professed utter ignorance of the subject. Some years before a small tribe of natives invaded the peninsula for religious rites. They came from a long way off in canoes, and wild stories were told concerning them. They burnt sacrifices, no doubt.

Scarlett turned his back contemptuously on this transparent tale. His curiosity was aroused. There must be some explanation, for Pierre Anton had been seen of men within the last ten years.

"There's something uncanny about this," he said to Tarrer. "I mean to get to the bottom of it, or know why."

"As for me," said Tarrer, with a cavernous yawn, "I have but one ambition, and that is my supper, followed by my bed."

III

Scarlett lay in the light of the fire looking about him. He felt restless and uneasy, though he would have found it difficult to explain the reason. For one thing, the air trembled to strange noises. There seemed to be something moving, writhing in the forest trees above his head. More than once it seemed to his distorted fancy that he could see a squirming knot of green snakes in motion.

Outside the circle, in a grotto of bones, Tito lay sleeping. A few moments before his dark, sleek head had been furtively raised, and his eyes seemed to gleam in the flickering firelight with malignant cunning as he met Scarlett's glance he gave a deprecatory gesture and subsided.

"What the deuce does it all mean?" Scarlett muttered. "I feel certain yonder rascal is up to some mischief. Jealous still because I paid his girl a little attention. But he can't do us any real harm. Quiet, there!"

The big mastiff growled and then whined uneasily. Even the dog seemed to be conscious of some unseen danger. He lay down again, cowed by the stern command, but he still whimpered in his dreams.

"I fancy I'll keep awake for a spell," Scarlett told himself.

For a time he did so. Presently he began to slide away into the lane of poppies. He was walking amongst a garden of bones which bore masses of purple blossoms. Then Pierre Anton came on the scene, pale and resolute as Scarlett had always known him; then the big mastiff seemed in some way to be mixed up with the phantasm of the dream, barking as if in pain, and Scarlett came to his senses.

He was breathing short, a beady perspiration stood on his forehead, his heart hammered in quick thuds—all the horrors of nightmare were still upon him. In a vague way as yet he heard the mastiff howl, a real howl of real terror, and Scarlett knew that he was awake.

Then a strange thing happened. In the none too certain light of the fire, Scarlett saw the mastiff snatched up by some invisible hand, carried far on high towards the trees, and finally flung to the earth with a crash. The big dog lay still as a log.

A sense of fear born of the knowledge of impotence came over Scarlett; what in the name of evil did it all mean? The smart scientist had no faith in the occult, and yet what *did* it all mean?

Nobody stirred. Scarlett's companions were soaked and soddened with fatigue; the rolling thunder of artillery would have scarce disturbed them. With teeth set and limbs that trembled, Scarlett crawled over to the dog.

The great, black-muzzled creature was quite dead. The full chest was stained and soaked in blood; the throat had been cut apparently with some jagged, saw-like instrument away to the bone. And, strangest thing of all, scattered all about the body was a score or more of the great purple orchid flowers broken off close to the head. A hot, pricking sensation travelled slowly up Scarlett's spine and seemed to pass out at the tip of his skull. He felt his hair rising.

He was frightened. As a matter of honest fact, he had never been so horribly scared in his life before. The whole thing was so mysterious, so cruel, so bloodthirsty.

Still, there must be some rational explanation. In some way the matter had to do with the purple orchid. The flower had an evil reputation. Was it not known to these Cubans as the devil's poppy?

Scarlett recollected vividly now Zara's white, scared face when Tito had volunteered to show the way to the resplendent bloom; he remembered the cry of the girl and the blow that followed. He could see it all now. The girl had meant to warn him against some nameless horror to which Tito was leading the small party. This was the jealous Cuban's revenge.

A wild desire to pay this debt to the uttermost fraction filled Scarlett, and shook him with a trembling passion. He crept along in the drenching dew to where Tito lay, and touched his forehead with the chill blue rim of a revolver barrel. Tito stirred slightly.

"You dog!" Scarlett cried. "I am going to shoot you."

Tito did not move again. His breathing was soft and regular. Beyond a doubt the man was sleeping peacefully. After all he might be innocent; and yet, on the other hand, he might be so sure of his quarry that he could afford to slumber without anxiety as to his vengeance.

In favor of the latter theory was the fact that the Cuban lay beyond the limit of what had previously been the circle of dry bones. It was just possible that there was no danger outside that pale. In that case it would be easy to arouse the rest, and so save them from the horrible death which had befallen the mastiff. No doubt these were a form of upas tree, but that would not account for the ghastly spectacle in mid-air.

"I'll let this chap sleep for the present," Scarlett muttered.

He crawled back, not without misgivings, into the ring of death. He meant to wake the others and then wait for further developments. By now his senses were more alert and vigorous than they had ever been before. A preternatural clearness of brain and vision possessed him. As he advanced he saw suddenly falling a green bunch of cord that straightened into a long, emerald line. It was triangular in shape, fine at the apex, and furnished with hooked spines. The rope appeared to dangle from the tree overhead; the broad, sucker-like termination was evidently soaking up moisture.

A natural phenomenon evidently, Scarlett thought. This was some plant new to him, a parasite living amongst the tree-tops and drawing life and vigor by means of these green, rope-like antennae designed by Nature to soak and absorb the heavy dews of night.

For a moment the logic of this theory was soothing to Scarlett's distracted nerves, but only for a moment, for then he saw at regular intervals along the green rope the big purple blossoms of the devil's poppy.

He stood gasping there, utterly taken aback for the moment. There must be some infernal juggling behind all this business. He saw the rope slacken and quiver, he saw it swing forward like a pendulum, and the next minute it had passed across the shoulders of a sleeping seaman.

Then the green root became as the arm of an octopus. The line shook from end to end like the web of an angry spider when invaded by a wasp. It seemed to grip the sailor and tighten, and then, before Scarlett's, affrighted eyes, the sleeping man was raised gently from the ground.

Scarlett jumped forward with a desire to scream hysterically. Now that a comrade was in danger he was no longer afraid. He whipped a jackknife from his pocket and slashed at the cruel cord. He half expected to meet with the stoutness of a steel strand, but to his surprise the feeler snapped like a carrot, bumping the sailor heavily on the ground.

He sat up, rubbing his eyes vigorously.

"That you, sir?" he asked. "What is the matter?"

"For the love of God, get up at once and help me to arouse the others," Scarlett said, hoarsely. "We have come across the devil's workshop. All the horrors of the inferno are invented here."

The bluejacket struggled to his feet. As he did so, the clothing from his waist downwards slipped about his feet, clean cut through by the teeth of the green parasite. All around the body of the sailor blood oozed from a zone of teeth-marks.

Two-o'clock-in-the-morning courage is a virtue vouchsafed to few. The tar, who would have faced an ironclad cheerfully, fairly shivered with fright and dismay.

"What does it mean, sir?" he cried. "I've been—"

"Wake the others," Scarlett screamed; "wake the others."

Two or three more green tangles of rope came tumbling to the ground, straightening and quivering instantly. The purple blossoms stood out like a frill upon them. Like a madman, Scarlett shouted, kicking his companions without mercy.

They were all awake at last, grumbling and moaning for their lost slumbers. All this time Tito had never stirred.

"I don't understand it at all," said Tarrer.

"Come from under those trees," said Scarlett, "and I will endeavor to explain. Not that you will believe me for a moment. No man can be expected to believe the awful nightmare I am going to tell you."

Scarlett proceeded to explain. As he expected, his story was followed with marked incredulity, save by the wounded sailor, who had strong evidence to stimulate his otherwise defective imagination.

"I can't believe it," Tarrer said, at length. They were whispering together beyond earshot of Tito, whom they had no desire to arouse for obvious reasons. "This is some diabolical juggling of yonder rascally Cuban. It seems impossible that those slender green cords could—"

Scarlett pointed to the center of the circle.

"Call the dog," he said grimly, "and see if he will come."

"I admit the point as far as the poor old mastiff is concerned. But at the same time I don't—however, I'll see for myself."

By this time a dozen or more of the slender cords were hanging pendent from the trees. They moved from spot to spot as if jerked up by some unseen hand and deposited a foot or two farther. With the great purple bloom fringing the stem, the effect was not unlovely save to Scarlett, who could see only the dark side of it. As Tarrer spoke he advanced in the direction of the trees.

"What are you going to do?" Scarlett asked.

"Exactly what I told you. I am going to investigate this business for myself."

Without wasting further words Scarlett sprang forward. It was no time for the niceties of an effete civilization. Force was the only logical argument to be used in a case like this, and Scarlett was the more powerful man of the two.

Tarrer saw and appreciated the situation.

"No, no," he cried; "none of that. Anyway, you're too late." He darted forward and threaded his way between the slender emerald columns. As they moved slowly and with a certain stately deliberation there was no great danger to an alert and vigorous individual. As Scarlett entered the avenue he could hear the soak and suck as the dew was absorbed.

"For Heaven's sake, come out of it," he cried.

The warning came too late. A whip-like trail of green touched Tarrer from behind, and in a lightning flash he was in the toils. The tendency to draw up anything and everything gave the cords a terrible power. Tarrer evidently felt it, for his breath came in great gasps.

"Cut me free," he said, hoarsely; "cut me free. I am being carried off my feet."

He seemed to be doomed for a moment, for all the cords there were apparently converging in his direction. This, as a matter of fact, was a solution of the whole sickening, horrible sensation. Pulled here and there, thrust in one direction and another, Tarrer contrived to keep his feet.

Heedless of possible danger to himself Scarlett darted forward, calling to his companions to come to the rescue. In less time than it takes to tell, four knives were at work ripping and slashing in all directions.

"Not all of you," Scarlett whispered. So tense was the situation that no voice was raised above a murmur. "You two keep your eyes open for fresh cords, and cut them as they fall, instantly. Now then."

The horrible green spines were round Tarrer's body like snakes. His face was white, his breath came painfully, for the pressure was terrible. It seemed to Scarlett to be one horrible dissolving view of green, slimy cords and great weltering, purple blossoms. The whole of the circle was strewn with them. They were wet and slimy underfoot.

Tarrer had fallen forward half unconscious. He was supported now by but two cords above his head. The cruel pressure had been relieved. With one savage sweep of his knife Scarlett cut the last of the lines, and Tarrer fell like a log unconscious to the ground. A feeling of nausea, a yellow dizziness, came over Scarlett as he staggered beyond the dread circle. He saw Tarrer carried to a place of safety, and then the world seemed to wither and leave him in the dark.

"I feel a bit groggy and weak," said Tarrer an hour or so later: "but beyond that this idiot of a Richard is himself again. So far as I am concerned, I should like to get even with our friend Tito for this."

"Something with boiling oil in it," Scarlett suggested, grimly. "The callous scoundrel has slept soundly through the whole of this business. I suppose he felt absolutely certain that he had finished with us."

"Upon my word, we ought to shoot the beggar!" Tarrer exclaimed.

"I have a little plan of my own," said Scarlett, "which I am going to put in force later on. Meanwhile we had better get on with breakfast. When Tito wakes a pleasant little surprise will await him."

Tito roused from his slumbers in due course and looked around him. His glance was curious, disappointed, then full of a white and yellow fear. A thousand conflicting emotions streamed across his dark face. Scarlett read them at a glance as he called the Cuban over to him.

"I am not going into any unnecessary details with you," he said. "It has come to my knowledge that you are playing traitor to us. Therefore we prefer to complete our journey alone. We can easily find the way now."

"The señor may do as he pleases," he replied. "Give me my dollar and let me go."

Scarlett replied grimly that he had no intention of doing anything of the kind. He did not propose to place the lives of himself and his comrades in the power of a rascally Cuban who had played false.

"We are going to leave you here till we return," he said. "You will have plenty of food, you will be perfectly safe under the shelter of these trees, and there is no chance of anybody disturbing you. We are going to tie you up to one of these trees for the next four-and-twenty hours."

All the insolence died out of Tito's face. His knees bowed, a cold dew came out over the ghastly green of his features. From the shaking of his limbs he might have fared disastrously with ague.

"The trees," he stammered, "the trees, señor! There is danger from snakes, and—and from many things. There are other places—"

"If this place was safe last night it is safe today," Scarlett said, grimly. "I have quite made up my mind."

Tito fought no longer. He fell forward on his knees, he howled for mercy, till Scarlett fairly kicked him up again.

"Make a clean breast of it," he said, "or take the consequences. You know perfectly well that we have found you out, scoundrel."

Tito's story came in gasps. He wanted to get rid of the Americans. He was jealous. Besides, under the Americanos would Cuba be any better off? By no means and assuredly not. Therefore it was the duty of every good Cuban to destroy the Americanos where possible.

"A nice lot to fight for," Scarlett muttered. "Get to the point."

Hastened to the point by a liberal application of stout shoe-leather, Tito made plenary confession. The señor himself had suggested death by medium of the devil's poppies. More than one predatory plant-hunter had been lured to his destruction in the same way. The skeleton hung on the tree was a Dutchman who had walked into the clutch of the purple terror innocently. And Pierre Anton had done the same. The suckers of the devil's poppy only came down at night to gather moisture; in the day they were coiled up like a spring. And anything that they touched they killed. Tito had watched more than one bird or small beast crushed and mauled by these cruel spines with their fringe of purple blossoms.

"How do you get the blooms?" Scarlett asked.

"That is easy," Tito replied. "In the daytime I moisten the ground under the trees. Then the suckers unfold, drawn by the water. Once the suckers unfold one cuts several of them off with long knives. There is danger, of course, but not if one is careful."

"I'll not trouble the devil's poppy any further at present," said Scarlett, "but I shall trouble you to accompany me to my destination as a prisoner."

Tito's eyes dilated.

"They will not shoot me?" he asked, hoarsely.

"I don't know," Scarlett replied. "They may hang you instead. At any rate, I shall be bitterly disappointed if they don't end you one way or the other. Whichever operation it is, I can look forward to it with perfect equanimity."

Introduction to Friend Island

Although not as well known today as many of her contemporaries, Francis Stevens (1883-1948) was a pioneer in the emerging dark fantasy subgenre. Born Gertrude Mabel Barrows in Minneapolis, she primarily wrote novels. Of these, she may be best remembered for *The Citadel of Fear* (1918) which features a lost Aztec city; *The Heads of Cerberus* (1919), a dystopian novel set in a future, totalitarian Philadelphia; and *Claimed* (1920), a supernatural work about a lost artifact capable of summoning an ancient god. Stevens also wrote several short stories, including the weird island tale presented here.

A story that takes place in a futuristic world in which women have replaced men as the dominant sex, "Friend Island" is both a quixotic feminist parable and a highly imaginative work of speculative fiction. In this borderline satirical tale, a male narrator details his conversation over tea and macaroons with an exceedingly strong-willed seafaring woman who, in turn, recounts her experiences as a shipwrecked passenger on a strange Pacific island. Stevens utilizes the island setting not only to critically examine traditional gender norms, but also to explore how individuals' subjective feelings may affect their perception of a nominally objective reality. "Friend Island" is also notable for its anthropomorphic characterization of a physical island. In this case, however, the island is most definitely a she!

FRIEND ISLAND
Francis Stevens

Being the Veracious Tale of an Ancient Mariness,
Heard and Reported in the Year A. D. 2100

It was upon the waterfront that I first met her, in one of the shabby little tea shops frequented by able sailoresses of the poorer type. The up-town, glittering resorts of the Lady Aviators' Union were not for such as she.

Stern of feature, bronzed by wind and sun, her age could only be guessed, but I surmised at once that in her I beheld a survivor of the age of turbines and oil engines—a true sea-woman of that elder time when woman's superiority to man had not been so long recognized. When, to emphasize their victory, women in all ranks were sterner than today's need demands.

The spruce, smiling young maidens—engine-women and stokers of the great aluminum rollers, but despite their profession, very neat in gold-braided blue knickers and boleros—these looked askance at the hard-faced relic of a harsher day, as they passed in and out of the shop.

I, however, brazenly ignoring similar glances at myself, a mere male intruding on the haunts of the world's ruling sex, drew a chair up beside the veteran. I ordered a full pot of tea, two cups and a plate of macaroons, and put on my most ingratiating air. Possibly my unconcealed admiration and interest were wiles not exercised in vain. Or the macaroons and tea, both excellent, may have loosened the old sea-woman's tongue. At any rate, under cautious questioning, she had soon launched upon a series of reminiscences well beyond my hopes for color and variety.

"When I was a lass," quoth the sea-woman, after a time, "there was none of this high-flying, gilt-edged, leather-stocking luxury about the sea. We sailed by the power of our oil and gasoline. If they failed on us, like as not 'twas the rubber ring and the rolling wave for ours."

She referred to the archaic practice of placing a pneumatic affair called a life-preserver beneath the arms, in case of that dreaded disaster, now so unheard of, shipwreck.

"In them days there was still many a man bold enough to join our crews. And I've knowed cases," she added condescendingly, "where just by the muscle and brawn of such men some poor sailor lass has reached shore alive that would have fed the sharks without 'em. Oh, I ain't so down on men as you might think. It's the spoiling of them that I don't hold with.

There's too much preached nowadays that man is fit for nothing but to fetch and carry and do nurse-work in big child-homes. To my mind, a man who hasn't the nerve of a woman ain't fitted to father children, let alone raise 'em. But that's not here nor there. My time's past, and I know it, or I wouldn't be setting here gossipin' to you, my lad, over an empty teapot."

I took the hint, and with our cups replenished, she bit thoughtfully into her fourteenth macaroon and continued.

"There's one voyage I'm not likely to forget, though I live to be as old as Cap'n Mary Barnacle, of the *Shouter*. 'Twas aboard the old *Shouter* that this here voyage occurred, and it was her last and likewise Cap'n Mary's. Cap'n Mary, she was then that decrepit, it seemed a mercy that she should go to her rest, and in good salt water at that.

"I remember the voyage for Cap'n Mary's sake, but most I remember it because 'twas then that I come the nighest in my life to committin' matrimony. For a man, the man had nerve; he was nearer bein' companionable than any other man I ever seed; and if it hadn't been for just one little event that showed up the—the *mannishness* of him, in a way I couldn't abide, I reckon he'd be keepin' house for me this minute."

"We cleared from Frisco with a cargo of silkateen petticoats for Brisbane. Cap'n Mary was always strong on petticoats. Leather breeches or even half-skirts would ha' paid far better, they being more in demand like, but Cap'n Mary was three-quarters owner, and says she, land women should buy petticoats, and if they didn't it wouldn't be the Lord's fault nor hers for not providing 'em.

"We cleared on a fine day, which is an all sign—or was, then when the weather and the seas o' God still counted in the trafficking of the humankind. Not two days out we met a whirling, mucking bouncer of a gale that well nigh threw the old *Shouter* a full point off her course in the first wallop. She was a stout craft, though. None of your featherweight, gas-lightened, paper-thin alloy shells, but toughened aluminum from stern to stern. Her turbine drove her through the combers at a forty-five knot clip, which named her a speedy craft for a freighter in them days.

"But this night, as we tore along through the creaming green billows, something unknown went 'way wrong down below.

"I was forward under the shelter of her long over-sloop, looking for a hairpin I'd dropped somewheres about that afternoon. It was a gold hairpin, and gold still being mighty scarce when I was a girl, a course I valued it. But suddenly I felt the old *Shouter* give a jump under my feet like a plane struck by a shell in full flight. Then she trembled all over for a full second, frightened like. Then, with the crash of doomsday ringing in my ears, I felt myself sailing through the air right into the teeth o' the shrieking gale, as near as I could judge. Down I come in the hollow of a monstrous big wave, and as my ears doused under I thought I heard a splash close by. Coming up, sure enough, there close by me was floating a new, patent, hermetic, thermo-ice-chest. Being as it was empty, and being as it was shut up airtight, that ice-chest made as sweet a life-preserver as a woman could wish in such an hour. About ten foot by twelve, it floated high in the raging sea. Out on its top I scrambled, and hanging on by a handle I looked expectant for some of my poor fellow-women to come floating by. Which they never did, for the good reason that the *Shouter* had blowed up and went below, petticoats, Cap'n Mary and all."

"What caused the explosion?" I inquired.

"The Lord and Cap'n Mary Barnacle can explain," she answered piously. "Besides the oil for her turbines, she carried a power of gasoline for her alternative engines, and likely 'twas the cause of her ending so sudden like. Anyways, all I ever seen of her again was the empty ice-chest that Providence had well-nigh hove upon my head. On that I sat and floated, and floated and sat some more, till by and by the storm sort of blowed itself out, the sun come shining—this was next morning—and I could dry my hair and look about me. I was a young lass, then, and not bad to look upon. I didn't want to die, any more than you that's sitting there this minute. So I up and prays for land. Sure enough toward evening a speck heaves up low down on the horizon. At first I took it for a gas liner, but later found it was just a little island, all alone by itself in the great Pacific Ocean.

"Come, now, here's luck, thinks I, and with that I deserts the ice-chest, which being empty, and me having no ice to put in it, not likely to have in them latitudes, is of no further use to me. Striking out I swum a mile or so and set foot on dry land for the first time in nigh three days.

"Pretty land it were, too, though bare of human life as an iceberg in the Arctic.

"I had landed on a shining white beach that run up to a grove of lovely, waving palm trees. Above them I could see the slopes of a hill so high and green it reminded me of my own old home, up near Couquomgomoc Lake in Maine. The whole place just seemed to smile and smile at me. The palms waved and bowed in the sweet breeze, like they wanted to say, 'Just set right down and make yourself to home. We've been waiting a long time for you to come.' I cried, I was that happy to be made welcome. I was a young lass then, and sensitive-like to how folks treated me. You're laughing now, but wait and see if or not there was sense to the way I felt.

"So I up and dries my clothes and my long, soft hair again, which was well worth drying, for I had far more of it than now. After that I walked along a piece, until there was a sweet little path meandering away into the wild woods.

"Here, thinks I, this looks like inhabitants. Be they civil or wild, I wonder? But after traveling the path a piece, lo and behold it ended sudden like in a wide circle of green grass, with a little spring of clear water. And the first thing I noticed was a slab of white board nailed to a palm tree close to the spring. Right off I took a long drink, for you better believe I was thirsty, and then I went to look at this board. It had evidently been tore off the side of a wooden packing box, and the letters was roughly printed in lead pencil.

"'Heaven help whoever you be,' I read. 'This island ain't just right. I'm going to swim for it. You better too. Good-by. Nelson Smith.' That's what it said, but the spellin' was simply awful. It all looked quite new and recent, as if Nelson Smith hadn't more than a few hours before he wrote and nailed it there.

"Well, after reading that queer warning I begun to shake all over like in a chill. Yes, I shook like I had the ague, though the hot tropic sun was burning down right on me and that alarming board. What had scared Nelson Smith so much that he had swum to get away? I looked all around real cautious and careful, but not a single frightening thing could I behold. And the palms and the green grass and the flowers still smiled that peaceful and friendly like. 'Just make yourself to home,' was wrote all over the place in plainer letters than those sprawly lead pencil ones on the board.

"Pretty soon, what with the quiet and all, the chill left me. Then I thought, 'Well, to be sure, this Smith person was just an ordinary man, I reckon, and likely he got nervous of being so alone. Likely he just fancied things which was really not. It's a pity he drowned himself before I come, though likely I'd have found him poor company. By his record I judge him a man of but common education.'

"So I decided to make the most of my welcome, and that I did for weeks to come. Right near the spring was a cave, dry as a biscuit box, with a nice floor of white sand. Nelson had lived there too, for there was a litter of stuff—tin cans—empty—scraps of newspapers and the like. I got to calling him Nelson in my mind, and then Nelly, and wondering if he was dark or fair, and how he come to be cast away there all alone, and what was the strange events that drove him to his end. I cleaned out the cave, though. He had devoured all his tin-canned provisions, however he come by them, but this I didn't mind. That there island was a generous body. Green milk-coconuts, sweet berries, turtle eggs and the like was my daily fare.

"For about three weeks the sun shone every day, the birds sang and the monkeys chattered. We was all one big, happy family, and the more I explored that island the better I liked the company I was keeping. The land was about ten miles from beach to beach, and never a foot of it that wasn't sweet and clean as a private park.

"From the top of the hill I could see the ocean, miles and miles of blue water, with never a sign of a gas liner, or even a little government running-boat. Them running-boats used to go most everywhere to keep the seaways clean of derelicts and the like. But I knowed that if this island was no more than a hundred miles off the regular courses of navigation, it might be many a long day before I'd be rescued. The top of the hill, as I found when first I climbed up there, was a wore-out crater. So I knowed that the island was one of them volcanic ones you run across so many of in the seas between Capricorn and Cancer.

"Here and there on the slopes and down through the jungly tree-growth, I would come on great lumps of rock, and these must have came up out of that crater long ago. If there was lava it was so old it had been covered up entire with green growing stuff. You couldn't have found it without a spade, which I didn't have nor want.

"Well, at first I was happy as the hours was long. I wandered and clambered and waded and swum, and combed my long hair on the beach, having fortunately not lost my side-combs nor the rest of my gold hairpins. But by and by it begun to get just a bit lonesome. Funny thing, that's a feeling that, once it starts, it gets worse and worser so quick it's perfectly surprising. And right then was when the days begun to get gloomy. We had a long, sickly hot spell, like I never seen before on an ocean island. There was dull clouds across the sun from morn to night. Even the little monkeys and parakeets, that had seemed so gay, moped and drowsed like they was sick. All one day I cried, and let the rain soak me through and through—that was the first rain we had—and I didn't get thorough dried even during the night, though I slept in my cave. Next morning I got up mad as thunder at myself and all the world.

"When I looked out the black clouds was billowing across the sky. I could hear nothing but great breakers roaring in on the beaches, and the wild wind raving through the lashing palms.

"As I stood there a nasty little wet monkey dropped from a branch almost on my head. I grabbed a pebble and slung it at him real vicious. 'Get away, you dirty little brute!' I shrieks, and with that there come a awful blinding flare of light. There was a long, crackling noise like a bunch of Chinese fireworks, and then a sound as if a whole fleet of *Shouters* had all went up together.

"When I come to, I found myself 'way in the back of my cave, trying to dig further into the rock with my fingernails. Upon taking thought, it come to me that what had occurred was just a lightning-clap, and going to look, sure enough there lay a big palm tree right across the glade. It was all busted and split open by the lightning, and the little monkey was under it, for I could see his tail and his hind legs sticking out.

"Now, when I set eyes on that poor, crushed little beast I'd been so mean to, I was terrible ashamed. I sat down on the smashed tree and considered and considered. How thankful I had ought to have been. Here I had a lovely, plenteous island, with food and water to my taste, when it might have been a barren, starvation rock that was my lot. And so, thinking, a sort of gradual peaceful feeling stole over me. I got cheerfuller and cheerfuller, till I could have sang and danced for joy.

"Pretty soon I realized that the sun was shining bright for the first time that week. The wind had stopped hollering, and the waves had died to just a singing murmur on the beach. It seemed kind o' strange, this sudden peace, like the cheer in my own heart after its rage and storm. I rose up, feeling sort of queer, and went to look if the little monkey had came alive again, though that was a fool thing, seeing he was laying all crushed up and very dead. I buried him under a tree root, and as I did it a conviction come to me.

"I didn't hardly question that conviction at all. Somehow, living there alone so long, perhaps my natural womanly intuition was stronger than ever before or since, and so I *knowed*. Then I went and pulled poor Nelson Smith's board off from the tree and tossed it away for the tide to carry off. That there board was an insult to my island!"

The sea-woman paused, and her eyes had a far-away look. It seemed as if I and perhaps even the macaroons and tea were quite forgotten.

"Why did you think that?" I asked, to bring her back. "How could an island be insulted?"

She started, passed her hand across her eyes, and hastily poured another cup of tea.

"Because," she said at last, poising a macaroon in mid-air, "because that island—that particular island that I had landed on—had a heart!

"When I was gay, it was bright and cheerful. It was glad when I come, and it treated me right until I got that grouchy it had to mope from sympathy. It loved me like a friend. When I flung a rock at that poor little drenched monkey critter, it backed up my act with an anger like the wrath o' God, and killed its own child to please me! But it got right cheery the minute I seen the wrongness of my ways. Nelson Smith had no business to say, 'This island ain't just right,' for it was a righter place than ever I seen elsewhere. When I cast away that lying board, all the birds begun to sing like mad. The green milk-coconuts fell right and left. Only the monkeys seemed kind o' sad like still, and no wonder. You see, their own mother, the island, had rounded on one o' them for my sake!

"After that I was right careful and considerate. I named the island Anita, not knowing her right name, or if she had any. Anita was a pretty name, and it sounded kind of South Sea like. Anita and me got along real well together from that day on. It was some strain to be always gay and singing around like a dear duck of a canary bird, but I done my best. Still, for all the love and gratitude I bore Anita, the company of an island, however sympathetic, ain't quite enough for a human being. I still got lonesome, and there was even days when I couldn't keep the clouds clear out of the sky, though I will say we had no more tornadoes.

"I think the island understood and tried to help me with all the bounty and good cheer the poor thing possessed. None the less my heart give a wonderful big leap when one day I seen a blot on the horizon. It drawed nearer and nearer, until at last I could make out its nature."

"A ship, of course," said I, "and were you rescued?"

"Tweren't a ship, neither," denied the sea-woman somewhat impatiently. "Can't you let me spin this yarn without no more remarks and fool questions? This thing what was bearing down so fast with the incoming tide was neither more nor less than another island!

"You may well look startled. I was startled myself. Much more so than you, likely. I didn't know then what you, with your book-learning, very likely know now—that islands sometimes float. Their underparts being a tangled-up mess of roots and old vines that new stuff's growed over, they sometimes break away from the mainland in a brisk gale and go off for a voyage, calm as a old-fashioned, eight-funnel steamer. This one was uncommon large, being as much as two miles, maybe, from shore to shore. It had its palm trees and its live things, just like my own Anita, and I've sometimes wondered if this drifting piece hadn't really been a part of my island once—just its daughter like, as you might say.

"Be that, however, as it might be, no sooner did the floating piece get within hailing distance than I hears a human holler and there was a man dancing up and down on the shore like he was plumb crazy. Next minute he had plunged into the narrow strip of water between us and in a few minutes had swum to where I stood.

"Yes, of course it was none other than Nelson Smith!

"I knowed that the minute I set eyes on him. He had the very look of not having no better sense than the man what wrote that board and then nearly committed suicide trying to get away from the best island in all the oceans. Glad enough he was to get back, though, for the coconuts was running very short on the floater what had rescued him, and the turtle eggs wasn't worth mentioning. Being short of grub is the surest way I know to cure a man's fear of the unknown.

"Well, to make a long story short, Nelson Smith told me he was a aeronauter. In them days to be an aeronauter was not the same as to be an aviatress is now. There was dangers in the air, and dangers in the sea, and he had met with both. His gas tank had leaked and he had dropped into the water close by Anita. A case or two of provisions was all he could save from the total wreck.

"Now, as you might guess, I was crazy enough to find out what had scared this Nelson Smith into trying to swim the Pacific. He told me a story that seemed to fit pretty well with mine, only when it come to the scary part he shut up like a clam, that aggravating way some men have. I give it up at last for just man-foolishness, and we begun to scheme to get away.

"Anita moped some while we talked it over. I realized how she must be feeling, so I explained to her that it was right needful for us to get with our kind again. If we stayed with her we should probably quarrel like cats, and maybe even kill each other out of pure human cussedness. She cheered up considerable after that, and even, I thought, got a little anxious to have us leave. At any rate, when we begun to provision up the little floater, which we had anchored to the big island by a cable of twisted bark, the green nuts fell all over the ground, and Nelson found more turtle nests in a day than I had in weeks.

"During them days I really got fond of Nelson Smith. He was a companionable body, and brave, or he wouldn't have been a professional aeronauter, a job that was rightly thought tough enough for a woman, let alone a man. Though he was not so well educated as me, at least he was quiet and modest about what he did know, not like some men, boasting most where there is least to brag of.

"Indeed, I misdoubt if Nelson and me would not have quit the sea and the air together and set up housekeeping in some quiet little town up in New England, maybe, after we had got away, if it had not been for what happened when we went. I never, let me say, was so deceived in any man before nor since. The thing taught me a lesson and I never was fooled again.

"We was all ready to go, and then one morning, like a parting gift from Anita, come a soft and favoring wind. Nelson and I run down the beach together, for we didn't want our floater to blow off and leave us. As we was running, our arms full of coconuts, Nelson Smith, stubbed his bare toe on a sharp rock, and down he went. I hadn't noticed, and was going on.

"But sudden the ground begun to shake under my feet, and the air was full of a queer, grinding, groaning sound, like the very earth was in pain.

"I turned around sharp. There sat Nelson, holding his bleeding toe in both fists and giving vent to such awful words as no decent sea-going lady would ever speak nor hear to!

"'Stop it, stop it!' I shrieked at him, but 'twas too late.

"Island or no island, Anita was a lady, too! She had a gentle heart, but she knowed how to behave when she was insulted.

"With one terrible, great roar a spout of smoke and flame belched up out o' the heart of Anita's crater hill a full mile into the air!

"I guess Nelson stopped swearing. He couldn't have heard himself, anyways. Anita was talking now with tongues of flame and such roars as would have bespoke the raging protest of a continent.

"I grabbed that fool man by the hand and run him down to the water. We had to swim good and hard to catch up with our only hope, the floater. No bark rope could hold her against the stiff breeze that was now blowing, and she had broke her cable. By the time we scrambled aboard great rocks was falling right and left. We couldn't see each other for a while for the clouds of fine gray ash.

"It seemed like Anita was that mad she was flinging stones after us, and truly I believe that such was her intention. I didn't blame her, neither!

"Lucky for us the wind was strong and we was soon out of range.

"'So!' says I to Nelson, after I'd got most of the ashes out of my mouth, and shook my hair clear of cinders. 'So, that was the reason you up and left sudden when you was there before! You aggravated that island till the poor thing druv you out!'

"'Well,' says he, and not so meek as I'd have admired to see him, 'how could I know the darn island was a lady?'

"'Actions speak louder than words,' says I. 'You should have knowed it by her ladylike behavior!'

"'Is volcanoes and slingin' hot rocks ladylike?' he says. 'Is snakes ladylike? T'other time I cut my thumb on a tin can, I cussed a little bit. Say— just a li'l' bit! An' what comes at me out o' all the caves, and out o' every crack in the rocks, and out o' the very spring o' water where I'd been drinkin'? Why snakes! *Snakes*, if you please, big, little, green, red and sky-blue-scarlet! What'd I do? Jumped in the water, of course. Why wouldn't I? I'd ruther swim and drown than be stung or swallowed to death. But how was I t' know the snakes come outta the rocks because I cussed?'

"'*You* couldn't,' I agrees, sarcastic. 'Some folks never knows a lady till she up and whangs 'em over the head with a brick. A real, gentle, kind-like warning, them snakes were, which you would not heed! Take shame to yourself, Nelly,' says I, right stern, 'that a decent little island like Anita can't associate with you peaceable, but you must hurt her sacredest feelings with language no lady would stand by to hear!'

"I never did see Anita again. She may have blew herself right out of the ocean in her just wrath at the vulgar, disgustin' language of Nelson Smith. I don't know. We was took off the floater at last, and I lost track of Nelson just as quick as I could when we was landed at Frisco.

"He had taught me a lesson. A man is just full of mannishness, and the best of 'em ain't good enough for a lady to sacrifice her sensibilities to put up with.

"Nelson Smith, he seemed to feel real bad when he learned I was not for him, and then he apologized. But apologies weren't no use to me. I could never abide him, after the way he went and talked right in the presence of me and my poor, sweet lady friend, Anita!"

Now I am well versed in the lore of the sea in all ages. Through mists of time I have enviously eyed wild voyagings of sea rovers who roved and spun their yarns before the stronger sex came into its own, and ousted man from his heroic pedestal. I have followed—across the printed page—the wanderings of Odysseus. Before Gulliver I have burned the incense of tranced attention; and with reverent awe considered the history of one Munchausen, a baron. But alas, these were only men!

In what field is not woman our subtle superior?

Meekly I bowed my head, and when my eyes dared lift again, the ancient mariness had departed, leaving me to sorrow for my surpassed and outdone idols. Also with a bill for macaroons and tea of such incredible proportions that in comparison therewith I found it easy to believe her story!

Introduction to In the Land of Tomorrow

Epes Winthrop Sargent (1872-1938) is primarily known for his work as a vaudeville critic and for his role in founding the Broadway trade journal, *Variety*. Born in Nassau, the Bahamas, where his father was a correspondent for the *New York Times*, Sargent spent his professional life in New York City. Aside from his work as a theater critic, Sargent authored books on the nascent film industry, including *The Technique of the Photoplay* (1913). Although he was not primarily a literary figure, Sargent also dabbled in short fiction.

Published in two parts in the December 1907/January 1908 issues of *The Ocean*, an early pulp magazine featuring male-oriented seafaring tales, "In the Land of Tomorrow" isn't the most literary of works, but it remains a simple, escapist pleasure. With both a story and a style reminiscent of Jules Verne, Sargent's novella features a down on his luck inventor named Grenville Carrisford, a man on the brink of suicide who is given a second chance at life upon Century Island, an uncharted territory somewhere in the South Seas. It is a land where past and present collide, where human ingenuity is appreciated, and where one is free to let one's imagination run wild. As Carrisford will soon learn, however, there is no such thing as a utopia and second chances often come at a steep price. Such are the perils of disembarking from the staid confines of modernity for a new life on the mysterious Century Island.

IN THE LAND OF TOMORROW
Epes Winthrop Sargent

I
THE DISAPPEARANCE AGENT

Carrisford half rose from his seat with an oath upon his lips.

"I am extremely sorry," began the stranger courteously. "It was very awkward of me to knock over the glass. Permit me to order another."

"Do you think that you can undo the harm by replacing the drink?" demanded Carrisford, the angry light still glowing in his eyes. "That was more than ordinary absinthe."

"But the drink I am about to order will be nothing more. Absinthe alone is quite enough of a poison for a brief chat. Perhaps when we have done, you will be glad that the mixture of chloral and absinthe which I destroyed was thrown to the floor."

"This passes the bounds of insolence," stormed Carrisford. "First, you brush my glass from the table, and then add to your offense by declaring that the drink was drugged."

"Mr. Carrisford has my apology—if the drink was not drugged. Let us say that it was not drugged and, by avoiding argument, come the sooner to our conversation."

"How do you know my name?" demanded Carrisford sullenly.

"Surely, the name and personality of Grenville Carrisford are not unknown," was the retort. "As for the rest, observing that you added to your drink from a vial, and knowing that this afternoon you failed to convince the Electric Development Company of the practicability of your current magnifier, the deduction was simple."

"Are you a detective?" demanded Carrisford. "By what right do you dog my footsteps?"

"I am not a detective," replied the other. "You will pardon me if, for the present, I refer to myself with some vagueness as a colonizing agent. You will perhaps recall the disappearance of Taylor Todd?"

Carrisford nodded. Taylor Todd and his disappearance on the heels of his disappointment with his air-ship had been a nine-days wonder.

"Like yourself, Mr. Todd was weary of life because of his inability to convince the public that his idea was right. He sought self-destruction, and found, instead, peace and appreciation."

"In the life beyond?" demanded Carrisford.

"Not in the life beyond the grave, but in the life beyond the confines of time. In the land of a hundred years from now. Would *you* voyage to this unknown country?"

Carrisford looked puzzled. There was no trace of insanity in the other's face. On the contrary, this strange man represented the best type of business man, alert, self-possessed, and well poised. Carrisford passed his hand uncertainly across his forehead.

"Your ideas of humor are somewhat obscure," he said coldly. "Do you wish me to believe that you are possessed of a time-machine?"

"Not a time-machine," was the ready answer. "But I am in earnest when I offer to move you forward a hundred years. You are hurt and disappointed because your invention does not appeal to the Development Company, and they will give you neither funds nor permission to work in their laboratory.

"One hundred years from now the magnification of the electric current will be well understood. Half a dozen cells and a magnifier will suffice to run an automobile or an air-ship. Today you are a dreamer because you are a hundred years ahead of your time.

"Century Island is also a hundred years in advance of the present day, but to get there you must vanish from the world as absolutely as though you had completed the rash act you were about to undertake when I stayed your hand. If you like, I will tell you more."

"I should be glad to complete my destruction," said Carrisford wearily. "As you say, I am a hundred years ahead of the times. Because my ideas are too great to be comprehended by the men who have capital, my lifework has gone for naught"

"Suppose we seek some place where we may talk more freely," suggested the stranger, "and meanwhile permit me to introduce myself."

He handed Carrisford a slip of cardboard on which was engraved the name:

GIDEON ROUTLEDGE.

There was no address. Carrisford bowed and thrust the card into his pocket.

"I am staying here in the hotel," he said. "We might go to my room."

"On the contrary," demurred Routledge. "Walls—and most particularly hotel walls—have ears. My car is outside. Suppose we take a spin in that? It is a fine night."

Carrisford nodded, and followed his new acquaintance from the café wondering what the next development would be. He did not fear violence; indeed, he would have welcomed death in any form.

For ten years he had been working on the device for multiplying the energy of the electric current. Every dollar he owned had gone into the experiments, and now that success was almost in sight, he found himself unable to command the small amount which would suffice to demonstrate the correctness of his theory.

He had approached the Electric Development Company last of all, assured that they would steal his ideas if possible, and he had found that they had not even considered his ideas worth the stealing. They had refused even to permit him to use their laboratory, though he had offered in exchange a half right to the completed invention.

He had no more than enough money to pay his bill at the hotel. To return home would be useless, since there was no one to whom he could appeal. He had sought to commit suicide, when Routledge had interfered, and it was without fear that he climbed into the touring-car that stood at the curb.

They soon came to the open country, and Routledge increased his speed until he came to an open space. On one side a cliff fell sheerly to the lake, a hundred feet below. The stunted undergrowth around them did not afford a hiding-place for a cat.

Routledge backed the machine close to the edge of the bluff and shut off the power. Carrisford looked at him inquiringly.

"This seems to be a safe place," explained Routledge, as he lighted a cigar and handed one to his companion. "What I have to say is not for the world in general. I want to be assured that it goes no further. I have your promise that, whatever the outcome may be, you will not divulge anything that passes between us?"

"You have that promise," said Carrisford.

"Unless I were convinced that you would be glad to accept my offer I should not speak at all," went on the other. "To be brief, I would recall to you the numerous instances in the past five years of the sudden disappearance of men who have advanced ideas too ambitious to be grasped by the average mind. The case of Todd is but one of a hundred or more."

"I recall an editorial in one of the papers at that time," said Carrisford. "It was intended to be humorous, and suggested that there must be a freemasonry among inventors of the crank class whereby their fellows expeditiously removed them from the world without the expense of a funeral."

"I remember the thing," said Routledge. "They had a very incomplete list—less than a score of names, all told. I am the agency by means of which they accomplish their effacement from the world."

"You!" Carrisford regarded his companion curiously, but without fear. Routledge puffed complacently upon the big cigar between his lips.

"You can understand now why my business is not engraved upon my card. I am the disappearance agent for Century Island."

"I have never heard of the place," said Carrisford.

"Naturally not. It is the land of a hundred years from now—the refuge of men who are so far ahead of their times that the world is too small for them."

"And it is near by?"

"I can say no more," said Routledge. "If you are fully determined to pass out from life; if you are ready to abandon your place in affairs; if death seems to you more desirable by far than life, I am prepared to offer to you not death, but life—a life in which you live for others as well as yourself, and realize to the full your dreams of conquest over the powers of nature.

"I am employed by the community of Century Island to keep watch over its interests here in America. There is another man, who looks after France and Germany. These three are the inventive nations, and from these we draw the citizens of Century Island. You are encouraged and helped in the development of your ideas, and this forms your contribution to the community.

"Some few of the inventions are given to the world, and these form the revenues of the island. In many ways your magnifier would form an addition to the resources of the island. It would, for instance, complement Todd's air-ship by providing him with the battery he needs for his motor.

"Are you willing to give up all claim to worldly fame, receiving in return perpetual provision for your comfort and all things needful for further experiments?"

Carrisford drew from his pockets half a dozen coins.

"This is all I possess in the world," he said. "They asked me to settle my bill at the hotel this evening, and it took all that I had except this. It was for this reason that I was about to commit suicide when you interfered.

"I cannot obtain employment, because I am regarded as a crank. Because I cherish a dream that other men cannot comprehend I am a visionary, and my knowledge of electricity is disbelieved since it leads me to so foolish a theory as the amplification of the power of a current. I am penniless, and without hope of obtaining employment from any source."

Routledge drew from his pocket a roll of bills.

"For a few days it will be necessary to remain here in town until I can arrange for transportation," he said. "Meanwhile, enjoy yourself and do not spare expense, for Century Island does not stint its guests.

"You will be taking your last look upon the world as you understand it. Two months from now you will be as much out of the world as though you had never lived. In return, I only require that once you become a member of the colony, you will not try to make your way back to the world."

For a few seconds Carrisford looked down silently upon the lights of the city, shimmering below them.

"Is it likely that I shall want to go back to that?" he asked bitterly. "But for your interference I should be out of it by now."

"I know how it is," Routledge admitted with a smile. "When you feel that way the world seems a veritable hell, and yet there comes a time when the call of your fellow man sounds louder than all else. But from Century Island there is no escape. Once you land there, you are dead to the world. In self-defense, the colony must guard against desertion lest their secrecy be betrayed.

"Until Thursday you will be free of all save the obligation of secrecy. On Thursday I will come for you, and from that time it will be too late to turn back. Should you attempt to escape, I would be forced to kill you, even though my own life should pay the forfeit."

Carrisford buttoned his coat over the money and laughed. "Have no fear," he said as Routledge turned the car in the direction of the city.

Nothing more was said until the hotel was reached. But as they clasped hands at parting, Routledge leaned forward and whispered in his ear:

"Think it all out before Thursday. Afterward will be too late."

II
THE ROAD TO THE LAND OF DEATH

Carrisford's interview with the electric company had taken place on Monday, and until Thursday there was no sign of Routledge. It was late on that afternoon when the disappearance agent sent up his card and followed it to the room.

"Have you changed your mind?" was his greeting. "Today is the day you take the veil of Science. Just as the novice assumes the veil before the altar of the church, so must you, in your own mind, assume the obligations before the altar of invention."

"I am sick of it all," said Carrisford. "I am sorry that I did not go with you on Monday."

"Think well," urged Routledge. "You are still a young man; not more than two-and-thirty, I should judge."

"I am thirty-three," corrected the inventor.

"Make it thirty-three," continued the other. "You are young, then, good looking and, until disappointment came, full of the joy of living. Your scientific attainments qualify you for membership in the colony, but are you certain that with content there will not come a yearning for the joys of the world you have left behind?"

"Entirely so," declared Carrisford. "I ask nothing better than to leave the world forever."

"You have no friends nor family ties. I have ascertained your debts and paid them in your name. We will leave for San Francisco this evening at five. I have a compartment in the sleeper. Will you meet me at the station or will you come in my car?"

"I will meet you at the station," said Carrisford. "I shall be only too glad to make the start."

"I have ordered some things for you," said the disappearance agent. "It will be best to pay your bill and leave your trunk here. You might take a car in a direction opposite to that in which the station lies. You can transfer to another line, and then turn toward the station. It will serve to confuse the trail slightly. I shall be waiting on the platform, and we will go at once to our compartment."

He shook hands and went out. At the door he turned and faced Carrisford again.

"I will see you tomorrow," he said loudly, as a chambermaid passed. "Come to the office about eleven."

Left to himself, Carrisford went through his trunk. There were a few papers of importance that he wished to carry. For the rest there was little that he regretted leaving.

He went down and paid his bill with a light heart and sauntered out of the hotel, taking a car, as Routledge had suggested. In half an hour he was at the station, and Routledge led him quickly to the compartment.

Before the train pulled out, Carrisford was dressed in a suit very different from the one he had been wearing, the beard had been shaved off, and the thick hair parted in the middle instead of on the side. He looked entirely unlike the man who had entered the compartment, and as soon as they had started he threw from the window the shaving-paper and the suit of clothes he had worn. They dropped into the river below, and Carrisford turned away with a happy laugh.

"Farewell to Grenville Carrisford," he said. "Who am I now?"

"Peter Waldron—until Century Island is reached," answered Routledge, with a smile. "After that you become Carrisford again."

"I don't want ever to hear of that failure," he said with a laugh. "I would rather remain Waldron."

"Wait and see," returned Routledge. "You may want to change your mind. Let's go in to dinner. The car is forward."

"Mr. Waldron accepts the invitation with pleasure," was the laughing response as the two left the stateroom.

As they sat in their stateroom after dinner, Carrisford again asked their destination. Routledge flicked the ash from his cigar with a smile.

"I am sorry that I cannot give you the information you ask," he said. "You must take us on trust. I leave you at San Francisco. From there you will sail for Australia. That is all that I can say."

"You mean that I am not to know where I am going until I arrive there?" demanded Carrisford.

"Almost that," admitted the agent. " You see, were some one to blunder by chance upon the island it would spoil everything. No living man knows just where Century Island is until he gets there. Perhaps a dozen of us can make a rough guess. That is all."

"At least, you can tell me what it is like," suggested Carrisford, and again Routledge laughed:

"I have never been there, else I should have stayed. Only the dead in life know just what the island is. We of the world serve the unknown for liberal pay. With that we must be satisfied. I hope that what I say does not dishearten you."

"Quite the contrary," retorted Carrisford. "I am the more anxious to see the place."

Not until San Francisco was reached was the subject even alluded to, and then only in discussing the telegraphic report of Carrisford's alleged death.

"The dead man had no relatives," concluded the report, after explaining that he had committed suicide because of his inability to place his invention with the Electric Development Company. "His remains will be buried by the college fraternity of which he was a member."

"That is odd," said Carrisford, pushing the paper toward Routledge.

The agent laughed.

"The numerous disappearances were beginning to attract attention," he explained. "One of the medical colleges had a cadaver much like you in appearance. Your disappearance was made complete."

"And tomorrow Peter Waldron will disappear from America," said Carrisford, with a smile. "I begin on the last lap of the journey."

Routledge only smiled, but when on the following day Carrisford swung away from the pier, Routledge knew what the inventor did not discover until much later. There were yet three stages of the journey to be taken.

Wellington was his objective point, but here he was met by another agent, who told him that in two days a smaller ship would start from New Zealand.

"I can't tell you where the end of the journey is," said the man. "I do know that the schooner stops at an uncharted island to the east of Antipodes Island. But you will see for yourself in a week."

The two days passed pleasantly enough, and on the third a trim auxiliary yacht bore him out of the harbor. The six men who manned the vessel, in addition to the captain, were all mutes, huge blacks, who went silently about their duties, with never a word or look toward the passenger sitting beside the skipper on the deck.

It seemed almost like a ship of death, and Carrisford wondered that the captain did not go mad. The skipper took his pipe from his mouth when he heard the suggestion.

"It's like a bit o' heaven," he returned. "I take it you're not married, sir?"

Carrisford shook his head. "Never had any inclination that way," he said.

"I was—for ten years," replied the other, as he replaced the short pipe between his teeth.

For three days they headed southeast, passing Antipodes Island, which approximately marks the antipodes of Greenwich, and late on the evening of the third day they ran into a sheltered cove. The captain pointed his pipe at a sheet-iron hut, on the beach.

"That's where you are headed," he said.

Carrisford looked about him in disappointment. In the moonlight the grim face of the cliffs that rose above the beach seemed less forbidding; but outside of the hut there was no sign of human habitation, and he dropped into the launch with many misgivings.

The interior of the hut was divided into two rooms, as Carrisford saw when lamps were lighted. In the outer apartment were utensils for simple cookery, a dinner table, and a small library. In the other room were two small iron camp beds, each nicely made up. The captain turned to his companion.

"I suppose you'll want to get to bed?" he suggested. Carrisford shook his head.

"I think I'll sit up to receive my hosts," he said with a smile.

The captain went over to a cellaret.

"Let us drink to your safe journey," he suggested, as he filled two glasses and raised one in a toast.

Carrisford took the other and tossed off the contents. The lights seemed to grow suddenly dim, and there was a roaring in his ears as of the pounding of surf in a storm. He fought desperately to retain consciousness, but at last he sank to the ground.

At a sign from the captain one of the mutes stepped forward, removed Carrisford's outer garments, and laid the inventor on one of the beds. Then they extinguished the lights and softly left the place.

When Carrisford awoke in the morning there was no trace of the schooner, nor could he even discover the footprints of the men in the soft sand. The appearance of the beach suggested a recent storm, though the skies were blue, and the vegetation above the sand-line gave no evidence of having been recently drenched.

Carrisford prepared breakfast from the food he found in the cupboard, and then wandered disconsolately about the beach. He had never felt so strangely lonesome. Before there had always been the feeling that other human beings were near. Now, even the birds were absent, and there was no hum of insect life. Once, far out at sea, a whale spouted, throwing up a great column of water, and Carrisford smiled at the thought that the ocean, at least, contained living animals.

He wandered back to the hut, getting an early lunch merely that he might have something to do. After the scanty meal he sought to occupy himself with a book. For an hour or more he turned the pages, though few of the printed thoughts occupied his mind, and then he suddenly dropped the volume. His quick ear had caught the faint sound of footsteps. He sprang toward the door, but before he reached it a man stepped through the opening.

"This is Mr. Grenville Carrisford?" he asked pleasantly. "Let me introduce myself as Masten Graves."

"Masten Graves!" Carrisford repeated. "The inventor of the turbine-torpedo?"

"The same," he smiled. "Don't look so shocked. You must be prepared to meet dead men on Century Island. Remember that you are dead yourself."

He held forth the clipping from the San Francisco newspaper, and Carrisford started.

"How did you get that down here?" he asked. "Is it magic?"

"Very white magic," explained Graves. "It is a part of your record sent on by our agent, Routledge. But we can talk more conveniently later on. Just now I only want to welcome you and tell you that I am glad to know you. Let us start for the land of the dead."

He led the way out of the hut, carefully closed the door, and started across the sand to the cliff. At the foot of the rock he turned and uncovered a hose, and a heavy spray of water soon obliterated their tracks. The beach was as hard and firm as though it had never been trodden upon.

"To prevent the millionth chance of discovery," said Graves. "Follow me closely, please," and he led the way into a cleft in the rock. "This is the worldly landing of the ferry across the modem Styx to the new land of death."

III
CENTURY ISLAND

Carrisford followed his guide into the cleft in the rock. To all appearances, it was a natural cave, roughly circular in outline, and some forty feet in diameter. At the rear was a second aperture, through which a dazzling white light gleamed, and toward this Graves led the way.

"I suppose you have seen demonstrations of the vibratory light?" he said. "We have it here in its most complete form. It is Breckenridge's contribution to the society of Century Island."

A cry escaped Carrisford as he led the way through the opening. The second cave was clearly the work of man. It was an arched tunnel one hundred feet across, and through the center was a canal in which lay a submarine. A traveling derrick ran down the center of the roof, but now it was at rest at the far end. Two men in white, short-skirted tunics, seated at the mouth of the submarine's hatchway, came forward as Graves approached.

"Our new comrade, Grenville Carrisford," said Graves, indicating the new arrival. "Mr. Carrisford, I wish to present George Hawley and Fergus McPherson."

The two men clasped his hand and led the way down the hatch into the interior of the boat. Graves went back to swing into place the section of rock that closed the entrance, and as the huge mass swung around, Carrisford looked with interest at the lights.

At either end of the tunnel were brass uprights, terminating in two rounded knobs, six inches apart. From these there named tongues of electricity so intensely white that it hurt the eye to look upon it. Graves laughed as he returned from the entrance.

"Plenty of time to study that when you arrive in Century," he said. "Suppose we start."

He helped Carrisford over the hatch and followed him down into the cabin, after making all secure. There was a whir from the motor, and then a slight vibration. Hawley took his place at the wheel, and Graves sank into a seat beside Carrisford.

"It speaks well for our planning," he said, "that for fifty years none has dreamed of the existence of Century Island. Now, those men on the schooner are as ignorant as you were of the means by which the material they bring is removed.

"They never see us. A letter in cipher, telling our wants, is placed in a secret cleft in the rocks. They bring what we send for and leave it in the outer cave. They imagine that we come in another schooner and take it away.

"Instead of that, we enter this island from the opposite side. The opening is forty feet below the surface, and the tunnel runs straight to the secret cave. The three of us can easily work the loading machinery, and in no time at all we are ready for the return trip.

"In ten minutes we shall emerge from the tunnel, and in eight hours we shall be at home, one hundred and sixty miles away."

"But do ships never come?" asked Carrisford. "Antarctic exploration is rather a fad now."

"They make for the known lands," was the explanation. "We lie apart from known routes, and a bank of fog is a perpetual screen. There is some warm current flowing toward the South Pole and, striking the colder waters, it creates the fog."

"But I should think that it would make the climate almost unendurable," objected Carrisford. Graves indicated McPherson.

"They say it was until McPherson came. He is the inventor of a plan for the prevention of fog. His suggestion was hooted at in London, but he has turned Century Island into a place of perpetual summer.

"We all contribute here. This boat, for instance, is my invention. Hawley improved it with the gyroscope that steadies it, and permits the use of a more powerful engine without increasing the vibration. With the aid of your invention we hope to make the boat complete by cutting down the size of the storage batteries."

"But where is the crew?" asked Carrisford. "Do you three represent the entire force?"

"Yes," replied Graves. "You see, we have very few servants. We discovered a race of mutes on one of the islands to the north, and when we need slaves we go and get a few of them. In our submarine they look upon us as gods, and it is not difficult to obtain all we need. But, of course, it is not wise to employ more than are necessary, and we have so arranged matters that machinery does most of the work.

"But you will see all that in a short time. Meanwhile, why not assume the costume of the country?"

Graves had thrown off the long black cloak he had worn when he had met Carrisford, and now, like the others, was clothed in the short tunic.

"The toga is our full dress," he explained. "You had better wear this until you take your place with the workers. A week is allowed in which to look over the place."

He brought out the garments and indicated an alcove where the change might be accomplished. In a few minutes Carrisford stepped out again, the transformation complete. His crisp black curls were well in keeping with the costume, which set off the finely cut features to far greater advantage. His fellows regarded him with approval.

"You will find it very easy," declared McPherson, whose brogue had long since disappeared. "The Scots were the wisest. They kept to the kilts long after the rest of the civilized world went over to breeches."

"Perhaps in the new athletic generation bare legs will become fashionable again," laughed Carrisford. "Golf is accomplishing wonders."

"Scots again," murmured McPherson, and they all laughed.

"McPherson is the one resident of Century Island," explained Hawley, "who will not grant that it is the most perfect spot on earth."

"I'm not saying that," protested the Scotchman, "but it has no lochs. We cannot have everything. I'm not asking that."

"I don't blame you for longing for your Scotch scenery," said Carrisford, with quick sympathy. "It is beautiful."

McPherson looked at him gratefully, and Carrisford had made his first friend in Century Island.

Graves moved about the place getting dinner, and presently he placed upon the table a steak cooked upon an electric broiler, while the other dishes and the coffee were also cooked by electricity.

"I rather imagined that you had tabloid meals in such an advanced colony," said Carrisford, as he gave testimony to the excellence of the dinner by eating heartily. Graves smiled.

"There is no necessity for it," he said. "We did try a food tablet in which the necessary elements were administered in a pure state instead of in combination with waste, but it is used now only when it is necessary to give the digestive organs a short rest. As a cure for dyspepsia, it is a huge success, but tabloid meals, or even synthetic food, is unnatural, and therefore unhealthy."

Graves rose from his seat when the dinner was over and an electric apparatus had washed and dried the dishes, and went into the tower. Presently Hawley nodded to him, and he threw over the lever that controlled the airtight seal. A moment later he had thrown back the hatch and stepped out upon the platform, calling to Carrisford to follow him.

They were moving rapidly through a thick fog. In the interior of the boat an automatic adjuster had maintained an equitable temperature, but in the open, even in spite of the fog, Carrisford was sensible of a marked increase of temperature.

The huge bulk of the submarine slipped through the water so smoothly that Carrisford scarcely realized that they were moving until, without warning, the boat shot out of the enclosing wall of fog and Century Island stood revealed.

The sun had long since sunk below the horizon, for it was winter in the southern hemisphere, and the days were short, but latticed towers crowned by vibratory lights gave an illumination almost equal to daylight.

The city was built upon a gentle slope, rising in terraces. At the foot of the hill ran a broad esplanade, gorgeous with flowerbeds. Along the rear was a one-story structure, apparently a mile and a half in length, pierced at intervals with wide gateways. Above this rose tiers of houses identical in design with the lower row save that here they were not more than two hundred feet long, with a fifty-foot space between each. At the top of the hill stood the Palace, or Administration Building—a large structure six stories high.

The esplanade was thronged with people who crowded eagerly about the basin in the center of the plaza, where rose a water gate. There was the sound of music, and as the submarine shot into view a cheer came faintly across the water.

"It is your welcome to Century Island," said Graves. "Quick; we must prepare for the reception."

Wonderingly, Carrisford followed him down the iron stairway. Now, McPherson was draped in the same kind of black cloak that Graves had worn at first when he had come to the new arrival. Graves' cloak hung over the back of one of the chairs. He slipped into this, and the two passed to the rear of the boat.

Here a handsome casket stood upon a pair of trestles, and over it hung a long cloth of black stuff. Graves caught this up and began winding it about Carrisford's shoulders.

"It is an ancient custom," he said. "Only the dead come to Century Island. The ceremony does not last very long, and you will find it interesting in the extreme."

As he was speaking he had wrapped Carrisford's legs, and now, catching him up in his arms, he deposited him in the casket.

"You may look," he counseled, "until you hear me call. Then close your eyes until you are commanded to open them again. Now lie quiet, for here come the bearers."

Eight huge blacks entered the hold through the hatch, which they had raised, and caught up the coffin. With this upon their shoulders, they moved over to an elevator in the center of the place. Graves and McPherson took their places behind them, and as the platform began to move upward the sound of a great organ, playing a dead march, pealed through the air.

Slowly the procession crossed the deck, and so across the platform of the water gate to the entrance, where they set down their burden upon a marble altar. In an instant all of the lights of the city went out save one torch at the head of the casket, and a man in a purple robe advanced toward the gruesome object.

IV
THE LAW OF THE ISLAND

With the extinguishing of the lights the music was hushed until it scarcely seemed sound at all. The man in the purple robe advanced to the side of the casket.

"Who lies here?" he demanded of Graves.

"One who in earth life was called Grenville Carrisford," answered Graves.

"He comes of his own free will?" Graves bowed.

"He comes because he has no further use for life on earth. Like us all, he has thought far in advance of his time, and he would die in life that he might reach that land where tomorrow is today and today is yesterday."

"And abandoning the world, as one dead, he comes willingly to our country of tomorrow, seeking the companionship of others who, like himself, have lived in advance of their time?"

"Even as one dead, renouncing the worldly pleasures for the greater joy of life among kindred souls."

"He has accomplished that which is worthy of our land?"

"He brings rare knowledge; thoughts so great that the earth men cannot understand."

The man in purple turned to the casket and looked down upon the man wrapped in his shroud of black.

"Grenville Carrisford," he said impressively. "But for those whom we maintain, already you would have passed the borders of the earth life. Even as your hand was raised against yourself did our agent intervene.

"We hold that we are entitled to the life that we have saved. Upon the body, upon the spirit we claim jurisdiction. Over thy actions in sleep or wakefulness, at work or at diversion, we claim entire control. For as we raised thee from the dead, so shall we take away that life as penalty for disobedience.

"We demand no vows, we ask no promises. Instead, we give assurance that even as we bring thee up out of the coffin, so shall we place thee therein forever if thou are not obedient."

Graves leaned over the casket.

"Close your eyes," he whispered, "and do not open them until the word is given."

Carrisford obediently closed his eyes, and the voice boomed out again. This time, Carrisford knew that he was addressing the people.

"Behold," he cried, "the body of Grenville Carrisford, who is dead on earth, but who shall live in the Land of Tomorrow. From the death of the ignorance of the world he rises to the fellowship of his equals, yielding obedience to the laws we have made and accepting the penalty thereof for his disobedience."

The voice ceased, and Carrisford felt them stripping from him his wrappings. Then he was raised up in the coffin, which had been moved in a quarter circle, and he was conscious of a flood of light against his closed eyelids.

"Open your eyes," called the voice. "Look upon those who are to be thy brothers."

At the command Carrisford opened his eyes and looked about him. The lights had been turned on again, and now the music swelled out in a new strain of gladness. Graves helped the man in purple lift him from the coffin, and as Carrisford stood up the entire assemblage raised their right hands high in the air in silent salute. Coached by Graves, Carrisford made reply and turned to be introduced to those on the platform.

The man in purple, he learned, was Paul Beardsley, the president of the island. Taylor Todd, with a broad band of purple edging his toga, was vice-president, and seven elderly men, who wore two narrow stripes of purple, were the council. The unofficial welcoming was soon over, and Carrisford, accompanied by McPherson, stepped down from the platform and made his way through the crowd.

As those nearest him clasped his hand in welcome, Carrisford marveled at the preponderance of men. Only here and there was a woman to be seen.

McPherson led the way through one of the gates in the long building, and Carrisford found himself ascending by a gentle grade a well-paved street. On either side were square buildings without openings of any sort save for the gateways that opened upon the streets running parallel with the harbor.

"In the morning," explained McPherson, "you will be assigned a permanent place. For tonight you shall be my guest. We turn here."

He led the way down one of the side streets and turned in at a gate. Carrisford could see now that the lights were enclosed in each courtyard. On three sides of the square were suites of rooms, consisting of a bath, a sitting room, and a sleeping room. On the fourth side was an open dining room on one side of the gateway, while on the other was the kitchen.

McPherson led the way into his own suite, and Carrisford noticed that the rooms were large and comfortable. There was no need of artificial light, though a vacuum tube ran around the four walls.

"The lights are turned off at eleven," explained the host. "After that the independent illumination must be used. Except by special permit, all lights must be out by midnight. Now, if you're ready, we'll go to your apartment. It's right next door."

He led the way through the arched passage into the next bedroom. It did not take Carrisford long to throw off his robes, and before the light in the court went out he was already sound asleep and dreaming that, instead of rising from the dead, the coffin had been lowered into the inferno.

He was wakened in the morning by a trumpet call, which seemed to sound in his very room. He jumped into the bathtub, and was getting into his clothes when McPherson came in.

"I'm to devote the day to showing you around," he explained. "I thought I had better start early. Was your bath too cold?"

"Rather chilly," said Carrisford with a smile. McPherson led the way into the bathroom and showed a dial on the wall.

"Set that overnight to the temperature you want," he explained. "It will be just right in time for your bath. The central station throws the current into the bath thermals at five. They wake you at seven by the music transmitter, and the bath is just the right temperature. Let's go to breakfast."

He led the way across the court to the dining room, where the rest of the company was already seated. Twelve men formed a house party and ate at the common table.

The food had been put into the electric cookers the night before by the slaves, who also set the tables. Now, the chops were cooked to a turn, the coffee was clear and fragrant, and even the biscuits were light and feathery.

As the meal was finished, a slave came in, cleared the table, and set about tidying the place. The others went about their daily tasks, but McPherson and Carrisford strolled through the city.

McPherson first led the way to the waterfront, where the laboratories were located in the long building. Here the scientists worked at their tasks, each in his own domain. Electricity was everywhere; it turned the wheels and provided heat for the furnaces. Apparently, the supply was inexhaustible, and Carrisford made inquiry.

"The radiations of radium," explained McPherson. "The island is volcanic, and President Beardsley devised a scheme for converting the rays directly into electrical impulse."

"There seems to be small need for my invention," laughed Carrisford. "No need to amplify the current when the direct product is so abundant."

"On the contrary, your idea is most welcome. It will relieve the pressure on the feed wires. Then, too, in the submarine we can develop greater power with the same storage capacity. Don't worry. You will find your place."

They went through the vast works, then climbed the hill for the interview with the president. The interview was satisfactory in the extreme, and as they came away Carrisford's face beamed. He had been given *carte blanche* to push his experiments to the utmost. He had been assigned a laboratory to himself, with the necessary helpers, and was to begin work as soon as he was ready.

What pleased him almost as much was his assignment to the quarters he had occupied the night before. He had conceived a genuine liking for McPherson, and was glad of his society.

They were descending the steps of the Administration Building, were congratulating themselves upon their good fortune, when a cry behind them caused them both to turn. Just behind, a girl, descending the steps, had slipped and, in falling, fell directly into Carrisford's arms.

For a moment he held the slender form in his arms, feeling her warm breath upon his cheek and scenting the fragrance of her hair. Then he had set her down, and with a blushing word of thanks she offered him her hand.

"I thank you very much," she said sweetly. "You are Mr. Carrisford, the new arrival, are you not? I am Clio Beardsley. I am glad to welcome you to Century Island."

She passed on down the steps with a pretty nod, and left Carrisford standing dumb with the pressure of his feelings. Carrisford had known many beautiful women in his day, but never before had he seen one so beautiful as Clio Beardsley. She was tall and slender, with great, serious eyes of unfathomable depths. Her face was a regular oval, framed in masses of golden hair, bound in the Grecian style with a purple band, and the robes, flowing in classical simplicity, were also edged with the purple of authority.

McPherson slapped him on the back.

"Come, lad," he admonished. "There is much to see this afternoon. You'll be wanting to have a look at your laboratory, and I want to show you my fog-dispeller."

They passed on down the steps, but Carrisford looked listlessly at the splendid laboratory placed at his disposal, and gave little heed to McPherson's explanation of the machine which had gained him admission to the colony. Even while he listened to the elaborate explanation of how the electrical currents dispelled the moisture of which the fogs were composed, he could see through the banks of mist the sweet girlish face.

In the middle of the explanation he broke in to ask whether it was Miss or Mrs. Beardsley.

"Miss Beardsley, of course," replied McPherson. "Now, you see how we keep the fogs away. Let's take one of the cars and go over to see the gardens."

They took a motorcar and rode out to where the vast fields provided the fruits and vegetables needed for the colony. They inspected the droves of fine cattle and sheep, and visited the vast poultry yard. It was all very interesting, but Carrisford was deep in thought of Clio Beardsley.

Late that evening McPherson stole into Carrisford's rooms.

"Are you awake, lad?" he whispered. Carrisford answered. He was too full of this new wonder of love to compose himself to sleep. McPherson sat himself down upon the edge of the bed.

"I wanted to tell you, lad," he whispered. "There's only one sort of vital statistics in Century Island. They are the deaths. It's like heaven in one way, for there is 'neither marriage nor giving in marriage.' To break the rule means death."

V
WHAT IS LOVE?

Carrisford half rose from the bed.

"Do you mean to say," he demanded hoarsely, "that marriage is not permitted here?"

"Just that," assented the Scotchman. "It is a wise provision, lad."

"It is unnatural," insisted Carrisford. "It is an outrage against the very law of the world."

"You don't understand," said McPherson pityingly. "You see, laddie, this is not a normal colony. Apart from the dumb slaves, we are all brain workers, men and women. The women, you see, have all contributed to the colony ideas of equal value with the men. There was a time when marriage was permitted, but from very horror the thing was stopped."

"I fail to see the horror in such a sacrament," said the younger man. "Why, we should have a race of intellectual giants here on Century Island."

McPherson shook his head.

"I saw some of them," he explained. "Too much intellect for the little bodies. They were all head, laddie—imbeciles. It was a pitiful sight."

"But Clio—Miss Beardsley; she is not abnormal."

"Very true, very true. But she is the only woman who ever came to Century Island who was not a scientist. If we made an exception in her case, all would demand it. No, it is wiser as it is. Most of us are content. The others know that death is the punishment for even speaking of love, and so we look to the earth people to populate our island. In return we give them our inventions when they are ready for them. The income from these goes to maintain our establishments for recruiting."

"And I am to bow meekly to the decree?" demanded Carrisford.

"Either that or death," responded McPherson. "Be careful, laddie. I speak only for your own good."

He patted Carrisford on the shoulder and slipped from the room.

No sleep came to Carrisford that night. In the darkness he could see the sweet face of Clio Beardsley as in a vision, and the more he looked the more determined he was that he should win her for his wife. There were some five thousand inhabitants on Century Island. Surely some of these must be intolerant of the same conditions. He might arrange a revolt.

He came to breakfast haggard and wan. McPherson, watching him anxiously, sighed. Once he had gone through the same experience, but he had come to realize that the existing order was the best.

"I must get over to the south side of the island," he said as they left the dining pavilion. "Some of the machines are in need of repair, and the fog is coming in on the vegetable garden. Go to your work, lad. You will find forgetfulness there."

The two men walked down the inclined street to the esplanade and as far as Carrisford's laboratory. There McPherson left him with a promise to look in on his way back, and went off to obtain a vehicle to carry him to his battle with the fog.

Carrisford went into the laboratory with far different feelings than he had anticipated the day before when President Beardsley had assured him that everything needed for his experiments would be forthcoming immediately.

The promise had almost overwhelmed him after the days of struggle in America, when a tool meant the sacrifice of a meal or two and the purchase of supplies was frequently delayed several weeks. He had left the reception chamber aglow with enthusiasm, but the meeting with Clio and the subsequent discovery of the law against marriage had thrown him into the blackest despondency.

And yet, once he became absorbed in his work he went rapidly about his task. Two skilled helpers had been provided, and he soon had his machine started.

The noon meal was served in the shops, and there was little delay. They were hard at work when some one entered the place.

"That you, McPherson?" called Carrisford without looking up. "Come over here; I'm fixing up the magnifier. I think I shall have it done by tomorrow."

"I am glad that Mr. Carrisford makes such excellent progress," said a deep voice behind him, and Carrisford sprang up to salute the president.

"I am very much interested in the invention," went on Beardsley. "It will simplify the wiring when additional power is needed, and in many ways it will work a revolution. My daughter was speaking of it last night. You have met Miss Beardsley," he added as Clio came forward.

Carrisford bent over the little hand with flaming face.

"I persuaded father to bring me down," she said in her low, clear voice. "I am studying electricity myself, you know. I feel so utterly frivolous in the midst of these thousands of clever people."

"I thought you had to be an inventor to obtain citizenship," he said. Clio smiled proudly.

"They needed father so badly that they waived the rule and let me come, too, though I am sure that I shall never invent anything. Will you show me your machine, please?"

Carrisford went over the details of his device, and was surprised at the intelligent appreciation she displayed. It was evident that she was possessed of a technical knowledge astonishing in a woman of her age, and he became so absorbed in his explanations that he did not realize how late it was until the electric apparatus blew its trumpet call for the cessation of work.

Clio started up with a little exclamation of surprise.

"I had no idea of the time," she said regretfully. "You must dine with us this evening, Mr. Carrisford, and complete the explanation then."

"We shall be most glad to have you," seconded the president, and Carrisford stammered out his acceptance.

Dressing for dinner was no elaborate undertaking on Century Island. After the bath a toga was put on instead of the short tunic. All of the garments were of the same cloth and made in the same fashion.

McPherson found Carrisford splashing about in his tub when he returned from his own work. He shook his head sadly at the announcement that Carrisford was to dine with the president, but he offered no objection.

He walked as far as the steps of the Administration Building with his friend, and as he took his leave, whispered a caution, but it is doubtful if Carrisford even heard it. He realized only that he was to dine with Clio, and he sprang up the steps with a beating heart.

The dinner was precisely the same as that served in every group house, but to the young inventor it seemed a banquet. Taylor Todd was also a guest, and the president carried him off after dinner to discuss some affairs of state.

"Suppose we sit in the court," suggested Clio. "Father will be talking with Mr. Todd for the rest of the evening. Mr. Todd wants to build an airship on a new principle."

They passed through the dining room out on to a covered balcony. The building was arranged around a square and the center was filled with a mass of luxuriant plants. Carrisford had already seen how the buried electrodes forced the growth, and merely marveled at the scientific development that maintained palms and other tropical vegetation a few hundred miles from the South Pole.

But the greater wonder was the glorious beauty of the girl beside him, and as they paced about the court he had eyes only for her. Presently she led the way through an arched passage to a terrace overlooking the town.

Seen from above, the greenery of the courts broke the monotony of the white granite-like composition which was the only material employed in the construction of buildings.

"Sometimes," she said, as they leaned against the balustrade, "I am afraid that I almost grow tired of this absolute regularity. I was such a little girl when I was brought here—not more than five or six, for father knew of radium long before the Curies announced that they had discovered it. I can just remember London, with the crooked streets and the smoke-stained buildings.

"Here everything is so orderly that at times I feel as though I must scream.

There are so many houses to a street, each the same as the other, and containing the same number of tenants; we all eat our breakfast at the same hour; we go to work and stop work at the same signal."

"You are unusual in longing for the world," said Carrisford. "Most of us have found the world too formidable a foe."

"I know," assented the girl, with a shudder. "It seems horrible to think that so many of the people here were saved from suicide. The ceremony of reception is a terrible thing."

"It is very impressive," he said, "and a warning against the infraction of the regulations. Yet I should think that Dan Cupid might make trouble at times."

"Dan Cupid?" she asked. "Is he in the electrical, mechanical, or minerals section?"

"He is everywhere—even on Century Island," Carrisford explained. "But he has never gone through the ceremony of reception. He is the god of love."

"Love," she echoed. "We know little of love here, Mr. Carrisford. I suppose you mean love for your friends. I have often wondered how it felt to be in love."

"Do you never read romances?"

"Romances are treatises upon love?" she asked.

"Not treatises," he said, with a laugh— "stories of persons who love. Sometimes they move heaven and earth before their tangled affairs are straightened out, and they are married and live happily ever after."

"The libraries here contain only scientific works," she said, with regret. "Only those parts of the magazines are reprinted which concern discoveries and inventions. Father is the editor. Did not Mr. McPherson show you a copy?"

"I have seen the abstract," he admitted, "but I thought that light reading might be permitted."

"It is prohibited," she said. "Mme. Ferrers once wrote a book. She wanted father to print it, but he scolded her and burned the manuscript. I asked her what it was about, but she said she dared not tell. Can you describe love?"

"It's rather hard," said Carrisford, with an uneasy laugh, "and it seems to be prohibited."

"But you will tell me," she urged.

"It is a feeling that there is one person worth more to you than all the world," began Carrisford. "He or she means more to you than even father or mother. For the loved one you are ready to go through any peril or sacrifice."

"It makes you feel strange when you see him?" she asked, placing her hand over her heart.

Carrisford nodded.

"And you want to be with him and help him? You are bashful when you meet him, and you are afraid that he will see that you like him, and then again you are afraid that he will not?"

"Something like that," he assented, the frown deepening on his brow. Clio already loved. There was no hope for him. "Love is a mass of contradictions."

"I know," she said. "You want him to kiss you, and then you know that you will die of shame if he does. I am in love. Is it not odd that I did not know what it was?"

"Not so very," said Carrisford gloomily. "Some people love for years and do not realize it until too late."

"I have only loved since yesterday," she said simply. "Only since you caught me in your arms there on the steps."

VI
REBELLION

For a moment the town seemed to whirl before Carrisford's eyes, and he clutched at the balustrade. Clio regarded him curiously.

"I have alarmed you?" she said. "I am sorry. Let us forget what I said. Perhaps it will pass."

"Forget!" he echoed. "Do you suppose that I want you to forget? Child, ever since that moment down there on the steps I have thought of nothing but you and the hopelessness of my love."

"You love, also?" she asked, as her hand slipped within his own.

"Heaven help us, I do!" he answered. "Don't you understand, dear, that love here, on Century Island, can bring only sorrow and pain?"

"Then, why can't we go away?" she asked. "You are so clever that you will find a way. Perhaps I could coax my father to let us go. He is president, and can do as he pleases."

"He cannot alter the law of the land," declared Carrisford. "If he did but imagine that I have come here to win you, he would kill me in a moment to hide the fact that you had fallen in love. It is perhaps wise in a measure that marriage is prohibited here. Not even for his own daughter may he overrule the law."

"Then, we must keep it secret," she said, "though it seems wrong to be ashamed of what God puts in our hearts. Perhaps in time we shall find a way."

"God grant that we may," he groaned, "else it were better that I had taken my life in that Chicago hotel."

"Do not say that," she pleaded. "It is better to have loved, even though we pay for it with our lives. We at least feel that we are for each other."

Slowly they retraced their steps across the terrace and through the passage leading to the court. The leave-taking was short.

The president regretted that the visit of Todd had caused an interruption, and promised that he would come to the laboratory in the morning to complete his inquiry. Then he escorted his guest to the head of the stairway and watched, with his arm about his daughter, while Carrisford went slowly down the broad flight. Then he turned to Clio.

"What did you and Carrisford find that was so interesting?" he demanded curiously. "You seemed much absorbed in your talk."

"He was asking of the city," she explained demurely, though her cheek still wore a delicate flush. "It was all so new and strange to him. We spoke of other things," she added, "but little that would interest."

The president raised the fair young face and looked down into the untroubled eyes.

"I fear that I acted unwisely in asking him to dinner," he said. "Young men fresh from the worldly life bring foolish notions into this happy country of ours. Be careful, Clio, and see him as little as possible, lest he fill your head with foolish thoughts. Come, child, let us go to our rooms, and think no more of this young man, who will be very useful to us if he possesses discretion to match his other qualities."

"He really is clever, is he not?" she demanded, anxious to hear him praised.

Beardsley shook his head.

"Almost too clever," he said. "I am afraid that even his invention, valuable as it is, will not excuse his introduction here."

Meanwhile, Carrisford was walking down the street toward the esplanade, lifting his feet heavily, as one half dazed. He could not go to his group house just now. He could not face the shrewd Scotchman in his present mood, and so he kept on until he reached the broad seawall.

The smell of the salt water was pleasant, and the light breeze cooled his healed brow. He walked hurriedly along to the east.

Here the esplanade ran into the broad road that led to the plantations, and presently he had left the paving and was hurrying along the macadam. He had gone perhaps a quarter of a mile when he came suddenly around a curve in the road to face two figures locked in an embrace.

For an instant, in the dim light, he thought that he had come upon a fight; but the next moment Taylor Todd came toward him with an upraised knife, and Carrisford saw that the other was a woman.

He was unarmed, but he was younger than Todd, and he had little trouble in gripping the hand that held the knife. Back and forth they struggled upon the smooth surface of the road, but, try as he would, he could not wrest the weapon from the other's grasp.

At last he succeeded in throwing his antagonist, and Todd's elbow striking the hard earth, the knife went flying across the road. Quick as a flash the woman had caught it up, and as the two men rolled over and over she watched her chance to strike.

Gaining new strength in his terror, Todd was besting Carrisford. With one hand he had pinned him to the ground and with the other was reaching for the knife the woman held, when Carrisford wrenched away the hand that was slowly strangling him.

"Hold on, you fool," he whispered. "Why do you want to kill me? I know that the president has given you permission to build a new airship. Now I know what you want it for. You need my help. Without my magnifier you can never make land."

Todd relaxed his pressure, but he held the knife threateningly against the other's throat.

"What makes you think I want to leave Century Island?" he demanded.

"It is death to remain here, loving a woman," answered Carrisford. "An airship is about the only real means of making an escape. Suppose I were minded to return to the world myself? We could go together."

"Perhaps it would be as well," muttered Todd; but the woman leaned over the pair.

"Perhaps he is a traitor," she whispered. "Perhaps he only seeks to accomplish our undoing. Strike, lest you regret it."

"Strike, and regret it, Mme. Ferrers," retorted Carrisford. It was a wild guess, but it struck home.

"You see, he knows my name," whispered the woman. "He has been set to watch us."

"It was perfectly natural," explained Carrisford. "I was told this evening by Miss Beardsley that a Mme. Ferrers had written a novel that the president would not permit her to print. There are so few women here who are not completely engrossed in their work that the inference was obvious."

"Clio Beardsley told you?" she asked.

Carrisford nodded. She turned away with a short laugh.

"He is safe enough, *mon ami*," she said to Todd. "He and the little Clio have learned to talk of love. It is but natural that they should wish to be fellow passengers."

Carrisford stared at her as he rose from the dust and shook the dirt from his garments. Mme. Ferrers was a rather gaunt Frenchwoman, whose dominant personality had swayed the less determined Todd. She had, he knew, been admitted to the colony because of her skill as a writer of scientific treatises rather than because of her scientific attainments.

She found the colony dull after her beloved Paris, and she was eager to make her escape. One after another, she had sought in vain to win the love of the three men who operated the submarine, and as a last resort she had turned to Todd, urging him to build an airship sufficiently strong to permit a passage to Australia or South America. He had fallen a victim to her wiles, and through his important position in the community he had obtained permission to construct a large airship.

"You think that you can help me with the ship?" demanded Todd as he turned to Carrisford, after a whispered conversation with the woman.

"I am certain that I can do so," was the confident reply. "How much power do you need?"

"I have not figured yet," he said, "but I am afraid that I cannot use electricity. The storage batteries would weigh too much, even in the improved form in which we get them."

"I can develop one horsepower with two gravity cells," said Carrisford. "The magnifier weighs as much as a third cell for each pair."

"You are certain of this?" demanded Todd excitedly. "You are sure that the supply of current will be constant?"

Carrisford smiled.

"I would suggest that you come to my laboratory tomorrow," he said. "There I can demonstrate my ideas to your entire satisfaction."

"Then we are indeed fortunate," said Todd. "In a little while we shall be free of all this and back to our own again. Glad indeed am I that the chance has come. Science is but a poor thing to love."

"Science takes all and gives nothing," said Carrisford. "I was not born to be a slave to science alone."

"Look!" Mme. Ferrers pointed to the city, where but a moment before the lights had been glowing. Now all was dark, and the buildings gleamed but faintly in the starlight.

"It is time to part," said Todd reluctantly. "Do you wait for me beyond the bend, Carrisford."

Carrisford walked rapidly toward the turning of the road and then more slowly until Todd caught up. Together they made their way back to the city, and as they walked Todd rapidly sketched a plan of action.

For the first time Carrisford realized that there was an electrified zone about the island, and that to attempt to pass this zone would be to give immediate warning to the watcher in the executive offices.

With the newly found power it might be possible to rise above this zone before heading away from the island, but this could only be accomplished were the authorities kept in ignorance of the power developed by the magnifier through the battery cells.

It was agreed that the magnifier should be developed for the direct current from the central generator, but that the experiments with the cells should appear to be a failure.

With this understanding they parted at Carrisford's street, and he turned up to his group house. At the entrance one of the mutes saluted, and Carrisford, thinking him one of those who filled the electric kitchens, passed in.

There was still a light in McPherson's quarters, and as Carrisford went past the open door the Scotchman followed him down to his own rooms.

"Where have you been, lad?" he demanded. "The president has called for you three times, and there is a man outside waiting for you—one of the mutes."

"I was only taking a walk," explained Carrisford. McPherson opened his mouth as though to speak, but at that moment the telephone bell rang, and Carrisford stepped to the instrument.

"Where were you, Mr. Carrisford?" asked President Beardsley.

"I went for a walk," replied Carrisford. "I went along the shore road for a space."

"Midnight walks are not to be recommended," said the voice at the other end of the line. "I trust that I am mistaken, Mr. Carrisford, but for the present it would be as well if you remained in your own apartments after dinner each evening."

Carrisford made reply, and hung up the receiver. He rapidly repeated to McPherson the gist of the message, and the Scotchman's face fell.

"It's but a poor beginning," he said, with a sigh. "Invited to the president's to dinner and then placed under surveillance. Here in Century Island life ends when love begins." McPherson went out, shaking his head.

VII
THE FLIGHT FROM CENTURY

There was little sleep for Carrisford that night. The knowledge that Clio loved him was tempered by the fact that the president suspected at least the affection that existed between them. No doubt they had both displayed their feelings in their faces as they came through the arch into the garden of the court.

That Todd could build an airship that would carry them to Australia or South America he did not doubt. Two small ships were in service on the island, though their heavy storage batteries prohibited extended flights. With his magnifier this obstacle could be overcome. But there was still the question how to get word to Clio when the time should be ripe, for he did not doubt that she would be watched.

He was entirely unprepared for the placing of a guard upon his own movements. As he came from the group house the following morning a huge mute stood beside the gate and silently fell in behind Carrisford, following him to the laboratory and placing himself unobtrusively within the place.

Paying no attention to him, Carrisford went quietly about his work, with the assistance of the two helpers who had been assigned to him. It was nearly noon when the president came, as he had promised, to complete his inspection of the magnifier.

That he was impressed was easy to be seen. He followed carefully the working of the crude model Carrisford had constructed the previous day, and nodded approvingly.

"I should be sorry to see the work abruptly terminated," he said as he stood beside the door when the visit was over.

"I should share your regret," said Carrisford simply. "I will not pretend to misunderstand your meaning, sir. McPherson explained last night."

"It will soon pass," said Beardsley, with a confidence that he did not seem to feel. "Look," he went on, waving his hand to indicate the vast shops. "All of these are men and women who have at some time been in love. Now they are absorbed in their work and are far happier than they could ever be if married. Do you recall Pschever, Mr. Carrisford? He gave wonderful promise at one time, but he married, and the scientific world knew him no more."

"I met them," returned Carrisford. "He made a fortune from his inventions. He is supremely happy with his wife and children."

Beardsley's brow clouded.

"That is the trouble here," he cried— "the children. Had you seen what I have seen, Mr. Carrisford, you would understand better. The ordinary man leaves his sons and daughters as a heritage to the next generation. The scientist leaves his inventions. Few there are whose children are aught but imbeciles."

"I might suggest yourself as a notable exception," said Carrisford, with a dark smile.

"I married first," explained Beardsley. "Absorption in my work came after my wife died. That does not prove the rule, Mr. Carrisford. Let us not argue the matter further. The laws of Century Island were made by wiser men than you or I, and I am merely here to see that they are enforced— not to upset the structure so carefully reared."

He turned away abruptly and hurried along the esplanade. Carrisford went to the edge of the broad walk and looked down into the water. The mute came silently to the doorway and stood there watching him. Taylor Todd, hurrying along, passed him with a short nod.

"I will run in this afternoon," he said loudly enough for the mute to hear.

"I have the president's permission to call upon you for some technical advice."

"I shall be glad to give it," replied Carrisford.

"I have a plan for a new airship," Todd went on. "It promises to be a little more difficult than I anticipated, but I am confident of my ultimate success. I will bring in some drawings to show you."

He hurried on, and Carrisford returned to his work much cheered. The words had carried a secret meaning to him. It was evident that Todd was aware of the espionage in which Carrisford was held and sought to give him hope.

This belief became a fact when Todd came in late in the afternoon. He carried under his arm a roll of plans, and immediately launched into a long discussion of the ship he intended to construct.

"The worst of it is," he said briskly, "that I cannot get away from the weight of the storage batteries. Now, you will see from this table that a ship of these dimensions cannot carry more than sufficient current for twenty-four hours operation."

He laid the plan on the bench and took out a smaller sheet. It contained a table of weights of the various parts of the airship. One set of figures particularly interested Carrisford. They were:

Weight of motor	537
Weight of storage-battery	973
	———
	1,510

He laid the table down upon a bench close to an electric furnace, and as Carrisford studied it an additional table was revealed on the paper. It ran:

Weight of motor	537
Weight of batteries	320
Weight of magnifier	?
	———

About sixty pounds here," said Carrisford, "giving a leeway of five hundred and sixty-three pounds."

"Then I think we can make it all right," said Todd, with a smile of satisfaction, as he slipped into Carrisford's hand a note folded within a second one. He rolled up his plans, and with the promise of a visit on the morrow, bustled out of the place.

Carrisford could scarcely wait until he returned to his apartment to open and read the letters. The first was a note from Todd, explaining that it was his idea to keep the matter of the batteries a complete secret until such time as they were ready to put them to use. Meanwhile, Beardsley would feel assured that the ship could not sail away from the current base on the island.

The second enclosure was Clio's first love letter—a faltering little epistle, half shy, half unconsciously frank. Carrisford reread the note until the words seemed engraved upon his brain. Then he tore it into minute particles and carefully burned the fragments with the other note.

Clio wrote that she was being closely watched, but that Mme. Ferrers had asked for a letter, and had told her of their hopes. She warned Carrisford not to attempt to reply, but promised to be ready at the appointed time.

It was with a more quiet mind that Carrisford sought his couch, and he awoke in the morning with his mind refreshed. By nightfall his first large magnifier had been tested and found to work admirably, and he was hailed as a worthy citizen.

The manufacture of the magnifier was commenced upon a large scale, and in the interest aroused by this novelty Todd's new airship was entirely forgotten.

But Todd was working with feverish energy. A huge barn had been erected at the end of the esplanade, and in this the machine was rapidly assuming form. It was of the double aeroplane type, without a gasbag, depending entirely upon air resistance and the power of its motors to keep it at any desired altitude.

He kept in close touch with Carrisford, and together they secretly constructed the cell batteries and a huge magnifier that would yield one horsepower for each pair of cells. This was hidden in the barn under some boxes of tools, and the public test was made with the usual storage batteries.

Todd also laid in a stock of diamonds artificially produced for use in drills, but as large and perfect as the best stones from the South African mines. The intense heat developed by the furnaces permitted the fusing of several smaller stones into a single large one, and since they were regarded only as material for tools Todd had little trouble in obtaining all he wanted. Platinum was the precious metal of Century Island, and this alone was used for ornaments.

It was four months after Carrisford's arrival that plans were at last completed. Todd met Mme. Ferrers for a final conference, and Carrisford was with him. He had long since been relieved of the espionage of the mute, but he knew that Clio was still watched.

Mme. Ferrers was like a child in her glee at the prospect of delivery from her long imprisonment, and babbled incessantly of what she should do when they were in Paris. She struck up a quaint old-fashioned song that Carrisford remembered having heard years before. It was probably the rage when she left the earth for Century, and he smiled as he thought of the difference she would find in her beloved city.

But as her shrill voice rang out it attracted the attention of a company of mutes on their way into the city with farm products, and the captain of the little band penetrated the grove to investigate the cause of the disturbance.

As he pushed his way into the little glade where the three had met, Carrisford caught sight of him. At his cry Todd also sprang up. The two raced after the intruder, who had already started to run back to the road and his companions.

Laying about them with branches picked up in their rush, Carrisford and Todd soon laid out four of the slaves. The other two did not stop to fight, but started on a run for the city, and were soon beyond reach.

In the emergency, Carrisford took command. Mme. Ferrers had followed them to the road, and now he caught her arm.

"Run to the barn," he cried. "It is our only hope."

Todd caught the idea, and they ran swiftly down the smooth road to the barn, where the airship was stored. As they worked over the exchange from storage to cell battery, Mme. Ferrers loaded the lockers with water and the food tablets that were sometimes used in an emergency.

They had almost completed their task when they heard the soft noise of bare feet on the road outside, and realized that a company of mutes was being rushed to the scene.

At the same time the city lights flared up and people began to rush down to the esplanade. Todd tested the motor, and they all climbed in.

"Too bad we cannot get Miss Beardsley," said Todd. "We had best make a straight dash out to sea."

Carrisford caught his arm.

"We shall do nothing of the sort," he declared sternly. "We shall make for the palace."

For a moment they struggled desperately, but Carrisford was both stronger and more determined. He forced Todd away from the wheel, and with a whir they were out of the barn and circling in the air.

As the ship rose, it headed for the hill. In the bright light, Carrisford could see that the inhabitants of the Administration Building were gathered on the roof watching the disturbance. His eyes were unusually good, and before he was recognized he had already picked out the purple-fringed tunic that he knew to be Clio's.

She was standing apart from the others. With a skillful touch he steered the machine close to that part of the roof on which she stood, and almost before the others realized that Clio had not come out simply to investigate the cause of the disturbance, Carrisford had swung the girl aboard the ship and turned toward the sea.

Half a dozen mutes came running toward the aeroplane, and one, leaping high in air, caught the lower edge of the platform. Lying down upon the platform, Todd reached over and wrenched loose the man's grip. Relieved of the weight, the car shot forward.

Century did not depend upon firearms for defense. The waters for ten miles about were wired with floats to notify the inhabitants of the approach of a ship, and long before the belt of fog was penetrated, the submarine could destroy the intruder with a torpedo.

Only the smaller air-ships could offer chase, but as they passed the water gate they could see the crew of the submarine preparing to follow. Carrisford leaned over and shouted a farewell to McPherson, who was just descending the hatchway. In answer to the hail came the reply:

"Good-by, lad, if you do get away; but I'm hoping that we catch you yet."

Then the aeroplane rose higher, and with a wave of the hand toward the glittering city Carrisford turned to the motor, giving the wheel to Todd.

VIII
MCPHERSON TO THE RESCUE

For a few minutes Carrisford busied himself with the buzzing instruments. There had been no time for adjustment before the start, and the magnifier was working badly. But presently the machine ran more smoothly, and the aeroplane shot up in the air as a result of the increased power.

They were above the fog bank now and were driving rapidly northward. The glittering walls of the town on Century Island were still visible to the south, and Clio stood at the edge of the platform looking backward upon the only home she had known save for the dimly remembered London of her infancy. Her eyes filled with tears as she looked back upon the Administration Building, where she knew that her father must still be watching the flight.

Carrisford slipped his arm about her.

"Do you regret this step?" he asked softly.

For answer she flung her arms about his neck.

"No," she cried. "When I saw that the aeroplane had started without me I felt as though my heart would break. It is not that, but because I shall never see my father again. He is as one dead, even as all are on Century Island. It is horrible that we should be regarded as criminals, deserving of death, because we love each other."

"Many things are horrible, dear," he answered as he wrapped about her the toga which was slipped over the tunic in the evening. "But soon we shall come to a land where marriage is a sacred institution and not a crime."

"And we shall be happy while life lasts?" she demanded.

"So long as life shall last," he declared. "There will be much that is new to grow accustomed to, but it will all come in time."

"I shall have you," she whispered tenderly. "The rest will not matter. Is it not strange, dear, the change that has already come? From that moment when I fell upon the steps I have known that life was larger and more beautiful than I had ever realized."

"We have seen the last of the narrow life of science," he said, drawing her closer to him. Even as he spoke a shaft of light rent the fog, and Carrisford leaned over the rail.

McPherson had started his fog dispeller, and the powerful machine had bored a tunnel through the fog through which gleamed the ray of a searchlight. In the face of the dazzling rays they could barely make out the outline of the submarine, now steaming along the surface of the sea.

"They are trailing us to catch us when we fall," shouted Todd. "They know nothing of the batteries and think that with the storage machines we cannot keep up long enough to make land."

"We shall lead McPherson a merry chase," laughed Carrisford. "He will stick until we land, that's one thing certain."

"He won't get us," declared Todd grimly. "I once saw a man who had sought to escape. They brought him back, and for seven days he lingered, while all were compelled to look upon him and take to heart the lesson. At last."

He broke off, and, with a white face, pushed over the lever and mounted higher in the air. It was clear that he was not minded to be taken. Clio leaned over to Carrisford.

"You won't let them take me back, will you?" she whispered.

"No danger of that," he said, with a laugh. "This aeroplane will take us clear through to New York if we want to go. Look!" he added as he pointed to the east. "Here comes the sun. At least you will not have to freeze now."

They had passed the fog belt, and now they could see the submarine slipping through the water directly underneath. McPherson sat on the tiny deck smoking his pipe, and as he caught sight of some one leaning over the rail he waved a good morning salute. Carrisford replied and turned his attention to the wheel, while Todd got out the food wafers.

It was a scanty breakfast at best, but Mme. Ferrers enlivened the meal by planning her first dinner in a Paris restaurant. At last Carrisford laughingly begged her to stop.

"I should be content with ham and eggs," he declared as he munched the tasteless compound of elements. "If you talk of truffled capon I shall certainly lose what little appetite I have for this scientific breakfast food."

"It will only be for a couple of days," said Todd. "We are heading pretty straight for New Zealand. We can do about five hundred and fifty miles a day, and it is about fourteen hundred miles away."

"It will surprise the New Zealanders to see us come fluttering down," said Mme. Ferrers.

"I hope they do not see us," said Carrisford. "I do not want to divulge the secret of Century Island, and it will be enough to explain our costumes without adding to our troubles with an airship. I propose to set the machinery in motion and let it fly off. It will be lost in the sea with no one to control it, and of course the metal will sink. It is different from a gas balloon."

"That is well," declared Mme. Ferrers, "but, *mon ami*, what of the jewels? Suppose that we have to disembark hurriedly?"

"Let's divide them now," proposed Todd. "Then we can each carry our share and dispose of just enough of them to take us to a place where we can sell them to advantage."

Clio packed the breakfast dishes away, and Todd brought out the bag and divided the jewels into four equal parts. These he tied up in portions of his toga, and each of the quartet fastened one portion about the body. Carrisford lay down to get some rest while Todd took the wheel again, and Mme. Ferrers and Clio curled up in the corner opposite Carrisford.

It seemed to Carrisford that he had been sleeping but a few minutes when Todd's voice wakened him. The sky was black as he opened his eyes.

"Is it night already?" he asked. "I thought that you were to call me in four hours."

"It's only about nine o'clock," explained Todd; "but we are running into a thunderstorm."

Clio had roused herself at the sound of Carrisford's name, and now her terrified cry awoke Mme. Ferrers. The two women, clasped in each other's arms, huddled in their corner, while Carrisford, with ashen face, bent over the motor. The machinery was so delicate that he feared that the natural electrical current might disarrange the magnifier. In such a case the puny batteries could not keep the propeller revolving, and they would inevitably be pitched into the sea.

The driving clouds came rushing toward them, and Todd let the aeroplane sink a little, for there were vivid flashes as the electricity shot from one cloud to another. Lower down it was barely possible that they might escape.

Lower and lower he sank, until they could almost feel the spray from the storm-tossed waters, and the submarine was clearly in view. The hatch was battened down, and the boat was struggling through the buffeting waves at slow speed. McPherson stood on the deck clinging to the railing and anxiously watching the aeroplane, now a little to the rear.

Presently the rain began to fall in torrents, great sheets of water driving into their faces, so that Todd could scarcely see to steer. Only through the compass was he able to keep his head to the storm, and as the wind beat against the inclined planes the aeroplane rose steadily upward, darting into the teeth of the gale like some huge albatross. The submarine would not have been able to keep up with them had it not been for the fact that the great masses of rain hammered down the surface of the sea.

Carrisford gave no heed to the storm. He was bending over the magnifier, adjusting the instrument, as the electrical waves threw it out of order, when a shout of encouragement from Todd caused him to look up. Far in the west the sky was lighter, a promise that the storm had nearly passed.

At that moment there was a blinding flash, a crackling noise, followed by a deafening reverberation, and Carrisford staggered back. A small bolt had struck the knobs of the magnifier, and the instrument was shattered, while the motor itself was burned out.

Half blinded by the flash, Carrisford staggered toward the corner where he knew Clio to be. As the aeroplane trembled and pitched forward he caught the girl in his arms.

"Small danger of going back to Century Island," he whispered. "The sea will end it all in a few moments."

"I am not afraid," said the girl bravely. "I die with you."

For an instant she pressed her lips against his, and, then, with a tremendous splash, the aeroplane struck the water.

Todd had adjusted the planes to break their fall as much as possible, and they were not carried very far under water. As they rose to the surface, Carrisford struck out, and presently he encountered an obstacle. Surprised that the aeroplane should be floating, he looked up. McPherson's huge hand grasped his collar, and in another moment the Scotchman had dragged Carrisford and his sweetheart on board.

They were passed down the hatch while McPherson rescued Mme. Ferrers. Todd had gone down with the aeroplane, and though they cruised about for an hour they could find no trace of him.

"It's no use," sighed McPherson at last. "He must have become tangled in the wires. Let's get under water, where it will be easier going."

He closed the hatch, and presently the pitching ceased as the boat sank beneath the waves. They sank as far as it was safe, but no sign of the aeroplane could they see in the murky depths. At last McPherson gave the command to go ahead.

"It is a pity that you did not let us drown with Todd," said Carrisford bitterly. "Better that than the tortures to which we are doomed."

McPherson turned, with the bottle from which he had been administering stimulant to the rescued ones still in his hand.

"Gren, lad," he said solemnly, "we did not find ye. There's only Graves and me aboard. Hawley did not get down to the dock in time. We decided hours ago that we would let you all drown if you should fall; but we've been good friends, lad, and I couldn't stand and see ye die."

"You mean—" Carrisford sprang from his chair.

"Ye all are dead," said McPherson solemnly. "We followed you until you all dropped into the sea, and then we turned and went home."

"And you won't take us back?" cried Clio. "Oh, it seems too good to be true."

"But it is true," said McPherson kindly. "Carrisford, here, is a fine man. It would be a shame to hold you down to the dry life of the island. You two were not made for science, but for love. I loved once, before I turned to science. I was happy for a little while. I pay that happiness back to you."

He took Clio's hand and placed it within Carrisford's.

"Take her, boy. Cherish her, and sometimes, in your happiness, think kindly of old Fergus McPherson."

With his left hand Carrisford clasped the other's.

"Won't you come with us, Fergus?" he pleaded. "Come and be happy again in the earth world."

The Scotchman shook his head, though his eyes grew wistful. "I'm too old to go back," he said. "Love is not for us old fellows. It is better that I should stay."

The following night the submarine crept up on the south coast of New Zealand. When the boat beached, McPherson walked with them to the shore.

"Ivercargill lies over there," he said, pointing to the west. "Get some civilized things before you get there. Work your way along the coast to Auckland. Don't go to Wellington, where our agent is. At Auckland you can get a steamer to Australia, and then—home."

His voice lingered over the last word, and for a moment the kindly eyes grew moist.

"You will need some money," he went on. "You cannot sell those diamonds in New Zealand."

He drew a bag from his tunic and handed it to Carrisford.

"That will see you through," he said. "It's the money that was left in the clothes of the new colonists. No one ever thought of the coins, and we just let them lie about the boat."

"You seem to have thought of everything," said Carrisford gratefully.

"Hush," was the embarrassed reply. "Can't you see that it's to my interest to keep you from being discovered. If word was to get back that three people in outlandish dresses were trying to sell diamonds, it would spoil the story I am going to tell in Century. And now, good-by, lad. Think well of an old man who thinks a lot of you, and be good to the lassie."

"That I will," promised Carrisford. "Won't you come with us, Fergus?"

"It's not for me," repeated McPherson. "Out with you for tempting an old man."

He wrung Carrisford's hand, and then turned to Clio and kissed her on the forehead. He shook hands with Mme. Ferrers, and caught Carrisford's hand again.

With a hungry look, he stepped back into the water to wade out to the submarine, but once more he turned back and beckoned Carrisford.

"If you're thinking of taking a wedding trip," he whispered, "Scotland's a bonny country. Take her there and think of old Fergus."

Introduction to The Isle of Voices

Robert Louis Stevenson (1850-1894) is best known for his ground-breaking contributions to the development of adventure fiction and the modern horror genre. Works such as *Treasure Island* (1883), *Kidnapped* (1886), and *The Strange Case of Dr. Jekyll and Mr. Hyde* (1886) are all now considered seminal works in English literature. Born in Edinburgh, Scotland, Stevenson long suffered from health problems that he attributed to the local climate. This was why he sought out a life in the South Seas, eventually living there and dying in Samoa at the age of forty-four.

Originally published in *Island Nights' Entertainment* (1893) "The Isle of Voices," is a work of short fiction that demonstrates Stevenson's knowledge of, and appreciation for, Polynesian culture. Unraveling like a fairy tale written for adults, "The Isle of Voices" is a strange island story that evokes in the reader a sense of both exoticism and resplendent wonder. Set in the Hawaiian Islands, Stevenson's tale traverses the realms of dark fantasy and folklore, all the while telling an exciting story about a man forced into a confrontation with the supernatural. As the reader shall soon learn, the titular isle of voices is a strange place indeed.

THE ISLE OF VOICES
Robert Louis Stevenson

Keola was married with Lehua, daughter of Kalamake, the wise man of Molokai, and he kept his dwelling with the father of his wife. There was no man more cunning than that prophet; he read the stars, he could divine by the bodies of the dead, and by the means of evil creatures: he could go alone into the highest parts of the mountain, into the region of the hobgoblins, and there he would lay snares to entrap the spirits of the ancient.

For this reason no man was more consulted in all the Kingdom of Hawaii. Prudent people bought, and sold, and married, and laid out their lives by his counsels; and the King had him twice to Kona to seek the treasures of Kamehameha. Neither was any man more feared: of his enemies, some had dwindled in sickness by the virtue of his incantations, and some had been spirited away, the life and the clay both, so that folk looked in vain for so much as a bone of their bodies. It was rumored that he had the art or the gift of the old heroes. Men had seen him at night upon the mountains, stepping from one cliff to the next; they had seen him walking in the high forest, and his head and shoulders were above the trees.

This Kalamake was a strange man to see. He was come of the best blood in Molokai and Maui, of a pure descent; and yet he was more white to look upon than any foreigner: his hair the colour of dry grass, and his eyes red and very blind, so that "Blind as Kalamake, that can see across tomorrow," was a byword in the islands.

Of all these doings of his father-in-law, Keola knew a little by the common repute, a little more he suspected, and the rest he ignored. But there was one thing troubled him. Kalamake was a man that spared for nothing, whether to eat or to drink, or to wear; and for all he paid in bright new dollars. "Bright as Kalamake's dollars," was another saying in the Eight Isles. Yet he neither sold, nor planted, nor took hire—only now and then from his sorceries—and there was no source conceivable for so much silver coin.

It chanced one day Keola's wife was gone upon a visit to Kaunakakai, on the lee side of the island, and the men were forth at the sea fishing. But Keola was an idle dog, and he lay in the veranda and watched the surf beat on the shore and the birds fly about the cliff. It was a chief thought with him always—the thought of the bright dollars. When he lay down to bed he would be wondering why they were so many, and when he woke at morn he would be wondering why they were all new; and the thing was never absent from his mind. But this day of all days he made sure in his heart of some discovery. For it seems he had observed the place where Kalamake kept his treasure, which was a lock-fast desk against the parlour wall, under the print of Kamehameha the Fifth, and a photograph of Queen Victoria with her crown; and it seems again that, no later than the night before, he found occasion to look in, and behold! the bag lay there empty. And this was the day of the steamer; he could see her smoke off Kalaupapa; and she must soon arrive with a month's goods, tinned salmon and gin, and all manner of rare luxuries for Kalamake.

"Now if he can pay for his goods today," Keola thought, "I shall know for certain that the man is a warlock, and the dollars come out of the Devil's pocket."

While he was so thinking, there was his father-in-law behind him, looking vexed.

"Is that the steamer?" he asked.

"Yes," said Keola. "She has but to call at Pelekunu, and then she will be here."

"There is no help for it then," returned Kalamake, "and I must take you in my confidence, Keola, for the lack of anyone better. Come here within the house."

So they stepped together into the parlor, which was a very fine room, papered and hung with prints, and furnished with a rocking chair, and a table and a sofa in the European style. There was a shelf of books besides, and a family Bible in the midst of the table, and the lock-fast writing desk against the wall; so that anyone could see it was the house of a man of substance.

Kalamake made Keola close the shutters of the windows, while he himself locked all the doors and set open the lid of the desk. From this he brought forth a pair of necklaces hung with charms and shells, a bundle of dried herbs, and the dried leaves of trees, and a green branch of palm.

"What I am about," said he, "is a thing beyond wonder. The men of old were wise; they wrought marvels, and this among the rest; but that was at night, in the dark, under the fit stars and in the desert. The same will I do here in my own house and under the plain eye of day."

So saying, he put the Bible under the cushion of the sofa so that it was all covered, brought out from the same place a mat of a wonderfully fine texture, and heaped the herbs and leaves on sand in a tin pan. And then he and Keola put on the necklaces and took their stand upon the opposite corners of the mat.

"The time comes," said the warlock, "be not afraid."

With that he set flame to the herbs, and began to mutter and wave the branch of palm. At first the light was dim because of the closed shutters;

but the herbs caught strongly afire, and the flames beat upon Keola, and the room glowed with the burning; and next the smoke rose and made his head swim and his eyes darken, and the sound of Kalamake muttering ran in his ears. And suddenly, to the mat on which they were standing came a snatch or twitch, that seemed to be more swift than lightning. In the same wink the room was gone and the house, the breath all beaten from Keola's body. Volumes of light rolled upon his eyes and head, and he found himself transported to a beach of the sea under a strong sun, with a great surf roaring: he and the warlock standing there on the same mat, speechless, gasping and grasping at one another, and passing their hands before their eyes.

"What was this?" cried Keola, who came to himself the first, because he was the younger. "The pang of it was like death."

"It matters not," panted Kalamake. "It is now done."

"And, in the name of God, where are we?" cried Keola.

"That is not the question," replied the sorcerer. "Being here, we have matter in our hands, and that we must attend to. Go, while I recover my breath, into the borders of the wood, and bring me the leaves of such and such a herb, and such and such a tree, which you will find to grow there plentifully—three handfuls of each. And be speedy. We must be home again before the steamer comes; it would seem strange if we had disappeared."

And he sat on the sand and panted.

Keola went up the beach, which was of shining sand and coral, strewn with singular shells; and he thought in his heart:

"How do I not know this beach? I will come here again and gather shells."

In front of him was a line of palms against the sky; not like the palms of the Eight Islands, but tall and fresh and beautiful, and hanging out withered fans like gold among the green, and he thought in his heart:

"It is strange I should not have found this grove. I will come here again, when it is warm, to sleep." And he thought, "How warm it has grown suddenly!" For it was winter in Hawaii, and the day had been chill. And he thought also, "Where are the grey mountains? And where is the high cliff with the hanging forest and the wheeling birds?" And the more he considered, the less he might conceive in what quarter of the islands he was fallen.

In the border of the grove, where it met the beach, the herb was growing, but the tree further back. Now, as Keola went toward the tree, he was aware of a young woman who had nothing on her body but a belt of leaves.

"Well!" thought Keola, "they are not very particular about their dress in this part of the country."

And he paused, supposing she would observe him and escape; and seeing that she still looked before her, stood and hummed aloud. Up she leaped at the sound. Her face was ashen; she looked this way and that, and her mouth gaped with the terror of her soul. But it was a strange thing that her eyes did not rest upon Keola.

"Good day," said he. "You need not be so frightened; I will not eat you."

And he had scarce opened his mouth before the young woman fled into the bush.

"These are strange manners," thought Keola. And, not thinking what he did, ran after her.

As she ran, the girl kept crying in some speech that was not practiced in Hawaii, yet some of the words were the same, and he knew she kept calling and warning others. And presently he saw more people running—men, women and children, one with another, all running and crying like people at a fire. And with that he began to grow afraid himself, and returned to Kalamake bringing the leaves. Him he told what he had seen.

"You must pay no heed," said Kalamake. "All this is like a dream and shadows. All will disappear and be forgotten."

"It seemed none saw me," said Keola.

"And none did," replied the sorcerer. "We walk here in the broad sun invisible by reason of these charms. Yet they hear us; and therefore it is well to speak softly, as I do."

With that he made a circle round the mat with stones, and in the midst he set the leaves.

"It will be your part," said he, "to keep the leaves alight, and feed the fire slowly. While they blaze (which is but for a little moment) I must do my errand; and before the ashes blacken, the same power that brought us carries us away. Be ready now with the match; and do you call me in good time lest the flames burn out and I be left."

As soon as the leaves caught, the sorcerer leaped like a deer out of the circle, and began to race along the beach like a hound that has been bathing. As he ran, he kept stooping to snatch shells; and it seemed to Keola that they glittered as he took them. The leaves blazed with a clear flame that consumed them swiftly; and presently Keola had but a handful left, and the sorcerer was far off, running and stopping.

"Back!" cried Keola. "Back! The leaves are near done."

At that Kalamake turned, and if he had run before, now he flew. But fast as he ran, the leaves burned faster. The flame was ready to expire when, with a great leap, he bounded on the mat. The wind of his leaping blew it out; and with that the beach was gone, and the sun and the sea, and they stood once more in the dimness of the shuttered parlor, and were once more shaken and blinded; and on the mat betwixt them lay a pile of shining dollars. Keola ran to the shutters; and there was the steamer tossing in the swell close in.

The same night Kalamake took his son-in-law apart, and gave him five dollars in his hand.

"Keola," said he, "if you are a wise man (which I am doubtful of) you will think you slept this afternoon on the veranda, and dreamed as you were sleeping. I am a man of few words, and I have for my helpers people of short memories."

Never a word more said Kalamake, nor referred again to that affair. But it ran all the while in Keola's head—if he were lazy before, he would now do nothing.

"Why should I work," thought he, "when I have a father-in-law who makes dollars of sea-shells?"

Presently his share was spent. He spent it all upon fine clothes. And then he was sorry:

"For," thought he, "I had done better to have bought a concertina, with which I might have entertained myself all day long."

And then he began to grow vexed with Kalamake.

"This man has the soul of a dog," thought he. "He can gather dollars when he pleases on the beach, and he leaves me to pine for a concertina! Let him beware: I am no child, I am as cunning as he, and hold his secret." With that he spoke to his wife Lehua, and complained of her father's manners.

"I would let my father be," said Lehua. "He is a dangerous man to cross."

"I care that for him!" cried Keola; and snapped his fingers. "I have him by the nose. I can make him do what I please." And he told Lehua the story.

But she shook her head.

"You may do what you like," said she; "but as sure as you thwart my father, you will be no more heard of. Think of this person, and that person; think of Hua, who was a noble of the House of Representatives, and went to Honolulu every year; and not a bone or a hair of him was found. Remember Kamau, and how he wasted to a thread, so that his wife lifted him with one hand. Keola, you are a baby in my father's hands; he will take you with his thumb and finger and eat you like a shrimp."

Now Keola was truly afraid of Kalamake, but he was vain too; and these words of his wife's incensed him.

"Very well," said he, "if that is what you think of me, I will show how much you are deceived."

And he went straight to where his father-in-law was sitting in the parlor.

"Kalamake," said he, "I want a concertina."

"Do you, indeed?" said Kalamake.

"Yes," said he, "and I may as well tell you plainly, I mean to have it. A man who picks up dollars on the beach can certainly afford a concertina."

"I had no idea you had so much spirit," replied the sorcerer. "I thought you were a timid, useless lad, and I cannot describe how much pleased I am to find I was mistaken. Now I begin to think I may have found an assistant and successor in my difficult business. A concertina? You shall have the best in Honolulu. And tonight, as soon as it is dark, you and I will go and find the money."

"Shall we return to the beach?" asked Keola.

"No, no!" replied Kalamake; "you must begin to learn more of my secrets. Last time I taught you to pick shells; this time I shall teach you to catch fish. Are you strong enough to launch Pili's boat?"

"I think I am," returned Keola. "But why should we not take your own, which is afloat already?"

"I have a reason which you will understand thoroughly before tomorrow," said Kalamake. "Pili's boat is the better suited for my purpose. So, if you please, let us meet there as soon as it is dark; and in the meanwhile, let us keep our own counsel, for there is no cause to let the family into our business."

Honey is not more sweet than was the voice of Kalamake, and Keola could scarce contain his satisfaction.

"I might have had my concertina weeks ago," thought he, "and there is nothing needed in this world but a little courage."

Presently after he spied Lehua weeping, and was half in a mind to tell her all was well.

"But no," thinks he; "I shall wait till I can show her the concertina; we shall see what the chit will do then. Perhaps she will understand in the future that her husband is a man of some intelligence."

As soon as it was dark father and son-in-law launched Pili's boat and set the sail. There was a great sea, and it blew strong from the leeward; but the boat was swift and light and dry, and skimmed the waves. The wizard had a lantern, which he lit and held with his finger through the ring; and the two sat in the stern and smoked cigars, of which Kalamake had always a provision, and spoke like friends of magic and the great sums of money which they could make by its exercise, and what they should buy first, and what second; and Kalamake talked like a father.

Presently he looked all about, and above him at the stars, and back at the island, which was already three parts sunk under the sea, and he seemed to consider ripely his position.

"Look!" says he, "there is Molokai already far behind us, and Maui like a cloud; and by the bearing of these three stars I know I am come where I desire. This part of the sea is called the Sea of the Dead. It is in this place extraordinarily deep, and the floor is all covered with the bones of men, and in the holes of this part gods and goblins keep their habitation. The flow of the sea is to the north, stronger than a shark can swim, and any man who shall here be thrown out of a ship it bears away like a wild horse into the uttermost ocean. Presently he is spent and goes down, and his bones are scattered with the rest, and the gods devour his spirit."

Fear came on Keola at the words, and he looked, and by the light of the stars and the lantern, the warlock seemed to change.

"What ails you?" cried Keola, quick and sharp.

"It is not I who am ailing," said the wizard; "but there is one here very sick."

With that he changed his grasp upon the lantern, and, behold! as he drew his finger from the ring, the finger stuck and the ring was burst, and his hand was grown to be of the bigness of three.

At that sight Keola screamed and covered his face.

But Kalamake held up the lantern.

"Look rather at my face!" said he.

And his head was huge as a barrel; and still he grew and grew as a cloud grows on a mountain, and Keola sat before him screaming, and the boat raced on the great seas.

"And now," said the wizard, "what do you think about that concertina? and are you sure you would not rather have a flute? No?" says he; "that is well, for I do not like my family to be changeable of purpose. But I begin to think I had better get out of this paltry boat, for my bulk swells to a very unusual degree, and if we are not the more careful, she will presently be swamped."

With that he threw his legs over the side. Even as he did so, the greatness of the man grew thirty-fold and forty-fold as swift as sight or thinking, so that he stood in the deep seas to the armpits, and his head and shoulders rose like a high isle, and the swell beat and burst upon his bosom, as it beats and breaks against a cliff. The boat ran still to the north, but he reached out his hand, and took the gunwale by the finger and thumb, and broke the side like a biscuit, and Keola was spilled into the sea. And the pieces of the boat the sorcerer crushed in the hollow of his hand and flung miles away into the night.

"Excuse me taking the lantern," said he; "for I have a long wade before me, and the land is far, and the bottom of the sea uneven, and I feel the bones under my toes."

And he turned and went off walking with great strides; and as often as Keola sank in the trough he could see him no longer; but as often as he was heaved upon the crest, there he was striding and dwindling, and he held the lamp high over his head, and the waves broke white about him as he went.

Since first the islands were fished out of the sea, there was never a man so terrified as this Keola. He swam indeed, but he swam as puppies swim when they are cast in to drown, and knew not wherefore. He could but think of the hugeness of the swelling of the warlock, of that face which was great as a mountain, of those shoulders that were broad as an isle, and of the seas that beat on them in vain. He thought, too, of the concertina, and shame took hold upon him; and of the dead men's bones, and fear shook him.

Of a sudden he was aware of something dark against the stars that tossed, and a light below, and a brightness of the cloven sea; and he heard speech of men. He cried out aloud and a voice answered; and in a twinkling the bows of a ship hung above him on a wave like a thing balanced, and swooped down. He caught with his two hands in the chains of her, and the next moment was buried in the rushing seas, and the next hauled on board by seamen.

They gave him gin and biscuit and dry clothes, and asked him how he came where they found him, and whether the light which they had seen was the lighthouse, Lae o Ka Laau. But Keola knew white men are like children and only believe their own stories; so about himself he told them what he pleased, and as for the light (which was Kalamake's lantern) he vowed he had seen none.

This ship was a schooner bound for Honolulu, and then to trade in the low islands; and by a very good chance for Keola she had lost a man off the bowsprit in a squall. It was no use talking. Keola durst not stay in the Eight Islands. Word goes so quickly, and all men are so fond to talk and carry news, that if he hid in the north end of Kauai or in the south end of Kau, the wizard would have wind of it before a month, and he must perish. So he did what seemed the most prudent, and shipped sailor in the place of the man who had been drowned.

In some ways the ship was a good place. The food was extraordinarily rich and plenty, with biscuits and salt beef every day, and pea-soup and puddings made of flour and suet twice a week, so that Keola grew fat. The captain also was a good man, and the crew no worse than other whites. The trouble was the mate, who was the most difficult man to please Keola had ever met with, and beat and cursed him daily, both for what he did and what he did not. The blows that he dealt were very sore, for he was strong; and the words he used were very unpalatable, for Keola was come of a good family and accustomed to respect. And what was the worst of all, whenever Keola found a chance to sleep, there was the mate awake and stirring him up with a rope's end. Keola saw it would never do; and he made up his mind to run away.

They were about a month out from Honolulu when they made the land. It was a fine starry night, the sea was smooth as well as the sky fair; it blew a steady trade; and there was the island on their weather bow, a ribbon of palm trees lying flat along the sea. The captain and the mate looked at it with the night glass, and named the name of it, and talked of it, beside the wheel where Keola was steering. It seemed it was an isle where no traders came. By the captain's way, it was an isle besides where no man dwelt; but the mate thought otherwise.

"I don't give a cent for the directory," said he, "I've been past here one night in the schooner *Eugenie*: it was just such a night as this; they were fishing with torches, and the beach was thick with lights like a town."

"Well, well," says the captain, "it's steep-to, that's the great point; and there ain't any outlying dangers by the chart, so we'll just hug the lee side of it. Keep her ramping full, don't I tell you!" he cried to Keola, who was listening so hard that he forgot to steer.

And the mate cursed him, and swore that Kanaka was for no use in the world, and if he got started after him with a belaying pin, it would be a cold day for Keola.

And so the captain and mate lay down on the house together, and Keola was left to himself.

"This island will do very well for me," he thought; "if no traders deal there, the mate will never come. And as for Kalamake, it is not possible he can ever get as far as this."

With that he kept edging the schooner nearer in. He had to do this quietly, for it was the trouble with these white men, and above all with the mate, that you could never be sure of them; they would all be sleeping sound, or else pretending, and if a sail shook, they would jump to their feet and fall on you with a rope's end. So Keola edged her up little by little, and kept all drawing. And presently the land was close on board, and the sound of the sea on the sides of it grew loud.

With that, the mate sat up suddenly upon the house.

"What are you doing?" he roars. "You'll have the ship ashore!"

And he made one bound for Keola, and Keola made another clean over the rail and plump into the starry sea. When he came up again, the schooner had paid off on her true course, and the mate stood by the wheel himself, and Keola heard him cursing. The sea was smooth under the lee of the island; it was warm besides, and Keola had his sailor's knife, so he had no fear of sharks. A little way before him the trees stopped; there was a break in the line of the land like the mouth of a harbor; and the tide, which was then flowing, took him up and carried him through. One minute he was without, and the next within: had floated there in a wide shallow water, bright with ten thousand stars, and all about him was the ring of the land, with its string of palm trees. And he was amazed, because this was a kind of island he had never heard of.

The time of Keola in that place was in two periods—the period when he was alone, and the period when he was there with the tribe. At first he sought everywhere and found no man; only some houses standing in a hamlet, and the marks of fires. But the ashes of the fires were cold and the rains had washed them away; and the winds had blown, and some of the huts were overthrown. It was here he took his dwelling, and he made a fire drill, and a shell hook, and fished and cooked his fish, and climbed after green coconuts, the juice of which he drank, for in all the isle there was no water. The days were long to him, and the nights terrifying. He made a lamp of cocoshell, and drew the oil of the ripe nuts, and made a wick of fiber; and when evening came he closed up his hut, and lit his lamp, and lay and trembled till morning. Many a time he thought in his heart he would have been better in the bottom of the sea, his bones rolling there with the others.

All this while he kept by the inside of the island, for the huts were on the shore of the lagoon, and it was there the palms grew best, and the lagoon itself abounded with good fish. And to the outer side he went once only, and he looked but the once at the beach of the ocean, and came away shaking. For the look of it, with its bright sand, and strewn shells, and strong sun and surf, went sore against his inclination.

"It cannot be," he thought, "and yet it is very like. And how do I know? These white men, although they pretend to know where they are sailing, must take their chance like other people. So that after all we may have sailed in a circle, and I may be quite near to Molokai, and this may be the very beach where my father-in-law gathers his dollars."

So after that he was prudent, and kept to the land side.

It was perhaps a month later, when the people of the place arrived—the fill of six great boats. They were a fine race of men, and spoke a tongue that sounded very different from the tongue of Hawaii, but so many of the words were the same that it was not difficult to understand. The men besides were very courteous, and the women very towardly; and they made Keola welcome, and built him a house, and gave him a wife; and what surprised him the most, he was never sent to work with the young men.

And now Keola had three periods. First he had a period of being very sad, and then he had a period when he was pretty merry. Last of all came the third, when he was the most terrified man in the four oceans.

The cause of the first period was the girl he had to wife. He was in doubt about the island, and he might have been in doubt about the speech, of which he had heard so little when he came there with the wizard on the mat. But about his wife there was no mistake conceivable, for she was the same girl that ran from him crying in the wood. So he had sailed all this way, and might as well have stayed in Molokai; and had left home and wife and all his friends for no other cause but to escape his enemy, and the place he had come to was that wizard's hunting ground, and the shore where he walked invisible. It was at this period when he kept the most close to the lagoon side, and as far as he dared, abode in the cover of his hut.

The cause of the second period was talk he heard from his wife and the chief islanders. Keola himself said little. He was never so sure of his new friends, for he judged they were too civil to be wholesome, and since he had grown better acquainted with his father-in-law the man had grown more cautious. So he told them nothing of himself, but only his name and descent, and that he came from the Eight Islands, and what fine islands they were; and about the king's palace in Honolulu, and how he was a chief friend of the king and the missionaries. But he put many questions and learned much.

The island where he was was called the Isle of Voices; it belonged to the tribe, but they made their home upon another, three hours' sail to the southward. There they lived and had their permanent houses, and it was a rich island, where were eggs and chickens and pigs, and ships came trading with rum and tobacco. It was there the schooner had gone after Keola deserted; there, too, the mate had died, like the fool of a white man as he was. It seems, when the ship came, it was the beginning of the sickly season in that isle, when the fish of the lagoon are poisonous, and all who eat of them swell up and die. The mate was told of it; he saw the boats preparing, because in that season the people leave that island and sail to the Isle of Voices; but he was a fool of a white man, who would believe no stories but his own, and he caught one of these fish, cooked it and ate it, and swelled up and died, which was good news to Keola.

As for the Isle of Voices, it lay solitary the most part of the year; only now and then a boat's crew came for copra, and in the bad season, when the fish at the main isle were poisonous, the tribe dwelt there in a body. It had its name from a marvel, for it seemed the seaside of it was all beset with invisible devils; day and night you heard them talking one with another in strange tongues; day and night little fires blazed up and were extinguished on the beach; and what was the cause of these doings no man might conceive.

Keola asked them if it were the same in their own island where they stayed, and they told him no, not there; nor yet in any other of some hundred isles that lay all about them in that sea; but it was a thing peculiar to the Isle of Voices. They told him also that these fires and voices were ever on the seaside and in the seaward fringes of the wood, and a man might dwell by the lagoon two thousand years (if he could live so long) and never be any way troubled; and even on the seaside the devils did no harm if let alone. Only once a chief had cast a spear at one of the voices, and the same night he fell out of a coconut palm and was killed.

Keola thought a good bit with himself. He saw he would be all right when the tribe returned to the main island, and right enough where he was, if he kept by the lagoon, yet he had a mind to make things righter if he could. So he told the high chief he had once been in an isle that was pestered the same way, and the folk had found a means to cure that trouble.

"There was a tree growing in the bush there," says he, "and it seems these devils came to get the leaves of it. So the people of the isle cut down the tree wherever it was found, and the devils came no more."

They asked what kind of tree this was, and he showed them the tree of which Kalamake burned the leaves. They found it hard to believe, yet the idea tickled them. Night after night the old men debated it in their councils, but the high chief (though he was a brave man) was afraid of the matter, and reminded them daily of the chief who cast a spear against the voices and was killed, and the thought of that brought all to a stand again.

Though he could not yet bring about the destruction of the trees, Keola was well enough pleased, and began to look about him and take pleasure in his days; and, among other things, he was the kinder to his wife, so that the girl began to love him greatly. One day he came to the hut, and she lay on the ground lamenting.

"Why," said Keola, "what is wrong with you now?"

She declared it was nothing.

The same night she woke him. The lamp burned very low, but he saw by her face she was in sorrow.

"Keola," she said, "put your ear to my mouth that I may whisper, for no one must hear us. Two days before the boats begin to be got ready, go you to the seaside of the isle and lie in a thicket. We shall choose that place before-hand, you and I; and hide food; and every night I shall come near by there singing. So when a night comes and you do not hear me, you shall know we are clean gone out of the island, and you may come forth again in safety."

The soul of Keola died within him.

"What is this?" he cried. "I cannot live among devils. I will not be left behind upon this isle. I am dying to leave it."

"You will never leave it alive, my poor Keola," said the girl; "for to tell you the truth, my people are eaters of men; but this they keep secret. And the reason they will kill you before we leave is because in our island ships come, and Donat-Kimaran comes and talks for the French, and there is a white trader there in a house with a veranda, and a catechist. Oh, that is a fine place indeed! The trader has barrels filled with flour, and a French warship once came in the lagoon and gave everybody wine and biscuit. Ah, my poor Keola, I wish I could take you there, for great is my love to you, and it is the finest place in the seas except Papeete."

So now Keola was the most terrified man in the four oceans. He had heard tell of eaters of men in the south islands, and the thing had always been a fear to him; and here it was knocking at his door. He had heard besides, by travellers, of their practices, and how when they are in a mind to eat a man, they cherish and fondle him like a mother with a favorite baby. And he saw this must be his own case; and that was why he had been housed, and fed, and wived, and liberated from all work; and why the old men and the chiefs discoursed with him like a person of weight. So he lay on his bed and railed upon his destiny; and the flesh curdled on his bones.

The next day the people of the tribe were very civil, as their way was. They were elegant speakers, and they made beautiful poetry, and jested at meals, so that a missionary must have died laughing. It was little enough Keola cared for their fine ways; all he saw was the white teeth shining in their mouths, and his gorge rose at the sight; and when they were done eating, he went and lay in the bush like a dead man.

The next day it was the same, and then his wife followed him.

"Keola," she said, "if you do not eat, I tell you plainly you will be killed and cooked tomorrow. Some of the old chiefs are murmuring already. They think you are fallen sick and must lose flesh."

With that Keola got to his feet, and anger burned in him.

"It is little I care one way or the other," said he. "I am between the devil and the deep sea. Since die I must, let me die the quickest way; and since I must be eaten at the best of it, let me rather be eaten by hobgoblins than by men. Farewell," said he, and he left her standing, and walked to the seaside of that island.

It was all bare in the strong sun; there was no sign of man, only the beach was trodden, and all about him as he went, the voices talked and whispered, and the little fires sprang up and burned down. All tongues of the earth were spoken there; the French, the Dutch, the Russian, the Tamil, the Chinese. Whatever land knew sorcery, there were some of its people whispering in Keola's ear. That beach was thick as a cried fair, yet no man seen; and as he walked he saw the shells vanish before him, and no man to pick them up. I think the devil would have been afraid to be alone in such a company; but Keola was past fear and courted death. When the fires sprang up, he charged for them like a bull. Bodiless voices called to and fro; unseen hands poured sand upon the flames; and they were gone from the beach before he reached them.

"It is plain Kalamake is not here," he thought, "or I must have been killed long since."

With that he sat him down in the margin of the wood, for he was tired, and put his chin upon his hands. The business before his eyes continued: the beach babbled with voices, and the fires sprang up and sank, and the shells vanished and were renewed again even while he looked.

"It was a by-day when I was here before," he thought, "for it was nothing to this."

And his head was dizzy with the thought of these millions and millions of dollars, and all these hundreds and hundreds of persons culling them upon the beach and flying in the air higher and swifter than eagles.

"And to think how they have fooled me with their talk of mints," says he, "and that money was made there, when it is clear that all the new coin in all the world is gathered on these sands! But I will know better the next time!" said he.

And at last, he knew not very well how or when, sleep fell on Keola, and he forgot the island and all his sorrows.

Early the next day, before the sun was yet up, a bustle woke him. He awoke in fear, for he thought the tribe had caught him napping: but it was no such matter. Only, on the beach in front of him, the bodiless voices called and shouted one upon another, and it seemed they all passed and swept beside him up the coast of the island.

"What is afoot now?" thinks Keola. And it was plain to him it was something beyond ordinary, for the fires were not lighted nor the shells taken, but the bodiless voices kept posting up the beach, and hailing and dying away; and others following, and by the sound of them these wizards should be angry.

"It is not me they are angry at," thought Keola, "for they pass me close."

As when hounds go by, or horses in a race, or city folk coursing to a fire, and all men join and follow after, so it was now with Keola; and he knew not what he did, nor why he did it, but there, lo and behold! he was running with the voices.

So he turned one point of the island, and this brought him in view of a second; and there he remembered the wizard trees to have been growing by the score together in a wood. From this point there went up a hubbub of men crying not to be described; and by the sound of them, those that he ran with shaped their course for the same quarter. A little nearer, and there began to mingle with the outcry the crash of many axes. And at this a thought came at last into his mind that the high chief had consented; that the men of the tribe had set to cutting down these trees; that word had gone about the isle from sorcerer to sorcerer, and these were all now assembling to defend their trees. Desire of strange things swept him on. He posted with the voices, crossed the beach, and came into the borders of the wood, and stood astonished. One tree had fallen, others were part hewed away.

There was the tribe clustered. They were back to back, and bodies lay, and blood flowed among their feet.

The hue of fear was on all their faces; their voices went up to heaven shrill as a weasel's cry.

Have you seen a child when he is all alone and has a wooden sword, and fights, leaping and hewing with the empty air? Even so the man eaters huddled back to back, and heaved up their axes, and laid on, and screamed as they laid on, and behold! no man to contend with them! only here and there Keola saw an axe swinging over against them without hands; and time and again a man of the tribe would fall before it, clove in twain or burst asunder, and his soul sped howling.

For awhile Keola looked upon this prodigy like one that dreams, and then fear took him by the midst as sharp as death, that he should behold such doings. Even in that same flash the high chief of the clan espied him standing, and pointed and called out his name. Thereat the whole tribe saw him also, and their eyes flashed, and their teeth clashed.

"I am too long here," thought Keola, and ran further out of the wood and down the beach, not caring whither.

"Keola!" said, a voice close by upon the empty sand.

"Lehua! is that you?" he cried, and gasped, and looked in vain for her; but by the eyesight he was stark alone.

"I saw you pass before," the voice answered: "but you would not hear me. Quick! get the leaves and the herbs, and let us free."

"You are there with the mat?" he asked.

"Here, at your side," said she. And he felt her arms about him. "Quick! the leaves and the herbs, before my father can get back!"

So Keola ran for his life, and fetched the wizard fuel; and Lehua guided him back, and set his feet upon the mat, and made the fire. All the time of its burning, the sound of the battle towered out of the wood; the wizards and the man-eaters hard at fight; the wizards, the viewless ones, roaring out aloud like bulls upon a mountain, and the men of the tribe replying shrill and savage out of the terror of their souls. And all the time of the burning, Keola stood there and listened, and shook, and watched how the unseen hands of Lehua poured the leaves. She poured them fast, and the flame burned high, and scorched Keola's hands; and she speeded and blew the burning with her breath. The last leaf was eaten, the flame fell, and the shock followed, and there were Keola and Lehua in the room at home.

Now, when Keola could see his wife at last he was mighty pleased, and he was mighty pleased to be home again in Molokai and sit down beside a bowl of poi—for they make no poi on board ships, and there was none in the Isle of Voices—and he was out of the body with pleasure to be clean escaped out of the hands of the eaters of men. But there was another matter not so clear, and Lehua and Keola talked of it all night and were troubled. There was Kalamake left upon the isle. If, by the blessing of God, he could but stick there, all were well; but should he escape and return to Molokai, it would be an ill day for his daughter and her husband. They spoke of his gift of swelling, and whether he could wade that distance in the seas. But Keola knew by this time where that island was—and that is to say, in the Low or Dangerous Archipelago. So they fetched the atlas and looked upon the distance in the map, and by what they could make of it, it seemed a far way for an old gentleman to walk. Still, it would not do to make too sure of a warlock like Kalamake, and they determined at last to take counsel of a white missionary.

So the first one that came by, Keola told him everything. And the missionary was very sharp on him for taking the second wife in the low island; but for all the rest, he vowed he could make neither head nor tail of it.

"However," says he, "if you think this money of your father's ill gotten, my advice to you would be, give some of it to the lepers and some to the missionary fund. And as for this extraordinary rigmarole, you cannot do better than keep it to yourselves."

But he warned the police at Honolulu that, by all he could make out, Kalamake and Keola had been coining false money, and it would not be amiss to watch them.

Keola and Lehua took his advice, and gave many dollars to the lepers and the fund. And no doubt the advice must have been good, for from that day to this, Kalamake has never more been heard of. But whether he was slain in the battle by the trees, or whether he is still kicking his heels upon the Isle of Voices, who shall say?

Introduction to Dagon

Born in Providence, Rhode Island, H. P. Lovecraft (1890-1937) is un-questionably a pioneer in the development of modern horror fiction. A pulp writer who is more popular now than he was during his short lifetime, Lovecraft successfully built upon nineteenth-century proto-weird fiction to create a whole cosmology in which the very laws of Nature were violently torn asunder, exposing mankind as merely a mere speck in a vast, uncaring universe. Highly prolific, Lovecraft authored numerous short stories, novellas, and a critical study of supernatural literature. He is probably best known for creating the Cthulhu mythos and for introducing readers to the "old gods," those otherworldly creatures from beyond the stars who lurk in the shadows ever ready to reclaim their dominion on Earth.

Originally published in the November 1919 edition of *The Vagrant* and reprinted in the October 1923 issue of *Weird Tales*, Lovecraft's "Dagon," although not as polished as his later stories, is nevertheless a formidable introduction to the themes and imagery that he would repeatedly turn to in his work. Written in the first person from the perspective of a distraught morphine addict, "Dagon" introduces the reader to an artificial, volcani-cally-created island somewhere in the Pacific. It is there that our mentally scarred narrator encounters not only the vestiges of a bizarre, lost civi-lization, but also to a hideous creature whose very presence causes him to lose his sanity. With elements of both high fantasy and supernatural dread, "Dagon" is an island story that, once read, is not soon forgotten.

DAGON
H. P. Lovecraft

I am writing this under an appreciable mental strain, since by tonight I shall be no more. Penniless, and at the end of my supply of the drug which alone makes life endurable, I can bear the torture no longer; and shall cast myself from this garret window into the squalid street below. Do not think from my slavery to morphine that I am a weakling or a degenerate. When you have read these hastily scrawled pages you may guess, though never fully realize, why it is that I must have forgetfulness or death.

It was in one of the most open and least frequented parts of the broad Pacific that the packet of which I was supercargo fell a victim to the German sea-raider. The great war was then at its very beginning, and the ocean forces of the Hun had not completely sunk to their later degradation; so that our vessel was made a legitimate prize, whilst we of her crew were treated with all the fairness and consideration due us as naval prisoners. So liberal, indeed, was the discipline of our captors, that five days after we were taken I managed to escape alone in a small boat with water and provisions for a good length of time.

When I finally found myself adrift and free, I had but little idea of my surroundings. Never a competent navigator, I could only guess vaguely by the sun and stars that I was somewhat south of the equator. Of the longitude I knew nothing, and no island or coast-line was in sight. The weather kept fair, and for uncounted days I drifted aimlessly beneath the scorching sun; waiting either for some passing ship, or to be cast on the shores of some habitable land. But neither ship nor land appeared, and I began to despair in my solitude upon the heaving vastnesses of unbroken blue.

The change happened whilst I slept. Its details I shall never know; for my slumber, though troubled and dream-infested, was continuous. When at last I awaked, it was to discover myself half sucked into a slimy expanse of hellish black mire which extended about me in monotonous undulations as far as I could see, and in which my boat lay grounded some distance away.

Though one might well imagine that my first sensation would be of wonder at so prodigious and unexpected a transformation of scenery, I was in reality more horrified than astonished; for there was in the air and in the rotting soil a sinister quality which chilled me to the very core. The region was putrid with the carcasses of decaying fish, and of other less describable things which I saw protruding from the nasty mud of the unending plain. Perhaps I should not hope to convey in mere words the unutterable hideousness that can dwell in absolute silence and barren immensity. There was nothing within hearing, and nothing in sight save a vast reach of black slime; yet the very completeness of the stillness and the homogeneity of the landscape oppressed me with a nauseating fear.

The sun was blazing down from a sky which seemed to me almost black in its cloudless cruelty; as though reflecting the inky marsh beneath my feet. As I crawled into the stranded boat I realized that only one theory could explain my position. Through some unprecedented volcanic upheaval, a portion of the ocean floor must have been thrown to the surface, exposing regions which for innumerable millions of years had lain hidden under unfathomable watery depths. So great was the extent of the new land which had risen beneath me, that I could not detect the faintest noise of the surging ocean, strain my ears as I might. Nor were there any sea-fowl to prey upon the dead things.

For several hours I sat thinking or brooding in the boat, which lay upon its side and afforded a slight shade as the sun moved across the heavens. As the day progressed, the ground lost some of its stickiness, and seemed likely to dry sufficiently for travelling purposes in a short time. That night I slept but little, and the next day I made for myself a pack containing food and water, preparatory to an overland journey in search of the vanished sea and possible rescue.

On the third morning I found the soil dry enough to walk upon with ease. The odor of the fish was maddening; but I was too much concerned with graver things to mind so slight an evil, and set out boldly for an unknown goal. All day I forged steadily westward, guided by a far-away hummock which rose higher than any other elevation on the rolling desert. That night I encamped, and on the following day still travelled toward the hummock, though that object seemed scarcely nearer than when I had first espied it. By the fourth evening I attained the base of the mound, which turned out to be much higher than it had appeared from a distance; an intervening valley setting it out in sharper relief from the general surface. Too weary to ascend, I slept in the shadow of the hill.

I know not why my dreams were so wild that night; but ere the waning and fantastically gibbous moon had risen far above the eastern plain, I was awake in a cold perspiration, determined to sleep no more. Such visions as I had experienced were too much for me to endure again. And in the glow of the moon I saw how unwise I had been to travel by day. Without the glare of the parching sun, my journey would have cost me less energy; indeed, I now felt quite able to perform the ascent which had deterred me at sunset. Picking up my pack, I started for the crest of the eminence.

I have said that the unbroken monotony of the rolling plain was a source of vague horror to me; but I think my horror was greater when I gained the summit of the mound and looked down the other side into an immeasurable pit or canyon, whose black recesses the moon had not yet soared high enough to illumine. I felt myself on the edge of the world; peering over the rim into a fathomless chaos of eternal night. Through my terror ran curious reminiscences of *Paradise Lost*, and of Satan's hideous climb through the unfashioned realms of darkness.

As the moon climbed higher in the sky, I began to see that the slopes of the valley were not quite so perpendicular as I had imagined. Ledges and outcroppings of rock afforded fairly easy foot-holds for a descent, whilst after a drop of a few hundred feet, the declivity became very gradual. Urged on by an impulse which I cannot definitely analyze, I scrambled with difficulty down the rocks and stood on the gentler slope beneath, gazing into the Stygian deeps where no light had yet penetrated.

All at once my attention was captured by a vast and singular object on the opposite slope, which rose steeply about an hundred yards ahead of me; an object that gleamed whitely in the newly bestowed rays of the ascending moon. That it was merely a gigantic piece of stone, I soon assured myself; but I was conscious of a distinct impression that its contour and position were not altogether the work of Nature. A closer scrutiny filled me with sensations I cannot express; for despite its enormous magnitude, and its position in an abyss which had yawned at the bottom of the sea since the world was young, I perceived beyond a doubt that the strange object was a well-shaped monolith whose massive bulk had known the workmanship and perhaps the worship of living and thinking creatures.

Dazed and frightened, yet not without a certain thrill of the scientist's or archaeologist's delight, I examined my surroundings more closely. The moon, now near the zenith, shone weirdly and vividly above the towering steeps that hemmed in the chasm, and revealed the fact that a far-flung body of water flowed at the bottom, winding out of sight in both directions, and almost lapping my feet as I stood on the slope. Across the chasm, the wavelets washed the base of the Cyclopean monolith; on whose surface I could now trace both inscriptions and crude sculptures. The writing was in a system of hieroglyphics unknown to me, and unlike anything I had ever seen in books; consisting for the most part of conventionalized aquatic symbols such as fishes, eels, octopi, crustaceans, molluscs, whales, and the like. Several characters obviously represented marine things which are unknown to the modern world, but whose decomposing forms I had observed on the ocean-risen plain.

It was the pictorial carving, however, that did most to hold me spellbound. Plainly visible across the intervening water on account of their enormous size, were an array of bas-reliefs whose subjects would have excited

the envy of Doré. I think that these things were supposed to depict men—
at least, a certain sort of men; though the creatures were shewn disport-
ing like fishes in the waters of some marine grotto, or paying homage at
some monolithic shrine which appeared to be under the waves as well. Of
their faces and forms I dare not speak in detail; for the mere remembrance
makes me grow faint. Grotesque beyond the imagination of a Poe or a Bulwer, they were damnably human in general outline despite webbed hands
and feet, shockingly wide and flabby lips, glassy, bulging eyes, and other
features less pleasant to recall. Curiously enough, they seemed to have been
chiselled badly out of proportion with their scenic background; for one of
the creatures was shewn in the act of killing a whale represented as but little larger than himself. I remarked, as I say, their grotesqueness and
strange size; but in a moment decided that they were merely the imaginary
gods of some primitive fishing or seafaring tribe; some tribe whose last descendant had perished eras before the first ancestor of the Piltdown or Ne-
anderthal Man was born. Awestruck at this unexpected glimpse into a past
beyond the conception of the most daring anthropologist, I stood musing
whilst the moon cast queer reflections on the silent channel before me.

Then suddenly I saw it. With only a slight churning to mark its rise to
the surface, the thing slid into view above the dark waters. Vast, Polyphe-
mus-like, and loathsome, it darted like a stupendous monster of nightmares
to the monolith, about which it flung its gigantic scaly arms, the while it
bowed its hideous head and gave vent to certain measured sounds. I
think I went mad then.

Of my frantic ascent of the slope and cliff, and of my delirious journey
back to the stranded boat, I remember little. I believe I sang a great deal,
and laughed oddly when I was unable to sing. I have indistinct recollec-
tions of a great storm some time after I reached the boat; at any rate, I know
that I heard peals of thunder and other tones which Nature utters only in
her wildest moods.

When I came out of the shadows I was in a San Francisco hospital;
brought thither by the captain of the American ship which had picked up
my boat in mid-ocean. In my delirium I had said much, but found that my
words had been given scant attention. Of any land upheaval in the Pacific,
my rescuers knew nothing; nor did I deem it necessary to insist upon a thing
which I knew they could not believe. Once I sought out a celebrated eth-
nologist, and amused him with peculiar questions regarding the ancient
Philistine legend of Dagon, the Fish-God; but soon perceiving that he was
hopelessly conventional, I did not press my inquiries.

It is at night, especially when the moon is gibbous and waning, that I see
the thing. I tried morphine; but the drug has given only transient surcease,
and has drawn me into its clutches as a hopeless slave. So now I am to end

it all, having written a full account for the information or the contemptu-
ous amusement of my fellow-men. Often I ask myself if it could not all have
been a pure phantasm—a mere freak of fever as I lay sun-stricken and raving in the open boat after my escape from the German man-of-war. This
I ask myself, but ever does there come before me a hideously vivid vision
in reply. I cannot think of the deep sea without shuddering at the nameless things that may at this very moment be crawling and floundering on
its slimy bed, worshipping their ancient stone idols and carving their own
detestable likenesses on submarine obelisks of water-soaked granite. I
dream of a day when they may rise above the billows to drag down in their
reeking talons the remnants of puny, war-exhausted mankind—of a day
when the land shall sink, and the dark ocean floor shall ascend amidst universal pandemonium.

The end is near. I hear a noise at the door, as of some immense slippery
body lumbering against it. It shall not find me. God, that hand! The window! The window!

Introduction to The People of Pan

Henry S. Whitehead (1882-1932) was a graduate of Harvard University, a newspaper editor, an ordained Episcopal deacon, and a prolific author of both supernatural and voodoo stories, many of which unfold on tropical islands. He wrote short stories in the emerging weird fiction genre for such pulp magazines as *Adventure*, *People's Magazine*, and most frequently, *Weird Tales*.

Originally published in the March 1929 issue of *Weird Tales*, "The People of Pan" takes place primarily on a fictional Caribbean island named Saona. Whitehead utilizes the setting of this supposedly uninhabited island to craft a heartfelt tale about how economic progress may impact an ancient, peaceful civilization. "The People of Pan," however, is far from a story of pure sentimentalism. It is also a decidedly uncanny tale replete with wondrous architecture, an ancient civilization long presumed lost to the ravages of time, and a stark climax in which the story's protagonist realizes the true cost paid for his financial success, one he obtains by exploiting the natural wonders of a strange little island.

THE PEOPLE OF PAN
Henry S. Whitehead

I, Gerald Canevin of Santa Cruz, have actually been down the ladder of thirteen hundred and twenty-six steps set into the masonry of the Great Cylinder of Saona; have marveled at the vast cathedral underground on that tropical island; have trembled under the menacing Horns of the Goat.

That this island, comparable in area with my own Santa Cruz, and lying as it does only an overnight's sail from Porto Rico's metropolis, San Juan, quite near the coast of Santo Domingo, and skirted almost daily by the vessels of the vast Caribbean trade—that such an island should have remained unexplored until our own day is, to me, the greatest of its many marvels. Through his discovery, Grosvenor is today the world's richest man.

How, under these conditions, it could have been inhabited by a cultured race for centuries, is not hard, however, to understand. The cylinder—but the reader will see that for himself; I must not anticipate. I would note that the insect life has been completely re-established since Grosvenor's well-nigh incredible adventure there. I can testify! I received my first (and only) centipede bite while on Saona with Grosvenor, from whose lips I obtained the extraordinary tale which follows…

"But," protested Grosvenor, "how about the lighthouse? Isn't there *anybody* there? Of course, I'm not questioning your word, Mr. Lopez!"

"Automatic light." The Insular Line agent spoke crisply. "Even the birds avoid Saona! Here—ask Hansen. Come here, will you, Captain?"

Captain Hansen of the company's ship *Madeleine* came to the desk. "Vot iss it?" he asked, steely blue eyes taking in Charles Grosvenor.

"Tell Mr. Grosvenor about Saona, Captain. You pass it twice a week on your run to Santo Domingo. I won't say a word. You tell him!"

Captain Hansen lowered his bulk carefully into an office chair.

"It iss a funny place, Saona. Me, I'm neffer ashore there. Nothing to go ashore for. Flat, it iss; covered down to de beach with mahogany trees—millions of mahogany trees. Nodding else—only beach. On one end, a liddle peninsula, and de automatic light. Nobody iss dere. De Dominican gofferment sends a boat vunce a month with oil for de light. Dar's all I could tell you—trees, sand, a dead leffel; nobody dere."

The captain paused to light a long black cigar.

Grosvenor broke a silence. "I have to go there, Captain. I am agent for a company which has bought a mahogany-cutting concession from the Dominican government. I have to look the place over—make a survey. Mr. Lopez suggests that you put me ashore there on the beach."

"Goot! Any time you made de arrangement here in de office, I put you on shore dere, and—I'll go ashore with you! In all de Seffen Seas neffer yet did I meet a man had been ashore on Saona. I t'ink dat yoost happens so. Dere iss noddings to go ashore for; so, efferybody sails past Saona."

The captain rose, saluted the agent and Grosvenor gravely, and moved majestically toward the narrow stairs which led to the blazing sidewalk of San Juan below.

It required two weeks in *mañana*-land for Grosvenor to assemble his outfit for the sojourn on Saona. He was fortunate in discovering, out of work and looking for a job, a Barbadian negro who spoke English—the ancient island tongue of the buccaneers—and who labored under the name of Christian Fabio. Christian had been a ship's steward. He could cook, and like most Barbadians had some education and preferred long, polysyllabic words.

The *Madeleine* sailed out of San Juan promptly at three one blazing afternoon, with Grosvenor and Christian aboard.

Grosvenor had asked to be called at six, and when he came on deck the next morning the land off the *Madeleine's* starboard side was the shore of Saona. The *Madeleine* skirted this low-lying shore for several hours, and Grosvenor, on the bridge deck, scanned the island with the captain's Zeiss glass. He saw one dense mass of mahogany trees, dwarfed by perspective, appearing little more impressive than bushes.

At eight bells Captain Hansen rang for half-speed, and brought the *Madeleine* to anchor off a small bay skirted by a crescent of coconut palms. Greensward indicated the mouth of a fresh-water stream, and for this point in the bay Captain Hansen steered the ship's boat, in which he accompanied Grosvenor and Christian ashore. They were followed by another and larger boat, loaded to the gunwales with their supplies.

The trees, seen now close at hand, were much larger than they had appeared from the ship's deck. A fortune in hardwood stood there, untouched it seemed for centuries, ready for the cutting.

As soon as the stores were unloaded, Captain Hansen shook hands gravely with Grosvenor, was rowed back to his ship, and the *Madeleine* was immediately got under weigh and proceeded on her voyage. Long before the taint of her smoke had faded into nothingness in the blazing glare of the tropic sun, the two marooned inhabitants of Saona had pitched their tents and were settled into the task of establishing themselves for several weeks' sojourn.

Grosvenor started his explorations the next morning. His map of the island was somewhat sketchy. It did not show the slight rise toward the island's center which had been perceptible even from shipboard. Grosvenor's kit included an aluminum surveyor's transit, a thermos-flask of potato soup—one of the best of tropical foods—and the inevitable mosquito-net for the noon *siesta*.

He started along the line of the stream, straight inland. He was soon out of sight and hearing of his camp in a silence unbroken by so much as the hum of an insect. He found the trees farther inland, in the rich soil of centuries of undisturbed leafage, better grown than those nearer the sea. As they increased in size, the sun's heat diminished.

Grosvenor walked along slowly. The stream, as he had expected, narrowed and deepened after a few rods of travel, and even a short distance inland, rinsing out his mouth with an aluminum cupful of the water, he found it surprisingly cool. This indicated shelter for a great distance and that the island must be very heavily forested.

A quarter of a mile inland he set up his transit, laid out a square and counted the trees within it. The density of the wood was seventeen per cent greater than what the company had estimated upon. He whistled to himself with satisfaction. This promised a favorable report. He continued his walk inland.

Four times he laid out a similar square, counted the trees, measured the circumference of their bases a little above the ground, estimated their average height. The wood-area became steadily denser.

At twelve-thirty he stopped for lunch and a couple of hours' rest. It would take him less time to walk back because he would not have to stop to lay out his squares.

He drank his potato soup, ate two small sandwiches of sharp Porto Rico sausage, and boiled a cupful of the stream water over a sterno apparatus for tea.

Then he stretched himself out on the long grass of the stream's bank under his mosquito-netting. He drifted easily into sleep, to the accompaniment of the stream's small rustlings and the sough of the trade wind through the millions of small mahogany leaves.

He awakened, two hours later, a sense of foreboding heavily upon him. It was as though something weird and strange had been going on for some time—something of which he was, somehow, dimly conscious. As he started, uneasily, to throw off the net and get up, he noticed with surprise that there were no mosquitoes on the net's outer surface. Then he remembered Captain Hansen's remarks about the dearth of animal life on the island. There was rarely even a seagull, the captain had said, along the island's shore. Grosvenor recalled that he had not seen so much as an insect during his five hours on the trail. He threw off the net and rose to his feet.

The vague sense of something obscurely amiss with which he had awakened remained. He looked curiously about him. He listened, carefully. All was silent except for the dying breath of the trade wind.

Then, all at once, he realized that he was missing the sound of the little stream. He stepped toward it and saw that the water had sunk to a mere trickle. He sat down near the low bank and looked at it. There were the marks of the water, more than a foot higher than its present level.

He glanced at his watch. It was three-thirteen. He had slept for two hours, exactly as he had intended. He might have slept the clock around! Even so, twenty-six hours would hardly account for a drop like this. He wound his watch—seven and one-half twists. It was the same day! He looked at the water again. It was dropping almost visibly, like watching the hour-hand of a huge clock at close range. He stuck a twig at its present level, and started to roll up his net and gather his belongings into a pack. That finished, he lit a cigarette.

He smoked the cigarette out and went to look at his twig. The water was half an inch below it. The many slight sounds which make up the note of a brook were muted now; the little trickle of water gave off no sound.

Greatly puzzled, Grosvenor shouldered his pack and started back to camp.

The walk occupied an hour and a quarter. The water grew lower as he went downstream. Before he reached the edge of the mahogany forest it had dwindled into a shallow bit of fenland. At the edge of the coral sand it was quite dry. He found Christian getting supper and bubbling over with long words which emerged out of a puzzled countenance.

"Doubtless you have remarked the diminution of the stream," began Christian. "I was fortunate enough to observe its cessation two hours ago and I have filled various vessels with water. It would constitute a very serious menace to our comfort, sir, if we are deprived of water. We might signal the *Madeleine* on her return voyage tomorrow, but I fear that if the lowering of the stream is permanent we shall be obliged to ration ourselves as to ablutions!"

Having delivered this masterpiece, Christian fell silent.

When Grosvenor arose the next morning the stream was at the same level as on the previous morning. It was as though this stream were subject to a twenty-four-hour tide. There was no means of judging now whether this were the case, or whether some cataclysm of nature at the stream's source had affected it in this extraordinary way. Grosvenor's instinct was all for another trip upstream to the source to find out what he could.

He made more of his tree-tests that morning, and after lunch the stream began to fail again. The following morning it was once more at its high level. That day Grosvenor put his wish into execution. He had plenty of time for his surveys. He would go exploring on his own account today. He started after breakfast, taking only the materials for lunch this time. The mosquito-netting had proved to be useless. There were no mosquitoes!

At nine he reached the spot where he had taken the first *siesta*. He proceeded upstream, and half an hour later the ground began to rise. The stream shallowed and broadened. The trees in this moist area grew larger than any others he had seen on the island.

His pedometer informed him he was getting close to the island's center. The ground now mounted steadily. He came to a kind of clearing, where the trees were sparse and great whitish ricks replaced the soft coral soil. Through these, the stream, now again narrow and deep, ran a tortuous way, winding about the great boulders. On this broken ground, without much shade, the sun poured in intolerable brilliance. He wiped the sweat from his face as he climbed the last rise to the island's summit.

As he topped the rise an abrupt change took place. One moment he had been picking his way through broken ground among rocks. The next he was standing on smooth stone. He paused, and looked about him. He was at the top.

At his feet lay a smooth, round lake, enclosed by a stone parapet. Beyond, a gentle slope, heavily forested, ran down to the distant sea on the island's other side.

He stooped down, rubbed his hand over the level surface of the stone. It was masonry.

All was silent about him; not even a dragon-fly disturbed the calm surface of the circular pool. No insect droned its fervid note in the clear, warm air.

Very quietly now, for he felt that the silence of this place must not be disturbed by any unnecessary sound, he started around the lake's circular rim. In twenty steps he had reached the source of the stream. Here the edge of masonry was cut into a U through which the water flowed silently out. He resumed his walk, and the circuit occupied fifteen minutes. He reached his starting-point, sat down on the warm rock-edge, and looked intently into the pool. It must be fed by deep, subterranean springs, he judged, and these springs, possibly, ebbed and flowed, a rhythm reflected in a rise and fall of the pool's surface; a consequent rise and fall in the water of the stream.

The sun was almost intolerably hot. He walked off to the nearest mahogany grove, pitched his camp in its deep shade, and sat down to wait till noon. Here he prepared lunch, ate it, and returned to the basin's rim.

The reservoir was several feet lower, the water now barely trickling through its outlet. He watched the waters sink, fascinated. He leaned over the edge of masonry and gazed into their still depths. A cloud passed over the sun, throwing the great pool into shade.

No bottom was visible. Down, down, his gaze traveled, and as he looked the rate of the sinking water-level increased and there arose from the pool a dim, hollow sound as some incalculable suction drew the waters down into the cylinder's depths.

An almost irresistible desire came over him to descend with the water. His scrutiny traveled about the inner surface of the great cylinder now revealed by the sinking waters.

What was that? Something like a vertical line, toward the other side, broke the cement-like smoothness of the chiseled surface. He started toward the point, his heart jumping as what he had vaguely suspected, hoped, became an actuality before his eyes. The vertical line was a ladder down the inner surface of the cylinder, of broad, copper-colored metal insets extending far down until he lost it in the unfathomable darkness below.

The ladder's topmost inset step was some three feet below the top. Looking closely from the rim above it, he observed semi-circular ridges on the rim itself, handholds, obviously, shaped like the handles of a stone crock, cut deeply into the masonry. A thin, metal hand-rail of the same material as the steps ran down straight and true beside them.

The impulse to descend became overpowering. He muttered a brief, fragmentary prayer, and stooped down, clutching the stone handholds. He stepped over the rim and down inside, and felt for the topmost step of the ladder with his foot. The step, and the railing, as he closed a firm right hand about it, felt slippery. But steps and rail were rigid, firmly set as though installed the day before. The metal showed no corrosion.

With a deep breath, he took one last look at the tops of the mahogany trees and began to go down the ladder.

At first he felt carefully for each succeeding step, clutched the unyielding handrail grimly, as the dank coolness of the stone cylinder closed in around him. Then, with custom, his first nervous vigilance relaxed. The steps were at precisely regular intervals; the handrail firm. He descended beyond the penetrating light of the first fifty feet into a region of increasing coolness and dimness.

When he reached the two hundredth step, he paused, resting, and looked down. Only a vague, imponderable dimness, a suggestion of infinite depth, was revealed to him. He turned his head about and looked up. A clear blue, exact circle stood out. Within it he saw the stars.

He descended another hundred steps, and now all was black about him. The blue circle above had turned darker. The stars glowed brilliantly.

He felt no fear. He had steady nerves, fortitude, a fatalistic faith in something he named his destiny. If harm were to come to him, it would come, here or anywhere else. He reasoned that the water would not rise for many hours. In that blackness he resumed his descent. He went down and down, step after interminable step ...

It was wholly dark now. The circle above was only the size of a small coin, the stars indistinguishable; only their flickering brightness over the surface of the tiny disk.

He had counted 1,326 steps when something happened to his left foot. He could not lower it from the step on which it rested. The very edge of a shadow of cold fear fell upon him, but resolutely he put it away. He lowered his right foot to the same step, and, resting his body's weight on the left foot attempted to lower the right. He could not!

Then it dawned upon him that he had reached the bottom of the ladder. Holding firmly to the rail with his left hand he reached for his flashlight with the other. By its light he looked about him. His feet were on a metal platform some twelve feet square. Just to his left, leading into the wall of the cylinder, was the outline of a lancet-shaped doorway. A great ring hung on a hinged knob near his hand.

He stepped out upon the platform, his muscles feeling strange after the long and unaccustomed strain of the descent. He took hold of the door-ring, twisted it to the left. It turned in his hand. He pulled, and a beam of light, soft and mellow, came through the vertical crack. He pulled the door half-open, and the soft light flooded the platform. He stepped over to its edge and looked down, leaning on the metal handrail which ran about the edge. Blackness there—sheer, utter blackness.

He turned again to the door. He had not come thus far to yield to misgivings as to what might lie behind it. He slipped through the opening and pulled the door to behind him. It shut, true and exactly flush with its surrounding walls and jambs, solidly.

He stood in a small, square room, of the same smooth masonry as the cylinder, floored with sheets of the coppery metal. The light came through from another doorway, open opposite the side where he stood. Resolutely he crossed the small room and looked through the door.

Vast space—a cathedral—was the first, breath-taking impression. Far above, a vast, vaulted arch of masonry. In the dim distance towered an amazing figure, so incredible that Grosvenor let out his breath in a long sigh and sat down weakly on the smooth floor.

The figure was that of an enormous goat, reared on a pair of colossal legs, the lowered head with sweeping horns pointing forward, some eighty feet in the air. About this astounding image hung such an air of menacing savagery that Grosvenor, weary with his long descent, covered his face with his hands to shut it out. He was aroused out of his momentary let-down by a sound.

He sat up, listened. It was a kind of faint, distant chanting. Suppressing a shudder he looked again toward the overpowering majesty of the colossus. A great concourse of people, dwarfed by the distance, danced rhythmically before the gigantic idol. The chant rose higher in measured cadence. Fascinated, Grosvenor rose and walked toward the distant dancers.

When he had traversed half the space between, the image took on a dignity not apparent from the greater distance. The craggy, bestial face was now benevolent, as it looked down upon its devotees. There was a grotesque air of benediction about the flare of the forehoofs as they seemed to wave in grave encouragement to the worshipers beneath. The attention of the throng was so occupied with their dance that Grosvenor remained unobserved. Clouds of incense rose before the image, making the head appear to nod, the forelegs to wave gravely.

Something more than its cadence seemed now to mingle with the chanting. There was something oddly familiar about it, and Grosvenor knitted his brows in the effort to place it. Then it came to him all at once. It was the words of the ancient Greek Chorus. Nearer and nearer he approached, his feet making no sound on the dull, russet-colored, metal flooring. It was like walking on solid lead. He stooped, at this thought, and with his sheathknife scratched its surface, dulled with the wear of countless feet. A thin, wire-like splinter curled behind his scratching knife-point. It was bright yellow on the fresh surface. He tore the splinter loose, held it close. It was soft, like lead—virgin gold.

He placed the sliver in his jacket pocket and stood, dumfounded, his heart pounding tumultuously. Gold! . . .

The chanting ceased. A clear, woman's voice detached itself; was lifted in a paean—a hymn of praise. The words now came to him clear and full. He stopped dead, trying, straining all his faculties, to understand. The woman was singing in classical Greek!

Something of modern Greek he understood from a long professional sojourn in the Mediterranean island of Xante where once he had been employed by the owner of a group of currant-plantations, and where he had learned enough of the Italianized Greek of the island to make himself understood. He hastened forward, stopping quite near the rearmost worshipers. This was no dialect. This was Old Greek, Attic Greek, the tongue of Hellas, of classic days, as used to celebrate the Mysteries about the altars of Zeus and the Nature gods; in the Sacred Groves; at Elis, and Dodona, and before the shrines of Apollo—and in the worship of Pan. Pan!—the Goat. The beginnings of an understanding surged through his mind.

In the ancient tongue of Homer and Aeschylus, this recitative now began to take form in his mind. It was, he soon perceived, a hymn to Pan, to the patron god of woodlands and wild places; of glades and streams and hidden groves; of nymphs and dryads ...

The people swayed to the cadences of the hymn, and at intervals the vast throng breathed out a few rhythmical words, a hushed, muted chorus, in which were recited the Attributes of Pan ...

Grosvenor found himself swaying with them, the notes of the chorus somehow strangely familiar to him, as though remembered after a great interval, although he knew that he had never before in this life heard anything like this. He approached nearer, without concealment now, mingled with the multitude pouring out its corporate soul to the god of Nature.

The hymn ended. Then, to a thin, piping note—the note of a syrinx—and with no confusion, a dance began. Grosvenor danced naturally with a group of four, and the others, in a kind of gentle ecstasy, danced with him, a dance as old as trees and hills, the worship of the Great Powers which through the dignity and grace of the dance seemed to promise strange and unknown joys ...

The dance ended, abruptly, on a note of the pan-pipes. Grosvenor, brought to himself, glanced quickly about him. He was conspicuous. The others were uniformly dressed in blue kirtles, sandals on their graceful feet. The people were very beautiful. Grace and dignity marked their every movement.

Behind the colossal image of the Goat a great recess was set off by an arch which towered aloft out of sight. Here stood an altar, about whose upper edge ran cameo-like figures: youths and girls bearing wreaths; garlanded oxen; children with torches; and, centrally placed, the grotesque figure of Pan with his goat's legs and small, crooked horns upon his forehead—Pan seated, his pipes at his lips.

Suddenly every eye turned to the altar.

There came from a recess a woman, tall and graceful, bearing in her hands a slender vase of white stone. From this, on reaching the altar, she poured out upon it a thin stream of golden-colored oil. An intense, reddish flame arose at once. The vast audience stood motionless.

Then a note on the pipe, and from the throng, quite close to Grosvenor, a young man stepped, and mounted broad, shallow steps to the altar. In his hand he carried a live beetle held delicately by the edge of elevated wings. Straight to the altar he proceeded and dropped the insect in the center of the flame. So silent was the motionless throng that the rackle of the flame devouring this inconsiderable offering was plainly heard. Bowing to the priestess, the young man returned to his place.

A sigh, such as proceeds from a large concourse of people who have been keeping silence, now arose from the throng, which forthwith broke up into conversing groups.

Then the first intimation of fear fell upon Grosvenor like a black mantle. For the first time since his arrival among this incredible company, a quarter of a mile underneath the surface of an 'uninhabited' West Indian island, he took sudden thought for his safety. It was late in the day to think of that! He was surrounded by these people, had intruded into their worship, a worship ancient when the Classics were composed. He was effectually cut off from any chance of escape, should they prove hostile. He saw a thickening group closing in about him—curious, incredulous, utterly taken by surprise at discovering this stranger in their midst ...

By a great effort, and in a voice hardly more than a whisper—for his danger had made itself overwhelmingly apparent to him—he spoke in his best attempt at pure Greek.

"I give you greeting, in the name of Pan!" he said.

"And to you, greeting, O barbarian," replied a deep and rich voice behind him.

The throng about him stirred—a movement of deference. He turned. The graceful priestess stood close to him. He bowed, prompted by an instinct for 'good manners'.

The priestess made a graceful inclination before him. Instinct prompted him a second time. He addressed her.

"I come to you in love and peace." It was a phrase he had gathered from the hymn to Pan—that phrase 'love and peace.' He continued: "I have sojourned in the Land of Hellas, the home of the great Pan, though no Hellene, as my speech declares."

"Sojourn here, then, with Pan's people in love and peace," returned the priestess with commanding dignity. She made him a summoning gesture.

"Come," she said, and, turning, led the way back toward the altar.

He followed, into the blackening gloom of the sanctuary, and straight before him walked his conductress without so much as a glance right or left. They passed at last between two enormous curtains screening an aperture, and Grosvenor found himself in a very beautiful room, square, and unmistakably Greek in its appointments. Two long couches stood at each side, along the walls. In the center a chaste, rectangular table held a great vase of the yellow metal, heaped with pomegranates.

The priestess, pausing, motioned him gracefully to one of the seats, and reclined opposite him upon the other.

She clapped her hands, and a beautiful child ran into the room. After a round-eyed glance at the stranger, he stood before the priestess, who spoke rapidly to him. He left the room, and almost immediately returned with a vase and two small goblets of the ruddy gold. The drink proved to be pomegranate-juice mingled with cold water. Grosvenor found it very refreshing.

When they had drunk, the priestess began at once to speak to him. "From where do you come, O barbarian?"

"From a region of cold climate, in the north, on the mainland."

"You are not, then, of Hispaniola?"

"No. My countrymen are named 'Americans.' In my childhood my countrymen made war upon those of Hispaniola, driving them from a great island toward the lowering sun from this place, and which men name 'Cuba'."

The priestess appeared impressed. She continued her questioning. "Why are you here among the People of Pan?"

Grosvenor explained his mission to the island of Saona, and, as well as his limited knowledge of Greek permitted, recounted the course of his adventure to the present time. When he had finished: "I understand you well," said the priestess. "Within man's memory none have been, save us of the People of Pan, upon this island's surface. I understand you are the forerunner of others, those who come to take of the wood of the surface. Are all your fellow-countrymen worshippers of Pan?"

Grosvenor was stuck! But his sense of humor came to his rescue and made an answer possible.

"We have a growing 'cultus' of Pan and his worship," he answered gravely. "Much in our life comes from the same source as yours, and in spirit many of us follow Pan. This following grows fast. The words for it in our tongue are 'nature-study,' 'camping,' 'scouting,' 'golf ,'and there are many other varieties of the cult of Pan."

The priestess nodded.

"Again, I understand,' she vouchsafed. She leaned her beautiful head upon her hand and thought deeply.

It was Grosvenor who broke a long silence. "Am I permitted to make enquiries of you?" he asked.

"Ask!" commanded the priestess.

Grosvenor enquired about the rise and fall of the water in the great cylinder; the origin of the cylinder itself: was the metal of which the floors and steps and handrail were made common? Where did the People of Pan get the air they breathe? How long had they been here, a quarter of a mile beneath the earth's surface? On what kind of food did they live? How could fruit—he indicated the pomegranates—grow here in the bowels of the earth?

He stopped for sheer lack of breath. Again the priestess smiled, though gravely.

"Your questions are those of a man of knowledge, although you are an outlander. We are Hellenes and here we have lived always. All of us and our fathers and fathers' fathers were born here. But our tradition teaches us that in the years behind the years, in the very ancient past, in an era so remote that the earth's waters were in a different relation to the land, a frightful cataclysm overwhelmed our mother-continent, Antillea. That whole land sank into the sea, save only one Deucalion and his woman, one Pyrrha, and these from Atlantis, the sister continent in the North. These, so the legend relates, floated upon the waters in a vessel prepared for them with much food and drink, and these having reached the Great Land, their seed became the Hellenes.

"Our forebears dwelt in a colony of our mother continent, which men name Yucatan, a peninsula. There came upon our forebears men of war-like habit, men fierce and cruel, from a land adjacent to Hellas, named 'Hispaniola.' These interlopers drove out our people who had for eons followed the paths of love and peace; of flocks and herds; of song and the dance, and the love of fields and forest and grove, and the worship of Pan. Some of our people they slew and some they enslaved, and these destroyed themselves.

"But among our forebears, during this persecution, was a wise man, one Anaxagoras, and with him fled a colony to the great island in the South which lies near this island. There they settled and there would have carried on our worship and our ways of peace. But here they of Hispaniola likewise came, and would not permit our people to abide in peace and love.

"Then were our people indeed desperate. By night they fled on rafts and reached this low-lying place. Here they discovered the cylinder, and certain ones, greatly daring, cast themselves on the mercy of Pan and descended while the waters were sunken.

"Here, then, we have dwelt since that time, in peace and love.

"We know not why the waters fall and rise, but our philosophers tell us of great reservoirs far beneath the platform where man's foot had not stepped. In these, as the planet revolves, there is oscillation, and thus the waters flow and ebb once in the day and not twice as does the salt sea.

"We believe that in times past, beyond the power of man to measure or compute, the dwellers of these islands, which then were mountain-tops, ere the submersion of Antillea and its sister continent Atlantis, caused the waters of the sea to rise upon them, and whose descendants those of Hispaniola did name 'Carib' were men of skill and knowledge in mighty works, and that these men, like one Archimedes of the later Hellas, did plan to restore the earth's axis to its center, for this planet revolves not evenly but slantwise, as they who study the stars know well. We believe that it was those mighty men of learning and skill who built the cylinder.

"Vessels and the metal of the floor were here when we came, and this metal, being soft and of no difficulty in the craftsman's trade, we have used to replace the vessels as time destroys them and they wear thin. This metal, in vast quantities, surrounds our halls and vaults here below the surface of the land above.

"Our light is constant. It is of the gases which flow constantly from the bowels of the earth. Spouts confine it, fire placed at the mouths of the spouts ignites it. The spouts, of this metal, are very ancient. Upon their mouths are coverings which are taken away when fire is set there; replaced when the light is needed no more in that place.

"Our air we receive from shaft-ways from the surface of the earth above. Their ground openings are among the white rocks. Our philosophers think the yellow metal was melted by the earth's fires and forced up through certain of the ancient air-openings from below."

The priestess finished her long recital, Grosvenor listening with all his faculties in order to understand her placid speech.

"I understand it all except the fruit," said he.

The priestess smiled again, gravely.

"The marvels of nature make no difficulty for your mind, but this simple question of fruit is difficult for you! Come—I will show you our gardens."

She rose; Grosvenor followed. They passed out through various chambers until they arrived at one whose outer wall was only a balustrade of white stone. An extraordinary sight met Grosvenor's eyes.

On a level piece of ground of many acres grew innumerable fruits: pineapples, mango-trees, oranges, pomegranates. Here were row upon row of sapodilla trees, yam-vines, eggplants, bananas, lemon and grapefruit trees, even trellises of pale green wine-grapes.

At irregular intervals stood metal pipes of varying thickness and height, and from the tops of these, even, whitish flares of burning gas illuminated the 'gardens.' A dozen questions rose in Grosvenor's mind. "How? Why?"

"What causes your failure to understand?" enquired the priestess, gently. "Heat, light, moisture, good earth well tended! Here, all these are present. These fruits are planted from long ago, and constantly renewed; originally they grew on the earth's surface."

They walked back through the rooms to the accompaniment of courteous inclinations from all whom they passed. They resumed their places in the first room. The priestess addressed Grosvenor.

"Many others will follow you; those who come to procure the wood of the forest above. Nothing we have is of any value to these people. Nothing they may bring do we desire. It would be well if they came and took their wood and departed knowing naught of us of the People of Pan here underground.

"We shall, therefore, make it impossible for them to descend should they desire so to do. We shall cut the topmost steps of the ladder away from the stone; replace them when your countrymen who drove the people of Hispaniola from Cuba have departed. I will ask you to swear by Pan that you will reveal nothing of what you have seen. Then remain with us if you so desire, and, when your countrymen have departed, come again in peace and love as behooveth a devotee of Pan."

"I will swear by Pan, as you desire," responded Grosvenor, his mind on the incalculable fortune in virgin gold which had here no value beyond that of its utility for vessels, and floors, and steps! Indeed he needed no oath to prevent his saying anything to his 'countrymen'! He might be trusted for that without an oath! A sudden idea struck him.

"The sacrifice," said he, —"the *thurìa*, or rather, I should say, the *holokautósis*—the burnt offering. Why was only an insect sacrificed to Pan?"

The priestess looked down at the burnished metal floor of the room and was silent. And as she spoke, Grosvenor saw tears standing in her eyes.

"The sinking and rise of the waters is not the only rhythm of this place. Four times each year the gases flow from within the earth. Then—every living thing upon this island's surface dies! At such seasons we here below are safe. Thus it happens that we have no beast worthy of an offering to Pan. Thus, at our festivals we may offer only inferior things. We eat no flesh. That is sacred to Pan, as it has been since our ancestors worshipped Him in the groves of Yucatan. That He may have His offering one or more of us journeys to the cylinder's top at full moon. Some form of life has always been found by diligent search. Somewhere some small creature survives. If we should not discover it, He would be angry, and, perhaps, slay us. We know not."

"When does the gas flow upward again?" enquired Grosvenor. He was thinking of Christian Fabio waiting for him there on the beach.

"At the turning of the season. It seethes upward in three days from now."

"Let me take my oath, then," replied Grosvenor, "and depart forthwith. Then I would speak concerning what I am to do with those others who follow me to this land."

The priestess clapped her hands, and the little serving-lad entered. To him she gave a brief order, and he took his departure. Then with the priestess Grosvenor made his arrangement about the wood-cutting force—a conversation which occupied perhaps a quarter of an hour. The little messenger returned as they were finishing. He bowed, spoke rapidly to the priestess, and retired.

"Rise, and follow me," she directed Grosvenor.

Before the great idol the people were again gathering when they arrived beside the altar. They stood, and the priestess held out her arms in a sweeping gesture, commanding silence. An imponderable quiet followed.

His hands beneath hers on the altar of Pan, Grosvenor took his oath as she indicated it to him.

"By the great Pan, I swear—by hill and stream, by mountain and valley, by the air of the sky and the water of streams and ponds, by the sea and by fire which consumes all things—by these I swear to hold inviolate within me that which I have known here in this temple and among the People of Pan. And may He pursue me with His vengeance if I break this my oath, in this world and in the world to come, until water ceaseth to flow, earth to support the trees, air to be breathed, and fire to burn—by these and by the Horns and Hooves of Pan I swear, and I will not break my oath."

Then, conducted by the priestess, Grosvenor walked through the people, who made a path for them, across the great expanse of the temple to the small anteroom beside the cylinder. Here the priestess placed her hands upon Grosvenor's head. "I bless thee, in Pan's name," she said, simply. He opened the door, passed through onto the metal platform, and pushed it shut behind him ...

He found the ascent very wearing and his muscles ached severely before he could discern clearly the stars flaming in the disk above his head. At last he grasped the stone handles on the rim. Wearily he drew himself above ground, and stretched himself upon the level rim of the cylinder.

Before starting down the gentle slope for his camp under the shade of the mahogany forest's abundant leafage, he paused beside one of the white rocks, laboriously heaving it to one side. Beneath it was an aperture, running straight down, and lined with a curiously smooth, lava-like stone. He had seen one of the air-pipes which the priestess had described. He knew now that he had not been passing through some incredibly strange dream. He stepped away and was soon within the forest's grateful shade.

He reached camp and Christian Fabio a little before seven-thirty that evening, finding supper ready and the faithful Christian agog for news. This he proffered in Christian's kind of language, ending by the statement that the stream "originated in a lake of indubitably pre-historic volcanic origin possessing superficial undulatory siphonage germane to seismic disturbance."

Christian, pop-eyed at this unexpected exhibition of learning on his master's part, remarked only: "How very extraordinary!" and thereafter maintained an awed silence.

The next day Grosvenor signaled the *Madeleine*, on her return trip, and taking Christian with him, returned to San Juan "for certain necessary supplies which had been overlooked."

From there he sent the company a long letter in which he enlarged on the danger of the periodic gas-escape and gave a favorable report on the island's forestation. He discharged Christian with a recommendation and a liberal bonus. Then he returned to Saona alone and completed his month's survey, doing his own cooking, and sleeping with no attention to non-existent insects. He did not visit the island's center again. He wished to expedite the woodcutting in every possible way, and disliked the loss of even a day.

The survey completed—in three weeks—he went back to San Juan, cabled his full report, and was at once instructed to assemble his gang and begin.

Within another month, despite the wails of '*mañana*'—tomorrow—a village, with himself as lawmaker, guide, philosopher, friend, and boss was established on Saona. Cooks, camp roustabouts, woodcutters, and the paraphernalia of an American enterprise established themselves as though by magic, and the cutting began. Only trees in excess of a certain girth were to be taken down.

By almost superhuman efforts on Grosvenor's part, the entire job was finished well within the three-month period. Three days before the exact date when the gas was to be expected, every trace of the village except the space it had occupied was gone, and not a person was left on Saona's surface. The great collection of mahogany he had made he took, beginning a week later, by tugboat to San Juan, whence it was reshipped to New York and Boston, to Steinway, and Bristol and other boat-building centers; to Ohio to veneering plants; to Michigan to the enormous shops of the Greene and Postlewaithe Furniture Company.

Grosvenor's job was finished.

In response to his application to the company, he was granted a month's well-earned vacation, accompanied by a substantial bonus for his good work.

This time he did not travel by the *Madeleine* to Saona. Instead he took ship for Port-au-Prince, Haiti, thence by another vessel to Santo Domingo City; from that point, in a small, coastwise vessel, to San Pedro Macoris.

From Macoris, where he had quietly hired a small sailboat, he slipped away one moonless evening, alone. Thirty hours afterward, he reached Saona, and, making his boat fast in a small, landlocked inlet which he had discovered in the course of his surveys, and with a food-supply for two days, he walked along the beach half a mile to the mouth of the stream.

He followed the well-remembered path until he came to the edge of the woods. He had not brought his gang as far as this. There had been more than enough mahogany boles to satisfy the company without passing inland farther than the level ground.

He walked now, slowly, under the pouring sunlight of morning, across the broken ground to the cylinder's edge, and there, temporarily encamped, he waited until it began to sink. He watched it until it had gone down a dozen feet or more, and then walked around to the point where the ladder began.

The ladder was gone. Not so much as a mark in the smooth masonry indicated that there ever had been a ladder. Once more, with a sinking heart, he asked himself if his strange adventure had been a dream—a touch of sun, perhaps ...

This was, dreams and sunstrokes apart, simply inexplicable. Twice, during the course of the wood-cutting operations, the People of Pan had communicated with him, at a spot agreed upon between him and the priestess. Both times had been early in the operations. It was nearly three months since he had seen any concrete evidence of the People's existence. But, according to their agreement, the ladder-steps should have been replaced immediately after the last of his gang had left Saona. This, plainly, had not been done. Had the People of Pan, underground there, played him false? He could not bring himself to believe that; yet—there was no ladder; no possible means of communicating with them. He was as effectually cut off from them as though they had been moon-dwellers.

Grosvenor's last man had left the island three days before the season's change—September twenty-first. It was now late in October.

Ingress and egress, as he knew, had been maintained by a clever, simple arrangement. Just below ground-level a small hole had been bored through the rim, near the U-shaped opening. Through this a thin, tough cord had run to a strong, thin, climbing-rope long enough to reach the topmost step remaining. He remembered this. Perhaps the people below had left this arrangement.

He found the hole, pulled lightly on the string. The climbing-rope came to light. An ingenious system of a counter-pull string allowed the replacing of the climbing rope. Obviously the last person above ground from below had returned successfully, leaving everything shipshape here. To get down he would have to descend some thirty feet on this spindling rope to the topmost step. He tested the rope carefully. It was in good condition. There was no help for it. He must start down that way.

Very carefully he lowered himself hand over hand, his feet against the slippery inner surface of the stone cylinder. It was a ticklish job, but his fortitude sustained him. He found the step, and, holding the climbing-rope firmly, descended two more steps and groped for the handrail. He got it in his grasp, pulled the return-string until it was taut, then began the tedious descent, through its remembered stages of gradual darkening, the damp pressure of terrible depth upon the senses, the periodic glances at the lessening disk above, the strange glow of the stars ...

At last he reached the platform, groped for the door-ring, drew open the door.

In the anteroom a terrible sense of foreboding shook him. The condition of the ladder might not be a misunderstanding. Something unforeseen, fearful, might have happened!

He pulled himself together, crossed the anteroom, looked in upon the vast temple.

A sense of physical emptiness bore down upon him. The illumination was as usual—that much was reassuring. Across the expanse the great idol reared its menacing bulk, the horned head menacingly lowered.

But before it bowed and swayed no thronged mass of worshippers. The temple was empty and silent.

Shaken, trembling, the sense of foreboding still weighing heavily upon him, he started toward the distant altar.

Soon his usual vigorous optimism came back to him. These had been unworthy fears! He looked about him as he proceeded, at the dun sidewalls rising, tier upon tier of vague masonry, up to the dim vault in the darkness above. Then the sense of evil sprang out again, and struck at his heart. His mouth went dry. He hastened his pace. He began to run.

As he approached the altar, something strange, something *different*, appeared before him. The line formed by the elevation of the chancel as it rose from the flooring, stone against dull, yellowish metal, a thousand paces ahead, should have been sharp and clear. Instead, it was blurred, uneven.

As he came nearer he saw that the statue's prancing legs were heaped about with piled stuff ...

He ran on, waveringly, uncertain now. He did not want to see clearly what he suspected. He stumbled over something bulky. He stopped, turned to see what had lain in his way.

It was the body of a man, mummified—dry, leathery, brown; the blue kirtle grotesquely askew. He paused, reverently, and turned the body on its back. The expression on the face was quite peaceful, as though a natural and quiet death had overtaken the victim.

As he rose from his task, his face being near the floor's level, he saw, along it, innumerable other bodies lying about in varying postures. He stood upright and looked toward the image of the Goat. Bodies lay heaped in great mounds about the curved animal legs; more bodies lay heaped before the sanctuary.

Awestruck, but, now that he knew, somewhat steadied by this wholesale calamity which had overtaken the peaceful People of Pan, he moved quietly forward at an even pace.

Something lay across the altar.

Picking his way carefully among the massed corpses he mounted the sanctuary steps. Across the altar lay the body of the priestess, her dead arms outstretched toward the image of the Goat. She had died in her appointed place, in the very attitude of making supplication for her people who had died about her. Grosvenor, greatly moved, looked closely into the once beautiful face. It was still strangely beautiful and placid, noble in death; and upon it was an expression of profound peace. Pan had taken his priestess and his people to Himself ...

He had slightly raised the mummified body, and as he replaced it reverently back across the altar, something fluttered from it to his feet. He picked up a bit of parchment-like material. There was writing on it. Holding it, he passed back through the sanctuary to the room behind, where there would be a clearer light. The rooms were empty. Nothing had been disturbed.

The parchment was addressed to him. He spelled out, carefully, the antique, beautifully formed characters of the old literary Greek:

"Hail to thee, and farewell, O stranger. I, Clytemnestra, priestess of Pan the Merciful, address thee, that thou mayest understand. Thou art freed from thy oath of silence.

"At the change of the seasons the sacrifice failed. Our search revealed no living thing to offer to our god. Pan takes His vengeance. My people abandon this life for Acheron, for upon us has Pan loosed the poisonous airs of the underworld. As I write I faint, and I am the last to go.

"Thine, then, O kind barbarian, of the seed of them that drove from Kuba the men of Hispaniola, are the treasures of Pan's People. Of them take freely. I go now to my appointed place, at the altar of the Great Pan who gathers us to Himself. In peace and love, O barbarian of the North Continent, I greet thee. In peace and love, farewell."

Grosvenor placed the parchment in his breast-pocket. He was profoundly affected. He sat for a long time on the white stone couch. At last he rose and passed reflectively out into the underground gardens. The great flares of natural gas burned steadily at the tops of the irregular pipes.

At once he was consumed in wonder. How could these continue to burn without there having occurred a great conflagration? The amount of free gas sufficient to asphyxiate and mummify the entire population of this underground community would have ignited in one heaving cataclysm which would have blown Saona out of the water!

But—perhaps that other gas was not inflammable. Then the true explanation occurred to him abruptly. The destructive gas was heavier than the air. It would lie along the ground, and be gradually dissipated as the fresh air from the pipes leading above diluted its deadly intensity. It would not mount to the tops of these illuminating pipes. The shortest of them, as he gaged it, was sixty feet high. Of course, he would never know, positively ...

He looked about him through the lovely gardens, now his paradise. All about were the evidences of long neglect. Unshorn grass waved like standing hay in the light breeze which seemed to come from nowhere. Rotting fruit lay in heaps under the sapodilla trees.

He plucked a handful of drying grass as long as his arm, and began to twist it into the tough string of the Antilles' grass-rope. He made five or six feet of the string. He retraced his steps slowly back to the room where he had read his last message from the priestess of Pan. He passed the string through the handles of a massive golden fruit jar, emptied the liquefying mass of corrupt fruit which lay sodden in its bowl.

He slung the heavy jar on his back, returned through the sanctuary, threaded his way among the heaped bodies, began to walk back through the temple toward the anteroom.

From across that vast room he looked back. Through the dim perspective the monstrous figure of the Goat seemed to exult. With a slight shudder Charles Grosvenor passed out onto the platform. He grasped the handrail, planted his feet on the first round of the ladder, and began his long, weary climb to the top ...

HUMAN
HORRORS

Introduction to The Sixth Gargoyle

An occasional contributor to *Weird Tales* and *Fantastic Universe* in the early 1950s, David Lewis Eynon published less than a dozen stories in his career as a pulp writer. Among them is "The Sixth Gargoyle," a deeply strange, Gothic murder mystery set in The Netherlands. First published in the January 1951 issue of *Weird Tales*, "The Sixth Gargoyle" unfolds in the coastal city of Veere, located on the island of Welcheren in the southwestern province of Zeeland. Although modern engineering techniques have allowed the Dutch authorities to connect Welcheren with the Dutch mainland, the island setting in Eynon's tale is fundamental to its impact upon the reader. Indeed, by utilizing a mysterious, geographically isolated setting in order to weave a chilling tale of murder, Eynon succeeds brilliantly in setting the mood for a story most strange.

THE SIXTH GARGOYLE
David Eynon

The tiny town of Veere sits snugly on the coast of Zeeland, huddled against the dunes which protect it from the harsh Nordzee winds. On the land side thick, serrated walls hide all but its rooftops and the tower of the Raddhuis which leans, ever so little, to the North, as if it had been bucking the gales for centuries.

A sea wall edging the harbor stands staunchly against the waves which come roaring in and, when halted by the huge gray stones, throw furious clouds of spray against the tiny houses that peep out over the quay. Stubby fishing smacks bob anxiously up and down and cluster together with squeals and groans, their nets blowing frantically from their masts.

The cathedral roosts on the hill, casting a benevolent eye over the village. It soars into the gray sky and sings minor liturgies to itself as the wind flies through its spires. Flying buttresses, crumbling with age, hang at its sides like town lace. In the cemetery sheltered under the south side of the cathedral are five graves, new, without headstones. Four of the graves are filled and show fresh mounds of earth. The fifth grave is waiting, open and expectant, for its occupant.

The fifth would be filled by morning, of that much Inspector Ter Horst was certain. Who it would be he could not say for sure, but the choice fell between two men—the murderer of the preceding four villagers, or the fifth of the murderer's victims. When the last gray light of evening dwindled and darkness and the North Sea wind took possession of the village streets the choice would be made.

"It was a matter of practicality," said the gray haired Burgomeister, "to have five graves dug instead of only four." The old man leaned back in his carved chair and pulled thoughtfully at his chin. The smoke from the bowl of his church warden pipe trailed upwards towards the ceiling and lost itself among the blackened beams of the ancient city hall. Jonkheer van Berendonk looked as quaint—and as timeworn—as a Rembrandt study. His silver chain of office, worn by ten generations of Burgomeisters of Veere, shone softly against the background of his black velvet cloak. Inspector Ter Horst waited patiently until, the old man spoke again.

"It is true," the Burgomeister went on, "that we have only four dead at present. Still, if your theory is correct, by morning we will have five. It is cheaper, then, that all the graves be dug at once, and so did I arrange it."

"Yes," said Ter Horst, "Mynheer is right. By morning we will undoubtedly need another grave. What would I not give to know, who it is that will lie in it!" Ter Horst spoke vehemently, irritated with his own failure to catch the murderer and apprehensive about the possibilities of a fifth crime. An idea crossed his mind and he spoke again to the Burgomeister.

"Pardon, Mynheer," he said, "but what if both the murderer and the victim both die this night? Then there will not be enough graves to go around."

"No," the Burgomeister admitted, "but in that case, the murderer would have to be buried elsewhere than the churchyard—in unhallowed ground—so it was still cheaper to arrange the matter of the graves as I have." The old man, pleased with his logic, smiled as he bent over to light the two candles on his desk. The clock in the city hall tower struck five and both men listened intently until the last sonorous note died out.

"Then, if the schedule is adhered to," said the Burgomeister refilling his pipe, "the architect should be murdered next?"

Inspector Ter Horst nodded. The schedule, he thought, would not be kept. It could not be kept. After all, wasn't he going to be at the architect's cottage, armed, on guard? And besides, he thought, it was impossible that any man could hope to complete a series of five murders, each a week apart, each but the first fully expected by the police.

Four killings perhaps. Certainly the killer had had luck so far. But five murders, never. This time the criminal would fail and, in failing, become the occupant of the fifth grave. Inspector Ter Horst turned to the Burgomeister and, more to clear his own thoughts than to be enlightening, reviewed the details of the case.

"It is unthinkable," he said, "that this madman could strike once again."

"Imagine, Mynheer, even the shrewdest madman—for we certainly deal with a madman—being able to kill five persons in accordance with a set plan and still escape capture. Especially when his identity is known."

The Burgomeister raised his eyebrows. "You know who the man is?" he asked.

"In a sense, we do," said Ter Horst. "His name, of course, not. But we know he is mad—and that is something. Then, we know he is of a family that has been here since the cathedral was built. He is agile, enough so to baptize each of the succeeding stone figures with blood, after he has destroyed their human counterparts. He is not, therefore, an old man."

The Burgomeister's wrinkled face arranged itself into a slight smile. He was amused at the way this policeman built up theories on nothing—houses of cards, he thought, that stood but a short time in the wind of reality.

Ter Horst continued talking, not noticing the old man's amusement. "A man of some education, I should say. Enough, at least to have made use of the records in the cathedral crypt. He must have traced records far enough to determine that each of his victims is a direct descendant of someone who helped construct the church. Our man knows Latin, at least."

The Inspector paused to light his cigar, which had gone out as he waved it about to illustrate his points. The Burgomeister got up for a moment to secure a shutter that had blown loose and was banging against the window frame.

"But this schedule," the Burgomeister asked, "on what is it based? How do you ascertain that the architect is next in his thoughts?"

"Ah," the Inspector chuckled. "A lucky accident, that. Pure chance that we noticed a spot of blood on the forehead of the first gargoyle. Just in searching the cathedral for a possible fugitive did we see it. Then, of course, certain facts fell into place and forced a conclusion.

"Imagine, six gargoyles straddling a flying buttress. Six little stone figures climbing toward the spires of the church. An artist, an engineer, a stonemason, a bricklayer and an architect."

The Inspector stopped and lighted a fresh cigar with one of the candles. He spoke between puffs. "One by one each is murdered."

"Except the architect," the Burgomeister inserted.

"Except the architect," Ter Horst nodded. But each of the others has been murdered, and in the order of his position on the buttress. Each man a direct descendant of, and in the same profession as, his ancestor who is represented in stone by the gargoyles.

"Imagine the uniqueness of the motive behind such a crime—if madness can be called a motive."

The Burgorneister leaned forward in his chair. "How," he asked, "do you know that the sixth gargoyle is the criminal? Why not, for instance, the fifth gargoyle?" With this he smiled laconically at the short, fat Inspector ...

Ter Horst was not impressed by the idea. He deprecated it with a wave of his hand and, noticing that his cigar was out again, leaned towards the candles. "It is," he said between puffs, "the sixth gargoyle because he is the only one who cannot be located. The first five are easily traceable. From the church records we know exactly who the first five men must be. And the subsequent deaths of the first five men must be. And the subsequent deaths of the first four hold exactly with our findings. Of the sixth gargoyle there is not a trace of information."

The Burgomeister settled back in his chair and mused to himself for several minutes. The crackling of the fire was almost drowned out by the wind's moan as it writhed around the tower of the Raddhuis. The Burgomeister looked up sharply at Ter Horst.

"This sixth stone figure," he asked, "what does it represent? What sort of figure is it?"

Ter Horst gently stamped out his cigar butt on the tiles of the hearth. "The sixth gargoyle," he said quietly, "is the figure of a man committing suicide."

"So," said the Burgomeister. His tone showed a heightened interest. "Then we *are* perhaps dealing with a madman." The old man's huge dog lumbered up from the hearth. He stretched himself laboriously and then stalked over to be petted. The old man rubbed the dog's neck gently and the animal groaned in appreciation.

"And just what do you do now?" the Burgomeister asked. "Is it necessary to wait until the architect is murdered to discover this madman's identity? Or do you wait until he kills himself, as he must, if your theory is correct."

"Two things I plan," Ter Horst said earnestly. "First, in the crypt below the cathedral, my men are pouring over the records to find any clue that remains which will point to our criminal."

"And if he has removed such records," smiled the Burgomeister, "when he made his own investigation?"

"Then," said Ter Horst, "there is a grave on the left side of the church, in unhallowed ground. Perhaps it may hold a clue, since it is, in all probability, the resting place of our original suicide."

"You would open the grave?" asked the Burgomeister. "There won't be much after four centuries."

"No," said Ter Horst, "but it is worth trying. If Mynheer would give his permission for such an act?"

The Burgomeister rubbed his leonine head, fingering the silver chain with his other hand. "I don't know," he said slowly. "It is an unusual request—and rather futile to search in any case, I fear. I would have to think it over. Besides, it is time for dinner," he said, noticing that his dog was nervously scratching at the door. "I will let you know in the morning."

"Of course, Mynheer," Ter Horst said, rising as the old man left the room and moved slowly down the stairs.

Ter Horst left the city hall and made his way over the slippery cobblestones to the architect's small cottage, just inside the city gates. The Inspector knocked and was admitted by the tall, thin architect who knew the stubby policeman from, the past weeks of investigation.

The host seated Ter Horst before the fire and took his coat. In a few minutes the policeman was nursing a glass of fiery Dutch "Geneva" and posting the architect on the latest developments of the case.

"As soon as we have the permission of the old Burgomeister," said Ter Horst, "we will open that grave. The Burgomeister is rather old-fashioned, you understand. He feels that it should be permitted only as a last resort, and we have to humor him."

"It is easy for old Berendonk to be conservative," the architect said with a smile, "where my life is concerned. Still, I don't think you would gain much in any case." He got up and went to a closet in the corner of the room. Opening the door, he drew out a raincoat and turned to Ter Horst.

"Since it is the night appointed for my demise," he said, "I feel guilty about wasting it in inactivity. Perhaps if we go to the cathedral I, as an architect, can help you in locating some information."

"If you're not nervous about going out," said Ter Horst.

"I will be less nervous if I am busy," said the architect.

On the slippery cobblestone road up the hill to the cathedral Ter Horst explained the circumstances of the crimes. He spoke loudly to be heard above the wind. Occasionally he had to repeat as he skipped along to keep up with the lanky architect.

"They were bludgeoned," he shouted as they reached the cathedral steps.

"What?"

"Bludgeoned, heads bashed in," Ter Horst said. They had stepped within the doors by now and his voice soared up into the roof of the darkened church. A policeman, on guard in the shadows, flashed his light on them. Seeing Ter Horst, he saluted.

"We're going down to the crypts," Ter Horst said.

The officer nodded and stepped back into the shadows.

As the two men descended the stone steps to the underground section of the church, their feet rang on the stairs. At the first doorway they were met by a young lieutenant.

"Ah, it's you, sir," he said, "I think we've got something."

Ter Horst introduced the architect. The young policeman showed obvious admiration for the man's nerve. "I can imagine you can make more sense from these documents than I can," the lieutenant said, handing the papers to the architect.

The architect took the sheaf of yellowed parchments and leafed through them slowly. At intervals he bent closer to scrutinize a poorly written phrase. Occasionally he muttered to himself. At the last page he chuckled and looked up at Ter Horst.

"You were indeed right, Inspector," the architect said. "Our madman has a unique motive indeed. It would appear that he, just as his victims, has followed the calling of his family—though how long this madness has lain dormant in his line no one knows."

"What do you find?" Ter Horst asked anxiously.

"This," said the architect, rustling the sheaf of parchment, "is the record of an unfortunate incident. It occurred during the construction of the cathedral, as you guessed.

"It seems that one of the casters—the men who made and installed the bells—went mad. Perhaps from the constant vibrations. In any case he

jumped from the tower one day. Not necessarily a suicide, you understand—it could have been an accident. However the priest was doubtful.
He called in the witnesses—an artist, an engineer, a stonemason, a bricklayer and an architect. On the basis of their testimony he decided that the
man was a suicide. Of course, he could not then be buried in holy ground."

Ter Horst thought for a minute. "You mean our murderer now takes revenge for an ancestor, who was buried without grace? Five murders for a
madman of the sixteenth century?"

"So it would appear," said the architect.

And even as he handed the parchments back to the lieutenant a stone,
dropped from the ceiling high above, fell directly on his head and crushed
his skull. The lieutenant had taken the sheaf of papers from a dead hand
and before he realized what had occurred the architect was slumped on the
floor with a widening pool of blood around his head.

The two policemen instinctively jumped back and then, seeing that the
architect was beyond aid, rushed up the long stairway to the floor level.

The ground floor of the church was empty. No one could have passed
out the door. Ter Horst ordered it locked and then beckoned the lieutenant
and his men to follow him up the stairway into the spire.

The exposed steps were mouldy with age and slippery with rain. The
wind's strength made going difficult. As they approached the level where
the still intact buttresses leaned against the church wall, Ter Horst stopped.

Across the stairway was a rod about six feet long. At one end it had a
knob. On the other was a bunch of feathers. The feathers were stiff and
dark with dried blood.

"So," thought Ter Horst, "we are not dealing with such an agile man after all. He has baptized the gargoyles with a tipstaff's rod."

He handed the rod to an officer at his side and walked, over to the edge
where he could see the six figures on the buttress. The moon went behind
the clouds at intervals. As he leaned over the edge it appeared again. In the
pale light he looked down the row of figures to the sixth gargoyle. Standing on the buttress was a huge dark figure that looked like an oversized
bat with its wings flung out.

As the moonlight came to full strength, Ter Horst could see the white
haired old Burgomeister clearly. His silver chain of office hung around his
neck, over the black velvet robe. The Burgomeister caught sight of Ter
Horst and laughed loudly. His laugh got more and more intense until it
shook his whole body. Ter Horst was about to call out when the Burgomeister lost his footing on the slippery stonework and tottered.

He fell a few feet and then his body was snapped up sharply. Ter Horst
saw that his chain of office had caught around the stone figure of the sixth

gargoyle. As the moon went behind the clouds once more, Ter Horst could see the figure of the Burgomeister swinging back and forth in the wind, his cloak flapping out behind him like the wings of a bat.

Introduction to Three Skeleton Key

George G. Toudouze (1877-1972) was a French writer and author of numerous adventure novels, children's novels, and short stories. He was born in Paris to a novelist father. In his lifetime, Toudouze was awarded both the Legion of Honor and the Prix de l'Académie française. He was also a resident of the Académie de France in Rome.

In the English-speaking world, however, Toudouze is best known for writing "Three Skeleton Key." First published in English translation in the January 1937 issue of *Esquire*, the action in "Three Skeleton Key" takes place in a lighthouse on a small island off the coast of South America. In blending elements of the modern ghost story with those of weird fiction, Toudouze has produced an unforgettably creepy story that delves deep into that universal human emotion: fear. As in many other stories included in this collection, this tale demonstrates how very much a remote island setting can test the most intrepid of men into a life or death confrontation with living nightmares. Also of note, "Three Skeleton Key" was adapted several times for radio, with the famous horror actor Vincent Price lending his voice to the project on three separate occasions.

THREE SKELETON KEY
George G. Toudouze

My most terrifying experience? Well, one does have a few in thirty-five years of service in the Lights, although it's mostly monotonous routine work—keeping the light in order, making out the reports.

When I was a young man, not very long in the service, there was an opening in a lighthouse newly built off the coast of Guiana, on a small rock twenty miles or so from the mainland. The pay was high, so in order to reach the sum I had set out to save before I married, I volunteered for service in the new light.

Three Skeleton Key, the small rock on which the light stood, bore a bad reputation. It earned its name from the story of the three convicts who, escaping from Cayenne in a stolen dugout canoe, were wrecked on the rock during the night, managed to escape the sea but eventually died of hunger and thirst. When they were discovered, nothing remained but three heaps of bones, picked clean by the birds. The story was that the three skeletons, gleaming with phosphorescent light, danced over the small rock, screaming....

But there are many such stories, and I did not give the warnings of the old-timers at the Isle de Sein a second thought. I signed up, boarded ship, and in a month I was installed at the light.

Picture a grey, tapering cylinder, welded to the solid black rock by iron rods and concrete, rising from a small island twenty odd miles from land. It lay in the midst of the sea, this island, a small, bare piece of stone, about one hundred fifty feet long, perhaps forty wide. Small, barely large enough for a man to walk about and stretch his legs at low tide.

This is an advantage one doesn't find in all lights, however, for some of them rise sheer from the waves, with no room for one to move save within the light itself. Still, on our island, one must be careful, for the rocks were treacherously smooth. One misstep and down you would fall into the sea— not that the risk of drowning was so great, but the waters about our island swarmed with huge sharks who kept an eternal patrol around the base of the light.

Still, it was a nice life there. We had enough provisions to last for months, in the event that the sea should become too rough for the supply ship to reach us on schedule. During the day we would work about the light, cleaning the rooms, polishing the metalwork and the lens and reflector of the light itself, and at night we would sit on the gallery and watch our light, a twenty thousand candle-power lantern, swinging its strong, white bar of light over the sea from the top of its hundred-twenty-foot tower. Some days, when the air would be very clear, we could see the land, a thread-like line to the west. To the east, north and south stretched the ocean. Landsmen, perhaps, would soon have tired of that kind of life, perched on a small island off the coast of South America for eighteen weeks, until one's turn for leave ashore came around. But we liked it there, my two fellow-tenders and myself so much so that, for twenty-two months on end with the exception of shore leaves, I was greatly satisfied with the life on Three Skeleton Key.

I had just returned from my leave at the end of June, that is to say midwinter in that latitude, and had settled down to the routine with my two fellow-keepers, a Breton by the name of Le Gleo and the head-keeper, Itchoua, a Basque some dozen years or so older than either of us.

Eight days went by as usual, then on the ninth night after my return, Itchoua, who was on night duty, called Le Gleo and me, sleeping in our rooms in the middle of the tower, at two in the morning. We rose immediately and, climbing the thirty or so steps that led to the gallery, stood beside our chief.

Itchoua pointed, and following his finger, we saw a big three-master, with all sail set, heading straight for the light. A queer course, for the vessel must have seen us, our light lit her with the glare of day each time it passed over her.

Now, ships were a rare sight in our waters, for our light was a warning of treacherous reefs, barely hidden under the surface and running far out to sea. Consequently we were always given a wide berth, especially by sailing vessels, which cannot maneuver as readily as steamers.

No wonder that we were surprised at seeing this three-master heading dead for us in the gloom of early morning. I had immediately recognized her lines, for she stood out plainly, even at the distance of a mile, when our light shone on her.

She was a beautiful ship of some four thousand tons, a fast sailor that had carried cargoes to every part of the world, plowing the seas unceasingly. By her lines she was identified as Dutch-built, which was understandable as Paramaribo and Dutch Guiana are very close to Cayenne.

Watching her sailing dead for us, a white wave boiling under her bows, Le Gleo cried out:

"What's wrong with her crew? Are they all drunk or insane? Can't they see us?"

Itchoua nodded soberly, looked at us sharply as he remarked: "See us? No doubt—if there is a crew aboard!"

"What do you mean, chief?" Le Gleo had started, turned to the Basque,

"Are you saying that she's the Flying Dutchman?"

His sudden fright had been so evident that the older man laughed:

"No, old man, that's not what I meant. If I say that no one's aboard, I mean she's a derelict."

Then we understood his queer behavior. Itchoua was right. For some reason, believing her doomed, her crew had abandoned her. Then she had righted herself and sailed on, wandering with the wind.

The three of us grew tense as the ship seemed about to crash on one of our numerous reefs, but she suddenly lurched with some change of the wind, the yards swung around, and the derelict came clumsily about and sailed dead away from us.

In the light of our lantern she seemed so sound, so strong, that Itchoua exclaimed impatiently:

"But why the devil was she abandoned? Nothing is smashed, no sign of fire—and she doesn't sail as if she were taking water."

Le Gleo waved to the departing ship:

"Bon voyage!" he smiled at Itchoua and went on. "She's leaving us, chief, and now we'll never know what—"

"No she's not!" cried the Basque. "Look! She's turning!"

As if obeying his words, the derelict three-master stopped, came about and headed for us once more. And for the next four hours the vessel played around us—zigzagging, coming about, stopping, then suddenly lurching forward. No doubt some freak of current and wind, of which our island was the center, kept her near us.

Then suddenly, the tropic dawn broke, the sun rose and it was day, and the ship was plainly visible as she sailed past us. Our light extinguished, we returned to the gallery with our glasses and inspected her.

The three of us focused our glasses on her poop, saw standing out sharply, black letters on the white background of a life-ring, the stenciled name:

"*Cornelius-de-Witt*, Rotterdam."

We had read her lines correctly, she was Dutch. Just then the wind rose and the *Cornelius-de-Witt* changed course, leaned to port and headed straight for us once more. But this time she was so close that we knew she would not turn in time.

"Thunder!" cried Le Gleo, his Breton soul aching to see a fine ship doomed to smash upon a reef, "She's going to pile up! She's gone!"

I shook my head:

"Yes, and a shame to see that beautiful ship wreck herself. And we're helpless."

There was nothing we could do but watch. A ship sailing with all sail spread, creaming the sea with her forefoot as she runs before the wind, is one of the most beautiful sights in the world—but this time I could feel the tears stinging my eyes as I saw this fine ship headed for her doom.

All this time our glasses were riveted on her, and we suddenly cried out together:

"The rats!"

Now we knew why this ship, in perfect condition, was sailing without her crew aboard. They had been driven out by the rats. Not those poor specimens of rats you see ashore, barely reaching the length of one foot from their trembling noses to the tip of their skinny tails, wretched creatures that dodge and hide at the mere sound of a footfall.

No, these were ships' rats, huge, wise creatures, born on the sea, sailing all over the world on ships, transferring to other, larger ships as they multiply. There is as much difference between the rats of the land and these maritime rats as between a fishing smack and an armored cruiser.

The rats of the sea are fierce, bold animals. Large, strong and intelligent, clannish and seawise, able to put the best of mariners to shame with their knowledge of the sea, their uncanny ability to foretell the weather.

And they are brave, these rats, and vengeful. If you so much as harm one, his sharp cry will bring hordes of his fellows to swarm over you, tear you and not cease until your flesh has been stripped from the bones.

The ones on this ship, the rats of Holland, are the worst, superior to other rats of the sea as their brethren are to the land rats. There is a well-known tale about these animals.

A Dutch captain, thinking to protect his cargo, brought aboard his ship—not cats—but two terriers, dogs trained in the hunting, fighting and killing of vicious rats. By the time the ship, sailing from Rotterdam, had passed the Ostend light, the dogs were gone and never seen again. In twenty-four hours they had been overwhelmed, killed and eaten by the rats.

At times, when the cargo does not suffice, the rats attack the crew, either driving them from the ship or eating them alive. And studying the *Cornelius-de-Witt*, I turned sick, for her small boats were all in place. She had not been abandoned.

Over her bridge, on her deck, in the rigging, on every visible spot, the ship was a writhing mass—a starving army coming towards us aboard a vessel gone mad!

Our island was a small spot in that immense stretch of sea. The ship could have grazed us, passed to port or starboard with its ravening cargo but no, she came for us at full speed, as if she were leading the regatta at a race, and impaled herself on a sharp point of rock.

There was a dull shock as her bottom stove in, then a horrible crackling as the three masts went overboard at once, as if cut down with one blow of some gigantic sickle. A sighing groan came as the water rushed into the ship, then she split in two and sank like a stone.

But the rats did not drown. Not these fellows! As much at home in the sea as any fish, they formed ranks in the water, heads lifted, tails stretched out, paws paddling. And half of them, those from the forepart of the ship, sprang along the masts and onto the rocks in the instant before she sank. Before we had time even to move, nothing remained of the three-master save some pieces of wreckage floating on the surface and an army of rats covering the rocks left bare by the receding tide.

Thousands of heads rose, felt the wind and we were scented, seen! To them we were fresh meat, after possible weeks of starving. There came a scream, composed of innumerable screams, sharper than the howl of a saw attacking a bar of iron, and in the one motion, every rat leaped to attack the tower!

We barely had time to leap back, close the door leading onto the gallery, descend the stairs and shut every window tightly. Luckily the door at the base of the light, which we never could have reached in time, was of bronze set in granite and was tightly closed.

The horrible band, in no measurable time, had swarmed up and over the tower as if it had been a tree, piled on the embrasures of the windows, scraped at the glass with thousands of claws, covered the lighthouse with a furry mantle and reached the top of the tower, filling the gallery and piling atop the lantern.

Their teeth grated as they pressed against the glass of the lantern-room, where they could plainly see us, though they could not reach us. A few millimeters of glass, luckily very strong, separated our faces from their gleaming, beady eyes, their sharp claws and teeth. Their odor filled the tower, poisoned our lungs and rasped our nostrils with a pestilential, nauseating smell. And there we were, sealed alive in our own light, prisoners of a horde of starving rats.

That first night, the tension was so great that we could not sleep. Every moment, we felt that some opening had been made, some window given away, and that our horrible besiegers were pouring through the breach. The rising tide, chasing those of the rats which had stayed on the bare rocks, increased the numbers clinging to the walls, piled on the balcony—so much so that clusters of rats clinging to one another hung from the lantern and the gallery.

With the coming of darkness we lit the light, and the turning beam completely maddened the beasts. As the light turned, it successively blinded thousands of rats crowded against the glass, while the dark side of the lantern-room gleamed with thousands of points of light, burning like the eyes of jungle beasts in the night.

All the while we could hear the enraged scraping of claws against the stone and glass, while the chorus of cries was so loud that we had to shout to hear one another. From time to time, some of the rats fought among themselves and a dark cluster would detach itself, falling into the sea like a ripe fruit from a tree. Then we would see phosphorescent streaks as triangular fins slashed the water—sharks, permanent guardians of our rock, feasting on our jailors.

The next day we were calmer, and amused ourselves by teasing the rats, placing our faces against the glass which separated us. They could not fathom the invisible barrier which separated them from us, and we laughed as we watched them leaping against the heavy glass.

But the day after that, we realized how serious our position was. The air was foul; even the heavy smell of oil within our stronghold could not dominate the fetid odor of the beasts massed around us, and there was no way of admitting fresh air without also admitting the rats.

The morning of the fourth day, at early dawn, I saw the wooden framework of my window, eaten away from the outside, sagging inwards. I called my comrades and the three of us fastened a sheet of tin in the opening, sealing it tightly. When we had completed the task, Itchoua turned to us and said dully:

"Well—the supply boat came thirteen days ago, and she won't be back for twenty-nine." He pointed at the white metal plate sealing the opening through the granite— "If that gives way—" he shrugged— "they can change the name of this place to Six Skeletons Key."

The next six days and seven nights, our only distraction was watching the rats whose holds were insecure fall a hundred and twenty feet into the maws of the sharks—but they were so many that we could not see any diminution in their numbers.

Thinking to calm ourselves and pass the time, we attempted to count them, but we soon gave up. They moved incessantly, never still. Then we tried identifying them, naming them.

One of them, larger than the others, who seemed to lead them in their rushes against the glass separating us, we named "Nero"; and there were several others whom we had learned to distinguish through various peculiarities.

But the thought of our bones joining those of the convicts was always in the back of our minds. And the gloom of our prison fed these thoughts, for the interior of the light was almost completely dark, as we had to seal every window in the same fashion as mine, and the only space that still admitted daylight was the glassed-in lantern-room at the very top of the tower.

Then Le Gleo became morose and had nightmares in which he would see the three skeletons dancing around him, gleaming coldly, seeking to grasp him. His maniacal, raving descriptions were so vivid that Itchoua and I began seeing them also.

It was a living nightmare, the raging cries of the rats as they swarmed over the light, mad with hunger; the sickening, strangling odor of their bodies—

True, there is a way of signaling from lighthouses, But to reach the mast on which to hang the signal we would have to go out on the gallery where the rats were.

There was only one thing left to do. After debating all of the ninth day, we decided not to light the lantern that night. This is the greatest breach of our service, never committed as long as the tenders of the light are alive; for the light is something sacred, warning ships of danger in the night. Either the light gleams, a quarter hour after sundown, or no one is left alive to light it.

Well, that night, Three Skeleton Light was dark, and all the men were alive. At the risk of causing ships to crash on our reefs, we left it unlit, for we were worn out—going mad!

At two in the morning, while Itchoua was dozing in his room, the sheet of metal sealing his window gave way. The chief had just time enough to leap to his feet and cry for help, the rats swarming over him.

But Le Gleo and I, who had been watching from the lantern-room, got to him immediately, and the three of us battled with the horde of maddened rats which flowed through the gaping window. They bit, we struck them down with our knives—and retreated.

We locked the door of the room on them, but before we had time to bind our wounds, the door was eaten through and gave way, and we retreated up the stairs, fighting off the rats that leaped on us from the knee-deep swarm.

I do not remember, to this day, how we ever managed to escape. All I can remember is wading through them up the stairs, striking them off as they swarmed over us; and then we found ourselves, bleeding from innumerable bites, our clothes shredded, sprawled across the trapdoor in the floor of the lantern-room—without food or drink, Luckily, the trapdoor was metal set into the granite with iron bolts.

The rats occupied the entire light beneath us, and on the floor of our retreat lay some twenty of their fellows, who had gotten in with us before the trapdoor closed, and whom we had killed without knives. Below us, in the tower, we could hear the screams of the rats as they devoured everything edible that they found. Those on the outside squealed in reply, and writhed in a horrible curtain as they stared at us through the glass of the lantern-room.

Itchoua sat up, stared silently at his blood trickling from the wounds on his limbs and body, and running in thin streams on the floor around him. Le Gleo, who was in as bad a state (and so was I, for that matter) stared at the chief and me vacantly, started as his gaze swung to the multitude of rats against the glass, then suddenly began laughing horribly:

"Hee! Hee! The Three Skeletons! Hee! Hee! The Three Skeletons are now *six* skeletons! *Six* skeletons!"

He threw his head back and howled, his eyes glazed, a trickle of saliva running from the corners of his mouth and thinning the blood flowing over his chest. I shouted to him to shut up, but he did not hear me, so I did the only thing I could to quiet him—I swung the back of my hand across his face.

The howling stopped suddenly, his eyes swung around the room, then he bowed his head and began weeping softly, like a child.

Our darkened light had been noticed from the mainland, and as dawn was breaking, the patrol was there to investigate the failure of our light. Looking through my binoculars, I could see the horrified expression on the faces of the officers and crew when, the daylight strengthening, they saw the light completely covered by a seething mass of rats. They thought, as I afterwards found out, that we had been eaten alive.

But the rats had also seen the ship, or had scented the crew. As the ship drew nearer, a solid phalanx left the light, plunged into the water and, swimming out, attempted to board her. They would have succeeded, as the ship was hove to, but the engineer connected his steam to a hose on the deck and scalded the head of the attacking column, which slowed them up long enough for the ship to get underway and leave the rats behind.

Then the sharks took part. Belly up, mouths gaping, they arrived in swarms and scooped up the rats, sweeping through them like a sickle through wheat. That was one day that sharks really served a useful purpose. The remaining rats turned tail, swam to the shore, and emerged dripping. As they neared the light, their comrades greeted them with shrill cries, with what sounded like a derisive note predominating. They answered angrily and mingled with their fellows. From the several tussles that broke out, they resented being ridiculed for their failure to capture the ship.

But all this did nothing to get us out of our jail. The small ship could not approach, but steamed around the light at a safe distance, and the tower must have seemed fantastic, some weird, many-mouthed beast hurling defiance at them.

Finally, seeing the rats running in and out of the tower through the door and the windows, those on the ship decided that we had perished and were about to leave when Itchoua, regaining his senses, thought of using the light as a signal. He lit it and, using a plank placed and withdrawn before the beam to form the dots and dashes, quickly sent out our story to those on the vessel.

Our reply came quickly. When they understood our position—how we could not get rid of the rats, Le Gleo's mind going fast, Itchoua and myself covered with bites, cornered in the lantern-room without food or water—they had a signal-man send us their reply.

His arms, swinging like those of a windmill, he quickly spelled out: "Don't give up. Hang on a little longer! We'll get you out of this!"

Then she turned and steamed at top speed for the coast, leaving us little reassured. She was back at noon, accompanied by the supply ship, two small coast guard boats, and the fire boat—a small squadron. At twelve-thirty the battle was on.

After a short reconnaissance, the fire boat picked her way slowly through the reefs until she was close to us, then turned her powerful jet of water on the rats. The heavy stream tore the rats from their places, hurled them screaming into the water where the sharks gulped them down. But for every ten that were dislodged, seven swam ashore, and the stream could do nothing to the rats within the tower. Furthermore, some of them, instead of returning to the rocks, boarded the fire boat, and the men were forced to battle them hand to hand. They were true rats of Holland, fearing no man, fighting for the right to live!

Nightfall came, and it was as if nothing had been done, the rats were still in possession. One of the patrol boats stayed by the island; the rest of the flotilla departed for the coast. We had to spend another night in our prison. Le Gleo was sitting on the floor, babbling about skeletons, and as I turned to Itchoua, he fell unconscious from his wounds. I was in no better shape and could feel my blood flaming with fever.

Somehow the night dragged by, and the next afternoon I saw a tug, accompanied by the fire boat, coming from the mainland with a huge barge in tow. Through my glasses, I saw that the barge was filled with meat.

Risking the treacherous reefs, the tug dragged the barge as close to the island as possible. To the last rat, our besiegers deserted the rock, swam out and boarded the barge reeking with the scent of freshly cut meat. The tug dragged the barge about a mile from shore, where the fire boat drenched the barge with gasoline. A well placed incendiary shell from the patrol boat set her on fire.

The barge was covered with flames immediately, and the rats took to the water in swarms, but the patrol boat bombarded them with shrapnel from a safe distance, and the sharks finished off the survivors.

A whaleboat from the patrol boat took us off the island and left three men to replace us. By nightfall we were in the hospital in Cayenne.

What became of my friends? Well, Le Gleo's mind had cracked and he was raving mad. They sent him back to France and locked him up in an asylum, the poor devil; Itchoua died within a week; a rat's bite is dangerous in that hot, humid climate, and infection sets in rapidly.

As for me—when they fumigated the light and repaired the damage done by the rats, I resumed my service there. Why not? No reason why such an incident should keep me from finishing out my service there, is there?

Besides—I told you I liked the place—to be truthful, I've never had a post as pleasant as that one, and when my time came to leave it forever, I tell you that I almost wept as Three Skeleton Key disappeared below the horizon.

Introduction to Good-By Jack

Author Jack London (1876-1916) is best known for his literary works chronicling the Klondike Gold Rush of the late nineteenth-century. The novels *The Call of the Wild* (1903) and *White Fang* (1906) and the short story, "To Build a Fire" (1902, revised 1908) are among the most read works in early twentieth-century American literature. London also authored a dystopian science fiction novel entitled *The Scarlet Plague* (1912) as well as numerous books of poetry.

In addition to his stories set in the Canadian north, London wrote numerous stories set in the Hawaiian Islands. Published in *The House of Pride & Other Tales of Hawaii* (1912), "Good-by, Jack" is a horror story of a different breed. Eschewing the supernatural for naturalism, London writes of an all-too-human horror, that of leprosy and the manner by which governments of the past have exiled lepers with their strange disfigurements, so as to render them effectively invisible.

Although a relatively short tale, "Good-by Jack" is the type of story that remains lodged in one's memory long after reading it. With its obsessive focus on death, it is a devastatingly sad tale that evokes despair in the reader. London's description of the leper colony on the Hawaiian island of Molokai, a land from which no one ever returns, is poignantly bleak: "There was much talk and feeling among the natives, fanned by the demagogues, concerning the cruelties of Molokai, where men and women, not alone banished from friends and family, were compelled to live in perpetual imprisonment until they died. There were no reprieves, no commutations or sentences. 'Abandon hope' was written over the portal of Molokai."

This island story is a fitting reminder of how island paradises can just as easily be transformed into island prisons.

GOOD-BYE, JACK

Jack London

Hawaii is a queer place. Everything socially is what I may call topsy-turvy. Not but what things are correct. They are almost too much so. But still things are sort of upside down. The most ultra-exclusive set there is the "Missionary Crowd." It comes with rather a shock to learn that in Hawaii the obscure martyrdom-seeking missionary sits at the head of the table of the moneyed aristocracy. But it is true. The humble New Englanders who came out in the third decade of the nineteenth century, came for the lofty purpose of teaching the Kanakas the true religion, the worship of the one only genuine and undeniable God. So well did they succeed in this, and also in civilizing the Kanaka, that by the second or third generation he was practically extinct. This being the fruit of the seed of the Gospel, the fruit of the seed of the missionaries (the sons and the grandsons) was the possession of the islands themselves—of the land, the ports, the town sites, and the sugar plantations. The missionary who came to give the bread of life remained to gobble up the whole heathen feast.

But that is not the Hawaiian queerness I started out to tell. Only one cannot speak of things Hawaiian without mentioning the missionaries. There is Jack Kersdale, the man I wanted to tell about; he came of missionary stock. That is, on his grandmother's side. His grandfather was old Benjamin Kersdale, a Yankee trader, who got his start for a million in the old days by selling cheap whiskey and square-face gin. There's another queer thing. The old missionaries and old traders were mortal enemies. You see, their interests conflicted. But their children made it up by intermarrying and dividing the island between them.

Life in Hawaii is a song. That's the way Stoddard put it in his "Hawaii Nei":

"Thy life is music—Fate the notes prolong!
Each isle a stanza, and the whole a song."

And he was right. Flesh is golden there. The native women are sun-ripe Junos, the native men bronzed Apollos. They sing, and dance, and all are flower-bejeweled and flower-crowned. And, outside the rigid "Missionary Crowd," the white men yield to the climate and the sun, and no matter how busy they may be, are prone to dance and sing and wear flowers behind their ears and in their hair. Jack Kersdale was one of these fellows. He was one of the busiest men I ever met. He was a several-times millionaire. He was a sugar-king, a coffee planter, a rubber pioneer, a cattle rancher, and a promoter of three out of every four new enterprises launched in the islands. He was a society man, a club man, a yachtsman, a bachelor, and withal as handsome a man as was ever doted upon by mammas with marriageable daughters. Incidentally, he had finished his education at Yale, and his head was crammed fuller with vital statistics and scholarly information concerning Hawaii Nei than any other islander I ever encountered. He turned off an immense amount of work, and he sang and danced and put flowers in his hair as immensely as any of the idlers.

He had grit, and had fought two duels—both political—when he was no more than a raw youth essaying his first adventures in politics. In fact, he played a most creditable and courageous part in the last revolution, when the native dynasty was overthrown; and he could not have been over sixteen at the time. I am pointing out that he was no coward, in order that you may appreciate what happens later on. I've seen him in the breaking yard at the Haleakala Ranch, conquering a four-year-old brute that for two years had defied the pick of Von Tempsky's cowboys. And I must tell of one other thing. It was down in Kona—or up, rather, for the Kona people scorn to live at less than a thousand feet elevation. We were all on the *lanai* of Doctor Goodhue's bungalow. I was talking with Dottie Fairchild when it happened. A big centipede—it was seven inches, for we measured it afterwards—fell from the rafters overhead squarely into her coiffure. I confess, the hideousness of it paralyzed me. I couldn't move. My mind refused to work. There, within two feet of me, the ugly venomous devil was writhing in her hair. It threatened at any moment to fall down upon her exposed shoulders—we had just come out from dinner.

"What is it?" she asked, starting to raise her hand to her head.

"Don't!" I cried. "Don't!"

"But what is it?" she insisted, growing frightened by the fright she read in my eyes and on my stammering lips.

My exclamation attracted Kersdale's attention. He glanced our way carelessly, but in that glance took in everything. He came over to us, but without haste.

"Please don't move, Dottie," he said quietly.

He never hesitated, nor did he hurry and make a bungle of it.

"Allow me," he said.

And with one hand he caught her scarf and drew it tightly around her shoulders so that the centipede could not fall inside her bodice. With the other hand—the right—he reached into her hair, caught the repulsive abomination as near as he was able by the nape of the neck, and held it tightly between thumb and forefinger as he withdrew it from her hair. It was as horrible and heroic a sight as man could wish to see. It made my flesh crawl. The centipede, seven inches of squirming legs, writhed and twisted and dashed itself about his hand, the body twining around the fingers and the legs digging into the skin and scratching as the beast endeavored to free itself. It bit him twice—I saw it—though he assured the ladies that he was not harmed as he dropped it upon the walk and stamped it into the gravel. But I saw him in the surgery five minutes afterwards, with Doctor Goodhue scarifying the wounds and injecting permanganate of potash. The next morning Kersdale's arm was as big as a barrel, and it was three weeks before the swelling went down.

All of which has nothing to do with my story, but which I could not avoid giving in order to show that Jack Kersdale was anything but a coward. It was the cleanest exhibition of grit I have ever seen. He never turned a hair. The smile never left his lips. And he dived with thumb and forefinger into Dottie Fairchild's hair as gaily as if it had been a box of salted almonds. Yet that was the man I was destined to see stricken with a fear a thousand times more hideous even than the fear that was mine when I saw that writhing abomination in Dottie Fairchild's hair, dangling over her eyes and the trap of her bodice.

I was interested in leprosy, and upon that, as upon every other island subject, Kersdale had encyclopedic knowledge. In fact, leprosy was one of his hobbies. He was an ardent defender of the settlement at Molokai, where all the island lepers were segregated. There was much talk and feeling among the natives, fanned by the demagogues, concerning the cruelties of Molokai, where men and women, not alone banished from friends and family, were compelled to live in perpetual imprisonment until they died. There were no reprieves, no commutations of sentences. "Abandon hope" was written over the portal of Molokai.

"I tell you they are happy there," Kersdale insisted. "And they are infinitely better off than their friends and relatives outside who have nothing the matter with them. The horrors of Molokai are all poppycock. I can take you through any hospital or any slum in any of the great cities of the world and show you a thousand times worse horrors. The living death! The creatures that once were men! Bosh! You ought to see those living deaths racing horses on the Fourth of July. Some of them own boats. One has a gasoline launch. They have nothing to do but have a good time. Food, shelter, clothes, medical attendance, everything, is theirs. They are the wards of the Territory. They have a much finer climate than Honolulu, and the scenery is magnificent. I shouldn't mind going down there myself for the rest of my days. It is a lovely spot."

So Kersdale on the joyous leper. He was not afraid of leprosy. He said so himself, and that there wasn't one chance in a million for him or any other white man to catch it, though he confessed afterward that one of his school chums, Alfred Starter, had contracted it, gone to Molokai, and there died.

"You know, in the old days," Kersdale explained, "there was no certain test for leprosy. Anything unusual or abnormal was sufficient to send a fellow to Molokai. The result was that dozens were sent there who were no more lepers than you or I. But they don't make that mistake now. The Board of Health tests are infallible. The funny thing is that when the test was discovered they immediately went down to Molokai and applied it, and they found a number who were not lepers. These were immediately deported. Happy to get away? They wailed harder at leaving the settlement than when they left Honolulu to go to it. Some refused to leave, and really had to be forced out. One of them even married a leper woman in the last stages and then wrote pathetic letters to the Board of Health, protesting against his expulsion on the ground that no one was so well able as he to take care of his poor old wife."

"What is this infallible test?" I demanded.

"The bacteriological test. There is no getting away from it. Doctor Hervey—he's our expert, you know—was the first man to apply it here. He is a wizard. He knows more about leprosy than any living man, and if a cure is ever discovered, he'll be that discoverer. As for the test, it is very simple. They have succeeded in isolating the *bacillus leprae* and studying it. They know it now when they see it. All they do is to snip a bit of skin from the suspect and subject it to the bacteriological test. A man without any visible symptoms may be chock full of the leprosy bacilli."

"Then you or I, for all we know," I suggested, "may be full of it now."

Kersdale shrugged his shoulders and laughed.

"Who can say? It takes seven years for it to incubate. If you have any doubts go and see Doctor Hervey. He'll just snip out a piece of your skin and let you know in a jiffy."

Later on he introduced me to Dr. Hervey, who loaded me down with Board of Health reports and pamphlets on the subject, and took me out to Kalihi, the Honolulu receiving station, where suspects were examined and confirmed lepers were held for deportation to Molokai. These deportations occurred about once a month, when, the last good-byes said, the lepers were marched on board the little steamer, the *Noeau*, and carried down to the settlement.

One afternoon, writing letters at the club, Jack Kersdale dropped in on me.

"Just the man I want to see," was his greeting. "I'll show you the saddest aspect of the whole situation—the lepers wailing as they depart for Molokai. The *Noeau* will be taking them on board in a few minutes. But let me warn you not to let your feelings be harrowed. Real as their grief is, they'd wail a whole sight harder a year hence if the Board of Health tried to take them away from Molokai. We've just time for a whiskey and soda. I've a carriage outside. It won't take us five minutes to get down to the wharf."

To the wharf we drove. Some forty sad wretches, amid their mats, blankets, and luggage of various sorts, were squatting on the stringer piece. The *Noeau* had just arrived and was making fast to a lighter that lay between her and the wharf. A Mr. McVeigh, the superintendent of the settlement, was overseeing the embarkation, and to him I was introduced, also to Dr. Georges, one of the Board of Health physicians whom I had already met at Kalihi. The lepers were a woebegone lot. The faces of the majority were hideous—too horrible for me to describe. But here and there I noticed fairly good-looking persons, with no apparent signs of the fell disease upon them. One, I noticed, a little white girl, not more than twelve, with blue eyes and golden hair. One cheek, however, showed the leprous bloat. On my remarking on the sadness of her alien situation among the brown-skinned afflicted ones, Doctor Georges replied:

"Oh, I don't know. It's a happy day in her life. She comes from Kauai. Her father is a brute. And now that she has developed the disease she is going to join her mother at the settlement. Her mother was sent down three years ago—a very bad case."

"You can't always tell from appearances," Mr. McVeigh explained. "That man there, that big chap, who looks the pink of condition, with nothing the matter with him, I happen to know has a perforating ulcer in his foot and another in his shoulder-blade. Then there are others—there, see that girl's hand, the one who is smoking the cigarette. See her twisted fingers. That's the anesthetic form. It attacks the nerves. You could cut her fingers off with a dull knife, or rub them off on a nutmeg-grater, and she would not experience the slightest sensation."

"Yes, but that fine-looking woman, there," I persisted; "surely, surely, there can't be anything the matter with her. She is too glorious and gorgeous altogether."

"A sad case," Mr. McVeigh answered over his shoulder, already turning away to walk down the wharf with Kersdale.

She was a beautiful woman, and she was pure Polynesian. From my meagre knowledge of the race and its types I could not but conclude that she had descended from old chief stock. She could not have been more than twenty-three or four. Her lines and proportions were magnificent, and she was just beginning to show the amplitude of the women of her race.

"It was a blow to all of us," Dr. Georges volunteered. "She gave herself up voluntarily, too. No one suspected. But somehow she had contracted the disease. It broke us all up, I assure you. We've kept it out of the papers, though. Nobody but us and her family knows what has become of her. In fact, if you were to ask any man in Honolulu, he'd tell you it was his impression that she was somewhere in Europe. It was at her request that we've been so quiet about it. Poor girl, she has a lot of pride."

"But who is she?" I asked. "Certainly, from the way you talk about her, she must be somebody."

"Did you ever hear of Lucy Mokunui?" he asked.

"Lucy Mokunui?" I repeated, haunted by some familiar association. I shook my head. "It seems to me I've heard the name, but I've forgotten it."

"Never heard of Lucy Mokunui! The Hawaiian nightingale! I beg your pardon. Of course you are a *malihini*, and could not be expected to know. Well, Lucy Mokunui was the best beloved of Honolulu—of all Hawaii, for that matter."

"You say was," I interrupted.

"And I mean it. She is finished." He shrugged his shoulders pityingly. "A dozen haoles—I beg your pardon, white men—have lost their hearts to her at one time or another. And I'm not counting in the ruck. The dozen I refer to were haoles of position and prominence.

"She could have married the son of the Chief Justice if she'd wanted to. You think she's beautiful, eh? But you should hear her sing. Finest native woman singer in Hawaii Nei. Her throat is pure silver and melted sunshine. We adored her. She toured America first with the Royal Hawaiian Band. After that she made two more trips on her own—concert work."

"Oh!" I cried. "I remember now. I heard her two years ago at the Boston Symphony. So that is she. I recognize her now."

I was oppressed by a heavy sadness. Life was a futile thing at best. A short two years and this magnificent creature, at the summit of her magnificent success, was one of the leper squad awaiting deportation to Molokai. Henley's lines came into my mind:

"The poor old tramp explains his poor old ulcers;
Life is, I think, a blunder and a shame."

I recoiled from my own future. If this awful fate fell to Lucy Mokunui, what might my lot not be?—or anybody's lot? I was thoroughly aware that in life we are in the midst of death—but to be in the midst of living death, to die and not be dead, to be one of that draft of creatures that once were men, aye, and women, like Lucy Mokunui, the epitome of all Polynesian charms, an artist as well, and well beloved of men—I am afraid I must have betrayed my perturbation, for Doctor Georges hastened to assure me that they were very happy down in the settlement.

It was all too inconceivably monstrous. I could not bear to look at her. A short distance away, behind a stretched rope guarded by a policeman, were the lepers' relatives and friends. They were not allowed to come near.

There were no last embraces, no kisses of farewell. They called back and forth to one another—last messages, last words of love, last reiterated instructions. And those behind the rope looked with terrible intensity. It was the last time they would behold the faces of their loved ones, for they were the living dead, being carted away in the funeral ship to the graveyard of Molokai.

Doctor Georges gave the command, and the unhappy wretches dragged themselves to their feet and under their burdens of luggage began to stagger across the lighter and aboard the steamer. It was the funeral procession. At once the wailing started from those behind the rope. It was blood-curdling; it was heart-rending. I never heard such woe, and I hope never to again. Kersdale and McVeigh were still at the other end of the wharf, talking earnestly—politics, of course, for both were head-over-heels in that particular game. When Lucy Mokunui passed me, I stole a look at her. She *was* beautiful. She was beautiful by our standards, as well—one of those rare blossoms that occur but once in generations. And she, of all women, was doomed to Molokai. She walked like a queen, across the lighter, straight on board, and aft on the open deck where the lepers huddled by the rail, wailing now, to their dear ones on shore.

The lines were cast off, and the *Noeau* began to move away from the wharf. The wailing increased. Such grief and despair! I was just resolving that never again would I be a witness to the sailing of the *Noeau*, when McVeigh and Kersdale returned. The latter's eyes were sparkling, and his lips could not quite hide the smile of delight that was his. Evidently the politics they had talked had been satisfactory. The rope had been flung aside, and the lamenting relatives now crowded the stringer piece on either side of us.

"That's her mother," Doctor Georges whispered, indicating an old woman next to me, who was rocking back and forth and gazing at the steamer rail out of tear-blinded eyes. I noticed that Lucy Mokunui was also wailing. She stopped abruptly and gazed at Kersdale. Then she stretched forth her arms in that adorable, sensuous way that Olga Nethersole has of embracing an audience. And with arms outspread, she cried:

"Good-bye, Jack! Good-bye!"

He heard the cry, and looked. Never was a man overtaken by more crushing fear. He reeled on the stringer piece, his face went white to the roots of his hair, and he seemed to shrink and wither away inside his clothes. He threw up his hands and groaned, "My God! My God!" Then he controlled himself by a great effort.

"Good-bye, Lucy! Good-bye!" he called.

And he stood there on the wharf, waving his hands to her till the *Noeau* was clear away and the faces lining her after-rail were vague and indistinct.

"I thought you knew," said McVeigh, who had been regarding him curiously. "You, of all men, should have known. I thought that was why you were here."

"I know now," Kersdale answered with immense gravity. "Where's the carriage?"

He walked rapidly—half-ran—to it. I had to half-run myself to keep up with him.

"Drive to Doctor Hervey's," he told the driver. "Drive as fast as you can."

He sank down in a seat, panting and gasping. The pallor of his face had increased. His lips were compressed and the sweat was standing out on his forehead and upper lip. He seemed in some horrible agony.

"For God's sake, Martin, make those horses go!" he broke out suddenly. "Lay the whip into them!—do you hear?—lay the whip into them!"

"They'll break, sir," the driver remonstrated.

"Let them break," Kersdale answered. "I'll pay your fine and square you with the police. Put it to them. That's right. Faster! Faster!"

"And I never knew, I never knew," he muttered, sinking back in the seat and with trembling hands wiping the sweat away.

The carriage was bouncing, swaying and lurching around corners at such a wild pace as to make conversation impossible. Besides, there was nothing to say. But I could hear him muttering over and over, "And I never knew. I never knew."

Introduction to The Isle of Doom

James Francis Dwyer (1874–1952) was an Australian writer born to Irish parents in New South Wales. He was a prolific contributor to early American pulp magazines such as *Black Cat*, *Short Stories*, and *Blue Book*. Unable to build a career in his native Australia due to a criminal conviction for fraud, Dwyer moved first to London before settling in the United States. A frequent traveler, he eventually settled in the French Pyrenees. Aside from his short story writing, he was also interested in promoting tourism and, with his wife, for a time published the *Dwyer Travel Letters* for an American audience.

Originally published in the April 15, 1910 issue of *The Popular Magazine*, "The Isle of Doom" showcases Dwyer's interest in exotic locales. More a strange story than a supernatural one, "The Isle of Doom" is both a crime story and an adventure tale, albeit one that strongly hints at forces beyond man's immediate control. In this story, a gang of thieves lands upon an island somewhere in the South Pacific. Soon enough, however, they discover that the island has its own plans for them.

THE ISLE OF DOOM
James Francis Dwyer

Kenyon lived on the outer fringe. He knew there were big cities—knew in the same indefinite way that the child born and bred in the slums knows that there are big open spots in the world, where the air is free from grime and smoke. There are a lot like Jack Kenyon on the unbeaten tracks. They are the world's trekkers, watching where the dawn shafts spring from space, and praying God to let the world fill up slowly so that they may die without being crushed for breathing space.

He told me this story one night in Banjermassin in a small grogshop opposite a little Dutch chapel near the wharves, where the puffs of wind prowling up the Banjar advanced cautiously, seemingly afraid lest they might lose themselves in the dark alleyways where the stenches fought eternally.

The minister of the church was speaking of eternal rewards and punishments, and his vigorous assertions burrowed into the air like sound projectiles. The thick shawl of night tried to smother them, but they cut their way through, and seemed to gain an increased penetrating power from the opposition. One pictured them as tangible things, red-hot, whistling missiles hurled against moral turpitude, ripping away down through the Java Sea and smiting the ears of the ungodly.

Kenyon had been silent for quite a while, his eyes fixed on the bottom of his glass. The heavy air did not encourage an animated conversation, and I was not disposed to break the silence. Presently he spoke.

"He's right!" he cried, "By gosh, he's right!"

My mind immediately suggested that Kenyon's remark referred to the ministerial declamations coming from the chapel, and I turned a listening ear to the sermon. The clergyman was repeating the Emersonian statement that crime and punishment grow on the one bough, and therefore come to the person who plucks the branch, and Kenyon shook his head sagely as he listened.

"That's so!" he cried. "He's got the hang of things sure as eggs."

He turned on me, with a quick movement that upset the glass, the liquor oozing slowly through the plaited Dyak mat that covered the table.

"Did I ever tell you the story of the *Queen Regent*?" he asked.

I shook my head, and Kenyon waited till the minister had rounded off his discourse with a broadside against sin that awakened the Malay bartender who was dozing in the corner.

"She ran into Port Darwin one day in eighty-nine," continued Kenyon, "the smartest seagoing yacht that ever heeled over before the trades, I was a boy working for 'Blackbirder' Benson, and the masts of the *Queen Regent* beckoned me like big white fingers. When I think of those masts I wonder why I didn't tell this story after it happened. It seems as if I had to go on that yacht; you wait and tell me what you think. It looks as if I was wanted as a witness to tell the thing over the world, yet I haven't spoken about it to a soul till tonight.

"I got a berth easy enough. The yacht was out of Liverpool, owned by an English baronet of the name of Sir Creswell Danersford, and she was on a cruise round the Marshall and Caroline groups. There were seven in the crew, including the captain and a deaf and dumb boy, who waited on the owner. Sir Creswell was a big, red-faced man, and just because his face was as broad as the war shield of a Kyan he tried to make it look broader by wearing side whiskers that stuck out like the hair of a Papuan belle.

"If I had been a man I might have been told something before we cleared Port Darwin, but I was only a boy at the time. That's why I had to sniff mystery for two days while we were beating across the Arafura. The five in the fo'c'sle—the mate, Fulton, camped there—talked of only one thing for those two days. They called that thing 'It.'

"We had the same brand of talk for breakfast, dinner, and supper. They were wishing all sorts of things about this 'It.' They were wishing the thing was lighter, handier, and more easily got at; and each of 'em had a spot in his eye where he reckoned he'd like to have the affair to keep him company.

"White, a cockney, voted for the Mile End Road; Fulton picked Suez as his choice; Beck had Glasgow in his eye; and the other two, Brennan and Camphin, wished that they had 'It' in a little kennel they knew of near the Liverpool docks. But they never said what the thing was. It was just 'It,' plain 'It,' and the talk got on my nerves.

"Was your mind ever that hungry to know the answer to a question that it fairly sprang upon the answer when it did come along? Mine was like that. It was ready to pounce on the slightest clue that came along, and on the second day the clue came. The deaf and dumb boy took ill, and the captain ordered me to clean up Sir Creswell's cabin. Then I saw 'It.' I knew the thing the moment I clapped eyes on it.

"I went back to the foc's'le and found White, Brennan, and Camphin sitting on a bunk and talking in whispers. I went across and sat near them. White was speaking, and, of course, 'It' was the topic.

"'I've just been dusting it,' I said, when he stopped for a minute to get his breath.

"The three looked at me and then at each other. White started to whistle, but Camphin leaned over and gripped hold of my sleeve.

"'Where?' he asked.

"'In Sir Creswell's cabin,' I said, and I knew by the way he looked at me that I had solved the puzzle.

"The three of 'em tried to keep from questioning me, but they were so full up on that matter that they couldn't keep their curiosity in check. The deaf and dumb fellow couldn't tell them much because none of them knew the sign language, and they just fell upon me with half a hundred questions.

"I had struck 'It' all right. Their fancy conversational topic was a black safe in Sir Creswell's cabin—a big safe with the Danersford arms painted on it. There were two gold eagles holding double-edged swords in their claws, and underneath were the words '*Quantum vis.*' Say, what does that mean, anyhow?"

"I think it means, 'As much as you will,' " I answered.

"H'm," grunted Kenyon. " 'As much as you will,' eh? That's funny. That bunch didn't know, and I've never asked anybody else. You see, I've never told this story before, but I should have done so. I know I should. I was sent on that yacht as a witness, and I've been a dumb one, more shame to me.

"They told me everything about Sir Creswell after I had satisfied their curiosity about the safe. The baronet had delusions. He carried all his money with him in sovereigns, and the big money box in the cabin held his fortune. It had come aboard at Tilbury, shipped straight from the Bank of England, and all the way out to Port Darwin the crowd in the foc's'le were guessing at the amount of coin inside it.

"You can picture them doing that guesswork, can't you? At Gibraltar they reckoned there were two hundred and fifty thousand sovereigns inside. At Suez they spun the figure up to half a million. The heat was beginning to stir their imaginations up, see? Slamming across the Indian it got between them and their sleep, and the figures went up with hundred thousand leaps. When I got the strength of the secret they estimated the contents at a million, and it was spilling over that figure while we were cutting through Torres Strait.

"Sir Creswell had 'em all right. He was mad, sure. He had written a book to prove that the Israelites had wandered into the South Seas, and he was going down to those old Nantauch ruins in Ponape to hunt up fresh proof. The captain was a short, fat man named Smedley, and he suffered from chapped hands and asthma.

"Did you ever see a man that suffered from chapped hands who was any way imaginative? Smedley wasn't. If he had one ounce of imagination he would have felt the curiosity wave that was coming out of the foc's'le. But be didn't; and Sir Creswell was thinking so hard about the wandering Israelites that he didn't worry about the thoughts of common sailor men.

"We were slipping past the Louisiades when the thing happened. Did you ever think how much piracy those islands of Oceania are responsible for? There was one of those little green, heart-pulling spots to leeward one morning, and it brought that thing to a head in five seconds.

"I don't know what was done. I came up the ladder to find that White and Camphin had lashed the three boats together and built a platform over them, while Fulton, Brennan, and Beck were busy rigging a tackle at the side, I didn't see the captain or Sir Creswell after that.

"Fulton ordered me down to give White a hand, and because I asked White a question he banged me on the side of the head with his hammer, and I rolled under the planking that he was fixing to the boats.

"When I recovered my senses we were on our way to the island, and that big safe was perched in the centre of the staging. I couldn't see the *Queen Regent*, so I guess where she had gone. Fulton was giving directions on the pontoon, and we were moving over a sea of glass toward the land.

"We were close in to the island when the fog came on us. It swept up from the south like a big, fat cloud rolling along that greasy, smooth sea, and a thing like that is pretty unusual in those parts, isn't it? It seemed as if it was galloping to head us off from the shore, and we couldn't move too fast. Ten minutes after we first sighted it coming, it was on us, and we lost our directions the minute it took us in its long white arms.

"Fogs are rather depressing at any time, but that white sheet crawling up out of a clear sky was worse than the ordinary. It sat on us, sort of bent our shoulders with the weight of it. We couldn't see a yard in front of us, and the five of them gave up pulling and stood with their hands on the safe, as if they were afraid it would walk away into that wall of mist. You couldn't guess how that safe had taken a grip of their minds.

"It must have been near dark when we struck land. We were swirling along in a current when the boats crashed into something and shot backward. We came forward again and bumped the second time.

"The staging started to splinter beneath the weight of the safe, and Beck let out a yell of agony. The deaf and dumb fellow would have yelled, too, if he'd only known how. The safe had crashed forward and pinned the two of them beneath it.

"Fulton started to roar and curse. There was a big danger of us being swamped or smashed to pieces against the shore, and he jumped overboard into the shallow water, and tried to drag the pontoon onto a bit of sloping beach. The rest of us got at the safe with levers, and when the boat grounded we toppled the big black money box forward, and over it went into about two feet of water.

"The raft shot back with such a jerk when the weight was lifted that the four of us who were lifting the safe were flung into the water, and before we had time to scramble to our feet the undertow sucked the raft into the wall of fog like as if a hand had gripped it.

"It was sudden, that. We couldn't see a sign of it or hear any voices. P'r'aps Beck was too much injured to call out, and, of course, the deaf and dumb fellow couldn't.

"The waves were washing round our legs as we stood by the safe trying to see the raft in the fog. We couldn't do anything else. You could hardly see two yards in front of you, then, and the man who started to swim round in search of the boats would have a mighty poor chance of getting back to land.

"'Get the safe up on the beach,' growled Fulton, and the rest of us levered it up out of the water.

"Fulton wasn't troubling much about Beck or the deaf and dumb fellow. He had a skull that went up to a point like a tomcat's, and I bet he was thinking that there were two less to divide the money with. He hadn't spoken to me since he ordered me down to help White; but when we got the safe on dry land he turned and gave me a cuff in the ear that sent me backward.

"'Pity you didn't drift away instead of Beck,' he said. But I didn't answer. There was precious little use of picking a row just then.

"A blear-eyed moon started to peep through the fog, and we began to get a dim idea of our whereabouts. The island seemed to be only a few feet over sea level, and the ground was moist. It was a little bit more than moist. If we stood for five minutes in the one spot we sank up to our ankles, and we kept moving round looking for dry places.

"It was White who noticed the safe. 'Quick!' he yelled. 'She's sinking!'

"And it was sinking. It had gone down about eighteen inches while we were pottering round looking for a dry place to stand in, and we had a job to dig it out.

"We rolled it about five yards farther inland, then we stopped and watched it. The moon was shining a bit stronger then, and we could see. The name of the manufacturers, the Britannic Safe Company, was lettered in gold about six inches from the bottom, and as we stared the name was swallowed up.

"'Hell!' roared Fulton. 'Get your sticks under her again.'

"We went twenty yards farther and watched the same thing happen. We went a hundred and saw the safe start its disappearing trick again. We went half a mile, testing every yard of the ground as we rolled the thing along, but we couldn't find a solid spot.

"We had to turn back then. The island was only half a mile long, and there wasn't three square inches of it that would hold a grown man five minutes. It was just a floating bed of lava cinders held together by roots of grass, and it was just as qualified to hold up that big iron safe as a rocking-horse is to hold the Chinese giant!

"I don't know how many times we moved the safe that night. I guess about four hundred. Two minutes was as long as we dared leave it in one spot, because if it got down any deeper there was a chance of it going for keeps. It was like standing on a big sponge. The holes made a sucking noise when we heaved the safe out of them, and that row didn't improve our nerves as we kept on the move.

"Fulton accused the others of blocking him when he wanted to open the thing on the yacht, and White and Camphin gave him the lie, and told him he was in too much of a hurry to get away from his own handiwork.

"It went on like that all through the night. The four of 'em cursing at each other every time we were compelled to move the thing. It was devilish the way that ground sucked at the safe. Did you ever see quicksand eating anything? Well, that island was alive. There was a mouth gurgling at each man's boots, and a big maw guzzling at the safe every time we stopped. Get on your nerves, that sort of thing, wouldn't it?

"I didn't work as hard as the rest on the transportation game. I had no hand in stealing the safe, and I didn't intend to take any of the money. But I had to help, or those four would have killed me.

"They worked like madmen. That safe had been on their minds ever since they left the Thames, and they were nearly mad to think of losing it, after what they had done. Nearly mad? I guess they were raving lunatics before the night was over.

"They kicked the island, and danced on it, swearing at the spongy cinders all the time. They got down on their knees, and clawed at the stuff with their fingers, and screeched when it started to swallow them as they knelt. Then the four of 'em would fumble with the lock of the safe and beat it with the pieces of wood. All the tools and food had been lost when the boats were drawn into the fog.

"The morning came at last, and we could see all over the island. It was only half a mile each way, and there wasn't a patch of grass, stone, or stick upon it. Anything heavy on that cindery cushion didn't stay there long. It just slipped through and went plumb to the bottom of the Pacific.

"We kept on rolling the safe. Sometimes one of the four saw a place that looked a little drier than the rest of the ground, and we'd roll the safe there in a hurry. But it was always the same. The moment we stopped, the mouth started to suck at the big box. Good God! I dreamed of those million mouths for months afterward. Every time we pulled our boots out of a hole we looked back and shivered.

"It was hot that morning. The Pacific was just beside us, and the ocean seemed to be lying there, watching us, quite pleased at the trap into which we had fallen. But Fulton didn't let us stop a minute. Up and down the island we went, without a rest, and the thing became a sort of nightmare, I wanted to throw away my lever and run, but there was no place to run to. That place, with its million mouths, was bound to get the safe, but those four couldn't bear to see it sink.

"Camphin gave in first. He was weak and his strength gave out about midday. He threw away his stick and laid down, but Fulton made him get up again. Then he fell down again, and he couldn't struggle onto his feet. We didn't stop to help him, and we didn't see him again.

"Can you picture the rest of us going backward and forward over that spot? They were all weak, but they wouldn't leave the safe. They had been guessing too long at the contents of that iron box.

"Camphin's odd disappearance didn't trouble 'em, but every time the safe started to sink they'd spring forward like fiends. The thing had a three-inch casing of mud on it then, and you couldn't see Sir Creswell's coat of arms and the gold letters of that motto of his. *Quantum vis*, eh? They were getting the true meaning of that motto just then.

"We kept staggering behind the safe all day, and then the night came down on us again. There wasn't a sign of a sail. The ocean was lying there quietly, like a wolf that has a man up a tree, and thinks that the end is pretty sure. I guess we were all insane, then.

"'Long about midnight, Brennan got tired of working, and Fulton punched him. Fulton was a devil. He had tore all his clothes off, so that he could work better, and his bare body was covered in a coating of mud, like the safe. When he fell down you couldn't tell him from the ground. We were all pretty near like that.

"Brennan began to cry when Fulton hit him, and he struck at the mate with his stick. Fulton sprang at him, and Brennan ran away. White and I kept the safe from sinking till Fulton came back. He brought Brennan's lever with him.

"Say, don't you think that parson was right when he said that crime and punishment grow on the same branch?

"We had to work a bit harder that night. The island was all mucked up with us tramping over it, and the safe couldn't be left a minute. I don't know whether it was my youth or whether it was because I didn't worry when I saw the cursed box slipping, but I was standing the fatigue better than White or Fulton. They could hardly stand, and the wonder is that they lasted through the night.

"The dawn was coming up from 'way over the Solomon Islands when White gave out. Money's the devil. He pushed the safe forward, and then fell down on his face, and stayed there. I don't know how long he stayed;

Fulton didn't give me time to look behind,

"Fulton was a shrieking maniac then. He rushed that ugly mass of cinders and wrestled with it like as if it was alive. *Quantum vis*, eh? I tried to run, but he knocked me down with his pole and stood over me till I got on my feet again. He seemed to have the strength of three men, and he rushed the safe up and down the island. He was blinded with the cinders. I could have killed him then, but it didn't seem worth the effort. The pace was too fast to last, and it looked as if the island would win in the end.

"I don't know what time it was when the safe stuck. It burrowed its way down, inch by inch, and the slush around it started to boil. Fulton yelled and cursed. He flung away his lever, and clutched at the thing with his bare hands. But the safe bad got a move on that time. The mouth sucked at it, and it slid away from his grip, looking like a devilish, human-looking horror as it went. It frightened me.

"'Let it go!' I yelled, but Fulton wouldn't. He sprang on one end of it, and tried to tip it over on its side by dancing on it, and he screamed out to me to lend a hand. Do you guess what happened? That infernal thing lurched over suddenly, tossed Fulton on the cinders, and before he could scramble out of the way it had pinioned his two legs!

"I remember that I kept rolling over and over, so as to save my strength and rest myself, and in the afternoon I staggered to my feet and looked out to sea. A schooner was so close to the shore that I thought it was a dream, but they saw me when I waved my shirt, and I tumbled into the boat before it touched the land.

"That's all. It was a copra boat, beating down to the Marshall group, and they nursed me for a week or two. But I didn't mention anything about the safe. I did wrong. I know now. Why, God dealt with that five like He did with the Egyptians in the Red Sea, didn't He? And I had a narrow shave, just because I didn't try to block the game."

Kenyon stopped and stared at the damp patch on the plaited mat where the liquor had soaked through. The Malay filled his glass, but he took no notice. Presently, he put his head down on the table, and, covering his face, he sobbed quietly. I stood up, paid the score to the sleepy Malay, and stepped out softly, leaving behind me the man who had seen a miracle and never reported it.

AN ADRIATIC AWAKENING
Jonathan E. Lewis

I

No man is an island. No matter how much we may like to pretend otherwise, our destinies are shaped less by unseen forces beyond our control than by the people we meet, the people we love and befriend, those people who, for one reason or another, for better or for worse, enter our lives.

That's something I used to believe. And even though in some ways I guess I still do, I now have my doubts.

I've been fortunate enough to meet many creative and unique people in my lifetime. Working in publishing in Manhattan, I've met my share of real characters, each making a lasting impression upon me, each shaping my ability to understand what makes people tick.

But there's never been anyone that I've let into my life—and I do mean anyone—quite like my friend Josh Stone. To this day, everything about his fate seems unreal, as if it were ripped straight from the pages of an old pulp magazine. His story is so fantastically odd, so very bizarre, so unbelievable that the mere suggestion that what he recounted to me the last time I saw him alive shakes me to my very core.

My mind keeps coming back to that last night at the steakhouse. It was an upscale establishment near Union Square. Josh had just closed a merger between two telecommunications giants. One was from Tokyo and the other from Milan. Putting these two companies together was going to create a big European-Asian partnership. He'd been exhausting himself over it for months. So when it was all done, with the documents signed, with the sleepless nights behind him, it was his time to shine.

In typical Josh Stone fashion, he had coined a catchphrase for the occasion: "Sushi Pasta."

Stupid, right?

That night he repeatedly shouted out that phrase—Sushi Pasta, Sushi Pasta—grinning ear to ear. While the bags underneath his eyes betrayed chronic stress, it was his eyes themselves that gave him away. How deep down he must have known how stupid it was for a late forty-something with an Ivy League law degree to be jumping up and down chanting that phrase like a frat boy. But there he was. Verbally projecting that extraordinarily infantile, yet undeniably catchy, sequence of words to all who would listen.

Me? I was happy for him—he was my friend after all—but I needed a drink and some quiet time to myself. So I sat myself down at the bar.

That's when I first noticed her. I was sitting on a stool nursing a beer that Larry—that was the bartender's name—had served me. She appeared out of thin air, sidling up next to me like a spider that seemingly appears out of nowhere. She pulled out the barstool next to mine. She sat down.

"Hi, the name is Lilly." Her voice was alarmingly seductive without a trace of an accent. Yet her syntax was strange, as if English were not her first language.

"James." I put out my hand to shake hers. She immediately seemed to spot my wedding band. She laughed, tossing her head back slightly.

"We're separated," I said. It was more of a declarative statement to myself than something intended for her ears. "She doesn't even live in New York anymore. She moved to Seat—"

Lilly interrupted.

"Oh, I don't remotely care. It's totally cool. Kind of cute, actually that you'd be so worried about something as trivial as that." Smiling wide, she took my hand in hers. It was pure warmth.

"Can I call you Jim?" she asked.

"That's fine," I replied.

Just then, Larry interrupted us, asking Lilly if she wanted something to drink. She asked for a beer, the same imported brand I was drinking. I put it on my tab.

"So where are you from?" I asked.

"Oh ... around," Lilly replied.

"Well that's enigmatic," I said playfully, feeling my pulse slightly rise.

"I try to keep people guessing." She laughed.

"Ah, I see, so tell me what's your passion?" I asked.

"My passion?" she asked as if she didn't comprehend the question.

"Yeah, what is that interests you? What makes your life worth living?" I asked, my fingers nervously peeling the paper labeling from the beer bottle in front of me.

"Well," she hesitated, "I really do love literature."

Oh, how we talked that night. Minutes flew by, disappearing like grains of sand washed back away into a vast sea. Mesmerized by her very being, I asked Lilly what brought her to that particular restaurant on that particular night, whether she knew Josh, where she was from, and what writers she liked. That part was the publisher in me, the part that loves to talk about books.

She said she didn't know Josh and that she absolutely loved poetry, that she devoured it. We spoke of decadence, of Baudelaire and Poe. We talked of the Renaissance poets and the Ancient Greek muses. We talked of epics penned at the dawn of human civilization somewhere between the Tigris and Euphrates. It'd been years since I'd felt so alive. I supposed her for a grad student. She just knew so much. She had a way with words that would have put other girls her age to shame.

When I attempted to ask her more personal questions, she demurred. She told me she was just in the area that night after a literary reading and didn't want to go straight home. So she stopped in for a drink and some conversation.

She was surely lying. As if I remotely cared.

I may have been legally married at the time even though a divorce was all but inevitable, but that didn't stop me from noticing everything about her. She was the type of girl who could hypnotize a room. Unlike a lot of the look-alike clones that frequent city bars in their little black dresses and fake smiles plastered on their faces, this girl had her own style, her own way of doing things. She was *different*. How her fiery auburn hair cascaded past her toned shoulders and flowed steadily ever downward, ending in a sea of curls on the small of her lower back. How her unblemished teeth contrasted so starkly with her crimson lips. And most of all, how her emerald eyes betrayed a deep melancholy, as if she had personally seen unspeakable things in her short time on earth, things that rested heavily on her soul.

"Last one, I promise!" It was Josh bellowing from the other side of the room. His outburst disconnected the rapport I thought I'd been building with Lilly. The two of us shifted around and turned our gazes to Josh. He was downing a shot of whiskey. Lilly smiled and took a sip from the beer I had bought her. She looked at Josh, blinked, and rolled her eyes.

Josh? He seemed aware enough of us, but he didn't particularly seem to mind our gawking at him. Dressed in a pinstripe suit, a disheveled white-collar shirt and a loosened red silk tie, Josh Stone, from every indication, was living out his existence to the fullest that unusually warm and muggy night in September.

"So, it was really nice talking to you Jim," Lilly said.

"You're going to head out for the night?" I asked.

"No, not exactly," she said, slightly biting her lower lip.

"What then? Was it something I said?" I asked, immediately regretting appearing insecure.

She put her hand on mine, slightly caressing my wedding ring in a circular motion.

"No, it's just that I kind of want to just, you know, meet some other people. But we'll definitely catch up before I leave. Promise," she said.

Her eyes seemed to be a less intense shade of green than just a few minutes ago. How very odd, I remember thinking.

It didn't take me very long to figure out what had happened. She'd seen Josh and was intrigued by him. How could I blame her? Josh always had a magnetic quality to him. So twenty minutes and one beer later, I realized Lilly was out of my reach. She and I were not to be.

I waved farewell to Josh, then headed to the men's room at the front of the restaurant. Just before I headed out the door to hail a cab, I spotted Josh out of the corner of my eye. He was standing by the *maître-d* station. Lilly was by his side. He had his arm around her waist, slightly resting his hand on her black jeans. I couldn't hear what he was saying to her over the music, but she was most definitely laughing. She seemed intensely focused on my friend, as if she had finally cornered her prey for the evening.

Truth be told, I didn't know exactly what I was feeling at the time. I thought it was a form of jealousy, an evolutionary impulse hardwired into the male brain. But now, I look back and I realize that what I was feeling wasn't jealousy at all.

It was dread.

When I first met Josh Stone some years before he had completed the merger, I'd been working at Seagull Books. It'd been only for a year at that point, but the board of directors liked me. When the higher-ups told me to find the best young hotshot lawyer out there who could help Seagull acquire a small publishing firm, I began my search for the most capable attorney we could afford.

I had asked around and one name kept popping up: Josh Stone at Katz, Miller, and Youngman. You've got to make an appointment with Josh Stone was what people told me.

So I did.

Looking back, it was his handshake that gave him away. Firm, solid, and masculine. Yet hesitant.

As if despite all appearances to the contrary, he didn't *really* want to be there. As if he had an urge to be somewhere else. Anyplace but the office where he spent nearly most of his waking life in a climate controlled, wall-to-wall carpeted suite.

I know now there was something I must have felt that time I first met him, something I couldn't quite put my finger on. Something I felt on a subconscious level that foretold that what fate had in store for Josh Stone wasn't going to be typical. His journey was going to take him down a road far less traveled.

We talked in his office for what must have been over two hours. He seemed like a guy who knew his stuff. He told me that he'd certainly be able to help Seagull with its acquisition. Soon enough, our conversation segued from the strictly professional to the deeply personal. He opened up to me. It was almost as if he saw me, a total stranger at the time, as his therapist. He told me about his time in law school, about his childhood in Maine. About how he used to sit and read books by Daniel Defoe and Robert Louis Stevenson while watching his friends play pick up games of touch football.

At the time, I thought it was his shtick.

That he was putting on the friendly, down home one-of-the-boys act solely to get the Seagull account.

But now, I know better. That it wasn't an act. That he just needed someone to talk to, someone who knew who Defoe and Stevenson were. The imaginative young boy from Maine who devoured tales of adventure and piracy lived on in Josh Stone's adulthood, a life hidden away under a swaggering exterior, silk ties, and pinstripe suits.

"Hey, it's getting late. What do you say about going out for dinner and finalizing our game plan?" he asked.

"Sure," I hesitated for a moment. "What did you have in mind? One of the steakhouses here in Midtown?"

"Nah. I know this amazing Balkan place out in Queens," he said.

"Balkan?" I asked, uncertain what that might entail.

"Oh yeah, when I first moved to the city, I lived in a studio over in Astoria. There are so many people from Eastern Europe there. It's ridiculous. Greece. Romania. Croatia. And because of that, there's a ton of these little hole in the wall restaurants, places you'd have no reason to know about, but that have the most amazing food. Plus it's a nice change of pace from Manhattan," he said.

I'd had Greek food a few times, but I didn't know anything about Romania. Let alone Yugoslavia. But I was open to doing something new, and I got the sense that Josh Stone was like me in one very important sense. We were both living in a large city, but at some level felt completely isolated. I didn't really have any close friends, and it'd been next to forever since I did anything besides go to work and come home to an empty apartment. So I agreed.

By the time we arrived in Astoria, the sun had performed its daily magic trick of disappearing down over the horizon in the sky. The vibrancy of late summer nights permeated the humid air like an electric current. Young white college students holding hands, elderly Asian women carrying bags of exotic vegetables, and old men with bronzed skin clasping onto newspapers all shoved their way out of the overheated subway car. We followed. As we passed through the exit turnstiles, walked up the concrete steps to ground level, and walked down the street, I couldn't help but wonder why I was so willing to have dinner with a man I barely knew.

It was an unassuming and nondescript restaurant, one that you could have easily walked past on the way to the subway without realizing it was even there. Tucked in between a late night joint selling greasy falafel and a grimy shoe repair store that looked as if it hadn't turned an honest profit in decades, *The Adriatic Diner* was pretty much what I had expected. A hole in the wall that catered to the yearning immigrant need for authentic hearty peasant food straight from the old country. A place where old men with thinning white hair could passionately argue about political developments taking place in the Balkan cities and towns where they were born and raised.

A place where someone like Josh Stone could easily sit by himself and have a plate of baked chicken and rice pilaf, immersing himself in a paperback novel, and—for a slight moment of time—tune out his identity as a corporate lawyer from Manhattan.

We seated ourselves at the small table furthest away from the kitchen.

"You want water first?" a voice asked in an accent as thick as it was pleasantly exotic.

I looked up. The waitress was a thin girl in her late teens. She was dressed in a white blouse and acid washed blue jeans. Her gaze met mine. She smiled.

"Sure, for both of us," Josh answered.

We ate well that night. We talked and we laughed as we ate large servings of seasoned chicken, brown rice, and steamed string beans. What was important was that I felt like I had made a new friend.

There was finally a natural lull in our conversation. Our stomachs full, our blood sugar rising, we began to lose steam. As I sat sipping bitter Turkish coffee, I noticed Josh looking across the restaurant, his gaze scanning the wide array of folk art paintings, outdated tourism posters from the Tito era, and a multitude of photographs decorating the light yellow walls.

"That's where I want to go," Josh said, pointing at the wall on the far side of the restaurant.

All of a sudden, I heard shouting coming from the open kitchen. It was the owner losing his temper at a short order cook, screaming at him in a language I couldn't understand.

"What were you saying? Sorry, that was quite a spat," I said.

"Oh, because of those two?" he said, gesturing to the kitchen. "He's always screaming at that poor son of a bitch."

"Charming," I murmured.

"Cultural differences, man. People from the Balkans are a more impassioned people than guys like you and I," he replied. "They're more *real* that way."

I had no reply so I said nothing.

Josh used his fork to stir up the remnants of brown rice from the far side of his plate, creating a small pile in the center. He set his fork down, loosened his golden yellow silk tie, and began to speak.

"See that photograph? That one over there?" he asked me. His tone grew oddly serious, almost urgent.

I set my cup down on the saucer and looked at the wall, uncertain which one Josh was referring to.

"You mean that one?" I asked, pointing to a framed color photograph of what looked to be a small island a million miles from nowhere. Apart from stone ruins, the island looked desolate. As if no human had disrupted the flow of Nature there for centuries.

"Indeed," Josh replied. He tapped his fingers on the table as if he were churning out a script on an electric typewriter.

"Well, what about it? You've been there?" I asked. My thoughts were focused on the natural beauty of the island's rolling waves of green grass. The way in which bright sunlight highlighted it in its entirety, highlighting the azure water that lapped up at the island's sandy edges, creating a natural demarcation between land and sea.

Josh stretched out his arms. "No, I haven't. It's just that—"

"—you really want to," I said.

"Exactly, exactly. There are just some days I wish I could be like Robinson Crusoe." Biting his lower lip, he blinked his eyes.

"Really? All alone in the middle of—where is this anyway?" I asked.

He answered my question with a question.

"Remember the name of the place you're in right now?"

Of course. It made perfect sense. *The Adriatic.*

"That's where you want to visit?" I asked.

"Not just visit," he said, emphasizing the final word. "Someday, I think I'd like to get away from this giant stinking pile of a city and live completely alone on an island. Where I can just be myself, do whatever I want to do. No rules," he said, his eyes lighting up with wonder.

"For real?" I asked.

"I don't know. Maybe when I make enough money," he laughed.

"Is there ever really enough?" I asked.

Josh laughed. "I don't know. But I have a feeling that someday I will."

Neither of us spoke much on the subway ride back into the city. Josh nodded off. I nudged him a couple of times, jolting him awake.

"You're falling asleep on my shoulder," I said.

"Sorry about that, it's just that I work ridiculous hours," he answered. "You know how it is."

I didn't, but I nodded in agreement.

As the train careened through a dark tunnel beneath the East River, the image of that small Adriatic island in the middle of nowhere resurfaced in my mind. Who had even taken that photograph? At that very moment, it occurred to me how I'd been living on an island without actively thinking about it. Who thinks of Manhattan as an island?

So Josh Stone wants to trade a densely populated island for a desolate one. I laughed to myself. I found it amusing. And at the time it was.

II

"So you've not heard from Mr. Stone in any fashion?"

"No, nothing. Nothing at all," I replied.

"You're sure about that?" he asked.

"I would absolutely tell you if I knew anything. He's my friend, you know," I answered.

The detective was clean cut, tall, and stern. Just like in the movies. He'd been in my apartment for about an hour, prodding me for possible clues as to the how, why, and where of Josh's disappearance. Whether there were any abnormal factors in his life, things that could have led him into owing money to some bad people. Problems like that.

It was now over a week into November. And my friend Josh Stone had vanished.

No one had reported having seen him. Well, that wasn't exactly true. There was a Border Patrol officer upstate who had sworn he had seen Josh, or at least someone who *looked* like Josh, riding as a passenger in a tractor trailer hauling produce across the border. But when pressed on the matter, the guy admitted he couldn't be sure.

"Honestly, I don't know what else to tell you. It's as much a mystery to me as it is to you," I said, adjusting some loose papers on my desk.

"Yes, but you were among the last people to see him, so that's why it keeps coming back to you," he replied.

I knew what he was thinking. It was up to me to provide the police with an explanation as to what happened to Josh Stone. It came back to Lilly. She had been with him at the steakhouse when I last saw him. No one could seem to locate her. It was as if she never existed.

Even stranger, Larry the bartender, the one who had served me a beer at the steakhouse that night when I met Lilly, swore he couldn't recall seeing me talk with a girl that night, or anyone else for that matter. At the time, I thought this was just plain nonsense. Either that, or that somehow she really was mixed up in all of this and had paid him to keep silent.

But why?

To the detective, I was beyond polite and only spoke when spoken to.

"If I think of anything, I'll be sure to be in touch," I said.

"Of course you will," he answered.

I wasn't sure how to take that. Did he suspect I was withholding something? Because what I didn't tell him was that I had been playing amateur detective myself.

What I refused to tell the detective was that I'd been having the most vivid dreams, dreams in which Lilly appeared to me. And what I dared not mention most of all, lest I find myself on the wrong side of the law, was that I had a plane ticket to Croatia stashed in my desk. What I refused to say was that I strongly suspected my friend Josh had really done it. That, after a month, it had occurred to me that maybe, just maybe, Josh Stone had fled to that island, the one in the photograph, the one he had been seemingly obsessed with years before his disappearance, the one from the *Adriatic Diner* wall.

Several days before, I had gone out to Queens, back to the place where Josh and I had dinner when we first met. Somehow it called me. The place was still there, somewhat worse for wear, but there. I asked the owner about that photograph. He told me exactly where the island was.

At that moment, I knew Josh was on that island. I felt it. Don't ask me how I knew. I just did.

There are over a thousand islands in the Adriatic Sea. Less than a hundred are inhabited. Others, with their untended lavender fields and grassy plains are beacons of natural beauty, all but untouched by human civilization. That's what I learned by reading a guidebook to Croatia on my overnight flight to Vienna.

From Austria, I took a connecting flight to Zagreb, the train to Split, and then the ninety-minute ferry trip to the island of Hvar, off the Dalmatian coast. A cold snap had hit the Adriatic that year, and the island seemed deserted. I asked the tourists and workers who remained if they recognized Josh. No one admitted to having encountered him. That's when I suspected Josh had paid them to keep quiet. I knew I had to go to that unnamed island on my own, hoping against hope that maybe, just maybe, I would find him there.

So I hired a local boat owner and asked him to take me where I needed to go.

Josh was my friend. Did I really have a choice?

III

"She wasn't human."

Those were his first words upon seeing me, as I got off the small boat, trudged up the sand and onto the grass, shouting out Josh's name on the top of my lungs. Not "hello" or "how are you?" No. Just "she wasn't human." And he repeated it. His voice more frenzied each time. The ebullience of "Sushi Pasta" had morphed into the monomania of "she wasn't human."

And the manner in which he spoke. It was as if he were desperately trying to convince himself of something. I was his friend. I had flown halfway across the world to a country technically still in the midst of a war to make sure he was okay. But at that moment, I didn't matter. My presence didn't really register with him.

The Josh Stone I found that unusually chilly day was no corporate lawyer. Haggard, dirty, and speaking so fast as to be almost unintelligible, Josh had clearly lost all sense of who he used to be. The man I found had been living in a small canvas tent that he had set up next to the ruins of what looked like a long abandoned stone fortress, a remnant of an ancient past long forgotten. He had obviously paid off some local officials to let him be. That was his style.

"It's me, Josh. It's Jim," I said, putting my hands on his shoulders, trying to stop his trembling. His worn clothes were unkempt. They smelled. He looked as if he hadn't eaten in days, as if he had looked into the abyss and that it had broken him.

"How did you find me?" he asked. His hands were shaking.

"I knew. I just knew," I replied. I tried very hard to ignore the odor that seemed to engulf his very being. It was clear he hadn't showered in weeks.

"I had to come here. You understand that?" Josh asked.

"Yes, but I'm here now. I'm here to take you home," I said, approaching him cautiously.

"No!" He fell to his knees and pounded his fists into the grass. "No! I can never go back. Didn't you hear what I said? Did you not hear what I told you? About her?"

"Who's her?" I asked, overlooking the obvious.

He looked up at me. "Lilly."

That's when I saw them—the hideous marks on his neck. It appeared as if a deranged person had taken a two-pronged object and had thrust it an inch or two below his jawline. The wound looked somewhat infected, with black and blue colors encircling it.

Perhaps I had lived a sheltered life up to then, but I'd never seen anything like it before.

"What about Lilly, Josh? What about her?" I asked, increasingly worried for my friend's health, both physical and mental.

"As I told you," he muttered, his voice nearly inaudible, "she wasn't human."

He stood up and looked around. It was as if he were worried she would hear him. But there was no one else on the tiny island. The place was just as eerily deserted as it had appeared in the framed photograph on the wall of the *Adriatic Diner*. It looked more or less the same. But my friend Josh didn't look anything like the man whom I had eaten dinner with that night in Queens.

Concerned for my friend's mental state, I indulged his fantasies. He spoke. I withheld judgment and listened.

"That night," he said, his fingers picking at unfathomably ugly scabs on his arm, "I went home with Lilly. You remember her?"

I opened my mouth to speak, then thought better of it. I merely nodded.

He told me that he had taken her home and that she had bitten him— bitten him!—in the middle of the night. He told me how he had woken up in the morning dazed and exhausted, with droplets of recently dried blood staining his pillow. He explained to me that he was sure she had put a spell on him, had given him visions of his destiny, and had disappeared at dawn. He spoke as if this insane fever dream had really happened. As if it weren't the product of a mind lost to the ravages of something I wasn't qualified to understand. I was in the publishing business, not psychiatry.

"Wow, that's ... that's incredible," I said not knowing what to say in a situation quite like this. Because I'd never been in a situation quite like this.

My friend had clearly lost his sanity. And I didn't know what to do.

Just then, he broke the silence that had engulfed us.

"Promise me? I'm asking you as a friend," he stammered, his voice nearly a whisper, almost completely drowned out by the rising wind. A storm was coming.

"Promise you what?" I asked. I felt a lump in my throat. Swallowing didn't help. It only made my mouth drier.

"That you will leave this island and never come back."

"Josh," I said, reaching for his shoulders, hoping to establish a real connection between us. "I can't do that. You're not well. I don't know how else to put it."

"Leave now," he said, his eyes burning with a frenzy that left me cold. He looked feral. It terrified me.

"Okay, okay," I said quietly.

He grunted.

Somehow I gathered up the nerve to ask him the one question that had been gnawing at me.

"Tell me," I said as calmly as possible, "what do you think Lilly was? You know, if she wasn't human, what was she?"

I couldn't believe I was indulging the ravings of a madman. But as I looked at the puncture marks on his neck, I found myself thinking the unthinkable.

He answered me with one word. It was a word I had never heard before outside of a few horror manuscripts I've read over the years.

Succubus.

Two hours later, the boat I had hired had returned. I was determined to get back to Hvar as quickly as possible and to let the police know what was going on. I wasn't going to let my friend Josh waste away all alone on that cursed island.

But it was not to be. By the time I was able to get a physician and a pair of policemen back there, Josh Stone was no more. Face down in the sand was how we found him. My friend Josh was dead, the culmination of a journey most strange. The official report confirmed Josh Stone had died of exhaustion and an infection stemming from two self-inflicted neck wounds.

But then again the official reports of post-communist countries in states of political upheaval don't always speak true.

On nights when sleep eludes me, when my mind returns to the unanswered question that still plagues me, I find myself going for walks around my neighborhood, past the mechanized street sweepers cleaning up the city's detritus, past bodegas, past the bagel shops preparing to open at the break of dawn. My mind races. It is a simple question that has no answer: Had my friend Josh Stone truly lost his mind, or was Lilly who—or what—he was convinced she was?

She did come out of nowhere that night at the steakhouse. This was true. She was uncannily seductive. This was also true. She appeared to carry the weight of centuries on her back. This was undeniable. But it's not possible. Demons don't exist. There are *no such things* as succubi, female demons that seduce men and drive them mad. There are no vampires, either. These are myths, vestigial legacies of a superstitious past that have no bearing on the present.

But then I think of my friend Josh Stone.

Of his crazed bloody face, of his gaunt frame as he waved me farewell. My mind wanders. I can't help it. I think of him that day we met, that day we went to the *Adriatic Diner*, of how his eyes widened with sheer delight when he spoke to me about how one day he would live a life free from the constraints of civilization. A life with no rules and no structure. An existence with no one to answer to. And I ponder whether maybe he was telling the truth. At least his truth.

Was Lilly—who or whatever she was—merely an excuse to do what he had always wanted to do? Did she somehow awaken a latent Robinson Crusoe fantasy? How long had he had a passport ready to use at a moment's notice and the cash stashed away to pay people off? I'm afraid I'll never have all the answers. Just questions. So many questions.

Sometimes, I take the train down to the East Village. I peer into tattoo parlors, scout out dive bars, and drink black coffee at all night diners, hoping beyond hope to catch a glimpse of Lilly. Hoping that maybe she would have the answers I've been looking for. Lilly. I think of her auburn hair and her crimson lips and the way she looked at both of us that night. Lilly. I think of the power she seemingly had over the both of us. And it haunts me. It haunts me still.

THE END

NOTES FOR FURTHER READING

For those readers who have not had the opportunity to read H. G. Wells's **The Island of Dr. Moreau** (1896), the Oxford World's Classics edition (2017) is a great starting point. It includes a superb introduction by editor Darryl Jones in which he puts Wells's work into its proper historical context. He discusses how the novel should be understood in relation to Charles Darwin's work in evolutionary biology and how even the geographical setting of the unnamed island in the story is an implicit reference to the Galapagos Islands. Wells's chilling tale about a scientist tinkering with evolution was most famously adapted to the big screen as **Island of Lost Souls** (1932), a remarkably sleazy pre-code horror movie. The film features Charles Laughton as Dr. Moreau and Bela Lugosi, best known for portraying Dracula, as the Sayer of the Law. Another black and white horror film, **Isle of the Dead** (1945), an RKO film produced by Val Lewton, may be of interest. The film stars Boris Karloff as a deeply superstitious Greek general temporarily trapped with a small group of other people on an island during a plague outbreak. The film effectively uses the island setting to create an atmosphere of dread and impending doom.

Daniel Defoe's **Robinson Crusoe** (1719), Robert Louis Stevenson's **Treasure Island** (1883), and William Golding's **Lord of the Flies** (1954), all of which were mentioned in the introduction to this anthology, would likely be of interest to those readers who want to read more island stories. Two more recent works, both of which became popular mainstream Hollywood films, are also worth a look. Michael Crichton's **Jurassic Park** (1990), which owes an obvious debt to Wells, is worth a read. A cautionary tale about the perils of genetic engineering, Crichton's novel was most famously adapted to the big screen by Steven Spielberg. **Jurassic Park** (1993), the film, is set on a fictional island off the coast of Central America and stars Sam Neill, Laura Dern, Jeff Goldblum, and Richard Attenborough. The movie was not only a blockbuster in its own right, but spawned a financially lucrative franchise. Similarly, Martin Scorsese's psychological thriller **Shutter Island** (2010), based on Dennis Lehane's novel of the same name (2003) utilizes an island setting to tell a story about a man's mental disintegration and his radical separation from society. Scorsese employs the island setting in the film to visually capture the supposed division between civilized, urban middle class norms and the mental patients imprisoned on the titular island. A neo-noir work that necessitates at least a second viewing, **Shutter Island** owes an indirect debt to those nineteenth- and twentieth-century authors whose works appear in this anthology.

H.G. Wells's "Aepyornis Island" (1894), which originally appeared in *Pall Mall Budget*, is often thought of as a science fiction story, yet is also a strange island story. The plot follows a man looking for the eggs of a now extinct flightless bird. Richard Connell's "The Most Dangerous Game" originally appeared in *Collier's* (January 19, 1924) and might be one of the most frequently reprinted short stories set on an island. More of a thriller than a strange island story, Cornell's story follows a man trying to escape a crazed hunter on an isolated Caribbean island. The story was famously adapted into a pre-code RKO adventure film by the same name (1932) starring Joel McCrea and Leslie Banks. H. P. Lovecraft's "The Call of Cthulhu" which was originally published in *Weird Tales* (February 1928) is set in part on the fictional sunken island nation of R'yleh in the South Pacific. Again, an island setting, albeit that of a sunken one, allows Lovecraft to craft an atmospheric tale that has become one of his most famous works.

For readers interested in island short stories that are not necessarily supernatural or weird, John S. Bowman's **A Book of Islands** (Doubleday & Company, 1971) is worth seeking out. As far as I can ascertain, it is one of the few literary anthologies that contains stories exclusively set on islands. It is not the easiest volume to find, but those readers who enjoyed the works included in **Strange Island Stories** might find much to appreciate in that anthology as well.

Jonathan E. Lewis is an editor and a writer who received his law degree from the University of Connecticut. **Ancient Egyptian Supernatural Tales,** his previous anthology for Stark House Press, was published in 2016. **Strange Island Stories** is his second anthology. His current projects include a stage adaptation of Louisa May Alcott's "Lost in a Pyramid, or the Mummy's Curse," a short story that appeared in his first anthology. Originally from Connecticut, he currently resides in Southern California.

Classic Fiction from

ALGERNON BLACKWOOD

Made in the USA
Monee, IL
23 February 2023

28503728R00193